Praise for *Summerland*

'A raffishly erudite amalgam of *The Great Gatsby* and Ford Madox Ford's *The Good Soldier* ... Astoundingly accomplished ... His clear-eyed vision and startling, depth-charged prose constitute a novel that should become as much a classic as the one he has remoulded'
Guardian

'As a remembrance of things past, Knox's novel is exquisite, blending a lyricism and exuberance of language with subtle undertones that point towards the denouement ... *Summerland* works on many levels and Knox is, quite simply, a fabulous writer'
Literary Review

'Knox's confident, ironic voice is completely his own, as he removes the veneer of his couples' charmed lives to reveal deceits and horrors ... Assured and gripping ... The growing darkness of the novel's vision is intensified against a background of relentless blue sky and sea, and the endless pleasures of the super-rich. *Summerland* is a compelling novel with a sinister undertow. Malcolm Knox has made an impressive debut'
Times Literary Supplement

'*Summerland* is a remarkable debut ... very good indeed, a noteworthy addition to the literature of princely pride before a fall ... Eloquent, savage and heartfelt, the novel ushers us into a world that is not glamorous at all but slippery with betrayal and deception'
New York Newsday

Jamaica

MALCOLM
KNOX

First published 2007 by Allen & Unwin, Australia

This edition published 2008 by Old Street Publishing Ltd
28-32 Bowling Green Lane, London EC1R 0BJ
www.oldstreetpublishing.co.uk

ISBN 978-1-905847-54-9

10 9 8 7 6 5 4 3 2 1

A CIP catalogue record for this title is available from the British Library.

Printed and bound in Great Britain by J. H. Haynes & Co. Ltd., Sparkford

The Jamaicans portrayed in these pages, and all those who exist there, are works of fiction. This book is dedicated to the facts who got out of the way of a good story.

Prologue

HUT SWAM ALONE only because none of the others would come with him.

The party was plumbing its eleventh hour when he gave up his station at the music system and stood in the centre of the sunken living room. The beach house looked as if ransacked by half-hearted burglars: furniture dislodged but not overturned, empty bottles unbroken on the tiled floor.

Stretching his arms showily above his head, Hut groaned as if answering a question: 'Taking a dip. Clean out the pipes. Anyone?'

He finger-combed his awning of orange hair—bloom of rust, the colour of heartbroken adolescence. Outside, the day was being dragged out of the dark, its rosy claws scratching the eastern blue; inside, there was also a reluctance to let go of the night. Pen, Nayce and Janey sprawled in a murmuring V on a daisy-chain of cushions and beanbags. Hut's announcement hung in the stale smoke, unbidden, unremarked. Pen dismissed her husband's offer with a distracted wave, her feet resting on Nayce's thigh.

Hut receded through the rubble-strewn coffee tables and dining suite: half-drunk glasses, good ideas at the time, discarded as if the evening had been a quest for some ultimate answer. 'Okay. Just me then,' he said with his customary brightness when taking no for an answer.

He found John and Susannah Bookalil sitting on the balcony, calves scissored on the glass table, sucking back champagne and orange. Smilingly they shook their heads at his invitation. Pongrass and Blackman, whom Hut had delivered to the house like a pair of trophies, had driven out an hour ago for an emergency resupply. *Comes a point*, Pongrass had said, *when the only answer is More*.

The methodical, urgent hedonism of parents on a night without children, Hut thought. Ten, twenty years ago they'd partied like there was no tomorrow. Now they went at it like there was not a moment to spare.

Down on the dewy beach, only a couple of fishermen had ventured out, well-spaced, in no danger of either entanglement or conversation. Jaundiced streetlight bounced off the sand-smeared road. Hut's hands were yellow and the shadows tinted, as if seen through smoked glass. The air smelt of salt, Norfolk Island pine sap, and the earth's night-sweat.

Big surfs seldom got up before dawn so Hut paid no attention to the waves. He dropped his towel onto the sand and considered taking off his rash vest, which he usually wore as protection from sunburn and mockery. With his redhead's complexion and tendency to buxomness, daytime beaches hummed with threat. In this solitary pre-dawn, he might have liberated himself, even swum nude in celebration of his diminishing torso. He didn't. The spandex skin coddled him, made him feel like one of the normal race, one of them.

Though no-one had come with him to the beach, Hut entered the water feeling jubilant and vindicated. It had been his idea to invite Pongrass and Blackman, his idea to abandon the Bookalils' overcrowded weatherboard and reconvene the holiday in the big house. His idea to leave all the kids, for one night, with Bookalil's parents. He'd come up with the week's five grand in rent: *Spare change*, he'd said, waving off the protests. The last eleven hours confirmed his wisdom: as his guests they'd whaled out—one of those unforgettable beach nights to add to the collection. He'd spent two thousand at the bottle shop as a guarantee of goodwill, Pongrass had unfolded his El Primo It, and everyone, in the end, after all the grumbling, had been up for it. Good old Papa Hut: they'd remember his generosity longer than their hangovers.

The darkness, and Hut's ecstatic indifference, threw a shroud over the sea like a sheet floating onto a bed. It wasn't until he was waist-deep that Hut felt the chunkiness of the current wrap his middle. He ignored it: although the break was further out than he could see in the half-light, the whitewater was frothy rather than steepling. He freestyled into a trough, enjoying his stretch and his kick too much to notice the sea's heft.

He had duckdived under six or seven broken waves before he realised he had been swept several 25-metre frontages to the north. The holiday house was now five doors down. Pen, as hostess, would be thinking about breakfast and cursing Hut for leaving her to clean up and cook. His legs reached beneath him and found the sandbank. As his toes touched the bottom, they skidded north. He breaststroked a little to save his breath; streetlights sailed southwards.

Rips didn't worry him. He reminded himself to go with it, let it take him out and drop him off, like a bus. The trick was to stay cool, get past the impact zone and not tire yourself fighting it. Seas were always calmer further out. Clinging to the sandbank, while seeming safe, exposed you to the combination punches of incoming waves. If you let the rip cart you into the deeper gutter,

3

you could relax, tread the calmer water and plot your next move. The key was not to pick a fight you couldn't win.

Even while rehearsing these thoughts, Hut heard them echo as in a draughty classroom, a hollow set of principles. *Principles.* There was a school camp when they'd gone solo sailing, aged fifteen or sixteen. Hut had told everyone he sailed—his family owned a yacht. Big-noting, he'd pretended he didn't need help. The truth was that his father sailed the boat and wouldn't let Hut do any more than perch in the cockpit and duck the swinging boom. In front of the class, on his knees, in his skiff, tangled among ropes and tiller, centreboard jammed in his hands, Hut had been blown straight back from the jetty to the headland. He fumbled and cursed. The other boys rolled around laughing. *You don't know how to sail, do you*, the pissed-off instructor called out. Face knotted, drifting towards the rocks, Hut retorted with that instinctive comic touch he used to be able to pull from the fire, defiant buffoonery, which could swing the mob and redirect their laughter against the haplessly furious teacher: *Sir, I know the principles!*

He knew the principles. He dogpaddled with the rip and was again surprised by the disproportion between the waves' macchiato tops and the deep force beneath. These were nuggety waves, stocky and packed. He found a lull between sets and coaxed himself into freestyle. But when the sets weren't breaking onto him there was a powerful drag, like an afterthought that is more persuasive and lingering than what's been said. He'd been in negotiations like this: the surface is unruffled but everyone's sitting there thinking: *Did that really happen? Are we at war here?*

It was when the next set arrived like a gang of pug-nosed brothers and Hut had still not reached the calmer sea that he realised maybe he was at war. Beyond the sandbank and unable to stand, yet inside the breaking zone, he took a gulp of air and braced

4

as the first wave collapsed onto him, hurled him up, then dragged him down. He let himself go limp, conserving energy. When he bobbed up he had time for one gulp of air before the next wave. Again, up, down: nature's empty-eyed even-handedness. On the rebound, he thought he could make it up for a breath. As long as you got one good lungful between waves, you would be all right. The set would pass. It was a question of maintaining your rhythm. Like a singer, you had to know when to breathe. More *principles*. But the milky greyness of the light confused him, and when he gave a strong dolphin kick he realised he was sending himself down, or across, not up. Bursting, he went ragdoll again, tumbled over, then found himself at the surface; but this time there was no chance for a breath as the next wave—the third-born, always the mean brother—came down in a great wrathful crump. Hut recognised the first colour of the day: a hope of green buried within the white of the falls, a keyhole, a ring.

The fourth of the set grabbed his ankle and shook him in its teeth. Spearing into the sandbank, he crossed his arms above his head to brace against the blow. The wave yanked him with a second wind towards the centre of the earth and reefed his rashie up his ribcage, peeling it halfway off. His arms flared to stop it but succeeded only in winding the vest around his neck, shoulders, and elbows. Trussed like a hostage, disarmed, he was thrown down again by the next wave. The shock of the situation—the rashie now acting as an effective binding of his neck and arms—robbed Hut of his composure. Being strangled by your own rash vest was not in the manual, as unnatural as a snake choked by its own half-shed skin. The freakishness of what was happening sucked the remaining calm out through his throat; he began flailing in a screaming blue panic.

Years before, he'd nearly drowned in the surf several times each summer, once a week at least. Like anything, he improved at panic with practice and had mastered his fear so that mountainous waves became less threatening than people smirking at his body on the beach (a malignant torment from which even the nastiest seas offered sanctuary). But that was twenty-five years ago, and he'd come into this surf as complacently as if his terrors, having once been subdued, were vanquished for good rather than, with death's infinite patience, simply lying in wait.

His arms were bound; another dumper dropped its load on him; a realisation of immense, authoritative clarity pierced his bursting chest: *I have nothing left. Don't pick a fight you can't win.*

It was as if God had spoken, with a matter-of-fact wisdom that suspended time, a voice that was steps ahead of him. *Giving up* presented itself as a seductive offer—a red, dreamless, hot bath filling him from inside. And so it came to Hut, with the calm and inviting brutality of a statistic, that this was it and he should wave life off, take his leave, with the glossy, slow-motion helplessness of watching himself in a car accident. It was all so easy. Pity—just as he'd glimpsed his first truth of middle age, he was going to die. What a waste. Drunk, stoned, high, tripping, his last contribution to the world's overflowing out-tray would not be (as he'd anticipated) the carnage of his financial affairs but a ripe and fruity toxicology report. *And with all that under his belt,* they would say, *he came for a swim, alone, before dawn, in a dangerous surf.* As if anyone needed proof of his stupidity. This *father of two.* This *employer.* As if anyone needed proof.

Immersed, forsaken, Jeremy Hutchison began to cry. Not literally—his literal shell was turning blue, indigo, and the ultimate colour, violet, his eyes distending in panic—but beneath his skin something of Hut retreated into the centre, circled his arms around his knees and began to bawl. His face, when they found him, would be black and sea-swollen, but his child face would be wrinkled into this woebegone tear-sponge. He cried and cried.

It was one of the fishermen who saw him. A sandblasted windcheatered man—not a local but a visitor from down the peninsula who'd heard about sand whiting on a run—had watched the round-shouldered redhead, twenty-dollar haircut on a ten-dollar head, trundle in, get carried down the beach on the rip, fight his way suicidally into the break, then after a moment's disappearance get spewed into the gutter between sandbanks with his arms twisted inhumanly above his head.

The fisherman would tell him he was lucky the sun had come up just then. 'I saw yer bloodnut, mate, yer red hair in the water. Five minutes earlier, yer'da been grey on grey and I'd nevera seenya.'

The fisherman waded into the gutter and dragged out the jellied figure, untwisting the rashie, bunching it and throwing it disgustedly onto the beach. Hut tried to walk away but his knees liquefied onto the blushing sand. Now, as his breath and colour returned, he did cry.

'Yawright, matey?' said the fisherman, face like a chewed caramel. 'Coulda been worse. Coulda been yer mum cryin'.'

Hut shook his head, on all fours, and emptied through his eyes and nose the tears collected beneath the waves. He folded in on himself and lay curled on the beach, his fleshy side crusting with sand, calling to his rescuer's mind the nice breading he'd give the whiting he'd caught.

'Wasn't worth the trip, eh matey?'

The fisherman, who didn't expect thanks, packed up and left before Hut had regained his feet.

Hut wobbled back to the holiday house on gelatinous legs. He used the outside shower under the balcony. His sobs had scoured him out and left him ravenous.

In full sunlight, the house had fallen quiet. The night's fun had soured into the day's chore. Hut drank orange juice in three shots from the last vessel in the cupboard above the stove, a Peter Rabbit egg cup. Pongrass and Blackman must have come back: half-snorted lines cross-hatched the kitchen table.

Hut padded through the house on bare feet and began pushing at the doors to the bedrooms.

Two days later, all the possible sources of his tears in the water were still jostling in his head like a creditors' meeting. They overwhelmed him. Nothing could bring on a crying jag like a fresh memory of near death. He was weeping again on the Monday morning, sitting alone on the beach in front of the house, remembering how, when that wave flipped him over and flattened him like a master pizza-maker working a pad of dough, he had heard the conclusion to his story: *I have nothing left.*

That voice had carried a warm and welcoming immensity, like a president inducting him into a club whose membership he had always craved. The Eternity Club. What brought him to tears now wasn't so much how close he had come to death as his grateful surge towards it. Like vertigo: it wasn't fear of falling, it was fear of seeing how much he *wanted* to fall. Was this him, was this Jeremy Hutchison? He couldn't escape the feeling that he'd given the incorrect answer to a crucial question. The vital part of him, the Hut part, had fallen out somewhere. Where? Whose was this acidic, death-loving voice? What had made him so fucking tired?

Hut's fists drove into the sand by his hips. He remembered the fisherman's dry Good Samaritan wit and wanted to punch the man's face. Hut didn't want to be saved. He wanted to save himself. He was as angry with the fisherman as his sons were when you did something for them that they were determined to do for themselves. Screaming at you to rewind the clock, let them start again. Daddy, *I* want to do it *myself*.

A sniffling fragment of a laugh: his boys.

He waited on the beach for the seas to rise. If Hut wished for anything, it was to be out there again, pressed under the ocean's thumb so that this time he could save himself. As he would have, if the fisherman hadn't stepped in. Wouldn't he? He needed to find that vital part, that Hut part, under the water. And then, maybe, if he could find that again, he could also have found something different in the bedrooms of the holiday house. Two failures coming so close together—he couldn't help feeling they were coupled, like the two parts of a tumbling lock.

But the heavy swell had subsided, leaving a pond with a guiltless sleeper's face. The two-faced sea.

He took his mobile phone out of his beach bag and called his company's travel agent to book the tickets for Jamaica.

Brace. Brace. Brace.

1

THE HOUR BETWEEN check-in and boarding was such a happy one for Jeremy Hutchison that he would revisit it with a warm throb of nostalgia. Moments of pure happiness were elusive; reliving them was like trying to trap a flea. He lived this one in the velvet-roped First-Class reserve of the frequent flyers' club at the international terminal of Sydney Airport.

Hut always got a lift out of airports. They contained the nasal thrill of jet fuel and the gravitational heft of things that cost three hundred million dollars; he felt warmed by proximity to such capital-intensiveness. But most of all, airports sighed with the relief of having *made it*. When you had checked in, you were scot-free. Nothing could touch you. In this way airports reminded Hut of prisons (places he'd been thinking about more and more). Prisons and airports put you beyond care, in a higher pair of hands. Hut could be as happy in either; which gave him something, at least, to hang on to.

He had found Justin Pongrass and Andy Blackman, tousled from the velocity of their check-in queues, in armchairs overlooking the main runway. Hut, holding a glass of Coke he'd poured at the open bar, pulled up a third chair to complete a semicircle before the sheet glass.

A pop tune, arranged for strings and wind, laid down a soundtrack to the tableau of Hut's satisfaction: a First-Class semicircle with these two mates and their retired-athlete bodies, staring into space, letting it sink in: the flight ahead, the escape, the holiday, the race, the *success* of it all.

Outside was the double-dealing of thrust and flap; but the boys weren't watching. Inside magazines and newspapers were pinwheeled on the glass coffee table; but the boys weren't reading.

The boys were neither reading nor watching, though Pongrass, in his way, was singing. Soft and surprisingly tuneful, Pong cooed with the muzak, one of those '70s choruses that Hut knew to be intimate with everyone except him. It wasn't that all popular music had passed Hut by. He knew the tunes. He just didn't know the names.

The muzak changed its tune, if not its mood. Pongrass's falsetto wafted over the First-Class lounge as Hut went to get a mineral water. He'd have liked a drink but didn't want to dehydrate— or didn't want to dehydrate yet. There'd be plenty of time for dehydration, for deep-vein-thrombosic languor, twenty-seven hours of it, and Hut demanded value for his First-Class fare. He'd do his dehydrating on a couple of flutes of something French, then a forthright Barossa red.

He watched Pongrass's once-famous face forget itself: 'Le-eh-eh-eh-ets! Let's stay togethah!'

His own eyes squeezed shut, and he joined in: 'Loving you whether/ Times are good or bad/ Happy or sa-a-a-ad/ A-a-a-ah . . .'

Carried away with the moment, Hut punctuated the last three beats with a slick pelvic thrust, his teeth gripping his lower lip with emotion. He opened his eyes to find a silent Pongrass and Blackman staring at him like a pair of magpies.

'Um,' Hut tried to laugh. 'Penny loves that song.'

There occurred a prickling instant when Blackman's and Pongrass's mouths both opened to pass comment on Hut's enthusiasm, and then, as they saw each other, their breeding reasserted itself in tightened lips and a change of subject.

Blackman spread his arms and groaned: 'Man, First-Class, long trip—be so good. Inhumane to let you travel anything else.'

Hut cleared his throat. 'I don't know how the others can do it. Economy. Christ.'

The last time he'd flown long-haul Economy was with Pen and the boys when they'd had to return from Europe at no notice for a funeral and there hadn't been any other seats. Two babies, twenty-six hours, noses red from blowing into cheap napkins: after that, ten K was loose coin well spent.

Blackman roused himself from the peaceable contemplation of his incoming Valium to shoot Hut a wink that anointed him with a full-body blush.

'Stick with us, son. Stick with the heavy stuff.'

Blackman and Pongrass were heavy hitters (Hut rolled the words around his mouth). He meant *heavy*. Money, Hut had learnt, was a heavy metal. It endowed weight, gravity. It embedded you in your earth, and when you grew large with money you earned not the power of flight but the power of mass: you were so heavy with it, you attracted other money. With sufficient money you weren't free from anxiety or obligation; that was the spiv's dream. Perhaps it had even been Hut's dream—to buy his way clear. If you observed real money, serious money, you learned that freedom was the last thing it wanted. It wanted to be weighty. Pongrass and Blackman were heavy as earth's crust. They weren't just rich for life; they were sedimented in it for several lives, inheritances before and to come. You couldn't spend your way out of that kind of money. You'd need too much imagination.

'Real cutlery,' Pongrass said. 'Right up the cockpit's clacker and they still give you steel knives. That's what First buys you. Respect. Common decency.'

'I've heard,' Blackman said, his self-oiling gaze brushing the floor-to-ceiling windows, 'that if you threaten a hijack in First-Class, as a joke, say you've got a bomb in your bag, you know what they do? They laugh. They get it.'

'Respect,' Pongrass nodded appreciatively, warmed by the fact that there remained places where the courtesies and traditions of the past endured. 'They ought to put up a sign: "WARNING: We don't take jokes seriously".'

Hut could get drunk on thinking about these guys. If Pongrass and Blackman were wines, they'd be the bottles you could only get a look at if you'd known the sommelier on first-name terms for fifteen years. Hut felt the rare privilege—the hairs in his erectile tissue stood up—of having friends of this calibre. When he had boasted of his friendship with Pongrass and Blackman—*the* Justin Pongrass, *the* Andrew Blackman—hoping to impress his parents, his mother had said in that dreamy, sedated way of hers: 'Ah! Theirs is a different world.' This was how the top half per cent regarded the top quarter per cent: a different world. The Hutchisons were rich by any measure, but relative deprivation—or 'aspiration' as it had come to be known—was a permanent mood.

'Dare you to try it!' Hut said, a quiver of delight jetting his words too forcefully over the coffee table. It happened again: Pongrass's eyes overshot Hut's to Blackman. They swapped something masonic, the pair of them, a micro-conference.

'Eh,' Blackman winked at Pongrass but directed his reply at Hut. 'You try it, pal. You try it. I swear, it'll be fine. They won't shit themselves—they'll *piss* themselves, yeah?'

Hut frowned hard at his nails. He'd seen the eyelids, the fluttering exchange. He had for most of his life been cultivating the disguise of an open-faced unsuspicious man who misses everything: a sound business trait he had learnt from his father. His real competitive advantage, though, the trait he inherited from his mother—his curse—was that he missed nothing.

When the boarding call came, Hut followed the weathered heels of Blackman's deck shoes down the sky bridge. The other three in the team—Nayce, Janey and Bookalil—were flying Economy. Hut was relieved he had avoided bumping into them on the way in, which would have been annoyingly awkward. He became troubled—or scratched his way down to existing troubles. An understanding flew through the nylon air and attached itself to him. He couldn't put his finger on when the happy moment had been whole and stationary, but he knew when it was on the turn.

Hut tried to shrug off this bleak flash. He would be happy. He would live, even if it killed him.

2

IN ROW 58, seat B, a breath downwind of the aft lavatories, David Nayce woke from a nap to read, on his seat-back video display, that the Time To Destination was two hours longer than it had been when he'd fallen asleep. The pleasant texture of his nap disintegrated. By the time he realised he was reading not Time *To* but Time *At*, he was feeling desperate and haggard, undone by a misread preposition.

He found long-distance travel a dislocating experience: it dislocated his neck from his back, his hips from his thighs, his jaw from his skull. How vivaciously the early hours passed, how miserably they matured, how malevolently they gummed up. In real life, the only comparison for your body falling apart was that the years accelerated and you got it over with sooner. But on an aircraft you had the worst of both worlds: as you slowed down, so did time. The last three or four hours of a long flight didn't drag; they had to *be* dragged. The only consolation was, it didn't matter whether you were in First or Cattle. The mulish last hours showed no respect for class.

He watched a movie and sank into his own dreadfulness. To his right, in 58C Janey Quested's eyes were compressed with what appeared to be the effort to inhale her headrest, and in 58D John Bookalil was dozing.

Nayce scratched his newly shaven head with both hands. A bad deal, shaving: you never knew what lay beneath.

His boyish crop of straight dark-blond hair had been one of his better points, greying imperceptibly over his pleasant if not quite handsome features. He hadn't shaved for the forty-year-old's standard reason: to thwart baldness by bringing it front and centre. (Though he liked the fact that the head-shaving craze had put neo-Nazis out of business; a skinned head these days meant not a swastika-worshipper but a middle-manager striking pre-emptively for male vanity.) Nayce had shaved because of the swimming race—shaving seemed a professional, Olympian act, bringing him skin-to-skin with the ocean. But he'd been regretting it. Shadowy remnants of stubble had disclosed an unexpected male pattern: on his forehead a pubic Tasmania detached from the mainland. In a horrible irony, the shaving of his head had revealed his bald patch. It had also uncovered a dark secret: a steep-pitched gabled skull marked with inexplicable gashes and knuckly lumps. Rather than a perfect globe, his head was a half-flat rugby ball with hives, a nineteenth-century criminologist's dream: the rear bumps for sexual deviancy, the pointed crown for avarice, the sloping front for murderous impulses. A bad deal, all up.

And to make matters worse, here, two movies into the flight, was the devil himself, freckly hands parting the curtain of the section before the section before Business, which was the section before First, now rowing himself along the headrests. His genial eyes sought out faces, warming the cabin with his smile, like a man receiving appearance money: a celebrity visiting the hoi polloi. He looked brown and almost wiry and, Nayce had to admit, fit.

Nayce braced himself. *Brace. Brace. Brace.* Like the flight attendants told you to do when disaster was imminent. The beautiful futility of it touched him somehow. Faced with a nine-hundred-kilometre-per-hour impact, what could you do but assume a good body position?

'Hey.' Hut's radiance betrayed simultaneously his relief at having a First-Class seat and his obligation to hide the fact.

'Mr A1 himself,' Nayce said, hooking his headphones around his neck and stretching to shake Hut's hand. These were handshaking men. Their fathers and their schools had taught them to shake hands. They did so genuinely, when they met; and ironically, such as now.

'My apologies. *Lord* A1,' Nayce corrected himself.

Hut was visibly fighting the temptation to gloat about First (steel cutlery, interactive games, respect, general awesomeness), but Nayce cut him short.

'What am I? You pay through me to sit in me.'

'Um.' Hut usually tolerated Nayce's fondness for wordplay, but there were only so many ways in which he was happy to have the piss taken out of him at once. 'No idea,' he sighed as if whatever the answer was, it couldn't matter.

'The nose.' Nayce tapped the side of his.

The seat to Nayce's left was empty. Its occupant, whose conversation had comprised a kind of public service announcement on the dangers of deep vein thrombosis, and who watched the seatbelt sign like a sprinter under the starter's gun, had leapt up hours earlier to 'stretch my legs and enjoy the view'. Before departing for the rear bulkhead, he had paused, giving Nayce a reproachful glare. People on planes were no longer satisfied with talking to you; they had to convert you.

Now Hut squeezed past Janey then Nayce and plonked himself into the vacant seat, causing the jumbo to sway minutely, or so it seemed. Although no longer a large man, Hut remained a large presence: his ghostly fat threw itself about, cleared a radius, shuffled and stretched and took its time arranging itself.

'Oi,' Nayce grunted abstractedly, as if Hut was interrupting important business. Hut was impervious to this kind of hint, however, particularly when it was feigned.

'Dave? Are you okay?' Hut was frowning at something above Nayce's eyes.

Rubbing his scalp, Nayce shrugged. 'Worse can happen. I guess.'

'But . . . are you okay?' Hut's voice trembled.

'Ask for clippers in haste, repent at leisure.'

'Oh. Oh. Right. I thought it might be, you know . . . medical.'

Nayce wondered if Hut was joking but could see the shine in his eyes. This was the trouble with the fucker. He let too much in. You had a haircut, and the next thing you knew Hut was offering a private room in the top hospital and a blank cheque for your bills.

Hut started inspecting the inflight magazine and safety cards, as if checking that they were suitably dog-eared and child-bitten compared with those in First. Nayce went back to his DVD. He had brought twenty DVDs and six books with him. What could he not pack into these five days, into this very flight? In the four years since he'd become a father, Nayce looked forward to trips away with a truant's excitement, almost a wild panic. When he stepped on a plane he could stand on time's brakes and forget he was married to Sophie, forget he was a father to John, forget he was forty; but only for a moment, before trailers loaded up with family, marriage, position, possessions and ambiguous unfinished love jackknifed into him. The excitement of going away begat a child of its own: guilt.

Why was he doing it, why had he been eating up that swimming pool as if it were his daily bread? He didn't need Sophie to tell him (though she did, and did) that it was all about mortality, about not wanting to let go, about proving his strength once more before it was too late. About, in her wifely nutshell, 'your midlife crisis'. What Sophie didn't realise was that she wasn't telling him anything he didn't know. He had caught an early whiff of death's hot breath and was swimming away from it. But what Sophie underestimated was the extent to which *everything*, now, was about mortality. The frenzy of the six books and twenty DVDs was about mortality. The 747 was about mortality. Jamaica was about mortality. The only time Nayce wasn't thinking about mortality was when he was playing with, or shouting at, or chasing around, or cleaning up after, his son. And so, more mixed feelings: he was euphoric to be escaping domesticity so he could contemplate his death in peace.

He wondered if he had any feelings left that he could take unmixed.

'What you watching?' Hut said as soon as Nayce had settled back down.

'Nothing.' Taking his headphones from his ears with an ostentatious sigh, Nayce offed the player.

'In First we've got a whole DVD library.'

'I don't know why you're down here then.'

'*I* don't know why *you're* down here. Twelve hours to LA, five to Miami, another hour and a half to Kingston—and you chose Economy? That's one whole day of your life with your knees against your chin.'

'Let's think of it another way,' Nayce said. 'It's only one day.'

They were continuing a kind of fraternal bickering that had been going on for thirty-three years. Their friendship circled inside the soiled cage of early impressions. Even in second grade Hut had seemed more of a child than anyone else: eager to please, innocent of consequence except when it affected him. More of a child, and also a born materialist, Hut had an innate grasp for the power of toys. At seven (at eight, at nine, at ten, at forty), Hut understood the magnetic pull of a home bulging with brands. Hut's house was the first place Nayce had seen a colour TV (Thorn); a dishwasher (Westinghouse); a video recorder (Sony beta); a computer game (Pong on Atari); a refrigerator with an ice-maker and cold water (some impossible German name); an automated swimming pool cleaner (Kreepy Krawly). At Hut's house Nayce and other friends were introduced to inventions such as the bidet (Nayce urinated in it by mistake); the jacuzzi (that too); the sauna; the handball court; and, by observing Hut's permissively 'European' parents (Ken Hutchison hailed from London's East End, but gold-and-white Ines was German), poolside nudity, the seven-hour lunch, adult conversation, the adult chunder, and, the next morning if Nayce stayed overnight, the mysteries of sweaty penitent adult exercise regimes circa 1979: starjumps, neckrolls, burpees, running-on-the-spot, as well as the timeless elegance of the push- and sit-up. Hut wore the newest manmade fibres in the latest colours, and second grade's first digital watch (Seiko, with calculator). Like an exclusive little club, the Hutchisons had family in-jokes and in-words. They always owned a basset hound named Fred. When Fred died, they replaced him with another Fred. Obese bassets didn't last long in the Sydney humidity, so there were generations of Freds; the Hutchisons didn't bother to distinguish them as Fred I, Fred II and so on. Just one eternal, reincarnated, wattly, panting Fred.

The in-jokes owed more to Hut's father than his mother. Ken Hutchison liked being captain of his little club, and his son was a loyal card-carrier. Ines Hutchison's wishes took him longer to read.

Later on, Nayce would come to think of the Hutchison house (Spanish hacienda: white stucco arches, terracotta tiles, hidden courtyards) as a kind of permanent technology expo, with Hut the resident PR flack. But for Hut—and this was always evident to his friends, who pitied it—his self and his possessions had been fused so that he never knew for certain whether his mates liked him or his toys. Ken was an importing entrepreneur, Ines (which Ken rhymed with 'penis') a retired TV lotteries announcer, twenty-two years in and twenty-two out of Dusseldorf. Cocksure and worldly, Ken fed Jeremy's fear with DIY aphorisms, loaded up with one constant subtext: *In the long run it's only your money that people like, so you'd better start shoring it up.*

'Why torture yourselves?' Hut said, shifting in his narrow Economy seat to make his point.

'What doesn't kill us makes us stronger.'

'Ha.'

Good old Nietzsche, the busy man's desk calendar. Nayce had read just enough gloomy German philosophy back at university to spread the impression that he was a dazzlingly educated man, a civilised merchant banker. This was how the businessman could earn his name as a Renaissance man: he couldn't quite raise an original idea, but he could work flavour into his commonplaces. The prudent fund manager left nothing to waste, not even the embarrassment of an arts degree.

'The difference between my ticket and yours,' Nayce said, 'is ten thousand dollars. If we're hitting a rough patch in Economy, I'll think about you spending ten grand for a couple of inches of leg room and wine in a real glass. When you're not eating, not watching a movie, not sleeping, not using real cutlery, you'll be paying ten grand to stare out the same-sized window at the same fluffy cottonwool clouds I'm staring at. I do think of you up there. It gives me a happy flight. And nothing makes me happier than to see you joining me down here. Did I tell you? I'm really pleased to see you, Hut.'

'You know what?' Hut closed his eyes for a short moment's long division. 'The difference is four-oh-nine dollars and eleven cents per hour. And if we get delayed, the longer it drags, the more the hourly difference comes down. Think about that.'

Nayce's mouth made a white hyphen. 'That'd take me ten minutes on a calculator, you bastard. You're a freak, Hutchison.'

They could say what they liked about him, and God knows they had, but no-one denied that Jeremy Hutchison had the Maths. The Maths was what had got him where he was. Or no—even he would admit that it was eight figures of patrimony that had got him, largely, where he was. But the Maths had saved him from pissing it away; the Maths had given him his self-made name, his ability to write in black ink. They all thought he was a buffoon, but they respected his idiot-savancy in simple (if not complex) mathematics. Calculus, matrices, the dark arts of irrational numbers—he'd had none of it. But give him addition and subtraction and division and multiplication, give him practical problems involving compound interest and if this costs this and that costs that—give him real maths, and he was a wizard, as proven by his topping the state—the state!—in school maths. All right, it was the lowest level. They'd called it vegie maths. But Hut was no vegetable. He'd taken pride in his inattention to every other subject, but they all knew he'd been the top vegie in the state. That was one of the upsides in still being friends with your schoolmates when you were forty.

'And then between flights,' Hut went on, 'what do you do at the airport? You don't even have a lounge to go to.'

He shook his head like a disappointed parent whose children are paying the price for ignoring him. After being with Pong Pongrass and Abo Blackman, it must have been unavoidably saddening for Hut to be with the Economy Three—as if they were transitories, penniless, lacking history, his heart sinking as he adjusted his thinking from many generations to one, from reserves to inflow.

'I'd have upgraded you all.'

'Ah, not that again.'

Hut had, two months ago, tried to upgrade Nayce, Janey and Bookalil to Business: another of those acts that had earnt him his reputation for generosity. Nayce had dismissed the offer with a double-edged laugh, as if it wasn't genuine or, if it was, it was insulting. In the usual upside-down morality of things, Hut, the rejected benefactor, was made to feel worse than Nayce, the cold-hearted repudiator. These convoluted transactions, over what Hut felt should have been a simple and heart-warming gesture, were the downside in still being friends with your schoolmates when you were forty.

Hut bleated on that the problem wasn't money. The problem was *division*. They were coming on this trip as a team, they'd trained as a team, they were doing the race as a team: the Fast Set, the Dirty Half-Dozen. The Economy Three were splitting the team.

'You want to be a team?' Nayce countered. 'Come and enjoy Economy.' Nayce didn't necessarily like the team congealing around him. Now that they were airborne over the Pacific he ventured to say that, though he could not quite will the 747 to go down, while Justin Pongrass and Andrew Blackman were aboard at least some good would come of it if it did.

As if seeking like minds, Nayce canted himself against his tray table to inspect row 58; he eyed two pubescent girls playing Grand Theft Auto. They were dressed in the fashionable retro Suzi Quatro style: denim jackets, tight jeans tucked into tooled leather boots, Zorro-masks of eye-shadow, feathery salt-and-pepper hair. The problem with that style, he thought, was that for a man of his age, born in the 1960s, it did not bring to mind Suzi Quatro but mature women whose best years had been spent aping Suzi Quatro and were now clinging to the memory. So these thirteen-year-olds made him think: *Lamb done up as mutton done up as lamb*.

But then, the real problem was that these girls weren't there for a man of his age and opinions. If his opinions had any point for such girls, it was that they be violated, offended, scorched from the earth.

Which was why he wanted them to smile at him, nothing more than to notice him, so badly he could have wept.

'Anyway. You're looking good,' Nayce said, giving his armrests a subject-changing slap, feeling a jolt of guilt for giving poor Hut the usual rough ride.

'Thanks, mate.' Hut's eyes glistened. The big lump turned on and off like a tap, and it was getting worse as he grew older.

'You think you can do the race?'

'It's all under control,' Hut said richly, as if pacifying doubts was all in a day's work.

'So how much have you been swimming?'

'Don't worry your pretty little head about that, my boy.'

'Where have you been training?'

'Never you mind, just look and learn. But thanks, mate, I'm feeling great.'

'You look a million bucks.'

Hut was about to pounce eagerly. 'Do I? Say something more!' But Nayce, alert to the kind of back-slapping session that came from nothing and went nowhere, said: 'Hey, I want to get some zeds before LA. You should too.'

'Sure, pal.' Hut's palm was again flat on Nayce's thigh: indulgent, like a father enjoying the cuteness of his son telling him to take care of his health.

'Just one thing,' Nayce said.

Suddenly conscious of the speed at which they were moving (almost the speed of sound in a tin bubble: poke your face out the window to enjoy the air and your brain-mist will drizzle over a whole island nation down there), Nayce hesitated before his friend's bright blue eyes. Hut palmed a hank of still-brilliant red hair off his forehead. Hut's sons had red hair too. Adults found kids with red hair cute, adorable even, unless they'd had to grow up with it themselves. You hate this thing your parents have given you, and they, having hated it in themselves, adore it in you. What's that all about? It was hard to feel ambivalent about redheads. Hut's mother Ines was red as well, though she dyed her hair that parodic platinum.

Nayce's stomach rose and fluttered, a helicopter beneath his ribs. How could Hut ever trust him? Wasn't that it? How could he ever trust Hut to trust *him*?

Nayce swallowed. 'Don't swim.'

'Don't swim?'

'Don't swim in the race. Come along, only . . . don't swim.'

Hut looked set to laugh, but something in Nayce's expression stopped him. A smokiness skidded across Hut's eyes.

'Eh, good one, mate.' Hut tapped Nayce on the cheek as he got up and straddled him to get to the aisle. Nayce made as if to knee Hut in the groin. Hut stopped, legs forked either side of Nayce's, and bent to his ear.

'Dave. Here's a deal. I won't swim,' he growled, movie-melodramatically, 'if you start telling the truth about yourself.'

Nayce suffered a flicker of confusion. The ironic mimicry of strong emotion was so habitual among his friends, the self-mockery so automatic, rooted in the friendships' histories, that it was almost impossible—and perhaps undesirable—to identify those moments when the play-acted emotion happened also to be real.

Hut straightened and thrust his pelvis into Nayce's forehead. Nayce flinched. They were locked in this coupling like a pair of ice dancers whose routine finishes with one's face in the other's crotch. *Freeze there and smile!*

'You know you want to,' Hut bowed to his ear again and purred. 'Just give in, Dave.'

Nayce gave him a push, and Hut stumbled into the aisle towards the curtain and commenced his odyssey through the sections before the sections before First. Nayce couldn't see his face, but knew that Hut would be grinning all the way to the nose.

The jumbo landed, disgorged, reloaded, upped, offed, made earth again. A thunderstorm delayed the landing in Miami, where the aircraft coughed out its human phlegm, some haggardly to a final destination, others to the unexpectedly skinny margins of their connecting flights. The men of First-Class made the shuttle flight to Kingston. Drunk and hungover at the same time, they eased their way through the purgatory of reclaim, clearance, transit and transfer to new boarding passes, new lounges, new bain-maries, newborn drooling jugs of orange juice.

As they boarded the Miami–Kingston shuttle, Blackman was asking Pongrass: 'So who would you write a letter to if the plane was going down?'

'Is it a rule that the plane can't crash until I've finished writing?'

'Sure,' Blackman tugged down the corners of his mouth, workshopping the idea. 'Whatever you like.'

'Right then,' Pongrass smacked his lips. 'I'd write a little thank-you note to every bunny I've knobbed. *Thanks for the lovin.* I'd be writing so long, we'd have to find an airport eventually!'

A titter escaped from Hut and floated above them like a curvaceous but slightly crass blimp.

'Um, who would you write to?' Hut asked Blackman.

'My soon-to-be-ex-wife,' Blackman nodded with compressed lips. He mimed a scrawl in the air: *'Dearest Maria. Wish you were here.'*

Pongrass laughed so hard he needed to go to the toilet. Hut laughed along but was internally restrained, trying to think up something funnier than the truth, which was that he'd write the kind of letter to Pen that he already wrote her every day, at least in his head. But the boys didn't want the truth. Or his contribution.

The Economy Three, meanwhile, met blockage. During the thunderstorm an elderly woman had vomited her teeth into her sick bag, and by the time she had conveyed this to her daughter, the sick bags had been thrown away. The feisty daughter, a mid-forties corporate blonde in a tomato-red pantsuit, was insisting that the flight attendants 'Go threw them awl'.

The crew members were seeking a satisfactory customer service response which didn't involve any of them angling in the swamp where sick bags went to die. In other words, Americans were passing the buck until somebody found a Guatemalan.

The blockage, like a colonic twist, was finally cleared, but then the carousel was reluctant to give up their bags. Nayce, Bookalil and Janey ran like rats through the maze of terminals for their Kingston flight, but were minutes late.

'Brilliant,' Janey said as they fetched up at the service desk. 'Ninety minutes till the next one?'

'The others probably waited for us,' Bookalil offered, looking around.

'Yeah right,' Nayce said.

'But the team . . .' Bookalil's natural optimism was sufficient to start but not complete his thought.

The team, Nayce thought but did not say. Any team involving Justin Pongrass and Andrew Blackman was unworthy of the name. Life was a race: this was a race, beating a traffic light was a race. He didn't hold it against them for rushing ahead to Jamaica. Why would they wait? They were born with the wind in their hair; it was their nature to seek out advantage. Nayce tried not to mind too much. The warmer air of Miami, his over-tiredness and the savage comedy of their missed connection put him in a temporary state of giddy loving-kindness. *After all*, he said to himself, *after all, you've got to admire them, they are what they are.*

'Janey? Can you wake me up when they call us to board?'

Nayce knelt beside his carry-on bag, plumping it up as his pillow, then lay on his back with his arms folded across his chest. He couldn't help thinking about the way Hut had behaved on the plane. His absolute predictability, his overflowing *life*, warmed Nayce, as it always had. He annoyed the shit out of you, but—it was like your children—when you were with him you stopped thinking about death. Hut stood, in some indefinable way, for the opposite of mortality, the opposite of death. It wasn't immortality—they were no longer children, though they could still act childishly with each other. It was death's other opposite. Love. That's what it was. Love. Or life. Whatever it was, Hut had always had more of it than Nayce.

Nayce lay on the floor of the gate lounge, drugged with Hut and love, keeping at bay the other thing, the thing that had opened up right out of the blue.

2

Welcome to Jamaica, have a nice day

3

Thirty-one hours after leaving Sydney, the Economy Three made landfall in the Caribbean.

Unlike Christopher Columbus, Nayce would never mistake it for any kind of new world. Jamaica felt ancient, a civilisation on its last legs. Listless men stood around Michael Manley International red-eyed, barely able to prop themselves up against their shadows. Uniformed women sank behind desks losing threads of conversation, their laughter as brief as a snapped twig. Even the taxi drivers were too inert to kidnap the arrivals' luggage and ransom it for a fare. As he emerged from the terminal (porters averting their eyes, taxi drivers finding some reason to wander off), Nayce felt as welcome as a West Indian entering a pub in Gympie.

Walking into the taxi concourse he was struck by two impressions that would lodge with him for the next five days. One was that Jamaica was a country with its own soundtrack. The other was that Jamaica was a country with its own scent.

The soundtrack was reggae: not unknown or generic reggae, but Bob Marley. From somewhere—a string section of cabs in the pit of the arrivals carpark—'Stir It Up' drifted, self-parodic in its lethargy. This was antique reggae, hackneyed, bone-weary, couldn't-give-a-fuck reggae, as if the Jamaicans hadn't realised that Bob Marley was just what an unresearched visitor would be expecting.

His dreadlock holiday. David Nayce didn't dislike reggae: he hated it.

Jamaica's scent also defied the visitor's wish to be surprised. Ganja overpowered aviation fuel at Michael Manley International and the ambient rotten-vegetable third-world understench. Nayce estimated that the ganja being smoked openly by the taxi drivers and porters was only fractionally responsible for the vigour of the scent. The ticketing and reservations officers must be smoking it, he thought. The baggage handlers must be smoking it. The engineers must be smoking it. Jesus, the pilots must be smoking it. And if they weren't smoking it, they had to be breathing it.

The scent wasn't just any ganja. It was old ganja, ancient, earthy and damp, buried in the impaired corners of Nayce's memory. It was late '70s, early '80s—the Bob Marley of ganja. These Jamaicans, he thought. Ganja, Marley, and three out of four men a beanie-topped Rasta. First impressions of a country always either rebutted or confirmed his prejudices. A new place was either just as or nothing like he'd expected. The only way out of this was not to expect anything (*Hut*, was where this thought led Nayce. *Hut*). Jamaica was exactly as Nayce had expected, only more so. In other words, it was nothing like he expected: when he was looking for national stereotypes he didn't expect the locals to go so far out of their way to help him. In London and New York, even a couple of times in Sydney, he'd come across expat Jamaicans. They'd struck him as cool, steady, ambitious and as desperate as any Westernised African or Indian or Turk to avoid being sucked back into the oppressive formulae of the old country. He now realised that they weren't getting away from war or corruption or arranged marriages or the trap of a caste system; they were getting away from Bob Marley and '70s ganja.

As he turned around and went back into the terminal, Nayce gave himself a mental slap, realising he was only projecting his disappointed perfectionism. A year ago, when Janey had first mentioned coming to Jamaica for the race, he'd conjured a picture-postcard image of the trip. It had been curling at the edges ever since: the insinuation of Pongrass and Blackman into the team, the late addition of Hut (which Nayce still believed might be a wind-up, possibly at his personal expense), the separation into First-Class and Economy travelling factions, again thanks to bloody Hut . . . and everything else besides, bringing new blisters and discolouration to Nayce's perfect picture . . . And if it couldn't be perfect, did he want it at all? Wasn't it ruined? He had to press down an impulse, petulant but powerful, to wish sabotage upon the whole thing.

Patting his moist bald head—his *new look*—as if settling a restive baby, Nayce returned to the terminal, where Book was making Janey laugh while standing guard over their luggage. Book wouldn't ever shave his head: it would regrow by dinnertime. His black mop was so thick and straight it looked like a wig, leaving a tow-path of forehead before his hedge of black eyebrow. Book wore a T-shirt and jeans, Janey a loose generic rugby jersey over a white T-shirt and ski pants. Janey favoured active sportswear that accentuated her resemblance to a slim, tanned, exceedingly pretty eleven-year-old boy. When she laughed, her whole body bounced as if it were travelling over a rutted road. Her raucous tomboy honk rebounded off the ceiling. Nayce knew no other woman who crossed gender lines with such abandon. Janey's was the kind of laugh that could win a woman popularity among men even if she had nothing else. But Janey had plenty more, all of it wasted, Nayce thought grimly, on her fellow travellers.

Still smiling at something Book had said, she looked questioningly at Nayce.

'We're in it on our own,' he said. 'It's sink or swim.'

Shaking her head at male incompetence, Janey went out and made herself impossible to ignore on the concourse apron. A taxi driver roused himself from an absorbing if glacier-paced conversation with a possibly deceased colleague under a palm tree to come to her aid, but only after looking around to see if anybody else, including the bundle of rags under the tree, wanted to go first. The competitive spirit seemed lacking. Nayce and Bookalil dragged their luggage, with spent force, after Janey, who removed her rugby jersey in the moist heat.

The driver's nom de guerre was 'Respect', or so it was deduced after he introduced himself with a proffered set of knuckles (Janey it was who showed the boys how, nudging her fist against the driver's and giving it a clockwise half-twist) and said:

'Respect.'

He did the same with Nayce and Bookalil, saying each time: 'Respect.' A crimson decal (bloody, dripping, boiling) on his back window said: 'RESPECT'. And then, in the car, Janey said: 'Okay, I'm Janey, and this is David, and this is John.' The driver tilted his forehead and said:

'Respect.'

Respect's sooty fifth-hand Ford Escort smelt of what hadn't occurred: cleaning. A rich indoorsy tang, reminiscent of raisins, brought to Nayce's mind old ladies in shut-up flats. After Janey told him which hotel they were going to, Respect puttered through Kingston's outskirt slums into the slums of the middle ring and the slummed-down cement and security ironwork of the garden suburbs, until finally entering the inner city, the hell that locals called the slums. Across the front seat Janey burbled away to Respect, whose corded neck and halo of hair, the colour, aroma and shape of a crystallised cloud of dope smoke, gave an occasional timeless nod.

'You going to Montego Bay, Negril?' Respect said without a glimmer of interest.

The more Nayce examined him, the more amazing Respect looked. Each of the features on his face boasted eons of world history. Left unattended on another face, any of these features would have dominated ruthlessly. Together, they maintained a nuclear-strength detente. The eyes, milky in the dark parts and black-blooded in the whites, surged from their sockets with a force suggesting someone had misread the pressure gauge while filling them up. The horizontal brow was furled thick as a weekend newspaper. The nose, an equilateral pyramid of gristle, had pores as big as nostrils and nostrils as big as mouths. And the lips, with their cusps and mouldings and vents and philtrum-sized vertical cracks, the lips that looked like the result of someone's effort to turn his whole head inside-out—Nayce didn't want to think about the lips.

'Uh-uh,' Janey shook her head. 'Negociante Classic.'

Respect let out a weary sigh. 'The swimming race.'

Life's guarantees: death, taxes, and the stupidity of foreigners. Nayce could have hugged the man.

4

A BUILDING THAT could not avoid being a hotel—two vast slabs of salmon-pink cement flanking a barred gate—pulled up alongside the taxi. The Wyndham Hotel, Kingston's premier bolthole. Ragged ghosts buttressed the wall with their worldly possessions, compact enough to pass through the needle's eye. They might have been beggars but none could be fucked putting his hand out.

Janey, whose radiance could outlive the sun, chirruped to Respect, who opened his boot for Nayce and Bookalil to take out their bags like a gentleman opening a door for ladies, before stalling his Escort in a dirt square opposite the hotel.

'What's he doing?' Nayce asked Janey.

'Oh, waiting for us.'

'Waiting.'

'Until we come out again later.'

'So the meter's running?'

'He and I struck a deal,' she smiled, showing both ranks of teeth. Janey's smile was a triumph of willpower: every man in her life had been a sinker on the corners of her mouth, and every smile was telling them—him?—that she would not be dragged down.

She hitched her short sleeves over her shoulders, giving her T-shirt the look of a gym outfit. Janey was too free-spirited and dazed by outdoor life to follow fashion, but her streaked dark-blonde hair, cut to kiss her shoulders, white T-shirt and ski pants also seemed to situate her within a cultural moment. Looking at her, Nayce thought that women, just now, had finally got it right. A historical zenith in the afternoon tropical sunlight.

'We pay him a hundred J-bucks to be our personal driver until tomorrow,' she said.

Nayce looked across the road. The sandy vacant lot, between a government building and a bank, was half-filled with parked taxis. In the bank's shadow and under a row of dusty palms, a pineapple-seller had set up, shaving fruit with a machete and handing out slices to the drivers, hustlers and hotel workers who had come out for a break. Two men in chef's uniforms laughed as they kicked a hackisack. A gourd-shaped woman held a chunk of pineapple in one upraised hand and a white Bratz doll in the other while she teased a bearded Rasta with a bump-and-grind against his unresponsive hip. In his car, Respect was bent over his dashboard, bright pink tongue lowering like a crane over the construction of a nine-paper bunger.

'We're going out again?' Bookalil yawned, stretching arms, neck, mouth. His beard had grown during the trip and glinted blue-black. 'Hotel looks inviting.'

'Maybe tonight, you never know your luck,' Janey said like a tour guide hiding cards up her sleeve.

'Speaking of which,' Nayce said, 'does anyone know what time it is?'

'Three,' Janey said.

'PM, I presume. What day?'

'Monday.'

'Date?'

'Eighteenth.'

'What day's the race?'

'Thursday the twenty-first.'

'Thank you.'

Nayce was ready for the scene in the hotel: Hut lounging with a poolside daiquiri, Pongrass stroking lazy laps, Blackman parenthesised by the dusky haunches of the house masseuse. But the First-Class Three were neither in the hotel lobby nor by the pool. Nayce said: 'Our earlybirds must be catching their beauty sleep.'

Nayce, Book and Janey took adjacent rooms on the second floor. After showering and changing, they reconvened by the pool and ordered cocktails. Book left the hotel and walked to a shopping mall to buy a road map of the island.

To shake out the travel kinks, Janey slipped into the pool in her one-piece and began stroking laps. Nayce sat in his banana lounge and watched her slide through the water with the ease of a bubble rising to the surface. Her strokes soothed his aches and brought back the perfect genesis of the project.

Twelve months ago, he had been stripping down for his daily forty laps at the Boy Charlton pool when he'd run into Janey. To dodge the awkwardness of the moment—she had come to Sydney without letting him know she was in town—she had told him with great enthusiasm about the Negociante Classic. One of her billionaires had swum in it or bought it or something. Nayce and Janey decided, jokingly, to train for the biennial Classic. She was taking a four-week holiday in Sydney and he had swum with her every day, managing to skip over the question of why she'd come home without telling him.

Nayce had researched the Classic on the Net—'a Fun Swim across treacherous tidal Straits' as the website put it. Piloted boats took teams of five swimmers from mainland Jamaica across the Straits of Negociante, where they would line up alongside 'the traditionally fifty or sixty competing teams'. The cross-current return swim measured seventeen kilometres and could take a relay of five anything from three to twelve hours. Their boat accompanied them. The rules were that each swimmer swam precisely thirty minutes, regardless of distance covered, then tagged over. This rotated through the five-swimmer team—everyone doing half-hour sets—until, after two rotations, in a rule-bend taking account of the insurance premiums the race organisers had to pay against swimmer expiry, any member could swim for any period. It was a great race, a 'Legendary race' (the website assured him; personally he hadn't heard of it, but he didn't follow these things).

In the ensuing months, after Janey flew overseas to go back to work, the crazy idea of training for the Negociante Classic gave shape to Nayce's solitary grind up and down the pool, or diverted it from the shape given it by other anxieties. He wasn't training hard every day because he was having a midlife crisis. He was training for a race: to achieve something. It was different.

Then, nine months ago, Nayce's second-oldest friend, John Bookalil, joined him at the pool and word by word they talked the race into existence, with a fixed date and the necessary planning. They'd needed a team of five, though, and on her next visit home Janey brought Andy Blackman, whose cousin was married to Janey's sister. Then Blackman brought Justin Pongrass.

Nayce knew Justin Pongrass and Andrew Blackman in the way that people at the big end of town knew each other, an extension of the way they knew each other at school and university. Beyond those horizons, Pongrass and Blackman enjoyed a wider, if timeworn, fame: they had been Olympic athletes, in rowing and swimming, two decades back. When Pongrass and Blackman joined in, the training took on a serious competitive edge. On Pongrass's first day, Nayce swam three kilometres, then sprayed his breakfast and morning tea on the boards. He swam seven days a week in the subsequent months, three k a pop, grinding his time down under an hour, under fifty-five minutes, plateauing at fifty-one (another gut-voiding exertion the day he broke fifty-two). He flabbed down and muscled up. He drank less and ate better.

Nayce had consoled himself in the solitude of the swimming, shared only with his own white light. He wanted to see how far he could stretch his body's elastic. His relentless will to self-improvement, or its estranged sibling, self-punishment, cogged his mental stopwatch to the timer on the wall. The five team members swam against each other yet also for each other, a perfect modern organisation with its internal parts engaged in a war that produced, as its collateral damage, efficiency. There was nothing shared about the swimming except the post-mortems, the lifts home, and the hell of the Friday lunches where they soon began talking about the race as if it were an actuality rather than a joke. Like a major crime, it evolved as one small step leading to another, without any real decision, before anyone could say no: a game of dare.

Janey climbed out of the pool and went to the desk to find the others' room numbers, but was told that Mr Pongrass, Mr Blackman and Mr Hutchison had not checked in.

Back outside, drawing up a banana lounge next to Nayce's, she asked: 'What do you think's happened to them?'

He pulled a grimace. 'Can't say I've been thinking about it.'

'You reckon they've gone off somewhere?'

'Maybe they've met a gang of murderers. I hope they've sacrificed Hut. Then we'd be back down to five swimmers.'

'That's what I like about you, Dave. Always seeing the bright side.'

'How can you say that?' he blinked.

'What? Oh, yeah, I forgot. The Ethical Investor. Capital with a

Conscience. Forgive me, Comrade.' She looked beyond his shoulder. 'Better chase up those Fair Trade fifteen-dollar daiquiris.'

As she got up and passed him, she dragged a fingernail over his sweat-slick head. Almost as a point of principle, as if to hold his line in the argument, he stayed his hand from touching the stripe fizzing from crown to nape.

She was quickly back with the drinks. 'What order do you think we should swim?'

Nayce grunted: 'Fucking Hut. The rules say five swimmers a team.'

'Gosh, how did we get the head-count wrong?'

'We never really sat down and talked about him, did we? About whether we were happy for him to come. And now it's too late.'

'Maybe you can quietly lose him somewhere between here and Negociante. Plenty of quiet rest stops in Jamaica.'

'I asked him not to swim, when we were on the plane.'

'You did?'

'He wasn't very responsive.'

Janey gave a smile, as if hearing a joke that excluded Nayce. 'I'm not surprised. We wouldn't even be here if it hadn't been for him.'

Nayce snorted. 'He got carried away with himself.'

'If not for Hut getting carried away with himself,' Janey said, 'you'd be swimming up and down the pool having happily postponed it until next time. Two years away? Perfect. All the more time to wallow in your midlife whatever-it-is.'

He knew what Janey thought: the race would have remained a fancy like all the other fads and notions that littered their collective past—their legacy, a garageful of costly toys gathering dust—if Hut hadn't stepped in and taken the idea all too seriously. Hut it was who had obtained the entry forms, paid the deposit, collected and sent off the required documentation.

'Crap,' Nayce said, giving his daiquiri an emphatic suck. Janey was the only person he'd allow to talk to him like this. If Sophie had said 'midlife crisis' one more time, he would have flipped. But Sophie was his wife, and Janey was Janey. 'We were about to register anyway, and he stepped in so he could make sure he was included. I should have put my foot down, said no.'

'Like you always do,' Janey smirked. 'Such a hard man.'

He didn't need to take the bait. He understood the rules of their social circle as well as she: bad form to pronounce a word as crass and confrontational, as pregnant with unknown consequence, as humourless, as *No*. Bad form to take the tongue out of the cheek. To speak directly from the heart was to blink, to lose the game.

'He looks fit though,' Janey said. 'Actually, he looks *great*.'

'He's going to fuck it all up. I don't know how, but he'll find a way.'

'One thing I've always loved about you,' Janey said, 'is your positive certainty about the future.'

'Fuck it.' Fuck Hut—fuckut—he mixed into his breath. He put on his headphones and shuffled through his iPod, thumb rotating and tapping, Parkinsonian convulsions.

Hut had never been part of the race, the team. Nearly three months before, as the team grew fitter and leaner, harder and browner, Hut had become involved. They'd started a Friday tradition of post-swim lunches at a restaurant on the harbour, and on the day they started talking about paying their five-hundred-dollar entry deposit for the Classic, Hut had shown up at the lunch and invited everyone to Palm Beach for a 'pre-race camp'. Nayce assumed Hut was an adjunct team member, a mascot only in it for the social climbing, until Hut appeared at the pool a week after Palm Beach with the entry forms and accommodation bookings, triumphantly 'all sorted'. The documents included the mark, ineradicable, of J. Hutchison in the new six-man team.

None of them said no. Pongrass had shrugged with the kind of broad indifference sometimes known as tolerance: 'Cunt's done the gophering . . .' Janey convinced Nayce that Hut wouldn't really swim. And so, without any discussion, without asking permission, with his bluffed air of entitlement, Hut had insinuated himself onto the team.

Nayce had swallowed his anger and tried to counsel the red-head to train. And Hut had. The first time, he stripped down to blancmange at the pool and rolled up and down with the surreptitious pull-along of the lane rope. Then he heaved himself up the steps and rewarded himself with three jam donuts while waiting for the others. Against all predictions, he showed up again at the next session, and the next, and the next. In line with all predictions, he swam a cumulative total of eight laps. Afterwards, he came to the team lunches and monologued about how his muscles ached but 'the pain will be all worth it when we're doing the race, eh guys?'

After Hut's fourth session, Nayce took him aside and said: 'Mate, this is no joke. This swim kills people. You can't faff about here, you've got to get into shape.'

'Yeah yeah,' Hut said airily, as if tired of answering such questions. 'It's under control,' he winked, implying that Nayce should know him better.

But Nayce did know him better, and that was the last they saw of Hut at training. Through the weeks leading up to the race Nayce repeated his warning at the Friday lunch, where Hut reliably was, but not at the pool, where he reliably wasn't. Hut only changed in one respect. He became browner, and trimmer, and lighter. A training athlete's spokes etched themselves around his eyes. His mandible, swaddled for forty years, unsheathed itself from its jowls. Hut was growing handsome, defiantly, and when he graced the harbourfront restaurant he slid into his seat with easy confidence and pulled himself closer to the table than any of the other men. A fortnight before the race, when he patted Nayce's knee and purred, 'It's under control, I'm doing my training somewhere else,' Nayce very nearly gave in to his desire to believe him.

5

JANEY WAS STILL swimming and Nayce was quietly rum-steeped by the time a check-in desk commotion alerted them to three men whose inquiries were strained with long-haul truculence. Nayce sat up in his banana lounge and watched the lobby choreography. Pongrass and Blackman stomped through the glass revolving door, intent on their Palm Pilots (which did look like pilots, guiding their owners into harbour). With itching hands Hut sloped in behind them, glancing from side to side in search of reinforcements. Pongrass and Blackman tore their attention from their devices long enough to bark at the desk staff; they signed their forms with lookaway scribbles and took their key cards to the lift. Hut remained at the desk, slump-shouldered and furtive, while the luggage was brought in. After tipping the porter he did not follow his buddies. Instead he came towards the pool patio. Through the glass his wrenched face uncoiled into frank relief when it met Nayce's.

Janey breaststroked to the near edge of the pool. 'We thought you'd checked in hours ago.'

'Oh, mate.' Hut shook hands with Nayce, waved at Janey, and fell into a banana lounge as dramatically as if he'd spent the afternoon at knifepoint. 'Those guys.' He shook his head. His nose issued a nervy sniff, exhausted by its search for the humour in the situation. 'It wasn't my fault.'

What had shaken Hut and sent the others in a fury to their rooms was nothing so heady as an attempted drug buy gone wrong (Nayce's guess) or an act of touro-terrorism. At Kingston airport, Hut had assumed responsibility for ground transport. He had wheeled and dealt with the denizens of Michael Manley International, outraged by the US-sixty-dollar and fifty-dollar offers from the taxi drivers, determined to show his mates his legendary maths nous, his street smarts. Jeremy Hutchison wouldn't be swindled on this or any other deal, no sirree. 'But we were all pretty ratty after the flight,' he said, First-Class pampering notwithstanding. Hut had found a shuttle bus that would get them to their hotel for eight dollars each—a clear saving of twenty-six dollars. Having secured the trio, the shuttle driver decided to fill his bus with six more passengers. Something about the three Australians had got onto the driver's wick; he dropped off his other passengers first. One lived in the Blue Mountains, inland of Kingston. A couple lived down south. A small family lived back out near the airport.

'Five hours.' Hut's fingers ploughed his hair, shimmering coppery under the patio lights. 'The last straw for Pong and Abo was seeing you two hanging out by the pool.'

'They're really pissed off, eh?' Nayce made no effort to tame his widening grin.

'Mate. I tried to tell Pong a joke and he just about laid some nut on me. I was scared.' Hut did look scared, and chastened. Nayce fancied he saw Hut's features struggle, under the fatigue and humiliation, with an admission that he wished he'd flown Economy; that he'd worked out that Pongrass and Blackman didn't really like him. Welling with pity to see Hut trying to force a smile through his twitching eyelid and rash-edged mouth, Nayce felt his friend's isolation. Yet the years—was it more than three decades they had been friends? Could this be remotely possible?—the years that gave Nayce his shortcut into Hut's feelings also fortified the wall between them, so that Nayce, the most natural person on whom Hut could unburden himself, was also the least likely.

'What do they want to do tonight?' Janey asked, hoisting herself out of the pool.

'How would I know?' Hut said. 'They're not talking to me.'

'Don't worry, you're here now,' Janey said, coming behind to give his shoulders a token rub with wet hands.

'Mate,' Hut gifted Nayce with a look of unusual candour. He looked five years older than yesterday. 'Cheap bastards, you should have flown First.'

6

AFTER FRESHENING UP in his room, Nayce returned downstairs for the evening poolside barbecue to find Pongrass and Blackman with Janey, Book and Hut.

Justin Pongrass, husbanding a scotch-rocks, was hammocked across his chair: back braced against one arm, legs looped over the other. His position looked awkward but its complicated physics neutralised opposing forces within his back. His impacted lower vertebrae ached like a clenched jaw; the intersection of ribs and spine was a multiple-fatality pile-up; his neck presented a wilier kind of pain, a taunting arthritic sponginess that chose its moments. Sometimes Pongrass wondered aloud if his attitude to all things these days was ruled—bent—by this, rather than the other legacy of his sporting career. He wore a cream-coloured sponsor's windjacket over a faded grey Lacoste shirt and bootcut blue jeans. A white-sandshod foot jiggled into the space beyond his armchair. The ice in his glass responded.

Andrew Blackman, who managed to be both bearlike and bearish—fearsome yet pessimistic, intimidating yet sullen—sank into his armchair with one foot resting on the other knee in the wide-apart, crotch-clearing triangular style. He was washing down a handful of Panadol with a healthy V-8 juice. Like Pongrass, he wore the casual uniform of men who looked as if they'd stepped off a yacht: wilted polo shirt, long twill shorts, and a windjacket so ancient that the chairman of the defunct company sponsoring the pocket had not only been convicted of fraud but had served his sentence and been released. His feet were encased by leather deckwalkers the size of carry-on luggage. His raised right foot also jiggled, while a secret smile waved off his post-flight pains with more confidence, and certainly more sincerity, than the many-toothed grin with which he had waved off the estranged-and-two after his supervised-access farewell the previous day. His wife, Blackman liked to say, could teach airports a thing or two about tight security.

They lined up at the serving tables with their plates. Bain-maries were labelled with the 'international menu' items: honeyed pork ribs, tandoori lamb cutlets, jerk chicken, piripiri chicken, filet mignon, and finally, in its saucy tray, butter chicken—only the stencil had cracked and lost its 'B'. 'I'll have the utter chicken, thanks,' Nayce said to the chef.

As a race, as a gene pool, they were tall humans. Privilege bred height. Blackman was six-four, Pongrass six-two, Hut about six-one. Among them, Nayce's five-ten felt runtish. Even Janey, at five-seven, sometimes felt taller than him. Only dark hobbity Book, at a buttery five-six, could make Nayce feel one of the genetic giants. The sense of being surrounded by tall timber, a splendid forest, would comfort him in the race, as if they had a design advantage. Perhaps tallness was the key to how people like Pongrass and Blackman saw the world. Above all, they were . . . *above all*.

The team shared a table and clicked cutlery over roasted meats dripping sweet sauces backed by steel drums. Nayce ate his utter chicken. Underemployed staff wandered aimlessly—the Wyndham's windows were mostly dark—with the languor of pupils running down the clock on a school Friday afternoon. Hut sat, uncharacteristically quiet, across the table from Nayce and worked on his beef. The music, the over-dressed food, the lingering ganjaroma were evidently as much Jamaica as Hut, battered by the flight, slaughtered by the shuttle bus, could take for now.

For the most part they talked about people they knew back home. There were only twenty private schools of a certain rank in Sydney; within those about fifteen per cent of students went on to Sydney University; within those about one-fifth had attended residential colleges; within those about one-third had maintained the network through adulthood, mainly in the financial services sector. This subset of subsets constituted 'everyone', so that when Janey said of a recent (or upcoming?) harbourfront party, 'everyone' was or would be 'there', the other five at the table knew whom she meant, as if 'everyone' was just beyond the hotel walls.

Janey was wearing a royal blue T-shirt crudely stencilled with the team's name: *The Fast Set*. Even though he had coined it, seeing the T-shirts gave Nayce a new pinch of resentment. Months ago, he and Janey had tossed around The Big End, as in Town, but Janey said 'people will think it refers to the size of our arses'. They'd settled on the name in recognition of a warning Janey's grandmother had once given her against 'socialising with the fast set'. The Fast Set—it brought to mind swimming training, and freighted its own self-ridicule, both as archaism and as inaccuracy. Nayce and Janey didn't see themselves as the Fast Set, so it was safe to call themselves this. And yet, once Pongrass and Blackman joined, the ironic undertone was stolen. Pongrass loved The Fast Set, he said, 'cause yeah, that's what we are'.

In Nayce's view, Pongrass was a man for whom double-meanings carried a threat of bitterness and complaint if not outright sedition. For Pongrass, anything on earth could be taken lightly; war, death, suffering, and certainly the day-to-day misfortunes of others were good for a laugh. Life's tough when you're born into an investment bank; how else are you to get by, if not to laugh at others? But Pongrass's oceans of good humour lapped limply against the granite bluffs of his self. Only one person in five billion could never raise a laugh from Justin Pongrass: the forty-two-year-old eminence of Justin Pongrass.

Pongrass and Blackman seemed vestigially angry with Hut about the shuttle bus. When they uncoupled their attention from their PDAs their eyes were magnetically repelled from him. Now, as if nobody but the two of them were there, Pongrass was telling Blackman a story about a coming of age.

'Leigh Something, older sister of an older friend. Or older friend of my older sister. Can't remember. I was only eleven. Anyway,' Pongrass leaned forward, his elbows on his knees as if putting a business proposal. 'There was no purchase. You know what I'm saying? The *air* in there. No suction. Ever had that?'

Blackman nodded, thoughtfully caressing his chin between thumb and forefinger. 'Bit like blowing into a Breathalyser: no resistance. It's just . . . whaaa.' Like a ham actor attempting a fit, he blew and coughed.

'But there was this circle of us having a go, and I was pulling away at her like an all-day sucker,' Pongrass continued, sweeping his eyes to include Janey in his audience. 'The other fellers were all fourteen. Cheering for me, like, "Look at the kid!" I was only staying down because I couldn't work out what was going wrong. And because nobody else said anything, I figured that this kind of air-mouth was how girls did it.'

'The original air-head,' said Blackman, who had never met Leigh Something.

Pongrass darkened and softened, fixing on Janey. 'So, next one I tongued, I took a deep breath and sucked on her like she was a snorkel. She was screaming her head off! Turned out I'd ruptured the webbing under her tongue. She needed stitches. They called me the Human Hoover and I was only eleven—seriously, what a way to start your life.'

Nayce was barely listening, chewing chagrin into his cheeks over The Fast Set, the theft of self-parody and its exchange for the printed, personalised blue T-shirts and peaked caps, supplied by one of Hut's companies.

He looked across the table to Hut, for support. But Hut had been woken by Pongrass's story and was snickering away. For a moment, Nayce failed to recognise him, literally, as if, assailed by a bout of Capgras Syndrome, he found himself a long way from home in the company of imposters. Nayce fought back the strangest urge to start crying. His bond with Hut was flawed, but as solid and permanent and reliable as blood. Was he jealous? Absurd as it seemed, he could only liken his sudden loneliness to the first tremors of a lover's panic.

7

'So what's the plan for tomorrow?' Hut asked Janey, the natural leader.

'It's a five-hour drive to Negociante Bay, and we don't check in there until late afternoon. So we might hang around and see the sights of Kingston in the morning. Unless you got enough sight-seeing done on your bus ride?'

Janey included Pongrass and Blackman in the question.

Hut, not daring to look at those two, shrugged. He hadn't retained any detailed impressions from that ordeal. Narrow rutted roads, kids in blinding white schoolshirts, coffee plantations, traffic police with handguns, and the rising tide of shame and car-sickness. 'Maybe we'll all sleep in,' he said with the stealthy eyes of a man flying below the radar. 'Keep ourselves fresh.'

A silence settled over the table. Staff removed plates and replaced cocktails.

After a while Pongrass put aside his Palm Pilot and his air of business. He stretched his Olympian arms above his head, knitting his fingers and turning his wrists inside out. A peacock fanning his tail.

'Damn, what I'd give for a bit of It.'

'Oh, sweet lord, yeah,' said Blackman.

With veiled eyes, Hut canvassed reactions around the table. Nayce and Janey swapped a glance.

'It. Outrageous,' Hut said with what he judged to be clever ambiguity.

The team had no strict game plan on the matter of pre-race substance abuse. Hut, in his innocence, had assumed all bets would be off until the race was swum, but this, like most of his assumptions, now seemed burred with question-marks.

It was a code word, coined by Pongrass, for cocaine. As in: Coke Is . . . All of the Fast Set had taken, or took, It. (There was no clear line between those who had taken and those who took. Who could say, after all, at which point hobby became habit?) They were wealthy white Sydneysiders in their early forties. Some had done coke as little as fifteen or twenty times, a special treat. For others, like Pongrass, It was a tenet of belief, a rock in a storm, a God, an ideology. After the weekly Friday post-training lunches, Pongrass would transform from his usual aloof cockiness into an intimate, winking co-conspirator; with a nudge he would guide each team member to the toilet with a personalised sachet. It was his one act of generosity, or mateship, as long as you didn't see it (as Nayce did) as the blind egotism of a man who couldn't bear to get high on his own. The It hour brought out Pong's charm, and every week the team allowed it, and It, to rope them in.

For Hut, the Friday lunches had begun to wash up at sunrise on Saturday. He was dipping his toes into the deep, dangerous water of Pong-world, and finding it surprisingly warm and welcoming. What was the point of it all if you couldn't be a bad boy once in a while? Hut felt light-headed with the thrill of unpunished obnoxiousness. Bad behaviour, like truth, beauty and heroism, was something he had always admired from afar. Risk scared him; he preferred to watch others tempt fate. But friendship with Pongrass and Blackman was luring him out of his timidity. Truth, beauty and heroism might be beyond him, but behaving like a brute was within reach, if he could raise himself to chance it. There was something honest, glorious and even heroic in true obnoxiousness. He couldn't quite understand why—and he sensed that this was an infatuation he ought to have passed through and left behind when he was ten years old—but the world smiled upon badness and it indulged shittiness and it was seduced by the unapologetic male principle, and Hut wanted a piece of that, if it wasn't too late. It helped, of course, if you had glamour. Justin Pongrass's glamour was an obvious thing. He used to be literally glamorous, world's best practice good-looking. A touch of Elvis: rosebud mouth tucked into round cheeks, eyes like black river stones. If, at forty-two, Pongrass looked a bit like Elvis at forty-two, that didn't diminish the essential glamour; he was a public celebrity, not just a local one, and no matter how much you played it down, fame couldn't but excite you.

Pen never exactly threw a coming-home party when he trotted bushy-eyed and bright-tailed into the house at 7 am, but he presented it as sacrifice in the name of a worthy cause. These were important new friends he was making. And he made it up to her by getting stuck into the housework.

So—It. Why not indeed? Tonight was Monday, the race was Thursday, and the Fast Set's arrival in Jamaica did seem to call for celebration. At least two Big Nights could be had before race eve. Hut saw a light on the hill.

'Let me take care of it,' he said, feeling instant popularity, warm as a pissed-in wetsuit, when Pongrass cried: 'Right on, Hut!' It—It—would be his redemption.

Hut skipped off to the wet bar, where he had been befriending floral-shirted Fidel, a tall open-faced man with a Slinky of silver hoops in each ear. Hut leaned into the bar, bobbled his eyebrows and murmured: 'Hey, Fidel. How's it hanging?'

Fidel finished decorating a cocktail, crouching to set his split strawberry on the rim and pierce the straw through a maraschino, rotating the glass 360 degrees before sliding it with cupped surgeon's hands to the edge of the bar, where it was escorted away by a colleague. Fidel took up a towel, swiped the mahogany counter and said, without addressing Hut visually, 'What I can do for you, sir?'

'Eh. Fidel.' Hut leaned closer. Knowing it was uncool to ask where he could get any, he said: 'Do you know, ah, what's the, ah, *seediest* bar in this part of town?'

Fidel ran a tap into his cocktail shaker and dismantled it for cleaning. '"Seediest", sir?'

'You know—where the, ah, low-lifes hang out.'

Fidel was doing his best not to look at the red-mopped guest, but let slip a puzzled glance. 'You don't want to be messing with low-lifes here, sir.'

'Hey, no worries, Fidel. But um, you know, I just wanted to know where we'd go if we wanted to have some *fun*. You know?'

Fidel now regarded Hut with open judgement and even hostility, but Hut, being Hut, failed to read the barman's direct stare. Fidel mumbled a list of 'the better-known nightspots'.

Hut persisted, in a heavy voice: 'No-no—somewhere *really seedy.*'

Unbeknown to Hut, Fidel was carrying three grams of cocaine in his shirt pocket and had been losing hope of selling them to these yuppies; but it was too dangerous for Fidel to assume that this was what Hut in fact wanted, and to take the initiative and offer it would break Fidel's personal code. He'd gladly have sold it, but he couldn't be certain what Hut was getting at. Why would these guys want to hang out with low-lifes? To appease the redhead, who seemed to want to take charge of the night, Fidel gave the name of the nearest disco: the Sly Mongoose. He suggested the Sly Mongoose because it was one block from the Wyndham and therefore posed the slenderest risk of these guys getting mugged. 'Real low-life bar,' he said.

'Cheers, mate.' Hut pressed a ten-Jamaican-dollar note into Fidel's pocket, narrowly missing contact with the still-for-sale baggie.

At the table, Hut mouthed to Pongrass: 'It's on.'

Pongrass sprang to his feet like a man who had just remembered an appointment. 'Right, who's in?'

Blackman, loyally, stepped up. Bookalil, sensing the wind's direction, gave a nod.

'I'm rooted,' Nayce said. 'Destination fart-sack.'

'No way!' Hut roared. Five minutes ago he was hoping to be swallowed by a hole in the ground; now he was pack leader. Hut and the desire for popularity enjoyed a special, if capricious and abusive, relationship. 'Sly Mongoose—how could you resist a place with a name like—'

'I can't tell you how much I'd love to join you,' said Janey, hand covering a yawn. 'But it's calypso collapso time for me.'

'I can't lift my feet. I can't even lift my voice,' Nayce said.

Hut was about to launch into an Agincourt speech in favour of the Sly Mongoose, but Pongrass interrupted him.

'Okay, okay, we're off. Skates, Abo.'

8

Fidel had been good to Hut's request. The Sly Mongoose was the seediest bar within walking distance of the Wyndham: a sombre, linoleum-themed joint on the ground floor of a blacked-out shopping mall. Beside its entrance, surmounted by a flickering purple neon rodent, were two security guards playing Texas Hold 'Em at a baize table with two Rastas. The Rastas made a token effort at selling the Australians some tourism-inappropriate wares: local lottery tickets, phone cards, TV guides. The guards' presence appeared to put paid to the kind of commerce Hut was looking for.

When the four members of the Fast Set entered, they increased the Sly Mongoose's clientele by two hundred per cent. The two regulars at the bar had not spoken for more than an hour, or perhaps a year, but their silence deepened to a new inkiness when the Australians waltzed in. Incautiously, Hut bought a round of Mai Tais, unmixed precipitates in smeared highball glasses. The boys slumped on their stools in the disinfectant-scented darkness. Blackman's finger pushed a brownish icefloe around the surface of his cocktail; Pongrass drummed a ready-to-leave beat on the bar.

Pongrass crossed the shadows to a jukebox but returned shaking his head bitterly. 'Forty-five pages of friggin' reggae.'

Hut kept drinking, feeling personally enlarged, moistened, by being able to fly on the wing of this grand Olympian who had rowed for Australia: bowsman of the Coxless Quartet, the Four Oarsmen of the Apocalypse who won gold at Buenos Aires. (Pongrass was the one with the eyes, the teeth, the packed lunch.) Pong's rowing was really a recreational interlude before the business of accumulation had to be taken in hand rather than merely left to happen. After retiring from the sport, Pong had become a broker in the trading firm owned—not managed, not directed, not partnered, but *owned*—by his father Duncan. From his job sitting on the phone talking to his mates Pongrass pulled down three hundred and fifty K, excluding bonuses, but this was just play money, almost a joke, something to keep him looking respectable and paying income tax while making plans upon the contingent asset of a dead Duncan.

As Pongrass and Blackman were shooting each other a let's-get-out look, Hut probed the barman about It but his hints fell on perhaps literally deaf ears. Finally, dropping the pretence and showing he could lose patience with the best of them, Hut jutted his chin and enunciated to the barman, loudly and slowly as if to someone very young or very old: 'Listen, man—mon—do you know where we can get any co-caine?'

The barman eyed Hut—or Hut's shirtfront—and said: 'You leave right now.'

Without finishing, or really starting, their Mai Tais, Pongrass, Blackman and Bookalil walked out. Hut drained his on principle, just to show the cut of his jib, and trailed out to the street where the others were in a taxi. One of the card-playing Rastas was behind the wheel, and Pongrass was telling a story.

'Ever tell you about my first nip?'

'Don't think so,' Blackman lied: an obvious, hence privately funny, denial.

'Sally Hudson. I was twelve. Just met her on a party phone call and made an arrangement for the sandhills. It was nothing much, a head of garlic; when I bit down she belted me on the ear. I was deaf for a day.'

Though Blackman's mouth wore the inverted-U he reserved for amusement so great it must be suppressed, Pongrass wasn't telling the story with humour, although with Pongrass it was sometimes hard to tell.

'I'm pissed off about that thick ear,' he said, rubbing as if it still hurt. 'I mean, why would a girl want to hit *me*? What's not to love?'

'Search me.' Blackman shook his head sorrowfully. 'Could only've been an accident.'

'Yeah!' Hut grinned. 'Could only've been an accident!' Since boyhood he had had a keen sense of what was better, by how much, and who looked down on whom from how high. All six of the group had gone to top private schools—but there were private schools and private schools; there were heights to which even the elites craned their necks with tingly awe. Pongrass and Blackman played rugby and rowed, whereas Hut and his schoolmates Nayce and Bookalil played soccer and cricket. Pongrass and Blackman went to university colleges to fuck and drink, whereas Hut's ilk had tried, for a time at least, to study. There were subtler financial distinctions too, flowing not from the quantity of money but from its age.

Hut's disposition towards all this was that of the pure enthusiast. Born rich, yet just far enough *outside* to feel like a visitor, Hut savoured the trappings like a collector.

Blackman exuded the Great Public Schools glamour that Hut had always found so intoxicating. Swimming, rowing, polo, B & S balls, the smell of horse hide. Financial markets, tuxedos, big-deal church weddings. Something soared when you were with

Blackman; and the guy was so down to earth, not the least bit snobbish. At check-in at Sydney Airport, even though he was as good as an Olympian swimmer—he'd been selected for the BA Games but pulled out with a badly cut hand—Blackman had locked onto everyone's eyes like gears meshing, and declared that he was going to be swimming for them—they for him. 'There's no I in team,' he'd said. Wherever they'd all come from, they had checked in as equals.

These days Blackman parked derivatives for Nomura. It was play money for him too, for he was seriously landed; his family bred polo ponies and stud Herefords, one of those clans who had a twig on half the large-cap boards in the country. There was a William Blackman, a David, a Robert, a Mortimer, even an Alison. You couldn't keep track of them all, but they'd bob up amid the trustees of some school or opera or symphony orchestra and you'd be made to feel a dill for not knowing it. Hut had had to absorb this kind of knowledge quickly and train himself in the *I-already-knew-that* look. The Blackmans never cropped up individually in Most Wealthy lists. They were, simply, The Blackman Family, worth somewhere between four hundred and ten million and five hundred million depending on seasonal farm prices. The current generation, Abo's, was thin on the ground. The oldest money kept the juice concentrated. Abo had only two cousins and was himself a forty-two-year-old only child, roosting on that stash like a seedy old Prince of Wales. His sun-blasted father Hilton kept a stable of floozies around the countryside but had always made sure, once the heir was born, to double-bag. As number one in a run of one himself, Hut approved. His own father emulated the higher orders in strategy, if not style.

But being rich was no substitute for being young. As Hut often said, he'd swap it all to be eighteen. After thirty, the problem was finding playmates. If you'd got ahead of the pack like Hut had, when you got a free week you'd look around for your old buddies and they'd be working, they'd have to go home to their brood, they weren't up for it anymore. You could get too far ahead.

This trip was an antidote to all that and Hut savoured it: for five endless days they *could* be eighteen again. Free as birds. What could beat that? In Jamaica he would party all night; dawn would signal crawling into bed rather than out of it; he would take drives into the coffee mountains, dives into the Caribbean shelf; he would encounter the culture, hear its music, trade in its stalls, speak its jive; he would replenish those friendships he was taking with him; and, as a pinnacle, he would swim the race.

'What's not to love?' Hut repeated. He had a penchant for repeating punchlines, over and over, until the last droplets of laughter had been squeezed out. 'What's not to love, yeah!'

The four Australians went to three more bars, in each of which Hut attempted to assert his place as quest leader, which in effect meant that he spoiled Pongrass's subtler, cannier endeavours to score. In the last of these places, an insipid hotel annexe that was insulin to Kingston's sugared rum, just as the realisation came upon Hut that this was Jamaica, after all, and you couldn't play fast and loose with the drug scene, so maybe it was time to drop the bit, he returned from the bar to an empty table. Figuring the boys were waiting for him outside, he gulped down two rum punches. He trailed out again, the pattern established in a string of dead bars (boys walk in, Hut buys drinks; boys walk out, Hut finishes drinks), but this time they hadn't asked their taxi to wait. Not even Book had spoken up for him. Or, he thought, there must have been some reason: taxi was too small. That'd be it.

He peered optimistically up and down the street but failed to conjure a car. Just like Sydney: they were never there when you needed them. But then it came to him that it wasn't like Sydney at all. The enormous singularity of being left there, in Kingston, alone after midnight, slowly dawned on Hut. Or rather, it hid from him; it hid behind his good nature and iron will to believe, at the worst of times, the best of his friends. When the soul's dark nights loomed, Hut irradiated mateship with a blaze of loyalty. He told himself a new tale. The guys had gone back to the hotel to wait for him. They trusted Hut to come up with the goods, with It. And so he would. He relished a challenge.

Like a moth he sought light. True, the light was only that thrown by yellow street lamps and low-heartrate neon; what he was doing was fleeing the peaty blackness of the Jamaican night. From housefronts pressed up against the footpath came the sound of laughter and reggae and the smell of frying chicken. The humid air cooled his cheeks. Cars slowed to observe the surreal sight of a redheaded white man walking alone. Even when the drivers called out to offer help, he bowed his face and clenched his fists like a madman. He was trying not to be in Jamaica; his mission was internal. Soon he found himself in a street lined with what looked like food stalls knocked together out of driftwood, except they were empty of food and filled with people. As he walked, he discovered that the boys' bar crawl had been an error of both location and timing. Location, because they'd been indoors when the action was al fresco. Timing, because they'd been out before one in the morning. It was clear now that nobody came out until the last hours before dawn; no wonder the locals had all looked so tired during the day.

A series of ambiguous but not terribly wrong turns took Hut into a writhing market street. His hearing flailed about between the approximations of jive talk—if he could only see it written, he could understand what they were saying, but he knew that the fact that he couldn't was its whole point—and the oil-and-water of two types of drumbeat, the beat that came from drums and the beat that came from machines. He arrived at a median strip where about a hundred men and women ground their way around a totem pole of speakers covered in green, gold and black cloth. A woman grabbed him by the hips and tried to dry-hump him. Grinning apologetically, unnecessarily and anachronistically—'Sorry, I'm happily married'—Hut fought free. He swam through the mass. People even had their children up, or someone's children. Pre-teens scampered under trestle tables and disappeared behind trees. Family night!

Hut melted into the clamour, unafraid. He would be afraid later, but too many sounds and sights and smells insisted themselves upon him now to leave room for fear. He felt privileged, as if he had stumbled into a carnival of vampires, a voodoo ritual in which he was the untouchable white ghost. Faces brushed him with neither curiosity nor animus, nulled by the music, by the hour, by the ganja. Perhaps, later, they'd be maddened by a white man's trespass. But now there were just phenomena: dope, reggae, teeth, hips, shouts, corncobs, stars, dirt, sweat.

He moved through the crowd with a smile on his face, a light-footed first-world private-school smile, which, as an outward expression of fear rather than calm, was both courageous and naive. It affirmed life. Hut enjoyed a transcendent moment: he might die at any second, but if this was his fate he welcomed it. There was nothing he could do; yes, the worst he could do would be to try to impose himself upon his surroundings. They would smell fear, or doubt: *phoniness*. He was the tamer in a dream lion-cage, testing his trust in himself and discovering a reserve of calm or grace that stood guard over him, like an angel. For some reason he thought of the fisherman who had dragged him out of the surf. *I never thanked him. I've got to find him one day and give him something.*

Hut found himself in a single-room hut, circled by young men in sheeny basketball outfits, their ventilated iridescence reflecting

candlelight and the flash of Bics. Hut took a joint and inhaled—
because it was offered, because it signified acceptance, because
of the marvellous newness of this night—and the next thing he
was sandwiched between a dancing woman's polished mahogany
flanks and a jukebox playing Marley's 'Jammin''. Eyes closed, Hut
was singing the words: 'Jammin' in de place of de Lord . . .' Around
him, boys were playing knife-fights: flicking their blades at the
walls of the hut, competing, it seemed, not to hit a target but to
pierce the wall with the most horizontal twang. Hut cavorted in
the centre of the room, a single thought-substitute in his head:
*This is so great, those other guys don't know what they're missing out
on, their problem is they're too scared, scared of the black man, scared
of the common people* . . . He cottoned on to the Marley lyrics
and continued excusing himself to women whose rumps would be
mortars to his pelvic pestle: 'Sorry—married.' 'Happily married,
love.' 'Father of two.' He doubted anyone could hear or understand
him, but that was, he figured, the beauty of it; *we're all just bodies,
just humans, no race, no class, no history, no religion* . . .

An indefinite period of time later, Hut was trying to buy drugs
off the basketball-shirted boys. They smiled gold ingots and asked
what he wanted.

'We call it It,' he said in what he hoped was a wised-up way. 'I
want It. You get me, ah . . . mon?'

A ringleader, a leader with rings on his fingers and through his
ears and nose and lips and eyebrows and, from what Hut could
see, through his teeth, took a hundred J-dollars of Hut's money
and asked if Hut wanted to 'ride with'.

'Nah, I trustja,' Hut waved him. 'Ya rip me off, man—er—mon . . .'
He tried to think of some jivish expression, but failed, reverting to
home patois: 'Fair cop, way of the world, yeah?'

In entering into a drug deal in a foreign country, Hut never
considered he was taking a risk. He felt shielded by an ambient

recklessness. The feeling resembled what he had felt during the two teenage car accidents he had been in, when, despite his nearness to death, he had seemed privileged to an articulated, bird's-eye-view of the suite of vectors and forces in action, and had known, well before the impact, that he was safe. Even in the second accident when his nose had come to rest less than twenty centimetres from the sheared-off blade of a lethally bent Children Crossing sign, Hut was unsurprised to be unscathed. Without touching his face or any part of his body, he had stepped out of the car and walked towards help.

Reinforcing his localised invulnerability, here in this bouncing den, was the knowledge of what was waiting for him back in Sydney. The worst that could happen here—the appearance of the Jamaican police, or a knife to his throat, the draining of his wallet—appealed as welcome diversions. Maybe being arrested and jailed here, or left destitute, would prevent him returning to Australia. Jail here or jail there—who was to say which was worse? What Kingston's might lack in hygiene, it would make up for in distance from certain people he knew. It wouldn't be such a bad outcome, when he thought about it. It would, at the very least, get right up the corporate regulator's nose.

Goldenteeth and two of his guards had disappeared with Hut's money. He lost track of them, indeed forgot the deal entirely, until some time later he was shaken from 'Iron Lion Zion' by a hand on his shoulder, a ringed smile and a palmed baggie.

'Now you get out of here,' Goldenteeth said.

'Hey, er, "mon"—we can party?'

The boy shook his head. The metal section percussed. 'It get light, it get hazardous for you.'

Something about Goldenteeth, conciding with the natural descent of his own three-hour-old high, put a chill on Hut.

'Okay, mate, okay, I'm, er, witja, is cool.' Hut pushed the bag into his chino pocket and backed out with palms raised.

He found himself in a more male and slightly paler-skyed version of the earlier street party, the atmospheric ganja having ceded meekly to the running-down-the-back-of-the-throat accelerant of amphetamine. The background noise was beginning to clarify: half-kidding shouts were rising into no-kidding shouts. The mixture had changed subtly but irreversibly, as if some self-feeding radioactivity had contaminated it. Patting the bag of drugs against his thigh, as if touching a talisman, he tried to locate the street he'd come up. But now, not only was he stoned and lost, he felt white again; he felt white all over. Eyes that earlier had skated over him now settled for an instant, registering. Fear remained suspended above him, but an abstract danger suggested itself. With detached surprise, like a moviegoer, he said to himself: 'Hey, the nasty bit has started.'

Much maler, now. The music more modern and harsh, less de place of de Lord. Growling voices, neo-Rasta madness. Hut quickened his step—but where to? He realised that the central market area, where he'd discovered the street party, was a star-shaped crossroads, a twinkling rotunda of radial exits. The terrain, though flat, resembled navigationally a mountain: only one peak, but numerous ways to get lost coming down. He strode along one street with the telltale determination of a man who suspects he has chosen the wrong one. He tried to calculate his best odds. Which was the right street? Any that led to a taxi. So there was no right one, in the sense that it was not a matter of finding the one he'd come in on. He just had to spin the wheel and hope like fuck for a taxi and a friendly one at that.

Hut had not left the shanty alone. He was more than vaguely aware that others had become more than vaguely aware of him. At first it was a handful of little boys, giggling, pointing. They collected others, until he moved like a comet, with a tail. Their numbers reached a kind of critical mass—there were so many of them that he had to quicken to get away from them. They achieved their own force: the tail wagging the cur. Hut stole a glance over his shoulder. He had become something he had never been before: a man with a following.

He broke into a run, and the jungle ran with him. It had been one big bluff, after all. You could fly, you could be a black man, if you believed it; but once you stopped believing it nobody else would believe it either.

Yet still there was an inviolable warm pool in his stomach and his pulse rose from exertion rather than straight fear. He smelt petrol, sweat, pineapple, rotten vegetables. Hut had gone under a local anaesthetic: he could see what was happening to him, or about to happen, quite obviously—he was about to be killed— but it failed to penetrate his feelings. He regarded his end with indifference.

But his indifference lasted only as long as he was able to box it in, laugh it off, brush it away: his *end*. People like Hut didn't meet *ends*. He'd realised that at Palm Beach two months ago. Whether long or short, the lives of men like Jeremy Hutchison were lived in open insurrection against finality. Around every corner lurked a new opportunity. The turn of the earth revealed ever-new horizons. If you were a Jeremy Hutchison, you could always spend your way out of death. Death was a hitch, a glitch, a momentary hold-up, a challenge, an opportunity—anything but an *end*.

And yet, as he rounded another cairn of crumbled concrete, it came upon him that he might in fact have wandered out too deep.

Since he had been running, a single pincer had been pushing him along. But every pincer has its mate, every finger its opposable thumb. Now the second pincer was closing in from the other side.

The second pincer wasn't in space, in Kingston. Tonight had its other half in time, a second loop closing around him, choking him down.

9

THEY—THE BOOKALILS, the Hutchisons, Janey, Nayce—had been staying for a week at the Bookalils' family place on Pittwater. It was meant to be a fortnight, the full school holiday, but the Bookalil house was too cramped for six adults and six children, and then there'd been Book's parents staying as well. Hut appreciated all the trouble the Books had gone to, but the shack was mostly weatherboard—walls like manila folders—and it was on the wrong side of the peninsula anyway. And the old scummed-up toaster. And the mothball-smelly beds. And the crinolene. And the rising damp. And the stone-hard water in the taps. And the children, children everywhere, a toddler madhouse. Beach shacks were meant to evoke the past, not flash back its night terrors.

On the middle weekend, as a surprise, Hut had invited Pong and Abo down, and he couldn't help it, when he saw the Bookalils' house with fresh eyes—Pongrass-Blackman eyes—Hut knew he'd be doing everyone a favour if he engineered a relocation.

The Hutchisons didn't own a house at Palm, but they'd rented the same beachfront each year when Hut was a kid. As luck had it, the current tenant, a British television comedy legend, had stormed off halfway through his fortnight, and the house came open at a hugely reduced price. Five grand for the week was a bargain after six nights in the Bookalil nuthouse. So, announcing it as a great happy philanthropic gift, Hut coupled the bulletin of Pong's and Abo's imminent arrival with the news that he, Pen and the boys, and Janey and Nayce if they wished, would give the Bookalils 'a bit of your own space' and relocate to the ocean side.

Pen was quietly furious with him, sucking her anger in through her cheeks. Hut couldn't work out why. Nayce, whose wife and son were in Adelaide with the in-laws, and so had no excuse for bad moods, spent a whole day not talking to him. Yet again. Nayce and his hair shirts: as if he *preferred* discomfort. But anyway, the quietly grateful looks of the Bookalil grandparents were enough to prod everyone along to the palatial beachfront—modern, nice-smelling, clean, airtight, six bedrooms instead of four, two storeys, and smack bang on the surf. Hut received a sheepish word of thanks from Book himself, who didn't seem at all sore to be getting his own house back. The elder Bookalils offered to look after all of the toddlers for one night: the truth was that it had been their adult guests rather than the young children who had been the hardest to host. Fully vindicated, Hut drove to the Pittwater bottle shop and stocked up for the party. Before the sun was up, he was a fluke short of dying in the surf.

When he started pushing at the bedroom doors, Hut knew he could not convey to anyone what he had just survived, and from then—whether it was what had happened to him in the surf or what happened when he started opening the doors, or somewhere in between, somewhere only the fisherman would have witnessed—his sense of the passage of time, his sense of himself in time, had begun to blister up. It hadn't started on the flight to Jamaica. That was when it started to hurt. But the wrong, the point when a space had opened up inside his skin and begun to fill with the water that a body cannot let out, had started earlier.

Those tears, these tears. Time itself had blistered around him. And as he ran from the mob, Hut cried again, his sobs feeding off themselves, cannibal heavings pouring into the burnt air between his two skins.

His complacency underwent no smooth escalation to panic. The quality of the pursuit sounds altered again—animal now, a roar not so much of anger as exasperation. Someone had finally had enough of his impertinence. Hut realised where he was. Kingston. Kingston. The city's name repeated like a tribal drumbeat. Kingston. Kingston. You don't fuck around in places like this. It's not a game here. You don't fuck around. Now he was in a thorough darkness. Smoky lights were coming on inside houses, doors were opening, and ever-larger figures were joining the hunt. Hut was the fox, and these roaring black men, fuelled by rum and ganja and several centuries of whip-scarred shoulders, were flaring their nostrils on his tail. In the alleys, under the railway tracks of Kingston, straws were breaking camels' backs. When every forebear of every man was a slave, what was the value of one fat white neck?

Like a silver ball in a shaken maze he turned corners—left, left, left again, hoping to circle back towards the light. Darkness would swallow him. Illuminated, he would be too visible to come to harm. But he had been running for minutes. He gagged on the tide of bile bubbling up his windpipe. His lungs and stomach furled up into a viscid red soup. A strange minty vapour swirled against the back of his throat, a taste he remembered from schoolboy cross-country races, the taste that heralded, one way or another, the end.

After him they were, a pandemonium. He rounded corners of painted concrete. Was the entire island concreted over? Were the palm trees concrete? Was the pink dawn a second concrete storey?

Faces stopped to watch him run by. His deckwalkers skidded on sand (on concrete). He heard the cruel deep new music of the beginning of the day, the end of the night, and behind him he heard shouting and laughter. But what was the nature of the laughter? What was the laughter of nature? He tripped and fell, and they still seemed to be chasing him rather than setting upon him. He found his feet and rounded a corner and, blubbering with abandonment, crossed a street and cartwheeled over the bonnet, over the roof, over the boot, of an oncoming car.

10

Nayce had had a bad feeling about it from the moment Hut had become overheated about It. As exhausted as he was, Nayce couldn't sleep in the Wyndham. He opened his sliding balcony door and listened to insects that buzzed like broken neon. Crockery clacked in the kitchen, mingled with the weary laughter of finished shifts. Nothing in the Jamaican night was exotic, or gave him the feeling of being on the far side of the world. The enervated chatter of the hotel workers, tired yet revved, interested in life again now that the guests were asleep, was both depressingly and comfortingly familiar. It could be any hotel, anywhere, and he couldn't be in Jamaica as long as he was stuck in himself.

He sat in an armchair in the lobby and waited. When those cunts—those cunts, even Book—came in at half past midnight without Hut, Nayce lost his temper.

Pongrass and Blackman, like dogs to their corners, went to their rooms. Book, shaking his head and asking aloud with his hands pressing his cheeks, 'What did we do? Wasn't he with us? What did we do?', stayed dressed and waited for Nayce to throw on street clothes and get money from his room. In the vacant lot opposite the Wyndham they found Respect snoring in his cab.

They were crawling the non-kerbs, the non-footpaths, the non-grids of Kingston's crumbling centre. Distantly there was music and human noise. Respect told them about the night street parties. Nayce, consumed with anger, found it hard to fix on any direction. No structure was higher than two storeys, and no road ran straight. Nayce's memories connected the city with Los Angeles: no there there, no here here.

'You man, he dead,' Respect kept up a cheerful singsong. 'You man, he dead.'

Nayce asked him to keep driving. 'Either way, mate, we're not going back to the hotel without him.'

While Book was fretfully powered by his guilt for having left Hut, Nayce found a motivation more his own. He wasn't out here to *look after* Hut. It might have seemed that way, and he was content for it to do so, but he wasn't here for Hut. Nayce, always, was motivated by loathing; he was here because of the way Pongrass and Blackman had chuckled and shaken their heads and gone up to their rooms to sleep off their jet lag. Cunts. The wish to save or protect Hut would never have given Nayce sufficient jolt to leave the hotel. Hut could go to hell. But Nayce was so enraged by those scum, those 'Olympians', he wanted to negate them, to find Hut's bleeding carcass and drag it back and throw it down on the end of Pongrass's bed.

Nayce ran a hand over his bald head: touching it had become a tic. Settled in his acidity, he grew comfortable. This was how he was: his enemy's enemy. He'd voted conservatively at university because he hated the greens and crusties. Then, when there were no greens and crusties around him, but only smug bankers and elderly self-justifiers, he voted Labor. In order to move, he needed

79

something to push against. (Physically, too: he loved running uphill, but felt sick running down; he loved to sail on tacks, not on spinnaker runs; he was relishing the upcoming swim because it would be a fight against a current.) So, to teach someone a lesson, Nayce could not deny that, while he was hoping to find Hut, he was hoping to find him hurt.

'Hey, Respect,' Nayce said.

The driver kept his counsel and wheeled his Escort around corners in fourth, too listless to gear down.

Nayce leaned forward between seats, his matte pate streetlight-yellow. 'Respect!'

The driver inclined his head a degree. 'Respect,' he rumbled.

'Where do you think we'll find him?'

Respect shook his head. Organic spores clouded out of his dreadlocks and formed cumulus billows in the headlights of a passing car. 'Kingston it be a big city in daytime,' he said.

'It's a needle in a haystack, yeah? He could be anywhere.'

'But in the night, Kingston it shrink into small island village. All the light it shrink into two, three blocks near the markets. You man he be there. He be dead, but he be there.'

'You seem pretty sure.'

Respect's shoulders rose and fell in two distinct and reluctant movements, a shrug of epic weariness. 'There be nowhere else to go.'

'For him?'

'For you.'

Nayce and Book raked the darkness from the back seat. Overloaded minibuses churned past them, mobile crowd-matter. Clumps of bystanders blocked the road from time to time and Respect slowed, without quite stopping or changing gears, to ask questions. Where had all these people come from? It was nearly dawn, and the place was pulsing. Nayce couldn't pick up the patois of inquiry or reply, but didn't need to. A shrug was a shrug, a lingua franca of indifference: shoulders up for *Don't Know*, shoulders down for *Don't Care*.

Nayce found it hard to keep his eyes from turning inwards. On the inside of the taxi window was a sticker. Its original message was: 'Please leave this taxi as you would like to find it.' Someone had scratched beneath it: 'In a fucking hurry.' Someone else had scratched: 'With your pants on.' Another sticker's original message read 'PRAISE GOD', but a scratcher had altered it to 'RAISE COD'. They reminded Nayce of his favourite serial scratchings back home: the road signs altered from 'HOW FAST ARE YOU GOING NOW?' to 'HOW . . . ARE YOU GOIN . . . ?' and the train carriage perennial, 'AT NIGHT TRAVEL NEAR THE GUARD'S COMPARTMENT MARKED WITH A BLUE LIGHT', doctored to 'AT NIGHT RAVE NEAR THE GUARD'S COMPARTMENT NAKED WITH A BLUE LIGHT'.

Through the window red eyes flashed malignantly from under tumbledown eyelids. Kingston was said to have the highest homicide rate in the world, but there seemed precious few individuals who could be bothered. If you felt any common humanity with these Jamaicans, Nayce wondered, what could you do but succumb to exhaustion? If these people could be fucked contemplating their death, he sensed that they would picture it less as a prospect than as a memory. Kingston was your afterlife if you had been very, very bad. Everything in the architecture seemed improvised—a roof served as a wall, a door served as a roof, a car served as a noise barrier, a satellite dish served as an outdoor bathtub—but not improvised in the Indian way, where you had to marvel at the invention mothered by necessity. Here, design and function were matters of happenstance. Things just stood where they'd been left. These benighted people, he thought: stolen from their home, fucked up on boats, fucked up in slavery, left for dead in this halfway house, this failed experiment.

He wasn't so sealed-up in the coffin of his solipsism that he wasn't aware that those windows also sheltered mothers nursing their babies, sons bringing care to their sick parents, families laughing together, lovers in each other's arms . . . But he suffered from a paralysis of vision. As if unable to break out of a stare, he was unconvinced that kindness and goodness were more than a rumour. He knew that the monsters out there were figments of the monsters *in here*; but he could not activate the muscles that might give him clarity. He was locked. And so he struggled to remember a city he'd hated, at first sight, so completely. Of course, after the brutality of a transglobal flight he was prepared to hate anywhere. In this mood he'd have hated Paris. But with Kingston, keeping an open mind would merely waste time. He and this place were dead-enders. The stored-up hatred in those red eyes felt—was—personal. Why wouldn't it be? What possible point could they have in existing if not to hate someone like David Nayce? He was a Westerner, a criminal. He had profited personally from the colonial rape. The only thing that puzzled him was the anti-gravitational force, like that which keeps the moon from plummeting into the earth, that stopped them setting upon the car right here, as Respect idled (the automotive verb had never been so apt) at a blocked intersection. What stopped them from setting upon Nayce and Bookalil and bludgeoning them to death? Surely not the law. There was no law. Surely not the reputation of their tourist industry—Kingston was already a global homicide capital. Surely not respect for human life. The only thing stopping them must have been that they couldn't be fucked. But it didn't make him feel any safer. Surely someone in this forsaken place could be fucked, and surely they would find him. If they hadn't already found Hut. It wasn't a pretty way to go, but at least it had

82

some leavening of geopolitical justice. Like blood and bone, your remains could fertilise a better future.

'Jesus Christ,' Nayce said across the back seat. 'I've caught myself doing it.'

'Doing what?' Book said without bringing his eyes inside.

'Preparing what I'd tell Pen.'

'If?'

'If—you know, something's happened.'

'Doesn't take you long to get to the worst-case scenario, does it?'

Nayce sniffed, his face taking a cruel cast as his nostrils opened. Book was right, as usual. Nayce was never sure where he was until he had hit the bottom, so in moments of uncertainty he dragged himself down to the worst. Keep a step ahead of death: go out to meet it.

'I'd tell her it was our fault,' he said. 'We abandoned him.'

'He's forty years old. You can't abandon a forty-year-old, and you can't keep him in his room. And he'll be fine anyway. I don't even know why we're having this conversation. Fuck it,' Book said out the window.

'But you know he's not really forty,' Nayce persisted. 'Forty's a man. He's Hut. He's a soft teddy bear and he doesn't have a clue what he's doing. He's spent his life in a zoo being fed steaks and lying around with someone shampooing his fur, and now he's in the jungle. And we're the ones who left the gate open.'

'Shut up. We'll find him,' Book said, not without a hint of menace. Though he was the straightest and most loyal individual in the group, Book always seemed to be bound up at a higher pressure than the others. After university he had gone into the family business, his dad's property development operation. Devotedly married to the family company, Book whinged about it nonstop; the most hardworking son a father could ever wish for, he continually threatened mutiny. This was the thing about Book:

83

he was absolutely consistent in his contradictions and predictable in his eccentricities. He belonged to a former age, the pre-self-improvement time, when you were who you were and you were lumped with it. Come to think of it, Justin Pongrass would never have thought of 'improving' or modifying himself for anyone. Even Janey didn't give a shit. It was a school thing.

'Jesus, I hate optimism. You think your goodwill can hold back all . . . that?' Nayce flicked a hand at a cluster of faces pausing to watch them pass.

'Shut up!' Book repeated. 'It's like you're *hoping* something bad's happened.'

Book knew him, at least.

'I just know we'll find him safe,' Book insisted.

'How do you know that? How? Christ, John, you always think your innocence is so fucking impregnable that nothing bad can happen to us. You're as bad as Hut. You think we can make the world in our image—but those people out there, look—they're not going to be made by us. They're going to do what they fucking well like.'

'Easy, Dave.'

'Fuck.'

'Careful you're not making them in *your* image.'

'Piss off.'

'Don't even joke about it. He's fine,' Book said, monobrow lowering to half-mast. Book, one of life's idealists, had always been the type to cry over tragedy. In fourth grade he'd got his parents to sponsor an Ethiopian. In sixth grade he'd been taken on a tour of the Spastic Centre to deliver funds raised in a school competition which he had won. He didn't make it through the tour, dissolving inconsolably and begging to be taken back to the bus. Book had an aura of innocence about him and a desire, or disposition, to take things at face value. It was the Books of Australia, Nayce thought, who fed that American idea that we were a national time-capsule of their '50s. (In Nayce's experience, if Americans wanted to find their own recent past they ought to look a bit more closely at America.) Yet, perhaps because his contradictions covered too much heat to suppress, there was also a simmering violence in Book. Nayce had never forgotten the time in sixth grade when Book—sincere, quiet, phlegmatic Book—had been caught by an accidental elbow in PE. He'd put the offender in hospital, jaw broken in four places. Everyone just stood around and said, 'Whoa, Bookalil.' Accidents tended not to happen around Book after that.

'Anyway,' Book said. 'I'm one of the arseholes who left him out there. Who actually did abandon him. And I know he's going to be all right.'

Nayce barred his arms across his chest and pointedly stopped looking out the windows. He could picture Hut lying in a pool of blood. He willed Hut to be hurt, to teach Book that optimism can't shut out the world, and to teach himself a lesson: that he was bad. That he had wished catastrophe into being, stamped his own corruption onto the blank black hearts of this city. Nothing short of the worst would satisfy him. The worst was what was needed to drag Book and Hut into his world—adulthood, fear, decay. Nayce was so sick of facing it alone.

'I should admire your determination to think the best,' he said.

'It's got nothing to do with that!' Book almost stamped his foot. 'I just know we'll find him.'

'But how? How?'

'Because there can be no other explanation for this crowd up here.'

While it would have had a certain symmetry if it was Respect's taxi, carrying Nayce and Bookalil, that ran over Hut, fate's involutions lacked poetry. Another taxi did the job, and nor did it quite run Hut over. By the time Hut's path had crossed with the taxi's, the driver had seen the ghost bullocking into the street with his retinue of cackling children. The car halted before impact. Hut, however, had attained a speed of about twenty kilometres per hour, so his impact with the taxi had the same effect as if it had run over him at that speed. Technically what happened was that *Hut ran over the taxi*. He hit the bonnet, spun on his hip, mounted the windscreen, hurdled the roof, bounced on the boot, and came down in a painful heap on his right side, scraping his temple on the exhaust pipe. A crowd of some four dozen circled him. Nobody touched. Some choked down giggles. Hut was trying so hard to stop crying that he lost control of a plaintive fart.

It was into the ensuing hilarity that Nayce and Book jostled, guided by Respect. Hut was sitting on the road, more embarrassed than wounded, his hand rubbing his hip not for therapy but to check that the bag of drugs was still in his pocket. Like a small child he sat in the dirt, his legs split in a vee in front of him.

'You all right?' Nayce knelt by his side and shaped to pick him up by his armpits.

'Mate . . .' Hut waved him away with groggy surliness, like a drunkard set on driving home.

'You come on.' Respect took an arm. Hut let the Rastafarian help him through the burbling crowd. Respect announced to general amusement, 'He bust he ass-bone!' before loading him, like a hostage, into the Escort's front seat.

Book, seeking atonement, massaged Hut's shoulders as they drove back to the Wyndham.

'Sorry, mate, I thought you were with us but the others wouldn't wait.'

'What the fuck did you think you were doing?' Nayce scolded.

'Mate,' Hut pleaded, mysteriously annoyed, it seemed, at Nayce.

'No, I'm serious. What were you hoping to prove?'

Hut gave a moue. 'My head's busting open. Is it bleeding?'

'Only on the inside,' Nayce said. 'You're fucked-up, you dill.'

'Man,' Hut grasped his skull as if to hold the plates together. '*Man*.'

'You're a fuckhead.'

It took a few more blocks for his groans to subside, then Hut reached into his pocket as if for a winning argument. 'I got this.'

Nayce regarded the bag. 'Weed. You risked your life for a quarter ounce of weed.'

Hut beheld the plastic bag with horror. This was the first time he had inspected it. The unspoken etiquette of the transaction had forbidden him from examining what he was buying.

'Damn, I thought they were getting It.'

'All that for a pissy bag of weed,' Nayce said. 'And this was to impress Pongrass? Those guys don't even smoke weed. They hate it. You've nearly killed yourself to impress those dickbrains, and all you got was some dirty old weed. Good work, champ.'

'Fuck!' Hut almost spat. In a swift motion he wound down his window and threw the bag out.

Their heads hit impediments—the seat backs, the dashboard—as Respect pulled his handbrake. The car rocked on its arthritic springs. Respect's rope-veined hand twisted the red-gold-and-green gearstick into reverse. He cast his nose, his lips and his eyes, in that order, over his shoulder and wove the Escort backwards.

'You don't want to be throwing the ganja out the window,' he said with the authority of Moses delivering a commandment.

He climbed out of the car and, showing his first sign of urgency since they had met him, crouched to the gutter to fetch Hut's bag. He crammed it into his shirt pocket and jogged back to the car.

'You don't like the ganja, you give it to me. Respect.'

He offered his knuckles, an act which made each of Nayce, Book and Hut, for their contrasting sins, feel a measure of forgiveness.

11

AT THE WYNDHAM, Book hugged Hut, whispering another apology, and went to bed. Nayce perched on Hut's banana lounge by the pool, siphoning him glasses of water. Dawn had fully broken and guests were nosing exploratively around the breakfast bain-maries.

'I mean it,' Nayce said. 'What did you think you were doing? I don't need to tell you how close you were to getting yourself seriously fucked up.'

'No, you don't need to,' Hut said as if setting the record straight. 'I wasn't scared—you ought to mingle more with these people, they're not as threatening as—'

'But why were you out there in the first place?'

'Hey. Dave. What is it you say? What doesn't kill us makes us stronger.'

'Fuck off.'

'Anyway, who appointed you Dad?'

They watched water boatmen skim the flat surface of the pool. The Jamaican dawn smelt like the Jamaican dusk. It smelt of ganja.

This, Nayce thought, was the problem with having the same

friends too long. He'd known Hut for four-fifths of his life. He couldn't remember what it was like to be seven, but he remembered the day he'd met Hut. On the first day of second grade, everyone was talking about this redhead, Hut (his nickname had arrived before him), who'd turned up at school wearing a watch with the leather cap fixed down with a press stud and a velveteen sloppy joe with a print of a surfer on the chest. His bronze shoes caught sunlight indoors. This Hut was a rosy-cheeked one-man show with wet inside-out lips and freckles (even on his eyelids) and buttery fat and orange hair that bouffed out rearwards the size of an extra skull. At recess, laughing kids gathered around him as he performed impressions of teachers. He exerted the magnetism of the unselfconscious, the schoolyard fitting him like a second skin. He could draw funny pictures and tell jokes and send himself up. He knew everyone's name. They couldn't yet name it, but their instincts detected that he had more of it—blood? breath? beans?—than anyone else.

He did have more money. Seven-year-olds may not know much about much, but they know about moolah. They know about toys and clothes and dads' cars. They know about class. Nayce didn't need French to know nouveau riche.

Nouveau riche needed you. Nouveau riche needed everyone, all the time. Nayce understood this much. At the first play lunch of that year, Nayce picked Hut in his team for brandings. That was all it took: lifelong loyalty for a game of brandings.

'What I don't get,' Nayce said, 'is why you think you have to impress them. They're arseholes, mate. You know they're arseholes. I can understand you being overawed by them when we were seventeen, but Christ, Hut, you've got more, I don't know, more heart in your fingertips than they have in their whole bodies. This is what I don't understand. You're so keen to impress people who are your inferiors.'

At forty Nayce felt silly trying to talk like an adult to Hut. Even if you'd forgotten why you liked each other, there was safety in remaining friends with your second-grade mates. You were known. You could relax. Old friends welcomed you back to a holiday in the comfortable, unpretentious, shorts-and-thongs shack where you'd retreated year after year. Old friends were a break from the performance, the tap-dancing in front of machine guns, of corporate life. Yet, like living in a village, old friends confined you inside your past; they wouldn't let you change; they mocked your efforts at reinvention. Whatever you did, your oldest friends knew you better. They were like your parents: they'd never take you more seriously than the boy they saw lurking behind your balance sheets, skulking in the skirts of your cash positions. Childhood was something you never got over; it was always in the way.

If Nayce and Hut were alike in their inability to see each other as grown-ups, the difference was that Nayce was sick of childhood, hated it, whereas Hut wanted to perpetuate it. Hut reigned in the glorious playground, and Pongrass and Blackman were cool new boys with great stuff. Hut would have given anything to be a kid again; Nayce would rather die.

Hut spent a long time looking at the pool, nodding slowly. Nayce blushed at his own candour; his pores prickling honesty. And now Hut's silence was reproaching him. Nayce knew what he was thinking: *The Team*. Nayce was betraying the cause, the Fast Set. (Which he was, but still, that was hardly the point.) Hut was taking—stealing—the moral high ground, condemning Nayce with the upright vigour of one of nature's born deputies. Above all else, Hut prized loyalty. Even when nobody else was loyal to him, he would die upholding his loyalty to them. Nayce should have known better. When you inform a loyalist that he's guarding an empty palace, he doesn't thank you for the information. He shoots you.

'And here we are in Jamaica,' Hut said with the quiet, gentle determination of one for whom the pieces have just fallen into place. 'You've come all this way to tell me you don't want to be in this team.'

'I didn't say that. I said you were trying to impress people who—'

'And *you* were trying to talk *me* out of swimming.' Hut stood. 'Maybe you're the one who should think about sitting out the race.'

He swivelled into a turn like a nib-busting full stop and crossed the pool deck, dirty chino-clad bum flouncing. Nayce's teeth sucked against his tongue. Hut had lost weight, but his walk, framed by the potted-palm glow of the hotel lobby, carried the phantom heft of an indignant waddle.

3

Whatever gets you through

12

Jeremy Hutchison wouldn't have called himself a calculating man; nor would anyone else. But he was a man who loved calculating, in the pure sense. In times of distress, such as during and after the five-hour shuttle bus odyssey, he soothed himself with mathematics.

The most therapeutic arithmetic was the calculation of individual worth. He knew within a five per cent margin the net asset value of each of his friends. He had Nayce's number: one-third of that pissy four-million-dollar ethical hedge fund he wanked about with. One point three mil might get old Nayce into heaven, but it wasn't going to get him a family home near the water. Numbers, naked, had the power both to arouse and calm Hut, but he knew enough to keep this little habit to himself. He did, after all, come from money. One generation was time enough to know what was done and what was not. What would Pong say if he could read Hut's thoughts? Hut shuddered, shivered, puked, to think. Of all his secrets, of all his shames, as bad as some of them were, Hut reckoned that this curiosity about exact values would be the last he'd ever surrender.

Yet when it came to personal wealth, the most fluid, the most elusive of tabulation, was Hut's own. He had no idea how much he was worth, but not in a good way. His personal value was uncertain in a sense that had nothing to do with maths and everything to do with hope and fear. His current net worth was a function of emotion, not addition.

He had done something very bad, which made him want to think of someone very good, so when he went to his room he opened his PDA and started thumb-typing a letter to his wife.

Sweetheart, he began, and stopped, a little overwhelmed. Hut was a sentimentalist. When he tried to send a message to Pen, he went twinkly and melty: then he became more twinkly and melty at the image of his own twinkliness and meltiness. Then even more so at that thought, and so on in an infinite regression, or progression, until he was slopping around in a cloying syrup akin to the loving stage of drunkenness, when everyone is *so* great and you love them *so* much that you don't know if you can take it anymore; you are inundating from within.

Well, he took a breath and typed, *the flight was good.*

He stopped and took another breath. There was more than the usual fluttering love shaking his fingers. He wondered if he could say anything now, frankly, to Pen.

They were set up at a wedding. A cliché, sure, but clichés can hit home with the force of unavoidable fate. That's what they're for, Hut thought: to give you a signal. Some clichés you don't mess with. There were men who would be embarrassed to admit they'd been set up with their wives at a wedding, but for Hut it was a boast, endowing his marriage with the weight of destiny, as if clichés existed to reinforce life, not diminish it.

He had gone to the wedding besotted with a woman he felt he had wanted since the day he was born. (It had been only a matter of months, but those months had telescoped painfully, like a tiny medical camera, into the root of his soul.) To save him from his doomed infatuation, the bride and groom (Susannah Greenfield and John Bookalil) had set him up with another girl, and as Hut would later tell it, the night became like a hunt in which he'd been aiming at a duck but missed, and hit a bull's eye. *The luckiest mistake I ever made.*

By the end of the wedding he was delivering the declaration of love that he had rehearsed, the only change being the identity of the listener. The fact that he'd known Penelope Lyons for fully three and a half hours was a barely relevant alteration, a concealed bobby-pin. When Susannah Bookalil tossed the bouquet, the other girl, the duck, had snatched it briefly until Hut hip-and-shouldered her, bouncing the flowers clear to Penny Lyons. They moved in together within a month, were engaged in a season, married in a year.

It was a given that Hut would mate with someone better (not different—*better*) than himself. He'd had few girlfriends, each slightly or unevenly his superior, but in Penny he had outdone himself—he'd married someone so incomparably better that in the early years his attitude to her was not companionable, or even, in the ordinary sense, loving. He loved her with adoration and wonder; its physical pose was genuflection.

He had kissed her that wedding night, in his car. Holding her hands between his, thumbs kneading her upturned palms, he entreated: *You know how much I know about women?* Penny shrugged. He hadn't even needed to say it. She was there ahead of him. Meeting Penny was like a dream in which he found someone who had known him all along, who relieved him of the burden of concealment.

'I hope you didn't think I was hanging around you like a bad smell tonight,' he'd said to her hands.

She bit her lip as if holding back some amusing thought. After a pause: 'You were . . . persistent. Just as well I'm not afraid of my own shadow.'

His heart wrung itself into a clump high in his throat. He had been tagging after her like a puppy. A shadow. 'I knew one thing: I wasn't going to let you leave without me.'

She gave him a smile that brought back, even now, more than a decade later, an unbearable fondness. Yet the smile wasn't something she *gave him*. That was its beauty. People were forever *giving* each other smiles, gestures for public consumption, expressions calculated for their expected return. Pen's face had creased against itself, a smile let loose in spite of her best efforts to keep it private. He had never felt so flattered.

'Shouldn't you be a bit more,' she struggled with a choice of words, you know, 'treat 'em mean . . . ?'

He nearly fell out of the car with the fantastical surprise of it. *She* was expecting *him* to play hard to get? He knew, from the exploits of Nayce and other friends better-travelled than himself, that to want a woman openly, with genuine need, was social death. Seduction relied on mystery and maltreatment and, as Nayce said in reference to North Shore private-school girls, *reassuring them in their certainty that they are shit*. But Hut had found that cruelty only worked when girls wanted you already. Treat 'em mean worked a treat for good-looking boys. If Hut ignored a girl he liked, she would be glad not to be pestered. He did have money—and as he looked at himself through Pen's eyes, maybe the Italian suit, the matching silk tie and cummerbund, and the expensive-smelling wood-and-leather interior of the car counted for something, or certainly framed him at his best—but he didn't see he had much else, other than his need. He needed her so completely, so irreversibly, that he had forgotten what he was meant to say. He had nothing to offer, he felt, except to implant in her the moral absolute that he wanted her more than anything in the world, and wanted her permanently. He would instantly give her inevitability, certainty until death. As an approach it was high-risk (wasn't pure and single-minded desire also what marked out the stalker?) but he was looking at love as a one-bid-only auction. Everything he had, first time.

Boomeranged back to herself by his silence, Pen said: 'You know, it's amazing we haven't met before. We seem to know the same people, go to the same parties. I'm sure I'd have noticed you.'

In a rush, honesty defeating strategy, heart quashing common sense, he yelped: 'You're out of my league. You just don't know it.' And began to cry.

Pen sat massaging his hands across the gear shift: her reply a frowning quaver in the neck. He felt like a fuckwit, hell-bent on ruining whatever hope he had with her, but Jesus, for once he had to tell someone how it was.

All he could hope was that she didn't open the door and walk away. He'd said too much, shown himself too raw. In this always-witty, controlled, sparkling banquet they moved in, where the highest virtue was *having it together*, was there anything more perverse than this human carpaccio of need he had just served her?

For a long time there was silence before Pen said: 'What a bubble you live in, Jeremy Hutchison.'

The sound of his name on her lips brought his face up, as if he'd been recognised from heaven. Her hazel eyes shone. Looking at her broad-bridged, slightly smashed-looking nose, vestigially pocked skin and lopsided smile, a wide face frothed in dark curls, he could still convince himself that her physical beauty, striking as it was, might have struck him alone. She was unusual-looking: a miraculous balance of imperfections; the type of beauty that flattered the beholder into believing he had cracked a secret code.

'You're joking, right?' she asked.

Eh? He could say no more. Fuckwit.

'You're joking. *Me* out of *your* league?'

She'd giggled. Hut hadn't known whether to be offended. Her hand went up to cheeks dusted with old acne pits that hinted, in a way that scared him, at mysteries of experience. He tried to laugh with her, but couldn't. Her laughter seemed older, and bruised; her face had the often-erased texture of someone who had tried a great many looks and other experiments on herself. A line of closed-up piercing holes along the rim of one ear; a tattoo-removal scar on her left shoulder. These whispers of Pen's history terrified Hut and he did his best, then and since, to shove them out of his mind.

Eventually she said: 'Any girl at the wedding, you could take your pick.'

'*Me?*' He started to think of all the evidence contradicting her, but stopped himself. She might still be winding him up. Amid her facial luminosity was a twinkling, juicy wryness ready for each moment's underside. She wasn't, really, a joking kind of woman like Janey Quested. A wisecrack wasn't as imminent as it looked. But he hadn't known that on the first night.

'You! That hair, those divine freckles—come on, girls have been swooning over you, stop lying to me, Jeremy.'

And that, he had to admit, was that. She was serious: she thought he was pulling her leg. He thought she was pulling his. She, this wonder of nature, believed he was beautiful—she made him feel beautiful. Hut was gone. Their first years together were studded with precious moments, a long gallery of stars, but that conversation in his car on the night of Book's wedding stood on his mental mantelpiece like an Oscar, a golden boy she had given him, to remember and cherish and strive to live up to. She was a once in a lifetime: a beautiful woman who thought he was beautiful. For her, he would glitter. No questions, no turning back. (While the kidding part of him thought, and the line he played to his friends asked: *Why hadn't I played the self-pity card before?*)

She'd slipped her hands away and, like a shell game, suddenly they were enclosing his. 'It's all right,' she said. 'You don't need to bullshit me.'

We're all in Jamaica now. You're going to love it.

From the scraps of guesswork and wild surmise that passed for his knowledge of women, he had learnt that there was some point, inside almost every one, where they were heartbreakingly not quite up to the task; where they just wanted to give it all away. Once you discovered that point in a woman, that onion-skin layer of the pathetic, you could die of pity for them. You could spend your life trying to console them. Pen did not have that layer. She was fully herself, a woman every moment of her age. Hut could never feel sorry for her, although she had no family she was close to, and the ones he'd met seemed like deadbeats. But she was too tough for pity: she pulled down one-fifty a year as a corporate lawyer. Never mind that she wouldn't need it once she had him, and never mind that she scorned her profession as a 'glorified Girl Friday'. Hut had seen her bonuses. She was a woman of six-figure substance. All his Christmases, New Years and birthdays had come at once. He fell in love worshipping her, forswearing all other gods and, like a pagan before the sun, sometimes did not dare to look at her squarely for fear of blindness.

I can't wait till you and the boys are with us.

He hadn't told her about Pongrass's reaction to his announcement that he'd invited his wife and kids to join the trip.

'You're fucking kidding,' were, to Hut's best recollection, Pongrass's exact words. Again Hut had miscalculated. He'd thought on a tour like this the guys would all want their womenfolk along. Pongrass had a girlfriend, Blackman was fighting with his wife but also had a new love, Nayce had Sophie, and Book had Susannah. There was no reason, Hut thought naively, not to make it a family trip. The resort! The kids playing in the sun! The relaxation! Until he realised, from Pongrass's and the others' reactions, that this was one of those trips from which women were expressly banned. This was a trip for *mates*, not mates. Its whole point was that it was a boys' trip (Janey, the exception that proved the rule, was here partly because she was one of the boys, partly because she was useful as cover, and partly because the swim had been her idea in the first place). Hut, in missing the point, had licensed Blackman to tag Penny 'Yoko'. At first Hut didn't mind that, because if Pen was Yoko, that made him John. But Hut wasn't John. He wasn't even Ringo.

Backtracking after this humiliation, Hut had asked Pen if she might modify her plans, so that instead of coming from the beginning, she'd come after the race. Pen had asked: 'Can't we come the night before the race?' As always, she offered a compromise instead of an argument. Hut couldn't say no. She would follow, with Charlie and Roy, arriving on Wednesday night. They'd be in Jamaica for the race itself, and then Hut would spend a week with Pen and the boys at the resort after the rest of the Fast Set had gone home.

I can't stop thinking about you guys.

He'd told bigger lies, he supposed. She would recognise it as a turn of phrase. Now, though, his options had expired. Circumstances were forcing him to act.

Is Roy-boy excited about going on the airplane? Is Charlie bringing his double-decker bus? I'm missing you like crazy.

Hut teared up again, but this time the rims of his eyes were the spillway of fast-rising anxiety, for the secret point of inviting

Pen and the kids along was not to have a holiday. It was to take her—take them all—out of the daily routines that stood as barriers to the news Hut had to deliver, about his *situation*. Jamaica would be a circuit-breaker, a fresh page. He could sit Pen down on a beach and be straight with her in a way that he couldn't be straight at home. He could point to the sands around them, the palm trees and the Caribbean—the far side of the world—and offer her the possibility of escape.

Love, Jeremy/Dad/Daddy.

He read back over his message: sentence by sentence, more of a wishlist than a letter. But Hut was full of forgiveness when it came to himself, and his marriage was all about giving himself something to aim up to. As wishful thinking went, its sentiments were if not fully frank then at least sincerely felt. He hit Send.

13

BY THE TIME Hut and Nayce crawled out of their rooms—one with roadworks jackhammering between his eyes, the other with a more complex set of symptoms—Janey had organised transport across the island.

At a morning summit with Respect, who was waiving his hourly rate in favour of a longer-term retainer, Janey agreed to employ a second taxi, a white six-seat minivan driven by a colleague whom Respect produced as if from out of his tea-cosy: the man they called Business. Business's name was also decalled on the back window of his van, and his greeting was to touch knuckles and intone: 'Business.'

In the Escort, Janey rode beside Respect while Nayce and Hut curled themselves foetally in the back. The convoy drove west out of Kingston, through Spanish Town. They cut a line through burning fields of sugar cane, caramelised smoke rising from treacly cane stubble, then geared down for the climb north through Bog Walk. Out of the city, the Escort climbing the island's spine like a beetle riding the plated back of a dinosaur, Janey noticed the churches—every village built around a cross.

'In Australia,' she said to Respect, 'when you strip it all down to the essentials, our civilisation consists of a pub and a post office. Yours boils down to a church.'

'Jamaicans are religious people,' Respect said, nodding towards a plain white-plastered church with blue eaves, placed by the roadside as if to make his point. 'We have the highest number of churches per capita in the world. We also have the highest number of murders.'

'You reckon they're related?' Janey smiled.

'Yah,' Respect said. 'We need the graveyards. No more shootings, the churches go out of business.'

Janey laughed and watched the island through the windscreen. The car wove down the two-lane highway, picking a helix between oncoming trucks and buses, potholes, and the stream of villagers beating flat the red dirt with their shoe leather.

'Everyone's going somewhere,' Janey said airily.

After a long silence, Respect replied: 'They going nowhere. Same steps everyday—they sleepwalking, Jamaicans. If we not an island, they all walk to America.'

'You think so?'

'Every Jamaican would leave if they could,' he said. 'They go to church and pray for the power to walk on water.'

'Why, when it's such a . . .' Janey struggled for the word '. . . a paradise on earth?'

Respect's stare made her feel like a bubbleheaded housewife.

'I'm sorry,' she said.

'You okay,' Respect said. 'But you a tourist.'

Pongrass and Blackman subdivided the back of Business's van while John Bookalil occupied the second seat and stared out of the window, his forehead reddening scarlike against the glass. The van slipped down streets lined with well-kept white colonial buildings.

Men in khaki uniforms with red braid and trim guarded the black iron gates, trying to ignore groups of neat, pretty women in navy-blue blazers who strolled past with linked arms and teased the guards with laughing comments. 'This the government quarter,' Business said to Bookalil, already knowing enough to separate him from Pongrass and Blackman. After last night, Book didn't want to be seen chumming too closely with those two. His optimism about finding Hut, as they'd driven around in the dark, had cloaked his shame at having abandoned him. Book knew it was only raw luck that had saved Hut from disaster and Pongrass, Blackman and himself from culpability. At least he knew it; those other two couldn't have given a fuck.

Pongrass was back on his favourite riff: his 'firsts'.

'First PE. Philippa Semple. She'd be anywhere for me, anytime. Modest offer. Tidy-looking, but sad, you know? An almost-Goth: black hair, white pancake, dark lips. Something had gone on with her oldfella, or her brother, or so everyone said. *She* said. So it wasn't just a rumour. She fucked like she'd been doing it for years.'

'Which shows,' Blackman said, 'incest has its benefits. Ha!' Noticing the stiff silence of Book and the driver, Blackman coughed and scratched his hair roughly. 'Only joking, boys.'

'No personality except when she had a knob in her,' Pongrass said, with apparent concern, or wonder, or nostalgic pleasure, like a retired psychiatrist remembering a curious case. 'First time she gave me a handie, you know what happened? My first ever PE. I go off in her mitts and all over her jumper. She told her dad a baby had been sick on her.'

'Most of us were going off on our own jumpers,' Blackman said. 'Consider yourself lucky.'

'Philippa Crevice, they called her. I still never told anyone. Never have. Makes me sad to think of her, Philippa. Someone told me she, like, topped herself before she was twenty-five.'

There was an awkward silence until Pongrass, as if to redress a lapse of taste, worked himself up to a happier story. 'Ever tell you about my first big let-down?'

Blackman shook his head, winking at Business's stony eyes in the rear-vision mirror as if to promise that things were about to improve.

'Ilona Dahl.'

'Ah! Who could forget?' Blackman said fondly; he and Pongrass could have been a long-married couple touching shoulders over their wedding album. 'The female Justin Pongrass.'

'Right, and my first crush: athletic, gorgeous, head of the pack at Queenwood. Remember the best thing about Ilona?'

'Fifteen-year-old frontie with a *Playboy* chest,' Blackman said. 'My biggest regret in life is, I appreciate it more now than I did then.' He gave Business a helpless shrug, man to man. 'Youth is wasted on the young.'

'Busted the seams of that Queenwood uniform,' Pongrass nodded seriously. 'She had everything but the staple in her navel.'

'You two were marked out for each other; nobody else had a chance.'

'Remember how she was really straight, though? She was a romantic. Like, it had to be almost marriage. When she was finally ready for it,' Pongrass said, 'like, the Big One, we couldn't go off during a party to the bedroom like normal chickies would, it had to be a whole fucking weekend in her parents' empty house, like a honeymoon. Ilona put this dinky classical music on and stayed in the bath for about a day. She'd bought this whole set of like sky-blue lingerie.' He pronounced it 'linjeray'. 'I got it off her and she *hums*, you know, as each stitch falls away. I'm down to her bra and set to feast. "Help yourself," she goes, she's lying back on the bed purring with her eyes closed and her arms folded behind her head. So I hoist them, two hands, out of the bra—and I lose it. Or lose them. Can't believe my eyes. She's got, like, *no tits*.'

'Ha-ha!' Blackman said as if he were responsible for the prank. 'But better men than you have fallen for the charms of a great pair of hockey socks.'

'Nah-nah. She has huge boobs, but no nips. Wormholes in an apple. On these huge knockers.'

'All boob, no tit.' Blackman shook his head with vicarious ruefulness.

'It just felt all wrong,' Pongrass wrinkled his nose. 'I was totally put off. Ilona wanted me to keep going, but I just couldn't. I told her I couldn't violate her if I wasn't prepared to make a commitment to at least getting engaged. I respected her too much.'

'And as soon as you got back to school you told everyone,' Blackman turned his mouth down, smiling. He would have laughed now, if he laughed, but part of Blackman's rural patrimony was a kind of manly restraint.

'Ilona All-Boob. Guys still went for her, but more from curiosity than anything else.'

'She was cream,' Blackman agreed. *Cream: rich and thick*. He couldn't suppress a mildly proud smirk: if he could call someone else cream, that meant he wasn't, right? 'Wasn't she the one who ran off and married one of her friend's dads when she was eighteen?'

'I know. Dirty old bastard. I mean, what a disgusting thing to do. Some people have no decency.'

Bookalil tried to catch the driver's eye, but the Jamaican drove as if none of this was any of his business.

They skirted the forested slopes of Mounts Diablo and Friendship before sliding down the Antilles-blown windward coast. Beyond was Cuba. There had been marathon swims between Montego Bay and Cuba, but the Classic would take place further along the coast in the heavily undertown chops between Jamaica and its satellite island of Negociante.

Janey was bringing Respect to the brink of laughter with her story of the Human Plug. A flight attendant during one of her serial rites of passage, Janey had been working on a jumbo that became depressurised when an improperly fixed toilet cap had come loose. Disaster was averted by the fact that a woman was sitting on the toilet at the time, but she'd become vacuumed to the seat. 'We couldn't get her off,' Janey let off her hoarse tomboy cackle. 'Mile-high colonic.'

From the back seat, Nayce watched her with a fondness that hurt his stomach. Like him, Janey had been a creature who belonged to an earlier time, pre-dating the escalation of private-school fees: the lower-middle-class non-scholarship child who happened by a combination of accident and geography to be part of the moneyed set. Janey's family were country but not landed. She'd grown up around the GPS guys, Pongrass and Blackman, yet her presence on this trip, Nayce thought, would be very hard to explain to an outsider, for her background and working life would normally have separated her from them. What held her in—inertia? History? Lack of alternatives? The boys were her friends because they always had been her friends, and Nayce knew how few other friends she had. Absurd as it would seem, these five oafs were her firmest links with her past and her place.

Janey—convent school, good marks, sporty, arts degree, boyfriends galore—now worked as a nanny. Or, to be fair, a governess. Her boss was one of the richest men in America. She spent eight months of the year in Vail, Monaco, the Seychelles and afloat in the Mediterranean, looking after billionaire brats, toiling below stairs. Then her boss gave her four months off to go canyoning, snowboarding, sailing, surfing, skateboarding—whatever athletic gerund was her current passion.

Or, as on this trip, swimming with the boys. Janey had been one of the boys, part of the furniture, ever since Nayce had known her. To these guys, Pongrass and Blackman, she was just Janey: a mate. She fitted in. Maybe it had nothing to do with the group's particularities, and was instead the universal chemistry of one female in a group of men. Janey had told him, years ago: *I don't really get on with other girls; I just love being with groups of guys; maybe I don't like competition*. She had no durable female friendships and rarely saw her family. Her varnish of independence, a woman making her own way in hostile territory, could give the impression that she had all she wanted. The truth, as Nayce knew it, was the other way around: Janey could fall straight through the cracks any day and be lost to them, someone they used to know. Her easy self-sufficiency, as cultivated as it was instinctive, was both her best safeguard against falling through and her one salvation if she ever did. They knew she'd be okay, whatever disaster befell her. Yet by wanting them to know she'd be okay, she was licensing them to treat her with blind, coldly good-humoured, casual indifference, which, Nayce knew, needed no encouragement.

Nayce, knotty and frayed, was the only glass-half-empty person in the group. In the eyes of a salesman like Hut, Janey represented potential, potential, potential: any day she could become engaged to a trillion dollars if it came stumbling below-decks with a headful of booze and coke. She had that up her sleeve. The way Hut saw it, she could end up richer than any of them and more important—the big man's wife, all power, no responsibility. Good old Janey. Those rich boys loved her to bits.

'But she did sue us later, and won. Got piles for her piles, we used to say.' Janey cackled and, without a breath, changed gear. 'Say, Respect, I've always wondered, what *is* Rastafarianism about, aside from smoking pot and being beautiful?'

She was thirty-eight and still sunnily gorgeous inside that flawless organ of hers, that sheath of golden skin you had to slap your hand to stop stroking. Nayce had met her when he was nineteen and she was dating a famous footballer. Janey Quested was the prettiest thing he'd ever seen: petite, open-faced, nut-brown, sniffing out the amusement in any situation. Unblocked. There was *nothing wrong with her*. That was the remarkable thing about Janey—she had nothing wrong with her at all.

He'd been fooled by that for a while. For six years, Janey and Nayce had been bound by a kind of soap-opera destiny. She two-timed the famous footballer, seeing Nayce on the sly. The understanding between Nayce and Janey had been immediate and astonishing, if subsonic: some shared genetic string of insecurity, guilt, thrill and surprise, a pair of spies who might be caught out at any moment. Neither quite belonged among the money, yet they had infiltrated too deeply to belong anywhere else. They had a shared ache, too: the strain of faking it. Their affair started the night they met, and the challenge of keeping it secret seemed to cement them together. If they could get through that, they could get through anything. Janey dumped the footballer and strung along a trail of rich chumps, while Nayce wove a thread of girlfriends into his tapestry. Why had they not come into the open? Nayce still didn't know. There was something profoundly romantic in the subterfuge, but that was Janey's choice, not his. It wasn't as if they were real spies, or that they'd lose a great deal by being openly together. Without hesitation Nayce would have dropped the sham and set up house with her, married her. Yet he never felt secure enough to ask. This was the thing about Janey: you could not talk to her squarely, directly, about matters of the heart. Something impervious in her self-reliance warded off sentimental dialogue. Nayce didn't push her. He told himself a story. Her slipperiness must have been her inbuilt survival instinct, how a poor girl got by among the rich.

As a couple, they were an inversion of the male–female cliché: Janey frustratingly elusive, incapable of emotional revelation, Nayce waiting for her to commit. He had lost count of the number of times he had wanted to cry in Janey's arms, tell her everything, confess, plead, console, offer. But there was no way through her laughter, her *making light*.

He had been able to tolerate that, as her lover, up to a point. And then he had outsmarted himself. Fifteen years ago, Hut's parents had hosted a twenty-fifth birthday dinner party for their son. Nayce, who made a clever speech, had been seated between Janey and Hut's mother. It was one of the last times Nayce had seen Ines Hutchison. He hadn't seen the Hutchisons a great deal since his mid-teens, and found them much changed. While Ken brimmed with his playboy decade, his last hurrah, Ines in her fifties seemed shrivelled, as if too much sun had microwaved her from the inside out. The wispy, enigmatic vagueness that Nayce remembered had descended (ascended?) into pure battiness. Ines kept squinting at Janey as if she didn't know who she was, and issued eye-rolling sarcastic splutters at everything Janey said.

Nayce, who hadn't had the courage to utter more than a polite word or two to Ines Hutchison, took the opportunity when Janey left the table to ask, softly: 'Why do you keep picking on her?'

'Why?' Ines said, avoiding his eye but snickering at some private joke. 'Why, why, why?' Nayce couldn't remember her being so animated. She finished her wine and shook her head, or perhaps it quivered of its own accord, an elderly lady's tremor.

'All right,' he said. 'Forget I asked.'

He felt a hand on his knee and jumped. Barely breathing—she seemed combustible, eccentric enough to say or do anything—he thought he was going to faint.

'If you want her, make her jealous. Get a girlfriend.'

Ah. Batty, but she saw. Of course she saw. She always did, even when he had nothing to do with her. To her he was still as transparent as the seven-year-old her son had dragged home.

Still mugging around the table as if for a staged photo, Nayce said with all the lightness he could muster: 'That old one? You reckon that works?'

'It saved my marriage.'

Feeling a blush flower across his face so alarmingly that it would be a miracle if the whole table didn't notice, Nayce inspected his napkin.

'I have lots of girlfriends. It makes no difference.'

'Then you . . .' the hand loosened on his thigh, slid up a span, lingered, and then, just as his confusion threatened to resolve like a cloud into a known face, gave him a condescending pat, 'you must marry one. See what happens then.'

He was a child, a twenty-five-year-old futures trader with a Dutch bank, an arts graduate, a private-school twerp. Janey was dating a university medallist in drinking. Anything Ines Hutchison said, however addled or manipulative or destructive, carried a kind of hypnotic truth-weight for Nayce. It wasn't that she spoke with the wisdom of experience, or any other wisdom. Her authority was purely local: Nayce-specific. She knew his future, was there ahead of him. She wasn't giving him advice. She was stating his fate.

Later that year he proposed to Sophie Grimes, the daughter of his boss at the Dutch bank. His big moment wasn't the proposal but the announcement to Janey: 'I'm getting married.'

She had fixed him with a Janey smile, so perfectly amused that it betrayed every other Janey smile, every laugh, every joke, before and since. She had clipped him gently over the ear and said: 'I never knew you had it in you.'

He kept finding reasons to postpone the wedding date. For three years Nayce waited for the coup de grace, the moment of revelation, when Janey would crack, the engagement would be broken, he would have his great love, and they would live happily ever after. As the engagement stretched and the questions grew awkward, he found himself oddly devoted to Sophie, even falling in love with her. Janey was working as a flight attendant, spending most of her time outside Australia. She never ruptured the perfect surface of her friendliness to Nayce, or acted as if anything abnormal had come to pass. He wavered; a new normality asserted itself. He did love Sophie, in his way, and if this was how Janey wanted it, he was in no position to argue. They wrote letters every few weeks and went out drinking when she came home. Every time he saw her he wanted to fall at her feet in tears and offer everything he had. He never said a word. Janey's conviviality was too high a wall.

He was twenty-eight when he married Sophie, the wedding speeches running like a horse-breeder's pedigree sheet at the Easter yearling sales. He'd married up, that was for sure. Janey was at the wedding—*absolutely thrilled to come*. Preserving the appearance of friendship was her gift to the couple: she would keep her secret watertight. But then, at the wedding, Nayce's father had said the worst possible thing. The Reverend Bill Nayce hadn't meant to be impolite. He just lacked tact, and he'd had three glasses of wine, thrice his weekly intake. He'd sidled up behind Nayce, tender hand on his shoulder. They were watching everyone dancing. Sophie waltzed with her father. Janey bounced up, grasped Rev Nayce's hand and said: 'Come on, homeboy, show me your moves!' Rev Nayce had tried to ward her off, but few men could resist Janey. He nodded her a watery grin and said, 'Just a moment.' Janey blew him a kiss, backing onto the dance floor, arms extended towards him, beckoning fingers fluttering. Rev Nayce pushed his parroty lips to his son's ear and said: 'I only wish you'd done this with her.'

Nayce hadn't needed his father to remind him. Something had gone terribly wrong. But if he told his father the truth—how it had come to this—the old man would never have forgiven him.

Eventually Nayce dozed, overcome by a greedy ten-tonne torpor. Janey soon slept, and so did Pongrass, Blackman and Book in the other car. At times it seemed that Business and Respect also slept, though they kept their cars motivated in a more or less forward direction. The only traveller who remained wide awake was Jeremy Hutchison.

Hut's hangover had an Attention Deficit Disorder quality. There were power-tool hangovers, bleached-out hangovers, road-tunnel hangovers, stomach-pump hangovers, spivvy seedy hangovers, wipeout hangovers, combine-harvester hangovers, dear-oh-dear remorseful head-cradling hangovers, concussive hangovers, collapsed-scrum hangovers, and whirling carousel hangovers. Hut had experienced them all. But this was an ADD hangover. Images chased each other around his head promiscuously and discordantly, like a maddening dream. His stomach tossed and twirled acrobatically and his heart fluttered like first love. It had to be the dope, he thought, and then he thought he remembered being in a casino on an ocean liner, and then he thought of bin-liners, and then of Bin Laden, and so on. It was the worst kind of hangover—a word-association hangover.

For five hours, giving off no sign except for irritably scratching his nose and fidgeting to change position on the narrow seat which was ribbed by a metal rod breaching its sponge defences, Hut went quietly mad. Sleep approached, but he grabbed at it too needily and scared it off. He tried the sleeping-draught of the fumes floating rearwards from Respect's cornucopian spliff, but the smell exhumed memories from the night before, and set him off again: dope, Dopey, Snow White, white powder, Cold Power, Cold War, Korea, North Korea, men with bad hair, hair with bad men . . .

He tried to compose a letter, in his head, to Pen. The thought of her and the boys steadied him for a moment. He thrashed towards them like a drowner for driftwood. Yet as soon as he lapsed into the usual euphemism (*Having a great time, wish you were here*), he lost his grip and was back in his maelstrom. He was only able to regain consecutive ideation when he attempted something quite novel: he imagined stripping the truth of its matrimonial varnish.

It wasn't as if his *situation* was a recent stroke of bad luck. It would seem such when the axe fell publicly, but (and here Hut's wretched state brought out uncommon frankness, if only to himself) the truth was that he'd been a liar, an exaggerator, a lily-gilder, all his life. Bullshitting was his blood, his oxygen, his language. What did Nayce say: 'You can't draw a straight line in curved space'. Right. Pompous prick, Nayce, but useful from time to time. In business, you had to bullshit. Bullshit made the world go round.

Hut's father loved to big-note, and worked hard to earn the right to drop names. Whether he was coaxing friends into his house for all-day drink-and-swim sessions, or coercing them to accept all-expenses-paid holidays with him and Ines, being able to big-note was the reward and consequence of Ken Hutchison's labour. Somewhere, in the transaction from Ken to Hut, the process had inverted itself. Whereas his father made money in order to big-note, Hut big-noted in order to make money. He was Hutchison 2.0, one generation cleverer. He'd observed that once people believed you were rich, they couldn't stop themselves from making you richer. Money's favourite pastime is to hang out with other money. How often he had heard Ken say, 'It's the paradox of money: the less you need it, the more everyone wants to throw it at you.' And vice versa, of course, but Hut hadn't known much about that until now.

His current troubles were not fresh. They were the accretion of the habits of a lifetime, like heart disease or lung cancer. You keep doing the bad thing and thrive on it, the picture of health, until one day you're suddenly fucked.

That would describe Hut's situation now. Suddenly fucked. He had invested in the no-brainers, the sure-fires, barely riskier than annuities, and they had generally, if not spectacularly, failed. After Ken had sold up, retired and passed the cashbox to him, Hut did the right thing, invested safely, but everything he touched turned miraculously to shit. He started feeling like a casino Cooler, the bad-luck contagion.

Nobody would have known this. Emboldened rather than chastened by his failures, Hut ascended to higher risks. Having bet on fifty-fifties and lost them all, he started placing skyscrapers of chips on long shots. He lost again, and threw good money after bad. Optimism had to be its own reward, didn't it? It had better be, because it was producing fuck-all else. Life became a round robin of papering over cracks, borrowing to pay off the first creditor. He moved fast, raising different funds simultaneously against the same collateral. He had liquidated and spent the high-value coin of his father's good name, turning 'Hutchison' from a T-Bill into a junk bond.

Pen had no idea. No idea in the world. Their pact, since that night in the car after Book's wedding, was No Bullshitting. He'd stayed true: rather than bullshit her, he created a reality in which the question of his solvency was never posed. He'd never had to lie. As such. He'd engineered things so that she'd never asked him the questions he couldn't answer truthfully.

For Pen, as Hut knew her, money was not a measurable or limited quantity. Money was an idea, a principle. You had money, so you spent it. If you did not have money, that was a bad thing. But if you had it, you could spend as much as you liked. As much as you possibly could. Much of his recent energy had been directed at keeping Pen's credit cards paid-up, concealing the situation from her. She was the ultimate creditor, the one who had to be snowed at all costs. His entire business philosophy could be summed up in the phrase *Keeping Up Appearances*, and appearances started at home. If all else was gone, you still had to maintain your lifestyle. He'd bought her a new car, a new kitchen, new plantation shutters, new dining chairs. Top of the line. He plunged mercilessly into consumption with a suicide's flair for giving it all away. He discovered the perfect diversion: prestige real estate. Every week, he took Pen to meet leased-BMW-driving agents who would oil them through ten-million-dollar houses. Palaces. Hut took contracts and held serious discussions about which one they might buy. Perfect, and free publicity! He made sure word got out. Whenever Pen asked how much they could spend, Hut kissed her perfect forehead and said, 'As much as you want. I mean, you can't take it with you, eh?'

You can't take it with you. Well, that was true, and even truer when you've pissed it all away. You can't take your debts with you, either. They stay with your family as a keepsake. Your legacy. If he'd gone under that taxi this morning, or been beaten to a pulp, he'd be leaving Pen with shame and debt. However long the shame would linger, the debt would outlast it. The shame wouldn't come with lawyers. The shame would take three cents in the dollar and go away. The debt would keep knocking until it took everything.

He couldn't go under a wave, or disappear down some Jamaican alley. He couldn't do it to Pen or the boys. Couldn't do it to himself! But that was no help, just a narrowing-down of the available options. The material fact. Hut was truly fucked. If he went home he was going to jail.

Yet he couldn't do that to himself either.

As he swung his Escort out of a weed-grizzled roundabout, Respect pointed his spatulate thumb at the last of the mountains, whose slopes they descended towards Negociante Bay and their destination, Sandals City, the thirty-five-hectare all-inclusive resort with marina, golf course, three pools, shopping centre, private beach and, just outside its confines (in case anyone exhausted Sandals' menu of entertainments), a beach bar called Slashing, which Janey's guide book named the 'hottest spot south-south-east of Havana'.

'You have to climb the volcano,' Respect said to Janey, his face cramped towards the turn-off they had not taken, as if repelled by the sight of the resort opening up below them.

'That's,' she consulted her guide book, 'Mount John?'

'It be the greatest spectacle in Jamaica.'

'It's still active, it says here.' The now-awake Nayce observed Janey from the back seat. She licked her fingers to turn the pages of the guide book. Her occasional giveaway tics, vestiges of nature rather than her rarefied nurture, melted his heart. They could only pose as ruling class for so long. Eventually they'd betray themselves. This, he told himself, was why he and Janey would always need each other.

'The volcano it be a show, you come this time of year, you come at sunset, and you see the Green Flash.'

'The Green Flash?' Janey looked to the index and shook her head. 'Is that a bar? Doesn't mention it here. They only talk about the famous Slashing.'

'That's why you have me,' Respect said. 'Me better than you tourist book.'

'So what's the Green Flash?' Janey said, reaching her arm across the back of his seat, unable to resist flirting. Nayce could see her mind working: Respect had the face of a *great man*. He was outside of 'everyone'. Why, Nayce wondered, did Janey's simple curiosity in Jamaica seem so heroic? Why did her possession of a guide book seem such exceptional intrepidity? Was it only that the rest of them were such fuckwits?

'You come up Mount John at sunset, you see the sun and the moon and the Green Flash,' Respect said sternly. 'Me say no more.'

'Sounds boring,' Janey narrowed her eyes. 'We'll have much more fun lying around the swimming pool.'

'You make sure,' Respect sighed as if he had heard an infinity of empty ironies before. His firm indifference spurred Janey. She tossed her hair and showed two rows of white teeth. None of this group had ever needed braces on their teeth. They had come out dentally blessed.

'You don't want to be missing it,' he said.

Deaf to this front-seat banter, twisting in the seabreeze pouring through a cracked window, Hut tried to rehearse how he would tell Pen. He would sit her down. No, he would take her out to dinner. No—dinner would seem a cruel joke, a last supper.

He would walk with her on the beach. At night. No. He'd gather her up with the kids and seek their protection—two toddlers to shield him from his wife. Because she'd flip out, she would, she'd be ropable. Incandescent. Not because he was in such a deep pit—she was, unfortunately, bigger than that—but because he'd been keeping it secret. Yes, that was the sclerotic heart of the matter, that was what she would never forgive him for, and that was what made it harder and harder to tell her. The act that would redeem him was the very act he could not commit. He could not confess. He would confess. The confessions of Hut. A confessional booth? Had he ever been in one of those? Yes—in Spain—on a trip—they'd had a fight—about the Pope—something to do with Poland—Polish sausage? Kransky? Krakow?

The word-association hangover snaked back on him and strangled, strangled, until Respect roused the car with the grave announcement.

'We here. Straits of Negociante.'

14

Hut's travel agent had booked three rooms in the all-inclusive Sandals Resort Negociante overlooking the bay's parabolic sweep. Pongrass and Blackman would share Room 1212, Nayce and Book Room 1214, and Hut and Janey the two-bedroom corner suite 1216 until Pen and the boys arrived, whereupon Janey would move into 1214 for the last night. But somehow the booking request had missed its mark: only 1212 and 1214 were reserved, the corner suite unavailable until Thursday night. Sandals was full of swim teams. Hut blamed the hotel staff, and the hotel staff reciprocated.

Janey went into Book and Nayce's twin room, the boys tossing a coin on who would sleep in the fold-out cot. Book lost. Hut would take the cot in 1212 with Pongrass and Blackman (no coin toss, no question that Hut would be punished).

Hut felt blessed in disguise, as if he had won a strategic victory underhandedly. Letting a staff member clip on his plastic fluorescent wrist bracelet—'Symbol of your entitlement to all you can eat and drink inside the bounds of the Resort and its private beach'—Hut tried to batten down his smile. He followed

Pongrass and Blackman up to 1212, guiltily thrilled. Pongrass and Blackman knew Hut as a man with sixty mil to play with. (Not as the fat freckly bloodnut who'd tried to buy his friends with snakes and thickshakes.) They knew Hut as the son of a successful North Shore importer. (Not as the fuck-up drop-kick never-good-enough son of lushos.) They knew him as a rich man, an enterprising capitalist. (Not, or not yet, as the man to whom half the investors in town would never again lend money as long as his arsehole was pointing to the ground.) These guys weren't bogged down in history and irony. He was always more comfortable with newer friends.

And it suited his purposes to spend more time with Pongrass and Blackman. This was, after all, a working trip for Hut. He had his Key Performance Indicators. From Nayce, he wanted submission. From Pen, he would want forgiveness, trust, and consideration for the options he was to put to her. From Pongrass and Blackman, he would want a substantial investment.

'Hilton, my man,' Pongrass bounced on his bed, eyebrows raised at Blackman. Squatting low in the folds of midlife Pongrass fat persisted one of life's pretty boys. 'Time to get wet.'

The team was planning a warm-up swim for the afternoon. Hut, who had been awake for seventy-two hours, subsided into the couch and covertly watched the others change. Pongrass's centre of gravity seemed to lie in his shoulders: masses of muscle gathered like a blockage, caught up in their passage to other parts of his body. His chest and arms were hairless, and his refusal to have an Olympian's rings and flag tattooed onto his arm or breast, as they all did nowadays, elevated him even further in Hut's eyes. Pong didn't need to signal what he'd done. He had nothing to prove. Those tattooed Olympians had just the one thing in their lives, the one moment. For Pong, the Olympics had been an enjoyable side-trip. Hut let his glance skid down to where Pong's pubes formed a neat moustache, as if trimmed. Hut caught a peek at his penis. There were willies and cocks and dicks and wangs, but Pongrass's tanned member was definitively (and, to Hut, somehow deservingly) a *schlong*.

'Ever tell you about my first slot?' Pongrass said, parading naked as he looked for his swimmers.

Blackman grunted from the bathroom.

'Name unknown,' Pongrass said in the tone of a policeman going through case files. 'I was fourteen. Palm Beach New Year's Eve party. I slipped down with a mate and a 500-ml bottle of Frigate OP.'

'That stuff,' Blackman winced. 'A hundred-and-thirty per cent alcohol.'

'First ever pass-out, too. We weren't allowed in the party so we sat on someone's catamaran and raced each other to the bottom of the OP. Missed the New Year, woke up about two in the morning with a bunch of nobodies around a beachfire. This frontie with, like, this curly black *minge* of hair on her head was, you know, cradling me in her lap. I woke up, instinct kicked in: unzip her fly, work the Pong-hand in. Pubes like lantana. When my mitts hit the slot I got this jolt of regret, or I sobered up suddenly, tried to pull away, but her hand came down and pinned me there. Jesus. I said I had to go off for a piss. As soon as I was clear I started running like my hand was on fire. Never looked back.'

'Nup,' Blackman chuckled, coming back into the room, 'you never looked back, Dunc old son.'

Dunc. Part of the exclusive allure of Justin Pongrass and Andy Blackman was their secret-society code of nicknames. Ever since they'd been bushy-haired, rousty man-boys at boarding school, Pong and Abo had reckoned each other by their fathers' names. The habit evolved from, and preserved, the peculiar sense of humour of adolescent male money—something irresistibly cheeky in naming teenage Pong after the patrician Duncan, and Abo after his born-in-moleskins, red-faced, dung-scented paterfamilias Hilton. Hut wished dearly that one day they might call him 'Ken'. It would be a crowning moment. But they'd shown no curiosity about who Ken Hutchison was. Maybe he should tell them. Maybe he should be grateful that they neither knew nor cared.

Blackman took off his shirt to reveal a second garment, an even pelt of grey-black fur from neck to ankle. Drooping pink nipples peered out like newborn suckling piglets, yet his physique still remembered a swimmer's proportions, the funhouse mirror stretchiness: wide shoulders, long back, narrow hips, no bum, dainty legs. His startlingly corpulent dick might have been a keel.

Hut yawned. 'Guys. I've got to get some kip. I'll catch up with you later.'

Blackman smoothed suntan oil into the neck and shoulders of Pongrass, who acted as if he hadn't heard. Blackman, however, paid Hut all too much attention. After Pongrass tried to return the favour but gave up—'Hilt, you could be on fucken Mercury and the sun wouldn't burn through that fucken forest'—Blackman crouched by Hut's face.

'Fall behind now, buddy, you'll never catch up.'

Hut tried to roll away, but Blackman scooped his hands under his ribs.

'Uh-uh, plenty of time for lazing about afterwards.'

'Mate, no, I'm rooted. You don't know what happened to me last—oi!'

Pongrass and Blackman, in swimmers and grease, were wrestling Hut upright. 'Come on, you redhead cunt.' He tried to fight back, but a grin betrayed him: he was loving it, like his sons when they succeeded in turning getting dressed into a game of wrestling. Any attention is good attention.

'Okay, okay!' he squealed. 'You win.'

Having won, they dropped him like a bag of trash and made their way out of the room. Hut changed cautiously, as if negotiating a trap. His surreal state—still awake, still half-insane—was brought to ground with the effort of locating and putting on his swimmers. He crept around the floor amid the spillage of his suitcase, grateful that the others weren't here to see him. He'd always felt awed by people who were comfortable in locker-rooms. Though he had this new body, this thin and trim phantom body, he still saw a fat man sucked into the loose coils of his belly. His non-belly. His non-arse. His non-love handles. Where had he gone? When he looked at his body, all he saw was what was missing. The skin was still there, puckering as if holding its breath. Its looseness, he felt, was a giveaway; the team would guess the truth the moment they saw him.

He stood before the bathroom mirror and saw his secret surrendered: he hadn't been training. He'd been dieting.

15

IN BRUISED SUNLIGHT on the Sandals private beach, Hut's five team-mates formed a tight crescent around a white man of about fifty wearing a baseball cap, sunglasses shaped like a horizontal hourglass, faded loose singlet (the yawning armholes as wide as waistbands), and salty goatee. Legs planted widely in the sand, folded arms forming the crossbar of his A-frame, he was chatting familiarly with Pongrass. The others were toggling their wrists and flicking their feet when Hut sloped up, unacknowledged. He was the only swimmer wearing a shirt.

Pongrass was finishing a story about his first job—or 'job'— apparently for the new man's benefit.

'So you can't disrespect short fronties. Jobber was four foot in her socks—perfect. Also, she had false teeth and took them out for you. It was like she was custom-built. She said it tasted like Ajax, but to her probably everything tasted like that. She was the school cleaner. Ha!'

Hut was the only one who laughed on cue, though Blackman gave a head-shaking chuckle. The story, demonstrating the coexistence of old-money and bogan-white-trash in the one Pongrassian form, confirmed Nayce's view that a fourth-generation millionaire could be as low-rent as anyone. For Hut, on the other hand, who was always learning goggle-eyed from Pongrass like a toddler watching his big brother, the flow was reversed. In Nayce's eyes, the trashiness of the story only darkened the taint on Pongrass. In Hut's eyes, the glamour of Pongrass made trashiness cool.

The man with the goatee shook his head with an ambiguous chuckle. 'Well, how about that,' he said. 'You're one funny Aussie.'

'Um. Rip,' Nayce said with a sour smell around his nose and his hand visoring his eyes against the particulate sunlight. Beside him Janey had listened to Pongrass's story with a fixed Janey smile. Embarrassed on her behalf in front of an outsider, Nayce felt like leaping on Pongrass and throttling him to defend her honour, yet knew that if he did this Janey would be the last to thank him. 'This is our last member—Hut. Rip's our race leader and pilot.'

Rip did an ostentatious head count—'You, you, you, you, you. That's five. And you,' he pointed at Hut, 'are number six.'

'Yeah well,' Nayce said. Jamaican sunshine seemed deflected, he felt, like the polluted milkiness of London or New York. The worst of all worlds. 'The race rules allow provision for a sixth team member.'

'As a reserve,' Rip said.

'We thought, nobody can accuse us of being one of the best teams in the race, so if we swim six I'm sure no-one will protest,' Nayce said, again shifting his face away from Rip.

'What do you guys think?' Rip addressed Pongrass.

'It's only a fun-run,' Pongrass said. 'Fun-swim.'

'And he did all the leg-work,' Blackman added. Then, to present both sides of the argument: 'Except he fucked up the rooms.'

Rip gave a shrug which conveyed a withdrawal of interest. His baseball cap crowned a sun-blossomed forehead, cheeks that were not so much wrinkled by the elements as pressed like a dried leaf, and a hard-working mouth clamlike between the bristles of his greying jowl pussy. 'Well, if he drowns, I ain't going back to get him. He's shark food.'

Hut's laugh, with his tongue hanging over his lower teeth, came out too loud. 'Rip, you'll be full throttle trying to keep up with me!' Wiping his eyes, Hut scanned the group but nobody laughed. He folded his arms across his Fast Set T-shirt. Fuck it. Fuckfuckfuckfuckfuckfuck.

'Okay, people, lemme see what I'm up against,' Rip said, turning towards the jetty.

Rip's motor launch, the twenty-eight-foot twin-engine Aquasmith, was attended by a shaven-headed Jamaican built like a decathlete.

'Jason. Yah, Jason. Jason.' He shook hands with each team member as he helped them onto the deck.

'Just gets worse and worse,' Janey said as she sat beside Nayce.

'What?'

She nodded at Jason's dorsal ripples. 'Jamaica.'

'Oh.' Nayce patted his own shadowy head, tacky with sweat, and wiped his hand on his thigh. 'Right.'

'Me no believe it, one of dem got a real name,' said Pongrass, who with Blackman had adopted an amateur blackface version of the patois.

'Aint no-one can beat Bidnid.' Blackman lowered his sunglasses like a boomgate from the crown of his head onto his nose.

Pongrass squinted across the hot glare of Negociante Bay. The light came stronger off the water than the sky. 'Is good Bidnid for eberybody mon.'

Hut, the last, waved Jason's helping hand away, but the boat shifted on an eddy as he stepped across and his bare foot missed the grained tread. Jason caught him before he fell into the drink. Flushing, expecting laughter, Hut brushed his sensors around the deck but nobody had noticed. For a second he considered going back and 'slipping' right off the boat—his staged pratfalls used to work such a treat, like when he'd 'fallen' screaming out of a first-floor classroom window into a hedge halfway through a German exam—but, like an old circus clown who had lost his edge, his timing, his audience (where? where? *when*?), Hut curled into himself, a flinching anemone, and sat quietly beside Book.

Jason fired the engine, pointed the Aquasmith into the bay and motored towards a red buoy. The team watched the marina and beach recede. Tourists cycled the bay on giant water-bikes or stood hopefully on becalmed windsurfers like commuters waiting for a bus. At the eastern headland, white-shirted staff swept out the beach bar, Slashing, the hottest spot south-south-east of Havana.

'Sounds hideous,' Janey said to Nayce. 'You pay ten J-dollars on entry and dance all night and drink as much rum punch as you like. My guide book says it's owned by Lawrence Rowe, the Test cricketer—I never realised he was Jamaican.'

'Whoever that is,' said Nayce, who hated cricket. It felt strange sometimes to be a man heading off cricket conversations with a woman, but there it was. He'd given up trying to make sense of either the game or Janey's liking for it. Janey had been infected by some boyfriend in her misspent youth. To her, the existence of someone called Lawrence Rowe was a reason to get drunk and fall face-down into sand. To him, it increased the appeal of a good book by the hotel pool. 'Here, give me that.' He grabbed a laminated nautical map from Bookalil.

Rip came down to the pit. 'Now.' Raising his nasal Kevin Costner whine above the engine noise, he couldn't help sounding querulous. 'You'll see that we're in pretty calm waters. When we do the race it'll be anything but. There's wind swell running in opposition to the current. It whips up the surface and fills your mouth and your eyes and three out of every four strokes you don't get a decent breath of air.'

'So we're genuinely fucked,' Janey said, deadpan.

'Oh, you're fucked all right,' Rip said, missing the irony, 'but that's the least of your problems.'

'What's the most of our problems?' said Janey.

'Depends,' Rip said. 'Anybody got a problem with seasickness?'

Hut looked around. Nobody put their hand up, so neither did he. He hoped he wasn't the only one lying. The last time he'd been outside Sydney Heads on his dad's yacht he'd spent the afternoon on all fours emptying himself out. Ken had said to his friends: 'This is why you never keep a gun on a boat. Because you'd rather shoot your son in the head than let him be like this.'

'We'll see,' Rip gave his cheek a sceptical chew. 'But it gets pretty rocky out there, and you can get sick just as easily while you're swimming as when you're sitting in the boat. And there ain't no cure for it, and we ain't coming in, so you're just gonna have to, as we say, green and bear it.'

Nervous throat-clearings passed around the boat. After gearing down and shutting the engine, Jason ran around the stern to uncoil chain and drop anchor by the red buoy.

'What about sharks?' Nayce said.

'Sharks?' Rip's eyes bulged. 'Did you say shark? Help! Help!'

The smiles were quick but humourless.

'Sharks,' Rip said, 'are like terrists. All I gotta say is, most of us get through our lives only seeing them on TV, and thank Jesus H. for that. But if your number's up, as we say, your number's up. No point worrying about it. They're the least of your worries, they really are.'

'That's a comforting thought to take into the water,' said Janey, who had swum in most of the world's seas in the course of her work, fretting about sharks every single time. 'I won't worry about it *at all* now.'

'But seriously,' Rip said.

'Since when were you not serious?' said Janey. The more urgent, real and serious Rip tried to be, the more American he seemed.

'Seriously, folks, you gotta problem with this current. It runs about eight knots through that channel. There are countervailing currents, refractory currents, the wind swell, any sea swell that's lounging about—a lot of complicating factors, which are good for you sometimes, because if that current was left alone to do its work, none of you would have a frog's chance in a blender of getting to the other side of the straits. It's a mean current. I know you say you're not the best team in the race, but you'll want to be solid swimmers, all five—all six—of you. Because anyone who's not solid will go sideways if not backwards. And if you start going off course, there's only one result.'

'A long day on the water,' Janey concluded.

'Time, my friend, is the least of your problems.'

'It's good that so many of these problems are the least of our problems,' Janey said.

'Who said babes couldn't be funny,' Rip said flatly to Pongrass.

'I'm not,' Janey said. 'Honestly. I'm not trying to be funny.'

Pongrass nodded at Rip: 'Believe her, matey. She's not funny.'

'Here's the rule,' Rip went on. 'If you guys swim off your line, this boat ain't coming to fetch you. This is how the race goes. Jason here and yours truly pilot this boat, but our job is easy. We navigate across the strait, trying to pick our way clear of the worst of the current. But let me repeat. *We* navigate the course. You don't. We do. So if you *choose*,' he stressed the verb and menaced the cabin with a fierce look, yet somehow actorly, as if learnt in a seminar, 'if you *choose* to swim off the line, away from the boat, then you can also *choose* to swim your way back to us. I'm not leaving my course, because my job is to get y'all to the other side, and I can't do that if I'm chasing you on whatever lines you choose to swim. Do y'all understand that?'

Silent looks passed like a joint around the boat.

'Okay, I won't tell you again,' Rip adjusted his sunnies. 'This is a serious freakin' business.'

Pongrass whispered something in Blackman's ear; they hid smirks behind nose-swiping hands.

'Wanna share it with us?' Rip said with the softness of rising hackles.

Pongrass waved him off.

'Okay, okay,' Rip said. 'You'll be telling me that one later. Anyway. As I was saying. This is a serious matter. A swimmer drowns in this event once every three races. We haven't had one in the last two races, so we're due. From the look of y'all,'—he said 'all' but glared straight at Hut—'you're a good chance to keep up our statistical average. All right? Yo—who wants a swim?'

16

After Rip's pep talk, the team couldn't get into the water fast enough. Hut stripped off his T-shirt and pencil-jumped in. The warm-up swim was only two kilometres, in the flat calm of the inner bay. But the team was thinking with one mind: finally. At last, at last they were under way. The water reminded them why they were here.

Swimming might seem a blurred or indistinct sport for the spectator. Unlike those laboratories of human emotion under high pressure—golf, cricket, baseball, tennis—swimming immersed the athlete beneath a fluid disguise. And tactically, swimming would seem to be one of those sports that offered least for analysis or individuation of the competitors. Tactics? Pace yourself, then go as hard as you can. There wasn't much more to it than that.

And yet, as Rip could see from the Aquasmith's bridge, each swimmer's temperament was revealed in the water as plainly as if they'd submitted to a personality test. Pretty Boy was out in front, brawnily pulling his body along, outmuscling the element. You didn't need to know his rowing history; his freestyle was a form of rowing, the hardwood torso as hull, the varnished brown arms as oars. Beside him, Hairy Sidekick was like one of those children's toys that need to be put in water to come to life. Cumbrous and effortful in his terrestrial middle-age, he was rehydrated by the sea. Of the six, he was exerting himself the least. His technique kept him high on the water, his slow stroke and kick pumping up a thick wave. Deceptively little was happening above the surface, but below, his hands were like the scoops of a waterwheel. He swam so languidly that he periscoped his neck above the water every few strokes to make sure he wasn't moving ahead of the others.

Perfect Skin exercised the straight-armed windmill stroke favoured by the top female racers, an unnatural stroke, hard to get right but highly propulsive. The mere fact that she could keep going with this tutored kind of stroke assured Rip that she was serious and fit, no concern at all despite her smart-ass comments. At her starboard flank the dark Moptop, the chubby one, appeared to be struggling, but after watching him for a minute or two Rip concluded that he just had a laboured, homemade stroke, a swimmer who'd improvised a style that worked for him but should never be taught or imitated. That much defiance of stroke correction bespoke a certain bloodymindedness that Rip knew could be either a great asset or a liability in a race like this. What Moptop lost in technique, he made up for in effort. His face was soon crimson, but he was swimming.

To Perfect Skin's port side, Baldy's style was more idiosyncratic still, but Rip soon detected its singular rhythm, if grudgingly. Rip didn't like this one: he saw trouble, an over-thinker. He recognised the type. They looked like a thumb with a face drawn on it but had too many ideas. Baldy's right arm, on his breathing side, came over much higher than his loose and lazy left. His lopsided stroke appeared to stop and start in each cycle. But the longer you examined it, the more it resembled an egg rolling down a hill. Not a ball—the Hairy Sidekick, the natural, had the smooth regular rotation of a sphere—but an egg, combining the attributes of asymmetry and unstoppable forward motion. Baldy could swim.

The team moved in a diamond-shaped pod: Pretty Boy and Hairy Sidekick at the nose, a three-strong centre of Moptop, Perfect Skin and Baldy, and a tail of the other, the redheaded reserve. The Monkey on their back. Rip didn't even like to look at the way the Orang-Utan was swimming. He hadn't had a drowner yet on the Aquasmith, and wasn't keen to start this year, no matter how much the fuckers deserved it.

He could feel a fight the way a dog can sniff a storm.

17

Hut had now been awake for seventy-four hours, some of that time pressurised, much of it both drunk and pressurised, some of it lost and humiliated in a minibus, much of it landbound but more drunk, some of it toxically stoned and walking the thinnest ice, and an embracing coalescence of it under the influence of anxiety and misery deflected by his reflexive, redemptive good humour. But all of it, every minute of it, he'd been awake. And now, in the water, he was his most awake yet.

He had been prepared to sink. Indeed, when he heard Rip intone the litany of dangers facing them in the race, Hut would happily have thrown himself into the sea with a lead choker. At least the bottom—of the sea, of your life—was solid, and nothing much else was solid out there. Yet when he stripped off his T-shirt and noticed the brief double-takes of the others, Hut received a reviving shock. They weren't laughing at him. They were admiring his buff shape. Even Janey, who'd never paid Hut more than a sisterly glance in twenty years, blew out her cheeks. 'Phew, Hutchison!'

When he landed in the water, Hut returned to life. He tingled, he fizzed. As he swam, his arms and legs seemed to know what they were doing. He felt himself lie back in his brain-centre and lace his fingers behind his head. He had never been able to trust his body, but his body, now, demanded trust. It asserted its own mysterious grace. It swam, allowing Hut's blissfully stunned consciousness to come along for the ride. How had he learned to swim like this? He wasn't asking. It was simply happening. He felt stationary while the water slipped beneath and around him. He slipstreamed behind the ghostly soles of Book and Janey, the froth and bubble of Nayce's wash. For a time he shut his eyes. He fancied he could take a nap. He swam like a swimmer swims. Even Rip, up in the boat, must have been a little taken aback.

He had to fight the urge to stretch out and swim ahead of the others: the sweetness of churning away, dropping them in his wake like bags of chum. But he had to throw a halter on his stroke, remain in formation. He couldn't help resenting it a little, if only for the effort. When you felt this good, swimming cost more energy at half-pace than flat-chat.

He concentrated on his stroke, drilling back into forgotten techniques. He dragged his fingertips across the water's surface, drawing parallel lines: the train tracks, or twin arrows, stringing his stroke along—nice. Under his abdomen, he forced the palms of his hands downwards—climbing on liquid steps. When he felt himself going too fast, he relaxed his kick from a four-beat to a two-, then, when he was still going too fast, a minimal quiver to keep his legs afloat.

He closed his eyes and opened his ears. You knew your stroke was smooth when you could swim with your eyes shut and not touch the lane ropes. (You were a god when you could tumble-turn without opening them.) Yet for some reason, the sound of the turbulence gave him nightmares; or rather, when he had nightmares, what he heard was this threshing of a giant moth's wings, the noise a brain would make if it started flooding with blood.

He gave it a voice—the roar of white pointers, of furious sea monsters, of giant squid, of killer whales, of unknown deep-sea nasties. He fed it into his motor like fuel. He was being chased; he swam from a predator, not a shark, no, something without a shape or a place in the animal kingdom.

Pen sometimes said he mixed up what he desperately wanted with what he already had; chased after something he could find if he only looked inside himself. But what she didn't get was that somewhere along the line he'd ceased running *to* and started running *from*; somewhere in the last few years carrot had turned into stick, and he dreamt less about what he desperately wanted and more about what he desperately *didn't* want. What he desperately feared. And he could run, or nail deals, or swim as fast as he could, in order to get away from this thing, but at the end of the day and at the end of the night it was still there, because it wasn't chasing him, nipping at his toes. Like what he'd wanted, it too was inside him. Or he was inside it.

Fuck it, Hut thought as he broke through to the front of the group and busted their formation. *I can't swim any slower than I am.*

18

NAYCE, MEANWHILE, SWAM into the past. What had Book said in Kingston, while they were searching for Hut? 'It's like you're *hoping* something bad has happened.' Too true. They'd found the fucker, but like a spike of coral pulled out of Nayce's foot, Book's comment had left its poisoned barb. The truth.

What was that Gore Vidal line Nayce loved? *Every time a friend succeeds, I die a little.* Beautiful. He loved to see his friends suffer, especially Hut. Nayce had always secretly cheered for suffering in all its forms, and expected some kind of ultimate punishment because of it. Yet being a merciless little shit had, in the contorted way of things, won him great popularity at school. He cheated disapproval by end-running it, winning the race to the most scabrous cynicism. 'You think I'm in an obnoxious adolescent phase,' Nayce, all of sixteen, had once declared to his father. 'What if this is just me?' Such honest self-appraisal could have won him some respite, or at least a discount off a sentence in hell, but Nayce was cynical about his cynicism. Two negatives did not make a positive; knowing you were a shit did not make you much less of one. Torturing yourself over your failure to be good was better than having no conscience, but only a little better.

In his twenties his nastiness caught up with him and he found himself descending into a premature midlife trough. Working in the Dutch bank, married for all the wrong reasons, Nayce gradually discovered that acerbic nihilism is no joke after adolescence. He spent the primetime of his twenties and thirties in an unbroken funk. Every morning he woke feeling homicidal, and from there the days only went downhill. At his wits' end at thirty-seven, he had decided to staunch his self-loathing by imitating the habits of a better man. His father, who had given up on inculcating a happy heart in David, said with monumental sadness: 'If you can't be good in this world, you might find peace by doing what good people do.'

It was a weirdly Machiavellian thing for a Uniting Church minister to say to his son. David's usual response to his father's advice was to mock it, relishing the adult son's satisfaction in breaking his dad's spirit. Rev Bill Nayce belonged to a church that was so tolerant, so inclusive and progressive, so well-adjusted, that by the turn of the century it stood for nothing more than Doing The Right Thing. 'The Uniting Church,' David loved to hector his father, had 'forgotten that churches are not *meant* to be likable; their existence depends on being doctrinaire. Otherwise we'd never notice them. Like we never notice you.'

But beneath what his father shrugged off as his 'pretty speeches', David was affected this time, perhaps by his father's observation that he needed to 'find peace'; a recognition that the keenest sufferer, beneath the overgrown-adolescent acerbity, was David himself. He resigned from his twelve-year job in the bank's futures arbitrage division to set up, with two friends, a hedge fund dealing only in products deemed 'ethical'. TBG Investments Pty Ltd ('There But for the Grace . . .') sourced and motivated financial backing for enterprises that set industry-best ethical standards in the environmental, biotech, educational, benevolent/philanthropic, medical and cultural fields.

His father, in his diffident way, approved. 'When the end comes,' Rev Nayce had said, 'you might hope that you will be judged by your deeds rather than your thoughts.' Again, his father had touched him, unexpectedly, with his recognition of *the end*. David had been so inured to Dad's sermons on the quotidian rather than the eternal—the Uniting Church's suburban mantra of 'community' and 'fellowship'—that he had forgotten that Dad might be as preoccupied with death and dying as was he. The son's belief that he was a pioneer, discovering insights of which his parents wouldn't have dreamt, blinded him to the obvious; David felt ashamed for assuming that a religious man would not have given serious thought to the afterlife. He wondered, for a brief but eye-opening time, where Dad ended and he began. Then he set up the ethical fund and discovered that nothing had changed.

Friends and colleagues had serenaded his 'middle-class guilt' with air-violins. Yet Nayce was scornful of middle-class guilt, it being both self-righteous and utterly self-referential. He knew TBG was all about himself and his own redemption, so his motives were self-referential; but he had not one self-righteous bone, not a single pious gland. Middle-class guilt? Fuck off. Nayce's professional life was mobilised by middle-class fear (of death); middle-class hatred (of arbitrage); middle-class contempt (of other middle-class people). He couldn't fool himself. TBG was another reaction: against his prosperous, monstrously self-absorbed society; against his schooling; against his peers, all richer than himself; against what was expected. All Nayce *felt*, it could seem, was the urge to react. As a church minister's son growing up among the rich, he was ideally placed to react upwards, against wealth, or downwards, against poverty. He could hate himself for being privileged; and he could hate those who were more privileged.

There were other reactionaries from his background who became 'compassionate conservatives'. Nayce was neither compassionate nor conservative. (He hated mushy compash-cons.) He preferred to label himself as an angry, aggressive liberal, a person who adopts the causes of the left with the scorched-earth bloodlust of the right. He had no heroes or models, but if he could have invented one, or invented himself as one, he would have been Dick Cheney, head of Greenpeace.

As they'd readied to dive, and Nayce was sealing his goggles into his eye-sockets with the violent heels of his hands, he spied Hut in an unguarded moment. A great many of Hut's moments were unguarded—he had an unguarded soul—but here his face had drained flat, creases ironed as if in a death mask. The freckles stood out from his nose and cheeks and he was seven again. The scratches on his face—from bushes, were they?—were the kind of scratches a little boy gets. Nayce paused, heart cavorting in his throat. This scratched Jeremy Hutchison, with the crackle of salt on skin and smell of sea, called up an old memory.

Between second grade and the end of school, for ten years, Nayce had spent every summer holiday with the Hutchisons at Palm Beach. Ken Hutchison was not part of the Palmie set, but his business dealings with the owner of an Ocean Road beachfront had led to a permanent summer rental. Ken didn't know that most of the owners deserted the beach at the summer peak, unable to resist the five-figure weekly rents and freedom from outsiders and other pollutants, but even if he had known, Ken, high-paying pollutant, wouldn't have given a stuff.

The house was known as the 'Pizza Hut' for its shingled faux-mansard roof. Built in the 1970s on a sandstone bungalow's grave, its construction had given birth to shock, horror and a local heritage society. The L-shaped layout suited the Hutchisons: a master bedroom on the north-eastern corner with sheet glass views; three other bedrooms spaced along the seaside wing; a large kitchen/living room with grand balcony in the crook of the L; and three bedrooms in a 'guest wing' extending into the bushland. Ken and Ines occupied the master bedroom, Jeremy and David hurling their bags into the adjacent children's rooms.

Young David Nayce tried simultaneously to drink in and spit out the glamour of holidays with the Hutchisons. Palm Beach parvenus they might have been, but compared to Nayceville they were royalty.

Nayce spent much boyhood energy keeping his family tucked under the carpet. Living free in the manse, it wasn't that they were shamefully poor (though his mother did need to work, as a kindergarten aide, to keep her son in private-school fees), but Nayce never invited friends home. Only later could he put a name to his embarrassment. His father's vice was excessive kindness. The Nayce gaze had something so blue and innocent about it, so unhurt, that its heir could only strive to muddy it. When Nayce's mother or father spoke, they regarded the listener with frank 1950s eyes: everything in life could be brushed off, put down to experience, rebirthed as a lesson or a tall story. Some people had expressionless eyes; the Nayces' had too much expression. His parents weren't proud of him as much as awed by him. Profoundly nice, if there could be such a thing, open-hearted and open-armed, his parents were his great shame. And he made sure they knew it. Why else would they send him to a private school they couldn't afford? Why else, when Nayce armoured himself with ruling class ways and sneeringly rejected his jocular parents, would they respond with chastened pride, as if bowing to their superior? They were frank and honest and their God was a placid old guy with a nice line in children's stories, and David couldn't bear their company for one minute.

His latest career move, into money's benevolent edge, was in no way a return or homage to his family's values. He moved into ethical investments not because he wanted to pay his respects to his parents' way of life, but because he wanted categorically to snub it. High-powered philanthropy and noblesse oblige were the repudiation of lower-middle-class humility, not fulfilling his Naycean roots but scorning them.

As a boy, he'd been transfixed by the Hutchisons. Cheeky, sandy Ken was a showy arsehole who Nayce could tell had become successful mainly by grinning and winking. Ken had one of those winsome smiles dominated by one front tooth that had charmed its way to the fore, an Artful Dodger tooth. It caught the light like a prow. As Ken aged, that tooth became his whole smile, his character. Though he'd grown up in Spitalfields, he resembled an aged surfer: sandy hair, sun-burnished handsomeness. As a boy you had to mock him, because that was what boys did, but you also had to respect what he'd done. Unlike the Reverend Bill Nayce, Ken Hutchison was a doer, Ken had been knocked around. If you were a boy, what was a kindly blue gaze next to a Thorn colour TV, a surf ski, a Merc and an MG, a Palm Beach holiday house?

Ines, in retrospect, seemed like a creature immobile in the aspic of her era. Were there any bronze-and-platinum blondes left? Did they all pour out of the north with Agnetha in 1973 before retiring into macrobiotics and meditation? Compared with the garrulous cocksparrow she'd married, Ines was a mystery wrapped in a vague and abstracted blear. Hers was the family with money; Ken had only married it and made it, striven for it and farmed it. Ines was unthinkingly *of* it. She never knew where anything was or how anything worked. Her response to the smallest household obstruction was to turn up her hands and say, 'Ken will do it.'

In the dining room, while Ken entertained the boys, Ines poked about dreamily, eating alone, after them, in the kitchen, unable to sit still at the table. Around the house she didn't walk so much as waft. Ken called her 'my freeloader'. Once, over a barbecue on the veranda of the Palm Beach house, Ken cawed: 'She's along for the ride—first sponging off her old man, now me.' Hut, who gulped down everything his father said, later told Nayce: 'Mum is like a pet—set her free in nature and she wouldn't know how to feed herself.' The sophistication and contempt in his tone, not to mention the truth of it, were too obviously parroted from his father.

And what was that Book had said, last night, about Hut?

When they were nine, Hut and Nayce had gone for a bushwalk on Barrenjoey Headland at the northern end of Palm Beach. They left Fred the latest basset at the house. Ines, wearing a filmy white sarong and espadrilles, platinum hair drawn into a half-hearted chignon, had escorted them on the marked path some of the way, but soon said she was tired and sat on a sandstone outcrop overlooking the sea. Mrs Hutchison was often tired, confusingly: Nayce had never seen her exert herself. She tucked her legs into her sarong and waved the boys on with a gluey negligence that would have looked studied were it not her natural state.

Braced by her trust, a nine-year-old man, Nayce forced aside the banksias and acacias fringing the headland. With Hut tagging, he left the track and thrust his way through the bush's acute angles, aiming to find the northernmost point where they could look out over Broken Bay.

'I don't know about this,' Hut said. 'We don't know where the edge is.'

Nayce's eyes thinned. 'We'll know where it is when we find it.'

Away from the parents, away from the house, Nayce could exploit his natural advantages over Hut. In the Hutchisons' home,

Nayce had the cunning to defer: he didn't want Ken to see his boy being number two. But away from the protection of family, Nayce led Hut.

'I don't think we should leave the track,' Hut said, fondling a banksia pod, his bottom lip shifting.

Nayce's look implied threat: *If you don't come, everyone at school will know about it.*

Damned if he did, damned if he didn't, Hut followed him into the deep bush. Their heels dug into the sandy soil as the land began to decline towards the cliff's edge.

Hut's ebullience had always been the kind that disguised timidity. Nayce loved the timidity more than the ebullience; it was truer. At home, the lively talkative funny Hut from school sank into his father's shadow. The kid wanted so badly to be like his dad, yet once you saw him at home you knew how much he took after his mother. Too disappointed to let it show, Ken strove to pump him up. No natural himself, Ken had pushed himself through barriers. Self-confidence was something his son could learn, if not earn; Hut's childhood was filled with the sound of his father telling him how great he was—how great they both were. Hut learned to suppress his mother's softness when he found it showing through.

But could he suppress those parts with any precision? What else was he holding down? That summer Ken had given him a set of new Taylor Made golf clubs, three lessons and an assurance that he was 'great'. Convinced he was an expert at the game, Hut took Nayce to the Palm Beach links.

'Here, have a go,' Hut said on the practice fairway.

'Don't you want to go first?' Nayce said. 'They're your clubs.'

'No, I want to see your style.'

Nayce, who had played golf since he could walk—the one leisure-class skill he owed his father—took six or seven practice swings.

'What are you doing?' Hut issued, hand over his mouth, the derisive pre-adolescent hoot. 'You're missing by a mile!'

Nayce gave him a puzzled look, then stepped up to the first ball and smacked it a hundred and fifty yards down the fairway. He hit two more, then handed the club to Hut.

'Okay,' Hut said. Nayce noticed Hut's hand tremble as he took the club. He squared up to the ball with a rigid, Z-shaped stance, fresh from the coaching clinic. His first swing: a robot with a faulty chip.

'That was my practice,' Hut said, reddening.

Hut skimmed the top of the ball and sent it over-spinning along the ground.

'Fuck these clubs,' Hut said. 'You mean you couldn't feel it? The weight is all wrong. Dad said he's taking them back.'

'Let me have another go.' Nayce stepped forward.

'I've got a better idea for you,' Hut said brightly, as if his purpose all along was to divert and cheer Nayce. 'This wind is fantastic—let's go home and get my new kite!'

Now on Barrenjoey Headland, they pressed through the sharp-clawed bush, Nayce holding down branches for the frowning, sweating redhead behind him.

'Nearly at the edge,' Nayce said. 'I can see the ocean.'

Soon they were at a pass between a knoll and the outermost tip of the headland. To reach the tip—which would bestow, like a blue ribbon, the view over north Pittwater and Lion Island up to the central coast—they would have to step across a narrow bridge of uneven rocks. The bridge itself was wide enough, but either side was a drop of thirty or forty feet, and then at the far edge, the precipice fell abysmally to the sea.

Nayce stopped. Hut came behind him and said: 'Told you it was a stupid idea. We can't make it to the edge.'

'What do you mean?' Nayce nodded to the rock bridge. 'It's only about fifteen steps.'

'Let's go back.'

Hut made to move into the bush, but wanted Nayce to lead him back through the nasty natives.

'We can't turn round now we've come this far,' Nayce said. He felt the silence as Hut paused behind him.

'No way,' Hut said, a knot in his throat.

'Come on. I'll show you.'

Nayce loved tests like this, not least because they gave him an opportunity to outpoint his friend. Hut may have had everything, but Nayce had courage. He took two steps onto the rock bridge and stopped when he heard a scuffle in the undergrowth.

'What are you doing?' Nayce turned.

On the sandy trail, Hut was pretending to balance, then crying 'Whoa!' and falling into the bushes. He got up, teetered, fell over. 'Whoa! Hard to stand up! Whoa!' He fell comically into a banksia and got up rubbing his cheek. 'Shit, scratched my face . . . Whoa!' He threw up his arms, as if hit by an earthquake, and fell the other way. 'Can't you feel that? Doesn't it make you dizzy? Is it just me, or is the ground moving? Don't you think?'

'Shut up,' Nayce said, smiling despite himself, and recommenced his crossing. He let his eyes slide from both sides of the bridge like hair flopping away from a centrepart. He knew that you weren't meant to look down, but this was another part of the challenge: to do what you were not meant to do. He was glad to have Hut as his witness. The story would get so much better at school.

Behind him, Hut had stopped throwing himself into the bushes. 'You know I went to America last autumn?'

Nayce shook his head rapidly, as if to scare off a fly.

'But see, they don't call it autumn there,' Hut went on. 'You know what they call it? Fall! *Fall!*'

'Shut up.' Nayce meshed his teeth against rising laughter. He probed a toe across the space between two boulders, rocked back and pushed off. His leading knee trembled and buckled, but held. He was three steps from the end.

'Did you hear that song on the radio?' Hut called, and sang with a surprisingly sweet voice that he never let show at school. Desperation was giving his precociousness a free head. *'I'll never fall in love a-ga-a-a-ain . . . I'll never fall in love again.* Ever *fallen* in love, Dave? Oh yeah! That ripper song, those garage band guys: *Ever fallen in love with someone, ever fallen, fallen, fallen in love with someone . . .* Hey—what about an old classic? *Raindrops keep falling on my head . . .'*

Despite himself, Nayce was getting the giggles. Was Hut trying to make him laugh so hard he'd lose his balance? With a half-lunge, he made it to the far side. He stood at the precipice and drummed his fists against his chest. He gave Hut the finger and surveyed the view like a captain on the poop deck, a hand shielding his brow. Hundreds of feet down and across the water, a lone yacht tacked in from the open sea.

'This is great. Come over, it's easy.'

Hut's face had clouded. 'You can die,' he said in a plump voice, as if Nayce had manipulated the whole episode to trap him here, on the wrong side.

'I made it over.'

'You still have to get back,' Hut scratched his armpits. 'And you'll die! I promise you, you will, you will!'

'Not funny anymore, Hut.'

'Go on,' Hut said, dropping to a whisper. 'Fall.'

Nayce stayed on the far edge as long as his patience permitted. The point was not to enjoy the view, anyway. The point was getting here. Now the point was getting back. Hut was chanting, clapping his hands in time: 'Fall! Die! Fall! Die! Fall!'

'Can you shut up? Serious.' Nayce stopped, halfway across.

'Fall! Go on! Fall!'

'Fuck off.'

'Fall!' Hut shouted with a boy's bitterness. 'Die! Go on! Die!'

Nayce came to the largest space between rocks, where he'd stumbled on the first crossing. Once again he looked down. It was only thirty feet of snags and crags, but thirty or three hundred, there wouldn't be much left of you.

'Fall! You bastard!' Tears clung to Hut's eyelids, fat enough to form but unconvinced about toppling down his cheeks. 'Go on, fall, you—you cunt!'

Hearing the word was nearly enough to shake Nayce off balance. He'd never heard one of his friends use it before. He'd heard Ken Hutchison use it to describe Ines, but it seemed desperate for Hut to repeat it here, now, so nastily, as if he really did want Nayce to die.

With a jump, arms stretched forward like a motorcyclist's, Nayce traversed the halfway gap. Hut fell silent, defeated. *Stuff him*, Nayce thought. *I'll tell everyone.* Hut deserved it for being such a shit.

Nayce was nearly across to the solid knoll when he glimpsed a white shape poised in the banksias. In an instant he saw what she saw: her son, weak, timid, resentful, wishing his best friend to die for being brave.

Ines's blank face was a coppertoned impasto. Nayce's first instinct, as always when surprised by an adult, was that he was in trouble: busted. If Nayce's mother had happened upon them, she would have smacked their bottoms and dragged them home by their ears, then burst out crying and hugged the air out of them. But Ines, Mrs Hutchison, just stood and watched, one hip turned out, silhouetted in her translucent sarong. Nayce couldn't drag his eyes off her as he took his last steps on the sandstone bridge. She didn't register her son; her eyes were on Nayce. Her expression, which he could only articulate as 'weird', was fixed and focused, the opposite of her usual fey gauziness. She stood there dead-still when usually she flitted like a leaf caught on a breeze. It would take him years to find a word for the look in her eyes.

With a grunt Nayce gained the knoll. As Hut turned to leave he finally saw his mother. 'Did you see what he did? Ha! He's so stupid! Did you see what he did?'

Ines ignored her son, who was now brave enough to storm past her into the fire-blackened banksia. She watched Nayce approach. He was nine years old, his chest welted with blushing scratches like the trunk of a scribbly gum, wearing nothing but a pair of board shorts, unabashed, defiant, muscular, at nine more manly than man. He stepped around her as coolly as if tempting death was all in a day's work. But if he could play a masculine role he was not quite able to shut out her silence. He couldn't resist turning around. Ines was picking her way through the bush, restored to her daydream. He waited until she was close, unable to avoid eye contact. When her cellophane blue eyes swept up, he winked and gave a little click: a Ken Hutchison gesture, disgusting, bluff, gladhanding. She stopped on an involuntary trip and frowned at her white-painted toenails as if they had let her down. Nayce inhaled, to keep himself taut, but his bubble was leaking. She seemed embarrassed on his behalf. With that cocky wink—where had it come from?—he had ruined everything. But what everything? What was it he had ruined?

Nayce finished the swim and accepted Jason's help back onto the Aquasmith, still immersed in a memory prompted by Hut's suddenly young face, the sea and the salt air.

Bullshit. Liar. Bullshit. It wasn't that long ago. That memory didn't need prompting; it was always chasing him, catching up with him whenever he came to a stop.

19

AFTER HALF AN hour in the water, Hut swam into Book's feet. Woken from his dream, he now found himself dying from shortness of breath. But he wasn't going to let them see. He'd proven himself. This had been his happiest half-hour in Jamaica, and he wasn't going to spoil it.

'Okay'all, up-up-up,' Rip was saying. Jason's arm like a length of shipping cable was winching each of the swimmers onto the Aquasmith. Blackman and Pongrass were quickly onto the bridge with Rip, sharing a joke, their faces fair and fresh. Book and Nayce were blowing a little more, and Janey was cracking some Red Stripes out of the cool box.

Blackman was telling Rip a story about Pongrass, who was nodding along.

'You know Pong came to Jamaica once for a rowing meet? They know him as "Nev" here. If you hear anybody call out "Hey Nev, how's it hanging?" don't worry, they've recognised the big guy.'

'Why Nev?' Rip asked, though the look on his face said he wondered if listening to these guys was part of his contract.

'You tell 'em,' Blackman said, but Pongrass, frowning magnanimously like a dignitary who didn't want to get in the way, waved his friend to continue.

'Okay, old Pong's prong has been out and about,' Blackman said. 'But the thing is, it's a covert operation. See, this was when he was engaged. He'd been the big family man in all the media, you know, "my bachelor days are over, blah blah blah", usual stuff, and he wants everyone on the team to get that image of him as well. So he's been very clandestine about it. And so on the last morning, when they're all in the minibus ready to go to the airport, the team manager looks around and says, "Where's Pongrass?" They're about to jump out and go searching for him, but at the last moment, here he comes, bolting out of the hotel, bag half open and all his stuff spilling out, but he's not stopping to go back and get it, he's just going hell-for-leather to get on the bus. I don't know if I can go on . . .'

Blackman subsided into the head-shaking fit of a man who knows what's coming next. Pongrass, quietly heroic, shrugged at Rip.

'Okay, okay,' Blackman painted the back of his hand with his nose. 'Pong comes bolting for the bus. The team manager's about to tear strips off him for being late, and for missing the curfew the previous night, when all of a sudden out of the hotel comes this big black bird, I mean, she's the size of a minibus, you know, she's all woman . . . And she cries out . . . and she cries out: "Neville! Neville! Don't leave me like this!"'

Pongrass bestowed a corroborative nod. 'My cover was blown, yep. My cover was blown.'

'Sure man,' Rip said. 'Neville. Hey, that's funny.' That American habit, to pronounce something funny without going to the trouble of laughing.

Hut had somehow made it to the stairs, struggled down to the toilet and shut himself in. It took all his strength to find pockets of air inside the walls of his chest. His face, he saw in the mirror, was porridge-grey. His eyes were red dwarfs. But it didn't matter—he hadn't embarrassed himself. He hadn't fallen off the pace. He hadn't drowned. He spun in the flow of gratified negatives, all the disasters he was proud to have avoided. The last thing he saw, as his head fell into the sink, was twin green streams—snot? upshafted vomit?—jetting out of his nostrils and forming a graciously symmetrical splatter pattern, like butterfly wings, on the vanity.

4

The other half

20

PENELOPE HUTCHISON WAS travelling halfway around the world to tell her husband that they needed time apart.

Was that ironic, or was ironic not quite the word? David, Professor Nayce, the anti-Hut, would pontificate that 'irony' was another false epidemic sweeping the globe, as when every headache was called a migraine and every runny nose the flu. Anyway, whatever it was, irony or just oddness, it saturated Pen's life. Going on a 'holiday' with a two-year-old and a three-year-old. Her certainty that becoming a single parent of two toddlers was going to make life easier than having a husband. It was, it had to be, ironic that she, product of a broken home—a shattered home, a nuclear family fissioned—who had clung to Hut for his stability, his family Christmases, his taking-for-granted of monogamy, the literalness of his till-death-us-do-part—ironic that she would now feel more secure alone.

She flew in the cranium, Business Class out of Sydney with Roy and Charlie in their own seats. Hut had wanted them to fly First—insisted—but Pen knew that your children produced only half of the stress of flying. The other half was created by the adults around you. The time you didn't spend coping with your kids you spent worrying about the tut-tutting and teeth-sucking.

Roy was three, Charlie two. That may not have been so bad if Roy had been nearly four and Charlie only recently two. But Roy was nowhere near four, and Charlie was just about three. They were her Irish twins: eleven months apart. She'd fallen pregnant with Charlie while Roy was still a toothless blob on her breast. And what was that about? Wasn't breastfeeding meant to be a contraceptive? When Pen and Hut had told Hut's mother about the pregnancy, Ines's glazed eyes had alit momentarily on Roy as if she'd never seen him in her life. 'What on earth was the thinking behind that?' she'd said.

Pen had groaned. What else could she have done, apart from cry? (She was doing enough of that. When she fell pregnant again, she cried for three months. A four-year stretch of bottles, nappies and sleep deprivation. Four years. You got less than that for killing someone.)

Hut had saved the day. 'Not much thinking behind it, Mum. Plenty of thinking after it.'

Hut had saved days, saved her, throughout that second pregnancy. He finally delivered on the promise he had not known he was making the night they met, at Susie and John Bookalil's wedding: to stand between Penny and the abyss. Her old abyss, her secret sickness. Hut loved the idea of a second baby. 'More of the same, please!' he crowed at the eighteen-week ultrasound: another boy. Having fertilised her with Charlie, he set about fertilising her with his happiness. In the last month, in the nick of time, Pen found that she, too, wanted her baby.

From there, though, it had been all downhill. Take this morning, one slice of the daily onslaught. Charlie woke at 4.30 am, turned on all the house lights and activated the burglar alarm. So Roy was up too, and by sunrise Pen felt she had worked a full day.

Roy threatened to hurl himself from the highest storey of the bookshelf if he could not wear his suffocating polar fleece jacket. Pen tried to talk him down. 'We're going to the beach, sweetheart, the beach!' She gave in. He could stifle in his bloody jacket if he wanted to. Roy assaulted Charlie with a toy trowel, then screamed—screamed as if she was trying to murder him—when the polar fleece jacket got anywhere near him. Interlocking with this narrative was Charlie's refusal to eat his breakfast. The little critter stored masticated Weetbix in his mouth for an hour and then, theatrically, looked her in the eye and released it in a molten cascade down his newly clean shirtfront. Then came his refusenik protest at helping Mummy pack, getting his toys together, getting out of the house, getting to the airport, getting onto the plane. Like his father, Charlie was a man: he hated transition. Like his father, Roy too was a man: he spent the two hours at the airport trying to wander off when her back was turned.

On a day when, normally, she would shelve any plans to leave the bunker, she was taking them to Jamaica. In Business Class, the boys were, if nothing else, businesslike. Roy found a way to the magazine rack and efficiently hand-shredded *The Economist*, *The Weekly Standard*, *The Bulletin*, *Time* and *The Monthly*. He posted the laminated safety cards between the seats. He upended his orange juice onto Charlie. He caused a security alert by charging the cockpit with a toy tank.

His younger brother, on the other hand, was a nightmare. When Charlie was overtired, he forced himself to be sick. He vomited into, around, under, and over the top of a roll of sick bags. He cried so persistently and violently that the flight attendants asked if Pen needed a doctor. When she said, 'No, he's not sick, he does this on purpose,' the flight attendants treated her with suspicion and distaste: heartless bitch, no right to be a mother, all her fault. Unlike Roy, who anyone could see was a complete shit, people

161

assumed the littlie was an innocent victim. The man in the row behind said: 'It's his ears, it's the pressure, all you have to do is kiss him on the mouth.' On the mouth? She held up Charlie and regarded his vomit-caked, snot-glossed lips. She presented him to the man behind and said, 'He's all yours.'

Two years before, Pen would have pined for Hut. If only their father were there. Hut was the answer. But that was the old Hut. If the current Hut were here, he'd make himself scarce. Or laugh it all off. The most insulting, offensive, marriage-fracturing thing he had ever said to her was, when she was complaining about another daylong Iliad with Roy and Charlie, 'Darls, live with it—you're a mother.' Then planted a kiss on her forehead. If she'd been able to unfreeze herself, she'd have punched him in the mouth.

If Hut was the answer now, it meant she'd asked the wrong question. Hut had been the world's best father for precisely eleven months: his dewy-eyed pride at Roy's birth, his fond and supportive days as a father of one with another on the way, right up to the arrival of number two. Then, when he realised that a second baby flushes out the father from his hiding place, all hands on deck day and night, Hut discovered that his business interests needed closer attention. If Hut were here now, he'd be creating new problems all his own. He'd try to work on his laptop. She was sure he never worked on his laptop when he flew on his own. He never wanted to work on his laptop except when he was with Pen and the boys. Grunting and tapping, he would inflame Pen by asking her to hush the kids, and bug her with questions. 'Why can't I get that document back? Can you do this? What the—what does this symbol mean? Damn, I've deleted it. Can you get it back for me?'

And yet these were the ordinary stresses of parenthood, or so she was told. Pen's friends' husbands were much the same. Having children turned them into children, competing with their offspring to be the first Me. To Hut's partial credit, he showered Pen with what he regarded as help: the weekday nanny, the visiting au pair, the groceries delivery, the suburban assault vehicle. And it did help. It saved her from the horror of raising two tyrants in poverty. It saved her, right at this minute, from Economy.

But for every quid there was a pro quo. Hut, in paying for all this assistance, believed he had discharged his responsibilities. He believed that the weekends he took Pen away from the boys made mothering easier—when any mother knew that a weekend off could be like sitting out part of a marathon to eat a hamburger and a plate of chips, then re-entering the race as the field accelerates. What Pen needed, and what the boys needed, was their father's regular, routine presence. What Hut thought, or told himself, they needed was his money. He believed his absence was a component in a mechanism of exchange that gave them 'a good life'. 'I have to make sacrifices too, you know,' he'd said, cuddling her.

Five hours in the air and the boys had started to settle. Pen could think about asking the flight attendant to bring her the hot meal she'd set aside. Roy was contentedly doodling in texta on wall-membrane and tray table. Charlie had discovered the fascination of cupping his hands and filling them with drool before emptying them onto his and Pen's lap. Whatever worked. She had tried to get them to watch videos or play electronic games, but their brains were too frisky to be tamed. Her father-in-law railed against television as 'a sop for failed parents'. Pen felt she was failing by *not* being able to get them to watch television. They didn't have enough attention to have their attention spans destroyed.

But they were quiet, at least. In the lull, the thought that broke through was *Hut, Hut, Hut*.

He wouldn't see it coming. She pitied him for that. He would be blindsided. But she hadn't seen it coming either—his change. How could she have? This was the boy who, from the night he met her, found it impossible to say goodbye. He drove her home from that wedding and burst into tears when she got out of his car. At first she was annoyed, thinking it a fit of petulance for her not going to bed with him. But he apologised: 'I know you have to go now, but I've never been so happy.'

The idea of making someone so happy was new to her. Pen's adolescence had been an ongoing survival campaign, the quest to imagine her way into a bearable existence punctuated by the seduction of razor blades. Happiness was such a forlorn hope for her, as a girl and a young woman, that Hut arrived in her life with the force of revelation: she had been looking for it in the wrong place. Happiness was not a state, but a gift. As cute as Danny Bonaduce and Ralph Malph put together—she had a thing for redheads—he was as plumped-up with life as a bag of kittens. Her previous boyfriends could only remind themselves they were alive with acts of casual cruelty. Hut had no time to play games. He ran in only one direction. He stuck to her, and when she wavered he stuck tighter. They went on three or four dates, and Hut talked all night, so glad with wherever they were, so uncritical, so *replete* with her company. He would drive her great distances to postpone the goodnight kiss. He would talk like the Ancient Mariner to distract her from evening's end. Eventually, she moved into his apartment because she couldn't handle the farewells either.

Hut fell in love with Pen first, but she was not long catching up. She fell for the background and the framing as much as the subject. Ken Hutchison was a jolly Cockney, holding himself back from the brink of constant amusement, and Ines was an airy beechwood-coloured German blonde who seemed of a piece with her walk-in fridge, her walk-in pantry, her walk-in wardrobes. They were so perfectly, intoxicatingly (and intoxicatedly) in their element. Pen's idea of herself was of a watch that never quite worked, some cog always out of whack. The Hutchison men *worked*. They neither asked questions nor looked rearwards, or inwards. Fatally, though (now she looked back on it), Ken and Hut had distracted her from Ines. In the male whirlwind, she'd never examined her mother-in-law closely. Nor had they. And nor had Hut examined her, Pen. It took her many years to stop and ask herself about this. Hut's lack of inquiry, his simple acceptance of her, had seemed such a blessing, such a relief. On one of those early dates she had tried to tell him about the teenage suicide attempts, the boyfriends begged for a cigarette burn, and about Tera. That had all been a long time ago, and she owed it to Hut to come clean. Her past couldn't scare him off, surely? But as she worried her way down to the grisly details, he stoppered her mouth with a long kiss. 'I don't care,' he said. 'I don't want to know.' She was so warmed by it that she had taken it for love, rather than more literally.

Hut's saturation with family suited Pen, who had none. When she was eight, her mother Angie had run off with her father's brother Griff. Pen and her younger sister Tera had stayed with their father, Stan; Angie had not contested custody. Stan was estranged from his entire family, not only because he could not stomach seeing Angie with Griff, but because the family, for some reason Pen could never work out, took Griff's side. So Penny and Tera were stripped clear of both families—their mother's, and their father's. Only when Stan walked off The Gap did Angie take them back.

Though nobody, least of all Hut, would have guessed it by her mid-twenties, Penny Lyons was strictly non-selective government school stock. Damaged goods saved by black-Irish looks and a sharp-clawed survival instinct. At fifteen Tera had taken the cutting thing too far, sucked into the black hole of Stan's absence. If her sister's death was going to mean anything, Pen had to turn her life into something. She ground through school into a university commerce course, earned high enough marks to transfer to law, worked as fiercely as a mature-age student and got into a big city firm. It was only persistence—she didn't kid herself, or wouldn't congratulate herself, that she was especially clever. She was a grinder. But along the way she picked up the gestures, the accents, of the people around her, with the same diligence she applied to her studies, so that by the time she met Hut, her colleagues and social set had little idea of the depth of the hole out of which she had climbed.

She was comfortable amid money. There were more of her type of female than she'd have expected. In Janey Quested, Pen found a mutual recognition. They weren't gold-diggers; they were survivors. And these men's peculiar insularity provided a good home for women who could survive. The boys just weren't *interested* in females in the same way they were interested in each other. Girls were givens. Sometimes she wondered how (or if) these boys maintained the kind of innocence they needed to steer clear of some physical expression of what she saw as an open-hearted homosexuality. Hut certainly had asked more questions about Justin Pongrass's sexual history in the last three months than he'd asked Pen about hers in twelve years of marriage.

But his incuriosity had been his appeal. He could have married any of those nice girls with Alice bands and sensible mothers and rich fathers—he didn't realise it, but he could have had his pick. Instead he chose her. And when he found out that, in defiance of appearances, Pen was from the other side, he was good enough not to care. He seemed even to prefer it that way. Much later, when she realised that Hut's father had married into money, she began to grasp that Hut got a competitive thrill from not having done the same. Somehow it soured the memory.

They had been at the Hutchisons' beach house when the engagement took place. That Christmas Eve, as he walked her along Palm Beach, folding her into him against the wind in that maritime way she loved, Hut murmured: 'What do you think you'd say if I thought about asking you to get married?'

'Ah. Ah. Ah.' She waved a finger like a windscreen-wiper. 'None of this hypothetical stuff, none of this what if, what if?'

'Oh. Right,' he said.

They walked halfway to Barrenjoey before Hut spoke again. 'Well?'

The word caught in his throat, touchingly, but Pen shook her head. 'I'm not letting you off that easily, buster. What are we going to say when our kids ask us how we got engaged? I'll say, "Dad eventually said, *Well?*"'

Hut chewed on that.

'You said kids. Does that mean it's a yes?'

With her, he was often shy. This was what she prized in him, in those days: the disconnection between public Hut, all bravado and bullshit, and the private Hut, her Hut. It seemed like a miracle, this meeting of bluster and softness with a crack in between that was only wide enough for her. He went to extremes in every direction, but his extremes of tenderness were reserved for Pen: their secret.

'I didn't say that,' she said. 'You haven't even asked yet.'

When they got back to the house, Hut found under the Christmas tree an envelope addressed to him in Pen's handwriting. He eyed her sidelong.

'Open it.'

Inside was a card with the question.

'*Tired of waiting*,' he read. '*Will you marry me?*'

'Snap.'

Their accounts of the engagement would differ. Hut claimed to have asked first, 'and lucky too, because I got in just before her'. Pen, out of respect for Hut's dignity, said: 'It was a dead heat.'

They prepared for their country wedding without mishap or

serious argument, Hut deferring: 'I'm only the groom. Way, way down the food chain.'

In those days his withdrawal from the efficiencies of daily life was endearing, and flattering, showing that he trusted her. He swore by her taste in all things, and she would hear him voicing opinions on art or interior design that were, verbatim, her own. He impressed upon her that he was the one who should feel gratitude. He told her, 'You're all there is between me and dying poor and lonely.' Pen would shrug this off: she, not Hut, was the one who skywalked without a safety net. And it was true. She had nothing. But he shook his head firmly, disagreeing and wanting to make sure she knew it. 'You have you, I mean, you'll always have this solid soul, this sense of who you are. Me, I might have the trappings and the family and all that, but when you take the crap away there's not much left.'

In front of two hundred weekend guests in the Hunter Valley, Hut stood on a platform and gripped her hands for dear life. He was four syllables into his vows when he broke down, nose streaming, red-eyed with love. He pressed on, his voice rising two octaves into a whimper, halting between words, half-laughing with the sheer embarrassment of it. When he was done, he and Pen found themselves surrounded by four hundred wet eyes, two hundred pink noses. There was more crying than at a funeral. When guests came to congratulate them, they burst into tears. When he got up to deliver his reception speech, he was off again, wailing like a child. It was passed around in the folklore of their circle, and their circle's radiating epicircles, as the wedding in which the groom lost it and the bride was cucumber-cool.

Charlie was now dozing against her right arm. In repose, he was the image of—who else?—his father. The little rat, the big rat. But a little rat was so much easier to love. His cheeks were rosy from crying, stained deltas down each side of his freckled nose. Like his father, he slept with his mouth open, snoring softly. To her left, Roy had decided to be Big, knuckling down with a favourite ambulance, rolling it up the six-lane freeway of his Business Class armrest. He issued a commentary from both sides of a conversation involving the driver and an injured passenger, who seemed to be his Daddy. Pen stroked his spun-gold hair and pressed her lips to his crown. She wanted to lift him up and cuddle him on her lap. This was the problem with the little buggers. All day she was dying for them to get to sleep or entertain themselves, wishing every long minute away, and then, when they settled, all she wanted was to get them up and play with them. Instant nostalgia.

One day she would wave them off into manhood. Maybe Hut's change was one of those biological rehearsals, programmed to toughen her for the heartbreak of losing her children. Yet Pen suspected that the recent changes in Hut had nothing to do with being a father. Being a father seemed to have less and less impact on Hut's personality. His sickness—she had no other word for it— was independent of the home, atrociously, barbarically indifferent. And there was the rub. If his recent behaviour had been a result of fatherhood, Pen would have forgiven him.

Goodbye. She rehearsed under her breath. She'd been surprised when Hut suggested that she and the children fly over to Jamaica; less surprised that he postponed her flight, pretending he wasn't under pressure from the boys, the team. That was Hut, good old Hut: bend over backwards to keep everyone happy, end up annoying them all. She would be in Jamaica in time for the race. And after it was over, she and Hut would have their sit-down.

The jumbo was eight hours over the Pacific and both boys were snoring. Pen asked the flight attendant if she could have her hot meal now.

21

As the earth averted its blushing cheek, David Nayce was enjoying an all-inclusive pina colada on the hotel terrace with Book and Janey. An afternoon sleep and the glow of the training swim had replenished Nayce's spirits, and he had refuelled with a room-service utter chicken—to which he was now addicted—and rice with a papaya salad. Janey wore her rugby jersey and jeans, Book a Sandals polo shirt from the lobby shop, and Nayce, as Janey remarked, 'TV—T-shirt under V-neck'. They shifted in cane chairs whose backs were canted at a frustrating mid-angle between upright and reclined. The crimson-painted cement terrace overlooked the halcyon bay and a palmy breeze rustled the hairs on their arms. Distantly the beach bar, Lawrence Rowe's Slashing, was emitting a faint pulse.

Janey and Nayce were joking about Hut passing out on the Aquasmith. He had been carried up the jetty and put to bed, where he remained. 'The funniest thing was Rip's face,' Janey said, though in earlier tellings the 'funniest thing' had been Hut's face, the state of the toilet, the group's efforts in carrying him out of the boat and cleaning him up, and eventually the funniest thing was the whole thing and the whole thing the funniest.

'That prick,' Nayce said, meaning Rip. 'He'd been so big on taking care, and first aid, and responsibility, and the moment Hut makes a mess on his boat it's "Oh fuck, you asshole, look what you've done to my vanity!"'

'Was his vanity broken?'

'Only wounded. Hairline fracture. You know what I told him? I said, "Rip, this is the least of your problems."'

John Bookalil was playing little part in the conversation. He stared pensively, listening to words that had not been spoken, in the direction of a puttering motor launch crossing the bay towards the island of Negociante.

'And he was swimming so well!' Janey laughed, as if this had been the most delicious irony.

'Was he?' Nayce said. 'I assumed he was riding in the boat.'

'Stop it,' she smacked his knee. Janey punctuated her speech with so many thigh-slaps and biceps-squeezes that Nayce sometimes worried that she was one touch away from a man who got the wrong idea. 'You really are *so* nice to him,' she said.

'I don't need to fuck him up. He does it all himself. He's made me surplus to requirements.'

'Ahh. Now, Nayce, where do you get a drink when you need one?'

With a wave of her fluorescent wristlet, Janey cast her face over one shoulder, then the other, exposing her slender tendon-fluted neck. Floral uniforms were seen scuttling into shadows.

'Only when you don't need one can you get one,' Nayce said. 'It's called the All-Inclusive Paradox. You can eat and drink as much as you can. But that isn't the same as eating and drinking as much as you'd like.'

'Damn. I swore I saw a waiter a minute ago.'

'That's because your glass was full a minute ago.'

'Fuck!' Book exclaimed with that startling bottled-up violence of his. 'I'm going to get them.' He leaped out of his chair and ran after a blurring shirt.

'What's up with Iron John?' Nayce said, ruffled by Book's remoteness.

'Maybe he really, really needed a drink,' Janey whispered, a strange barb in her voice, as if she really, really needed one too. Nayce felt a beat of nausea. Just when he'd begun feeling better, his paranoia sneaked back in, a wave of suspicion that he was on the wrong side of a silence.

They watched the sky darken, the sea lighten.

Never comfortable in dead air, Janey turned Nayce a solicitude-painted face and inquired, for the first time this week, about Sophie and little John.

'They're great,' he said. 'We're all great.' Nayce squirmed under the hypocrisy of extolling his wife and son with a gusto that could only come from knowing that they were at home and he was here, with Janey.

'I'm so happy for you,' she beamed.

'They mean so much to me,' he carried on, hoping to lather on the sarcasm thickly enough to force Janey to react. Yet knowing she wouldn't. 'I feel lucky every day of my life.'

What he would have preferred to admit was that he had a far more ambivalent relationship with every day of his life. At home, time was held in a boxer's clinch. With a relatively demanding wife and child (he'd conducted a straw poll; he'd come out poorly), Nayce nickel-and-dimed his privacy into minutes here, seconds there: a deep breath and back unto the fray. He hated that tightness, the family man's treadmill. The pleasure and the release of these five days without family or job—and with Janey—stretched out like oceans of time.

'That's so great,' Janey said, the forced breadth of her smile prepared to go with him lie for lie. Would she stop when he stopped? Was she challenging him to be, after twenty-some years, *straight* with her for one second? No. Or not yet. He knew Janey too well for it to be a simple matter of coming out and saying it. The entire purpose of their jocular conversational formula, it could seem, was to air the exact opposite of the truth. It gave them a species of comfort: as long as they kept lying and telling nothing but lies, each knew where the other stood.

Book returned, cuddling three voluptuous pink drinks. 'Fuck,' he muttered as he sat down.

'You okay?' Nayce said.

Book shrugged.

'Is that a Yes shrug,' Nayce said, 'or a No shrug?'

'I'm fine.'

Normally that would be enough. In this group, it suited everyone's emotional palettes to take responses at face value. You could be fracturing into small pieces, tears spurting from your eyes, but if you said 'I'm all right', your respondent would give you a clap on the shoulder and say: 'Righteo!' And yet here in Jamaica they were out of their element and stuck with each other, and persiflage would no longer do as camouflage.

'Seriously,' Nayce leaned forward and rapped Book's thigh. 'A Jamaican dollar for your thoughts?'

A baleful sigh, seeming to originate behind Book, blew through him. 'Sorry, guys. It's hard.'

Janey stroked Book's back with her knuckles. 'It's all right, John.' Her voice was thick with complicity.

Nayce felt dizzy, as if being pushed through an automatic car wash, the blows raining down from all sides. 'Come on,' he said. 'Both of you. What's it about?'

Book scratched his nose and examined his fingertips as if for oracular guidance. 'I spoke to my dad today,' he said.

'Oh shit,' Nayce said. 'Is he okay?'

'Dad? Dad's fine.' Book blinked suspiciously as if Nayce might know something he, Book, didn't.

'So . . . ?' Nayce said, curling it into a question.

'Ah, I don't know if I should be telling you this. It's kind of commercial-in-confidence.'

'A trouble shared is a trouble halved,' Nayce said, struggling to control his impatience and anxiety.

'Shit,' Book said and took a breath. 'Um, Dad said he'd got a phone call from a lawyer about Hut.'

'Your dad?' Nayce sat forward, unable to make the connection. 'What lawyer?'

'You know these old-boy networks,' Book said. 'Dad's known Ken Hutchison from way back. Looks like there've been some calls going round.'

'Hey,' Nayce said. 'Hut's got lost in a taxi, been stoned out of his brain, got hit by a car, nearly been beaten to death and passed out in a pool of vomit after swimming a slow two k. And I've never had a bad feeling about any of it until now.'

'It's not funny,' Book said with a sharpness that reminded Nayce, like a cryptic warning, of schoolyard ambush.

'Shut up, Nayce.' Janey's fingers brushed the back of his hand.

'It's not funny at all.' Book's Adam's apple nodded.

There was a disturbance in the bar area. Two large white men in Hawaiian shirts and cargo shorts, hair slicked down and white-framed sunglasses pushed back on their crowns, were barging through with armloads of creamy cocktails. Nayce's heart sank.

'Oi,' Pongrass said when he made it to the terrace. He bent down and tenderly unloaded six daiquiris onto the cane table. 'It's the only way you can guarantee to get refreshed around here. You gotta have all you can drink in the first round.'

'Lead with your trumps,' Blackman said, following up with another six.

Pongrass and Blackman pulled up chairs, ritually shook hands with Nayce and Bookalil, and filled in the circle, their backs to the view over the bay.

'We were just debating,' Pongrass said at large, like an MC who presumes he is on permanent duty, 'if there's any such thing as a bad job. Abo says there isn't, but I remember clear as a bell my first bad job. Petra Farkis. Petra was a real trier, you had to say that for her. I was sixteen. Sweet sixteen and never been . . . Well, never been nothing, really.'

'Oh, Petra,' Blackman said. 'Went down like the sun—on a daily basis.'

'Right, so after my episode with Jobber (strictly a one-off, or two-off as it happened), I zeroed in on Petra. I thought about jobs all day long. I didn't care if I never fucked anyone. Why would you when there were jobs? Why did fronties even *have* fronties? So I got an introduction to Petra Farkis and she took me to her office.'

'Oh, that fucken Catholic graveyard,' Blackman said. 'They said you'd get a curse on you if you went down there.'

'I never went *down*!' Pongrass said, all rehashed misunderstanding and offended innocence. '*She* did! Without so much as a howdyedo, Petra buckled down and got to work. I stood there reading about Florence Someone who died in 1925 and Esmerelda Somebody who kicked it in 1949 but was only born in '44. Tragic. I was totally put off.'

'Death,' Blackman shook his head profoundly, and left it at that.

'Nah, not the graves,' Pongrass laughed. 'What put me off was Petra. Chowed down like she was packing bags at Woolies. That's why everyone called the graveyard her office. She went to work on you like she was getting six bucks an hour.'

'Ear-nose-and-throat specialist,' Blackman said glumly. 'That's what they called her.'

'Where was the art, where was the subtlety? She was an over-achiever,' Pongrass said, as if regretting a protégé. 'I pulled her head away—not, it has to be said, without resistance—and said, "Oi, can't you just paint the tree for a bit?" And Petra goes, "Yuk, no way do I do that".'

The evening air thickened. Pongrass looked around, clearly annoyed at Nayce and Book for not supporting him with laughter or murmurous solidarity. His look was all tough pride, the only man with the balls to tell it the way it is.

Nayce, who could think of nothing to say to Pongrass, perhaps ever again, was hanging on to what Book had been verging on revealing about Hut. Book, interrupted, stared down onto the marina, seeing nothing. Nayce cleared his throat to ask if Hut was still asleep upstairs.

'Didn't notice,' Pongrass said. 'Cunt's moved his cot out onto the balcony. Hey Abo, want anothery?'

Blackman finger-combed his bosky thorax, wrist undulating as if strumming a guitar or having a wank. 'Another daiquiri and I'm ready for commitment.'

While Pongrass and Blackman began to semaphore the staff, Nayce studied Book, as if he might learn from his friend's fidgets and frowns what was the matter with Hut. It had to be money. Money was the taboo, the anti-subject. It opened up the cracks. Between Book and Janey. Between Nayce and Hut. Between them all and Pongrass and Blackman. As a group, they could only pretend they had anything in common if they stopped themselves thinking about, or mentioning, money. But could Hut really be in trouble? Nayce had always imagined and even willed possible disasters for Hut, but in these fantasies Hut always escaped, scathed but untouched in spirit. Hut was a dunderhead, but his ink was black, not red. The guy topped the state in maths. Vegie maths, but still maths. Behind the bluster, he was a conservative investor. The possibility that he might be in real trouble inverted thirty-three years of knowledge.

In time, more drinks arrived. As Pongrass and Blackman prattled on, maddeningly unaware that they were in the way, Book started thumping the arms of his chair. There was something so honest and true in Book, Nayce thought, some perfect balance of loyalty and simplicity, that it was only human to take him for granted. He had changed the least since boyhood. Yet the danger in treating your most loyal friend as part of the furniture was that you might deprive yourself of the best of his nature. As Nayce looked at his poor friend, pregnant with bad news, he was struck with admiration for how grown-up Book was: this dark stranger, this capable authoritative man amongst them. This guy who had lived in the same suburb his whole life, had never been overseas for more than two-week business trips, still ate a meal with his parents every Friday, went to the same job every day and home to the girl he'd taken to his school formal, prepared the same breakfasts every morning and read the same stories to his daughters every night, a real girls' dad; this guy who had experienced no hardship, no great unhappiness, gone nowhere, done nothing—when had it happened? When had Book become a man? And how had he managed to leave the rest of them behind?

Pongrass was finishing a story about his 'first Westie'. 'You remember, the one at the ice-skating rink, we were about fifteen, scraggy little chickie, black T-shirt, yellow hair, white face, grey freckles.'

'Can't remember,' Blackman said. 'You wouldn't stoop that low, would you?'

'Research purposes only.'

177

'God help us,' Nayce hissed under his breath and scratched his bald head furiously with both sets of nails. In a movie, he would have stood up and confronted Pongrass, chest-to-chest, and told him to shut up. Here in Jamaica, where it was not a movie, Nayce scratched his scalp almost hard enough to break the skin and said nothing.

'Fuck!' Book exclaimed again. Without a further word, he left the terrace and stalked into the hotel. Nayce got up to follow but Janey placed a restraining hand on his arm. She shook her head urgently. Nayce sat down, wondering what the hell was going on.

Alcohol had entered its contractual partnership with the customer, to stimulate or depress, and the customer was always right. While Nayce sank, Pongrass and Blackman were bouncing for a night on the town. Pongrass was on a roll, freshly effervescent. There was an additional explanation. That day Rip had emerged as a promising conduit in the provenance of It, hinting at a post-race surprise. For tonight, he had given Pongrass 'a coupla names of a coupla places'. Pongrass and Blackman, brimming with all the cocktails they could drink and a happy hour's worth of Red Stripes, were ready to riot.

With a laugh that was not altogether kind, Pongrass looked towards the hotel lobby and exclaimed: 'Dude! The old man of the sea!'

'Hey guys. Dudes,' Hut corrected himself, crossing the terrace. 'What's going on?'

One side of his face pillow-wrinkled, Hut was dressed for an evening out on the North Shore: Oxfords, chinos, blue chambray shirt.

'Um . . .' Pongrass looked at Blackman. Blackman looked at Pongrass. Nayce, raging with impatience, looked at Janey. 'Nothing,' Pongrass said.

'You guys are out of your trees.' Hut twinkled. He had a bleary blinky look, having been profoundly asleep for three of the twenty-four catch-up hours he needed. Both well-rested and dog-tired, he'd evidently decided he was not going to be able to sleep again until he had lived a little. 'We going out? A Slashing night?'

Blackman and Pongrass exchanged a look. Whether too drunk to construct a lie, or seeing the potential entertainment, they came to an unspoken accord. Blackman slung a paw around Hut's shoulder.

'Wouldn't you like to know?'

Hut chuckled, warming up, and looked to Nayce. 'Coming?'

Three cocktails leaden in his soles, Nayce shook his head. He could not abide the sight of Hut until he knew what was going on.

'Me neither,' Janey smiled. 'I need sleep.'

'You guys are such pikers,' Hut whined, clearly happy, nevertheless, to be going off alone with Pongrass and Blackman.

'C'mon,' Pongrass said. 'Sleeping's cheating. Vamoose!'

Alone with Janey, Nayce spoke. 'Bottom line?'

'On?'

'Hut.'

'Search me.'

'Don't tempt me.'

She shot him an arch look. All week he had been trying to ignore the impression of something brewing beneath her silken surface. It worried him in the same foggy way that many events were beginning to worry him—*Is it me or is everything just a little more fucked-up each day?*—but Janey was not made of the same stuff as the boys. Under heat, while the boys cracked and split and flared, Janey just glowed. There was a piece waiting to be spoken, but he'd been waiting for it too long to expect it now. Janey would speak when—if—she was ready. Trouble was, she had the mettle to go right through her natural term without saying it.

'What Book was about to say about Hut,' Nayce said. 'You know what it is, don't you?'

'Hey, I feel like a walk on the beach. It's our third-last night.'

'You're right.' He clapped his thighs, ready to push back his tiredness. 'Let me get my other shoes.'

'Nayce.' She patted his arm indulgently, as if he was an old man. 'I didn't say I wanted company.'

Throat dry—was this some kind of moment?—Nayce stammered about the dangers of going out alone. Janey interrupted him.

'It's a private beach owned by the resort. Now, you go inside and do the right thing, phone your wife or have a toss or something, and I'll see you bright and early.'

'Don't patronise me, Janey.'

Her two rows of teeth glowed in the dark. 'Nobody could patronise you, Dave. Now. It's not for me to spread rumours. If you want to know what's going on, why don't you ask him?'

'He stormed off. I don't know where he's gone.'

'I don't mean Book, silly. Just ask Hut.'

'But—but, he's gone,' Nayce stammered. 'With those guys.'

'Oh yeah, Hut's with the big boys,' Janey said. 'See it as a lesson, Dave. Sometimes you have to take your chances and speak up. It's not so scary. If you've got a question, just ask it.'

She stood on her toes and kissed his reddening cheek. 'Goodnight!' Watching her cross the terrace and punch in the security code to go out the cane gate to the beach, Nayce was revisited by the thought that had come to him in Kingston: *They've got it just right*.

Wallowing under fatigue, paranoia and anxiety, he considered going after Hut. But the truth was, Nayce felt intimidated, out of his depth. The mercantile class were different from Nayce.

There were certain words they could use, certain conversations they could have, as smoothly as spreading honey on their morning toast. No matter how long Nayce worked with money, he could never earn that fluency. He was a minister's son. He disapproved. And what he disapproved of was what scared him.

And yet, in reply to this feeling (this friendship could seem like a lifelong argument between Nayce and himself), he felt a throb of fear. Running through his feelings towards Hut, like a metal thread woven into a fabric, sparse but the strongest, was a fear that what Nayce wished for might actually occur. Last night, when it had seemed that Hut might indeed have met with some kind of injury, Nayce had felt this same pang. It was all very well to wish for some tragedy to harden or inoculate Hut, but what if Hut, lacking an adult immune system, had no defences against adult pain? What if it was too late for a painful lesson?

He went up to the room. Book wasn't there. Rather than go look for him, Nayce lay on his bed and turned to his iPod for a lullaby.

22

Pongrass, Blackman and Hut exited through the hotel forecourt
and strolled across the road to the dirt park where Business and
Respect were toasting corn and smoking cob-sized reefers.

'Bidnid, ma mon!' Pongrass declaimed.

Hut felt queasy in Business's smoke-filled minicab, but his
friends were roaring. As he slowly woke, Hut came to an executive
decision. He had only one life to lead. You can't take it with you.
Keep up appearances. Look to the future.

'Business,' he said. 'Can I have some of that?'

Pongrass raised an eyebrow at Hut with flattering curiosity, as if
there might be more to the redhead than met the eye.

'Got to catch up,' Hut said.

The minivan headed out of Sandals City, in the opposite
direction from Slashing, towards the outskirts of Negociante
around the foot, or the toenails, of Mount John, where the
local populace of service employees retreated to a thriving
dormitory township of timber shanties and half-built cement
brick shells centred on an Anglican church and a sewage
treatment plant. The air smelt rich with pineapple juice and

human turds. Business was driving. Pongrass was talking.

'Yeah, eighteen, going to college, it just got a little wild, didn't it? What's the collective noun for front-bums? A blur of fronties?'

'A daze of fronties,' Blackman offered.

'Up till then I could still list them off by heart. Every frontie I'd done. I'd, like, catalogue them in my head when I was rowing or doing weights training, and it took the mind off the pain. Sometimes I'd want to go out and row or swim or run ten k just to give myself the headspace to go back over my, like, album.'

'You're a nerd, Dunc. Bet you alphabetise your CD collection,' Blackman said with fond gruffness.

'I'm a collector.' Pongrass issued a tight-lipped nod. 'I value them all. This is why I have a bit of regret over those uni years: the fucks at formals, the midnight raids on the women's college, the gribs taken on dares . . .'

'A case of Johnnie Blue or a gram of Lou Reed for schtupping the ugliest frontie in the bar,' Blackman clucked.

'I ticked off the Women's Eight, ditto the Women's Four, ditto the Women's Pairs. Forget the Women's Singles—dyke-sculls,' Pongrass said earnestly. 'Then branching out into other sports. But you know, they tumbled, literally, ha, like, helter-skelter so I barely got a chance to sit back and remember them. I ought to've taken photos. In my head I couldn't link the right body with the right face, the right nips with the right tits, the right taste with the right name. The important things, you know? I have my regrets, just like anyone else.'

Hut looked out the window. The smoke tacked his tongue to the roof of his mouth. They had left the populated area and were driving along an ill-lit one-lane road through what would have been an industrial zone if there had been any factories or warehouses. Instead there were vacant lots, a bus depot and piles of abandoned building materials. He reached forward for another toke on Business's spliff.

183

'I do remember my first hooker. Heike the hooker. That was weird. Remember those guys at college who went in for hookers?'

'Oh yeah,' Blackman said. 'They talked about them like they were the last word. I could never figure it out.'

'I know!' Pongrass said. 'Why would you pay for it if you didn't have to? Didn't only cripples or Kerry Packer pay for it? But I was curious, I guess. This bunch, they were all those brainiac medicine guys, held hooker dinners every Thursday: piss-elegant restaurant, five-hundred-dollars-an-hour dates. If things got out of hand, all the better, they could do swapsies. I couldn't say no. But I didn't know any hookers, so I asked some girl I knew—Leah Wurst, remember her?'

'That the one who works in Canberra now?'

'Right. Advises the PM. I asked her to come along and said, "if anyone asks, you've got to tell them you're a pro". But it backfired: someone else who worked for the Liberal Party recognised her.'

'How embarrassing,' Blackman said. 'You were with a chick you weren't paying.'

'Right,' Pongrass nodded. 'So for the next hooker dinner, which happened to be a special one—it was Christmas week—I trawled the Escorts section until I found one who didn't sound too rough. I told her what I needed. So Heike the hooker came out. She did so well at the after-party, I saw her another six or seven times. Until her number was disconnected. I never found out why.'

'Shit. Maybe she was knocked off.'

'Maybe silicon poisoning. Size of honeydews. Plastic fantastic.'

'Any good?'

Pongrass stroked his jaw, like a wine judge quizzed over a '68 shiraz. 'I wouldn't go silicon valley again by choice. It was kind of weird—I kept thinking, I'm Heike-ing up the Alps. The thing nobody tells you is, they're fucken *hard*: hers felt like a couple of knees pressed up between her arms. I kept getting a bump—oi, is she pushing me off?'

'You ever wonder if she was actually pushing you off?'

'Nah, I wasn't paying her for any rough stuff,' said Pongrass, who couldn't think of any other reason a woman might want to push him off. 'They looked awesome. But felt shit.'

'Opposite of a cunt, really.'

'You speak the truth, Hilton my man. You speak the truth.'

They were pulling up at a low concrete building with a circus-style neon fringe, all bulging pink arcs and flags and big tops. Business wheeled his van to rest by a flying fish stall set up for passing pedestrians, that is, the pedestrians expected to emerge later in the night. For now, the traffic was all inbound.

'Palais Royale,' Hut read.

'Abandon hope all ye who enter here,' Pongrass snickered.

'Eh?' Hut said, feeling the corners of his lips pulled as if by a puppeteer.

'What Rip said about it.'

'This Palais Royale, it a bad bad neck of the woods.' Business reached above the sun visor for his rolling papers. 'I wait here.'

Hut giggled. 'I'd love to stay with you, Biz, but the boys are going in.'

'You be careful,' Business said soberly, and commenced work on a twelve-paper bunger.

A ring of astonishments closed around them.

Hut had been in strip clubs, but back home these places saddened him. He empathised with few people—he was deficient in empathy—but he could empathise with strippers and prostitutes, for some dark unexamined reason. He still let Pongrass drag him along occasionally on Friday nights, but the taste for strippers came and went like Big Macs. Every so often, he'd want nothing but that

185

(a Big Mac, a strip joint). Having consumed it (the hamburger, the spectacle), he would wonder how he could ever have wanted it.

But this place, this Palais Royale, was different. Oh, it was different. At first Hut didn't recognise it as a strip club. Tables and chairs were arranged around a broad central bar under the canopy of stars in an open-air garden. About a hundred men and women were in the club, drinking Red Stripe or rum punch, talking loudly. The music was contemporary American rock. The smell was ganja. Just another Jamaican nightspot. Hut followed Pongrass and Blackman to the counter, where they ordered a jug of rum punch from a big clean-cut man with glisteningly hollow temples.

It wasn't until they sat down at a plastic furniture set that Hut registered the true tone and texture of the Palais. At each end of the courtyard was a stage, backed with mirrors. There were mirrors everywhere, on the walls, flanking the pillars, on the bar itself. On each stage were six or seven topless girls, dancing in an absent-minded way, talking among themselves. There was no gyno row, no press of eager viewers, nobody offering paper money for special pleading. No patrons were paying much attention at all to the dancers, who were mutually indifferent. The dancers were wallpaper, or television, music videos, optional extras to a normal, congenial bar.

No sooner had the three boys taken their seats than a statuesque woman in a startlingly white slip twitched her hips across the floor. She made straight for Pongrass and straddled his lap, bearing her weight on white stilettos, as she laid her hands theatrically upon his shoulders, fingers splayed as if her silver nailpolish was still drying. Her shoulders twinkled galaxies of glitter; the mouldings of her lips and eyes loomed over him in ebony cornices. She bowed to tickle a curtain of hair across his cheek, then tilted his face aside with a platinum-tipped index finger and whispered into his ear. When she pulled away, Pongrass's round face rippled moonbeams. She rose, pirouetting on one long leg and lifting the other with a flourish, and walked towards the flank of the club, which, Hut's adjusting eyes now made out, was scalloped with velveteen semicircular banquettes. Pongrass somnambulated in her slipstream. She chose a banquette with a flick of her neck, and Pongrass sat, wide-legged, hands falling palm-up beside his thighs. She draped her legs over his lap and knit her fingers around his neck. They commenced a deep conversation. But beautiful, in its way. Their immediate ease, Hut thought, came as quickly as if they had a prior understanding: the secret, democratic, culture-crossing language of beings who fuck at will. There was something timeless and sculptural in the way the muscled black woman arranged herself over the receptive white man.

Well-stoned now, Hut tried to engage Blackman in some kind of nod or wink, but the big grazier was smiling to himself.

'Quick mover,' Hut said above the music.

Blackman looked around the club and downed his rum punch. He raised his empty glass to Hut, signalling another round.

Hut made his way to the bar. The mix was about 60:40 men to women, none white. Hut guessed that the women there were working. He swam between bodies and bought another jug of rum punch from the man with the hollow temples. As he reached out for it, he felt more conspicuous for his fluorescent orange Sandals bracelet than for the colour of his skin.

Never much of a rum drinker, Hut was loving this Bajan Mount Gay. He carted the jug and plastic cups back through the crush to the table, where his place had been taken by another Amazon in a dress like a half-sloughed snakeskin. She was enjoying a joke with Blackman. As coolly as he could manage, Hut poured fresh drinks and resumed his seat.

It was a nice place, no doubt. If strip joints were all like this, he might have a problem. If he was running a strip joint, this was what it would be like. More like a club than a show, you didn't feel you had to watch, and nobody made too big a deal of it. Everyone was cool. It would be nicer, true, if the girls had descended on him as rapidly as they had on Pongrass and the big bear Blackman, but (Hut reminded himself) he was a married man and would have to disappoint them. Maybe the girls sensed this: he wore a forcefield of matrimony, they could tell. Then again, Blackman was married too. But differently. Hut loved Pen. He worshipped Pen. He might be about to lose Pen.

Turning away from this sickening spectre, Hut scanned the club. He worked out the purpose of the mirrors. No matter where you were sitting, you could see nipples. Nipples bounced off the walls, nipples bounced off the cladding on the pillars. Nipples bounced from one end of the club to the other, like pinballs, hitting five, six surfaces before alighting upon Hut. That was the beauty of the Palais. You didn't have to watch the stage to see the show.

Blackman and his new friend were strategising the potential outcomes of their cultural exchange. Hut sipped punch and observed the mirrors. The stage girls hardly bothered to dance. They strolled as if waiting on a street corner, sliding past each other, dreamily smiling, parading more than performing. Their skins occupied the full spectrum from milk-coffee to peaty pitch, untraceable Asiatic–Incan blends, hook-nosed ancient Mixtecs, profound Africans. Their heights ranged from four-six to six-four, their hair from electrified frizz through every geometric patterning of cornrow and braid to a kind of frightened, bullied straightness. The only uniformity was in their uniforms: Dayglo cat's cradles of string and triangle. These girls weren't sad, oppressed or junked-out, and the club was firmly their territory. Hut felt incidental; these girls would be hanging about, passing comments with their eyeballs and eyebrows, whether he was here or not. A numb conviviality settled over him. Below the belt, nothing: No news, good news.

This place took him back to the earliest days of adolescent dreaming, to where he could believe that these women offered a choice, a variety of experience; or maybe this had something to do with being white. Hard to forget. He was white all right.

The music humped its bass-load along and the air misted with sweet ganja and the acrylic scent of smoke machine. The denizens of the Palais Royale were ignoring Hut; he was growing used to that. Ignoring the white guy was Jamaican-cool. But he knew they knew he was here. He knew that even the dreamy girls sleepwalking on the stage knew he was here. He was a character, he was a somebody. He didn't kid himself that his skin colour gave him any power or sexual allure. But it gave him, within these mirrored walls, something to which he'd never presume at home: celebrity.

Blackman had his hands all over his girl, who was alternately snubbing him and nibbling his ear like an ex unable to resist one for the road. Hut imagined Blackman and Pongrass must have been here already—such was their instant fame with the girls—but realised how absurd that was. Of course they couldn't have been here. Of course this was what the girls were paid to do. It was the same as Nayce at that brothel all those years ago: some men just had it.

Of course Hut was stoned. Alone with his rum punch, he watched the larger of the two stages. Occupying the central position, solacing a steel pole, was the most beautiful female shape he had ever seen. Hut had heard somewhere that beauty could be quantified by mathematical ratios of hips to waist and waist to ribs and breasts to thighs. He would have liked to wrap her in measuring tape, because she was the benchmark, the Napoleonic metre, the divine proportion of the female form. A short glossy fringe flopped over her forehead. Her skin showed its iridescent facets to the circling spotlights, the depth of cooking chocolate to the shadows. She wore high-hipped sequinned pink bikini pants and pink stilettos. Her breasts defied description. They brought a tear to his eye. Such breasts, he thought, shouldn't be allowed in a place like this. It was an abuse. He began to feel sad again.

She coaxed her way around the pole. There was a fugitive aspect to her, as if she used the lighting and props to obscure her nakedness. The secrets of her body were more elusive than if she had been clothed. Soon Hut was mildly exasperated by her insinuations. The realer part of him, the corporeal part, wanted her standing still with her hands by her sides, defenceless, vulnerable, aching for the comfort of his touch.

'Eh! Wake up!' Blackman was slapping him more painfully than strictly necessary on the side of his neck.

Hut tilted away, almost letting a scowl show before he caught it. 'What happened to your little friend?'

'Ah, places to go, people to see. Where's Nev?'

Hut raked the walls for Pongrass, who had disappeared from his banquette.

'We ought to watch each other's back,' Blackman said.

'What should we do?'

'Ah, he's probably okay. VIP room.'

'Shall we go look?'

Blackman glanced up and said, 'Christ, who let heaven into the room?'

He was looking at the girl at the pole in the pink bikini.

Hut felt unaccountably possessive. 'I'd say she's for lookee, no touchee,' he said, trying to sound worldly.

Blackman was about to respond, but reconsidered, then said, 'Wouldn't you like five minutes with every one of them?'

'Every one in the room? It might take a while,' Hut said.

'Every one on the island,' Blackman said, sniffing lopsidedly. 'I'm getting a drink.'

Hut sat back and counted the mirrors in which he could spy the girl in pink. She had a shyness that made him feel a surge of violence towards Blackman. Don't be ridiculous, he told himself. You are being ridiculous. Think of Pen.

But as the stone from Business's spliff settled in, Hut could not think of Pen. Nor could he think of the boys, nor any of the troubles he had put behind him. They were a construct, a false memory: he was a robot created this minute. Nothing behind him was real. *Now* was real. For a flash the girl in the pink bikini had been looking at him. He watched her closely. Maybe she hadn't. He convinced himself that she was looking everywhere but at him, which meant that she was, in effect, outlining him by evasion; he was the man whose presence she felt. A charge of desperate schoolboy hope pulsed through him. What would he do if she came down? What would he say?

Ridiculous. You cunt. There's only one cunt in the room, and that's you.

Blackman appeared at his shoulder, leading a kind of cavalry charge. 'Buddy, I'd like you to meet, ah, Jewel, Marisa, Zelda, and, sorry darling, you are . . . ?'

A little voice said a big word. Hut instinctively stood up to offer chairs, the perfect host.

'Ah, ladies, ladies. Can I get you drinks?'

They spilt giggles into their hands. Heartbreak again—they were children, possibly eighteen, more likely fifteen. The older Hut got the younger eighteen-year-olds seemed—but that was optimism's diabolic whisper. They were thirteen, twelve: tiny girlie voices and miniature girlie hands. This might have been what Blackman wanted, instead of the onyx giantess he had been cradling; but it was definitely, certifiably not what Hut wanted. What Hut wanted was on the stage and wore a pink bikini. What Hut wanted was, right now . . .

Cunt. Cunt.

'Rum punches all round?'

'Go for it, buddy,' said Blackman.

As Hut oozed towards the bar, his mind was on an exit strategy. He could see how events might corner him again. One thing, as they say, leads to another, and he was a married man. A married man. He pictured himself ordering the drinks for the table, then, pretending to slip off to the bathroom, dashing outside and crying: 'Business! Sandals, and on the double!'

But as he contemplated his escape, a hoarse laugh peaked above the low plateau of bar talk. Hut thought he was hallucinating. He blinked, shook his head and refixed a keen squint along the brushed-tin surface. Wearing a black off-the-shoulder jersey and silver hoop earrings, Janey, Janey Quested, was amusing two Jamaicans. Hut worked his way along and grasped her elbow.

'The fuck are you doing here?'

'Hey, Hutski! I've never known what Single White Female really meant until now!'

Hut grabbed the drink out of her hand. Janey snatched it back. The two Jamaicans inflected their faces away.

'Respect?' Hut said. 'Business?'

'*You're* having a go at the company *I* keep?' Janey grimaced towards Blackman. 'I came with Respect, and we bumped into Business eating a flying fish burger outside. They get in free if they bring a white girl. And,' she made a joint-smoking gesture, her thumb and forefinger pinched on the invisible roach, 'they figured it was a good idea to come in and keep an eye on you, Hut. They were worried about you.'

'Me? What about you? What do you think you're doing?' Hut heard himself sounding like a father, but couldn't help it. The part of him that was not protective of Janey's safety was terrified of being caught out, dobbed in. Janey wouldn't tell Pen she'd found him here, would she?

'Oh, come on.' Smiling parentheses framed Janey's mouth, but her eyes skidded. She was more drunk, or stoned, than he'd noticed at first. 'You don't think I'm going to sit on the sidelines all week and let you boys get all the action?'

'You're . . . you're—what about the race?' Hut spluttered.

'Even you know how weak that sounds. Anyway,' Janey's eyes skirted around the Palais. 'This place is cool. Where's Pongo-bongo?'

'I don't—come on, let's just go.'

'Fuck off, Hut!'

This time a streak of distaste crossed her face. She pushed his chest. 'Just because I'm a girl, I can't enjoy myself? You're always trying to stop me having fun in *gentlemen's establishments*.'

'That?' Hut knew what she was talking about. 'That wasn't a strip club. Anyway, you didn't really want to go.'

'All the more reason for me to be here now. This is just harmless fun, right? Come on, come and have a rum punch with me and our fleetboys. They'll take care of us, don't worry.'

Hut paused over the bar stool behind Respect. The drivers ignored him and chatted with Janey. He'd never seen the two men so animated; their mouths even moved. Hut tried to spot Pongrass in the banquettes but failed. Blackman was entertaining his little troupe in the courtyard.

Janey, whose memory was fitted out with a barbed tip, had been referring to an incident years earlier, in a country town when she, Hut and Nayce were on a road trip during the last year of uni. Having checked into their motel, lacking the imaginative powers to while away an evening in the country, Nayce had dug out a Yellow Pages and found the town knockshop. He and Hut waited until Janey was asleep and sneaked out, walking the three miles to a wide-porched wooden house with an untended yard at the edge of town. Nayce tapped at the door, and a middle-aged woman with her hair pulled back in a bun let them in. As Hut's latest celibate run had extended to twenty-four months compared with Nayce's twenty-four days, they agreed that Hut got first choice.

There were no girls available on arrival, so the bun-haired woman led Nayce and Hut to a couch in an overheated flock-wallpapered sitting room where cricket murmured from a portable television. She offered cups of tea in such a way as to indicate that it was not part of the service and acceptance would not be welcomed and might even jeopardise other privileges. Little was said other than mild passing remarks about the game. Hut's eyes darted when the door grunted in its frame and came open with a twang. A girl entered, and Hut hungrily eyed her, his mind short-circuiting with snap calculations while he affected absorption in the cricket. His torment ended when she revealed herself to be part of middle-management rather than the frontline staff, as it were; she left after a word with the older woman about keys and book-keeping.

A half-hour passed, two wickets fell, the door coughed and a fake-tanned woman in her late thirties came in and perched on the arm of Nayce's couch.

'What's the score?' she said, reaching across Nayce, steadying herself with a hand on his knee, to light a cigarette from a box of matches on the coffee table. A red strapless gown trussed the slim, tired figure of what Hut imagined was a mother making ends meet. Her voice rasped like a junky's. Her breasts, Hut speculated, were either silicon-filled or naturally standoffish, separated like a cow-girl's saddle-sore thighs. Normally the fake ones tried to look real. These could be real ones trying to look fake. Matching the ribbed hollow of her chest was a big tooth-sized gap between her front teeth. She blew

194

smoke up into the ceiling light, an overbright perspex gravepit of moths and gnats, and exchanged terse commentary with the older woman, whose knitting needles were conjuring a pastel baby's jacket.

'Three for two hundred-odd,' Hut said.

The woman in the red dress appraised Nayce, then, briefly, Hut, and paid Nayce a return visit. Nayce nodded her towards Hut.

'What's it to be then, bubs?' she said, intent on Nayce. *It's you or nothing, bubs.*

Hut, dry-throated, felt not a drip of desire. He felt sorry for her, and pity was a hard-on's antidote. But there was also the obvious charge passing between her and Nayce. It was as if they, or their bodies, recognised each other. Astoundingly, they seemed to want each other.

'I'm all right.' Hut aimed a magnanimous smile at Nayce, who did not need a second invitation.

Hut stayed in the sitting room watching the cricket. He didn't much like cricket, but he liked it more than he liked the woman in the red dress, and more than any of the other girls who dribbed and drabbed through the place. If Nayce had been with him, Hut would have felt pressured. But alone, he glanced up benignly at each girl, then returned his attention to the television. He felt quite comfortable opting out. The middle-aged woman made him tea. The cricket droned. After two hours, Nayce emerged, unaltered apart from a slow-fading red wrinkle like a scar alongside his right eye, and the odd impression that his chin-stubble had grown.

As they walked back to town, Nayce said: 'Mate, that was fucking outstanding. Outstanding fucking. How did you go?'

'Yeah-no,' Hut said. 'Outstanding. Same.'

Nayce, reverberant inside his own pleasure, did not ask Hut another question, and Hut never told him what he'd done. What he hadn't done.

At the motel, Janey was awake and indignant. Nayce told her everything. He even said, ignoring Hut's hapless silencing gestures, that Hut had 'bitten from the fruit' as well. Duncelike in a corner, Hut shoved his hands in his pockets, unable to work out whether he would be more shamed by the truth or the lie. Rather than disapproving, Janey made some sarcastic remarks about why they hadn't invited her along. For the rest of the trip, she and Nayce only communicated via ironic one-lines diverted through Hut. It was the nearest he'd ever seen to Janey and Nayce fighting. But they couldn't quite come out with it; their emotions were constipated. In the end, feeling dreadful about the whole incident, Hut apologised to Janey. She winked: 'I'm only kidding. Don't you ever get it?'

No, he thought. He didn't.

Janey, Business and Respect were enjoying the show, Business pointing out sights, Respect's face split into a disconcertingly horse-toothed grin. Other Jamaicans around the Palais Royale, and the girls on the stage, were pretending to be incurious about the white woman. Hut wanted to run Janey outside and take her back to the hotel, but couldn't work out how to ask Business or Respect for help.

Then he saw, with unexpected relief, the shape of Pongrass in his banquette. The woman in the white slip was back astride his thighs. Hut had a jug of rum punches sent to Blackman's table and, taking a Red Stripe for himself, went to the banquette.

'Where'd you get to?' he sat next to Pongrass.

'Just washing my hands,' Pongrass winked, as if making a double entendre. Or maybe, Hut thought, he was.

'You see who's here?' Hut nodded towards Janey.

Pongrass cast an indifferent look. 'What's the world coming to,' he said.

'So what's happening?' Hut said brightly, trying to be as casual as Pongrass, pretending the woman wasn't there.

'This and that,' Pongrass said.

Hut remembered how Pongrass liked jokes. 'Hey, Pong. What's got sixty-four teeth and holds back a monster?'

Pongrass shrugged as if to get it over with quickly.

'Your fly!' Hut laughed, then, when Pongrass failed to react, thought: That sounded like I was talking about his dick. 'I meant . . . I mean, *my* fly!'

Now Pongrass was looking over his shoulder.

Hut thought: God, that's worse. I meant . . . 'Eh.' Desperately, Hut winked, leaning close and flicking his eyes towards Pongrass's companion. 'You like a bit of the old shoe polish?'

Even as he said it, Hut shuddered at his misjudgement. Pongrass shot him a sneer of disdain and disgust. These guys—they didn't go in for racism. Racism was a lower-middle-class kind of thing, like state politics and pop culture. Racism was not their bag; nor was any other form of intolerance. Indifference, on the other hand . . . Indifference was their thing. You had to cultivate it to keep up.

'Listen,' Hut said, anxious to move the conversation along. Now seemed as good a time as any. 'I was wondering if I could put something to you.'

'Oh fuck.'

Pongrass wasn't speaking in reply to Hut. His eyes rolled back in his head as the meat-grinder of the woman's hips went to work.

Pressing on, feeling the need to be casual, Hut said: 'See, I think I need a favour.'

'Oh, Jesus.'

'Hush you mouth,' the woman said to Pongrass. 'You no blaspheme in my house.' Gravely, she began mauling his neck.

'I'm, ah, I don't know how to put this,' Hut persisted. 'I need some legal representation, but don't want to go through the normal channels.'

'Aieee!' Pongrass leapt as if electrocuted. The woman bounced, then landed, and let out a low, generous laugh.

'See,' Hut said, 'there are these—I can't believe it, it's nothing, but the charges are criminal, not civil, and it could go on for a while . . .'

'Ar fuck,' Pongrass said, in a weary tone, as if he'd left something important back at the hotel. The woman was riding his waist, her hands pressed down as if onto a pommel. The hem of her white slip fluttered around his chest. Her thighs shimmered and his bare belly caught a flash of lights from the stage.

'I'll be able to pay you back.' Hut was streaming sweat. 'No worries. But in the short term it's a good criminal legal team I need and the backing, you know, it can drag on, you know, and I can't afford to let my old man get caught up in it, or the wife . . .'

Here was Hut's moment, the pointy end of the trip. He rolled into his pitch. 'I know you're wondering why I'm asking you, but the most important thing right now is discretion, and I know I can trust you . . .'

'Ar fuck, will you shut the fuck up?' Pongrass's teeth were bared: animal, not human.

Hut dropped his eyes. 'Sorry, mate, I just . . .' Hut glimpsed Pongrass's bare belly as it caught the light. 'Oh. Oh.'

Pong's shirt was raised to his diaphragm and his trousers were, Hut now registered, stretched to splitting point across his knees. The woman's buttocks: a pair of medicine balls.

'Oh sorry,' Hut said. His throat crackled, paper-dry. 'I didn't know.' He laughed weakly. 'Maybe we'll chat later?'

Pongrass was fucking her. Right here. Sitting in the banquette. It wasn't a lap dance. He was fucking her. He was fucking her. The guy was. It wasn't R-rated. It was X.

'Just piss off for once in your life, will you?' Pongrass snarled, but gently, as if to a child he wanted to get rid of but not upset.

'Sure, Justin, no worries.' Hut backed away, as if walking backwards might rewind the past few minutes.

'Hush you mouth,' he heard the woman say to Pongrass. 'You no blaspheme.' She gave Hut a look over her sheeny shoulder. 'And if you need a lawyer, you got no business here, boy.'

Hut bumbled against chairs, dizzy. Janey was clapping and cheering in front of the stage, whistling with two fingers in her mouth. Flanking her, Respect and Business were shaking their heads mellowly. He'd have sought the exit but could hardly keep his balance. He knocked a couple of shoulders, hips. A man gave him a shove. He felt the thinness of the ice beneath his feet.

'Oi, steady on, bud.' Blackman was guiding him by the elbow. He sat Hut down at the plastic table setting with the four young girls.

'You all right?' Blackman said. 'Hey, did I introduce you to, um, here's Zegna, this one's Ammonia, and, um, Jewellery I think, and . . .'

'It's okay,' Hut waved an unsteady hand. His strategy had been to ask both Blackman and Pongrass if they could help him. Now he just wanted to run off and bury himself. 'It's okay. I need to go to the loo.'

'Cool bananas,' Blackman said. 'But be careful. I've got your back. We're all waiting for you out here. Open arms, eh girls?'

Hut got up and staggered towards the large stage. He passed by Janey, ignoring her. He'd been wanting to protect her, but the futility of that was now lost in his hall of mirrors. He was the one needing protection.

A neon-lit corridor fed the bathrooms. Heavy men crusted the walls, looked at him with the neutrality of overwhelming but unusable force. Hut barely noticed them. He pushed the door and went to the urinal. He tried to piss but could not: could not bring himself to piss in another man's piss. He found a cubicle, pulled the door, lowered the seat, sat and let his face fall into the soft cradle of his hands.

Because it was too unbearable to contemplate the other thing, the worse thing—the worst thing—Hut fixed upon the lesser shock.

He'd led a sheltered life. He'd have liked to be as bad as those guys, but maybe he was more prudish than he wanted to admit. Wasn't it all meant to be simulated? By going beyond, from R into X, Pongrass had severed a tie: he was not fully human in the way Hut understood it—or maybe Pongrass was *too* human, his human-ness overflowed. He was naive, he knew, in the ways of men like Pongrass. Do they fuck everything? *Do they simply fuck everything?* Either way, Hut's unqualified admiration could only stretch so far. No matter how hard he tried, he'd never be one of them. He lacked the brass. He shouldn't have come. He just shouldn't have come.

He pushed himself to his feet, flushed the toilet for appearances' sake, and re-entered the Palais. The types along the walls would not meet his eye. Hut was getting used to this inversion. To make eye contact and nod or smile was an insult. To ignore was a compliment. Respect, as Respect would say.

Hut brought a new jug of rum punch to the table, where Blackman was capering with his four friends. Stingingly aware of Pongrass still humping unabashedly in the banquette, Hut shunned that side of the bar.

'Hey dude, come join the fun,' Blackman said.

Crisply, bitterly sober, Hut took his seat. One of the little girls pounced onto his knee. Hut nodded to her burbling and made hollow remarks: 'Is that so?' 'How about that?' He felt seventy years old, a dirty uncle, but that was all right. That was better.

He could feel himself beginning to relax, after a fashion, but the girl on his lap began plucking at his crotch like a child taunting a hamster.

'Steady on,' he said, edging her onto his knee.

She persisted, chattering in her girlish singsong.

'No, I don't want that,' he said.

She slipped in a quiet and forbiddingly adult whisper: 'But you do want that, see?'

And Hut could see too, or feel. 'I'm married,' he said as sternly as the circumstances allowed. 'Wife.' He held up his wedding ring. Guiltily he shot a look towards Janey. She was on her feet now, on the dance floor between the stages, bump-grinding in a sandwich of Business and Respect.

The girl gave Hut a mock-hurt frown, as if he was trifling with her emotions. 'But look,' she said.

Hut didn't need to look. He didn't want to look. Looking might only encourage it.

'Mixed messages, ignore it,' he said. 'I am married.'.

'Me married too!' she said.

'No, this is different. I love my wife.'

'Yah,' she nodded with a kind of earnest happiness, as if sharing with him a joyous view of the world, 'and you love me too!'

'I'm going to go now,' he said. 'Bye-bye.'

With the heavy regretful roughness of a firing squad shooter called to duty, Hut climbed to his feet. The girl, challenging him to hold her, refused to move off him; she broke her fall against a plastic chair and muttered viciously. Hut felt disgusted looks dumped on him like an upended garbage bin.

'Hey, where you going?' Blackman called from beneath a scrummage of ruined adolescence.

'Back to the hotel. Have a good time.'

Blackman's girl pinched his chin and rotated it away from Hut, who had become a kind of hex, an evil ghost.

Hut made his way through the bar towards Janey and the drivers. New girls seemed to condense out of the humid air, grabbing at his crotch, pulling and squeezing, a stage crew with only a few seconds to change the scenery. He wanted to say, 'It's a fake, it's like you all, it's just a fake.'

But, when he was almost at the dance floor, he came up against a contradiction of his good intentions.

'Hello,' she said.

'Oh no.'

'What is your name?'

Hut choked on a word.

'My name is Iliana. What is your name?'

She had put on her bikini top, luckily. She blew her fringe out of her eyes. Below, Hut noted an orchestra of hydraulics and pulleys and winches and inflationary forces conspiring to undo him.

'Ah. Hut,' he said. He closed his eyes to stop the tears.

'You having a nice night, Hut?'

Seldom accused of being a great judge of character, Hut tended to play to his strengths: hearty good cheer, humour, ebullience, skating the surfaces, winning over rather than seeing into. But with this girl, he saw something, as if his receptors were open for the first time. And what he saw, from her accent and her eyes and the recitation of her speech, was that she was thunderously, record-breakingly, achingly, tragically simple. Her body, her breasts, her skin, her proportion and perfection, were a travesty: she was a simpleton, she was the Mentally Handicapped, and the very fact of her in this place was an abuse.

'You want to come to the VIP room?' she said.

Hut remembered another reason why, when he was in that brothel with Nayce, he hadn't been able to go with any of the women. His maths—all that was left of him, it seemed right now—came to his rescue. Nayce had slept with so many girls, women, that two hours with a prostitute were only going to account for a fraction of his lifetime's sexual experience. Guys like Pongrass and

Blackman—likewise. For twenty-five years they'd been fucking anything with a pulse. What dilution would some playtime with these locals work on them? Nothing. By morning, they'd have forgotten. Pong would have forgotten those hurtful things he'd said. *Neville, don't leave me like this!* If caught, these guys could say, 'It meant nothing.' And they'd be telling the truth. Nothing.

But for Hut, the maths were different. He had only slept with two women. The first, at uni, no more than four times. The second was the mother of his children. If he did anything with this girl, with the hookers in that country town, they would account for one-third of his lifetime sexual partners. They would tower in his memory. They would haunt those hours of the morning when he woke with a galloping heart. What this simple, sad Iliana was offering him was not a moment's forgettable fun; she didn't know it, but she was offering to tilt his world on its axis. She was offering to become thirty-three-and-a-third per cent; to water down Pen from a controlling fifty per cent to a minority shareholding. He couldn't do that to Pen. He couldn't do it to himself. And that was without thinking of what he couldn't do to this poor girl.

'No,' he said.

She slithered up and pressed her naked belly against his contradiction.

'You want me?' she said, as a question, but rhetorical, meant as an assertion.

'You may think I do,' he said, 'but I don't.'

'You want me,' she repeated, getting her intonation right.

'See you.' He bent and aimed a kiss at the pale line where her fringe parted from the crown of her head.

'Fuck you.' She twisted away. He watched her enter the crowd like a monarch, afloat on her dignity.

Janey intercepted him before the door.

'I saw that,' she winked. 'Smooth.'

Hut couldn't care, now, what she'd seen or not seen. He would give away everything he owned for eight hours' sleep.

'I'll come with you,' Janey said, huddling into his side. He stiffened away from her.

Respect drove them back to the hotel, saying how wise they were to have an early night. 'It is only two in the morning. You get you beauty sleep.' Respect's voice was almost sub-sonar, the frequency of his laryngeal waves so low that Hut could hear each individual vibration. It was a voice that vindicated smoking, vindicated cancer.

They passed through a thumping street party, smaller than the one Hut had got caught up in in Kingston. This island of nocturnal beings was taking on the quality of a dream. The dancing crowd flashed gemstones, sequins, teeth, glossy limbs. Would Hut wake up in his bed at home, beside Pen, safe and warm?

In the fuggy Escort, Respect offered a toke on his travelling reefer. Janey shook her head. So vivacious inside the bar, as if proving a point, she was now gazing inscrutably and, Hut thought, morosely, out the car window. She had made her point; but what now? What did she want next?

'No thanks,' Hut said to Respect. 'We've got a race to swim in.'

'Hut,' Janey said. Across the vinyl seat she clasped his hand. He didn't like the feel of this. 'Book told me this afternoon.'

Hut's instinct was denial, bright innocence: *Told you what? What do you mean?* But his weariness—a sense that he had reached the end of the night, of his adventure—overcame him. Janey wouldn't look at him, her face coated in the dark mustard of the passing streetlights, sightseeing in the void.

'Who else knows?' was all he could say. If Jamaica wasn't real, maybe this conversation wasn't either.

Janey shook her head. 'Book's dad told him. Back home, it's getting around.' She paused and stroked Respect on the shoulder.

He passed her the joint. She took a pull, rolled down her window, and hung her face outside like a dog. Her eyes closed against the night wind. She wound her window back up and, still without looking at Hut, said: 'Is it as bad as it seems?'

'Depends,' Hut said.

'I heard jail.'

'Worst-case scenario. But possible.'

She squeezed his hand with a lover's strength. It was a long time before she spoke; they were entering the Sandals carpark, the electric light whiter.

'Why are we here?' she said. 'Why the fuck are we here?'

Hut shrugged. 'I had a plan. Sort of.'

'Jesus, Hut.' She laid her head on his shoulder and kneaded his arm. Respect wheeled the Escort into the porte-cochere. Janey said: 'Is there anything I can do?'

Hut answered with a question. 'Does Nayce know?'

'No. I don't think so.'

'Then that's what you can do for me.'

'You want me to tell him?'

'I want you to *not* tell him. You and Book. Make sure Nayce doesn't know.'

'Can I ask how come?'

'I don't know.' Hut unclipped his seatbelt and eased Janey away. 'It just seems important to me right now.'

Hut pulled his cot bed out onto the balcony of room 1212 and slid shut the glass door. He curled inside a blanket and imagined it to be his wife's arms. He tried to cry himself to sleep but was too empty for tears, too sad for words, too tired for sleep.

A few hours later, a crash and a domino effect of brightly coloured oaths signalled the return of Pongrass and Blackman. They switched the television on, and before long its black-and-white old-movie theatrics were being sound-mixed with heavy-hitter snoring. Hut tried to listen to the waves lapping in the bay but could not find their rhythm. They seemed perversely jagged, unwilling to lull. Rigging clinked in the marina and, more distantly, the beach bar, Slashing, spooled out another long night of regrettable acts. The sky was growing pale before Hut's strength failed him, and the worst, the whole unspeakable business he'd been trying to keep out, poured through.

23

THE AQUASMITH BUSTLED through taffeta waters towards the strait. Behind them, the cone of Mount John was ruptured by clouds that oozed steamily down the volcano's slopes. The white gables of Sandals, and the broader flat roofs of the town behind the resort, receded behind the trees until the entire settlement contracted into a thin band between mountains and sea. Ahead, the wilderness island of Negociante slept on the horizon like a blue dog, haunchy with folds and jointed bones. Overhead some ornamental clouds broke up the baby-blue sky. You could be forgiven for thinking you were in paradise. Jason took the wheel. Rip chaired a team meeting around the cabin table to explain what he called 'the context of the race' before they took their 'orientation swim'.

Rip, 'California-born, Florida-raised, still heading towards the sunrise', told them how he had 'found peace' in Jamaica. To Nayce, most of what came out of Rip's chap-lipped mouth sounded stale, with the counterfeit flavour of the too-often-told.

Moving from memoir to travelogue, Rip went on: 'Negociante used to be called St George, who you all might associate with England and dragons, but he's also the patron saint of syphilitics.

Which proves that five hundred years ago they had a sense of humour.'

St George, he explained, was 'a pimple on the haemorrhoid of the prolapsed asshole of the earth. Think of the Bronx when everyone was killing everyone for a pipe, and then think of the worst part of the Bronx. Then think of the worst crack house in the worst block, and you're nowhere near how bad it was here.'

To the blank looks, Rip shook his head and said: 'Okay, think of downtown Baghdad.'

Renamed Negociante after its third and most homicidal lieutenant-governor, the island off Jamaica's north coast had been the 'refuge for the refuse' of Caribbean slavery, Rip said, a prison within a prison where the 'paedophiles and monkey-fuckers' were dumped and left to rot. 'Even the monkeys were scared to live on this island,' said Rip, warming to his task. 'They knew the rough stuff that was waiting for them.'

And rot the prisoners did. The bay oozed cholera, the streams were suspensions of diarrhoea. There was no law, no family, no humanity—Negociante was, Rip said grandly, a 'laboratory for what happens when evolution is allowed to travel backwards'.

The bay over which they were travelling became 'one of the world's richest shark-breeding grounds'. As ritual punishment on the island, miscreants were nicked with blades and, with their blood as seasoning, thrown into the water. Spectators gathered on the headlands. The resultant shark frenzy was 'these people's version of the Super Bowl'.

Nayce thought most of this lay between wild exaggeration and pure fantasy. Some Americans couldn't get through the day without fancying themselves the hero of a Hollywood three-act adventure, striding boldly within a 16:9 frame. Rip was the type of character over whom Nayce and Hut would, in happier times, enjoy a good laugh. But Hut wasn't with them.

Nayce cast his eye around the table. Book was frowning at Rip's story, typically literal-minded. Book was Rip's ideal listener, gullible, ready to repeat back home this history and its modern-day redeemed wanderer/hero. Beside him, Janey was also listening, though with more politeness and effort. Janey knew all about big-noting men. Rip belonged, like her, below stairs, to the proletariat who moulded adventure from the rough clay of working lives as janitor and grease monkey. The difference between Janey and Rip was that she was not condemned for life. Unlike a ship's pilot, a nanny could still (just, at thirty-eight) harbour Cinderella hopes of life above deck. Or she could come home and re-boot with someone who'd never stopped loving her.

Across the table, Pongrass and Blackman rode on Queasy Street. Both boys had left their marriages. It had often struck Nayce as something worth studying in their faces: the effects of divorce. Excruciatingly married, Nayce had been thinking a lot about divorce, of which Pongrass had been a pioneer: the first of Nayce's contemporaries to burn that bridge. A landmark event, it was, to be able to say that a guy your age was divorced. Blackman was divorcing too. It was in the air. Nayce had noticed it at his son's pre-school: couples became alternating-weekend singles. Forty, emerging from the early-childhood woods. You reached a stage of life. The divorced man had a *usedness* about him. Or maybe the strain around the eyes and the intimation of old age came from sticking with a bad marriage too long, and the divorce was a reprieve.

Pongrass and Blackman had to remain outwardly attentive to Rip, partly because he was their pilot but mainly because he'd promised to secure three grams of It for Thursday night. They had to stay on Rip's good side. But they were struggling. His stories could not divert them from the Aquasmith's pitch and roll. The previous night's activities had watered down their already limited powers of concentration. They looked as if they regretted getting out of bed. If Rip had an ounce of empathy, he would have interrupted himself and said, 'You guys don't give a shit about any of this, do you?' And he'd have been right. They didn't. But they were making a show of it. For It.

Which was more than could be said of Hut, who had remained cot-bound when the group left the marina at nine that morning. As Rip had brought the Aquasmith to the jetty, Pongrass and Blackman, hardened to working through hangovers that would cripple an elephant, had emerged from the hotel with pouchy eyes and mouths greasy from fried eggs. Nayce, who'd had a full night's sleep, was doing some stretches on the decking. When Nayce asked where Hut was, Blackman shook his head ponderously. Pongrass said: 'We shouted in his ear, we tried to tip him out of his cot, we punched him in the guts. Abo dribbled his toothpaste all over the guy's face. But our motivational tactics were to no avail. Lazy cunt.'

'So where is he?' Nayce asked.

'Still in his cot, still on the balcony, where he'll be when we get back later.'

'Morning, Neville!' Janey and Book came down to the jetty together. Nayce had looked for them around the hotel, but they'd gone for a walk on the beach. Now, arriving on the marina to hear Pongrass's last words, Janey laughed and tweaked his bicep. Disconcerted, Nayce studied her. Something had shifted overnight, a cold change. Her smile was dazzlingly opaque as she snuggled—*snuggled*—up beside Pongrass.

'We had to lock him on the balcony,' Pongrass said regretfully, as if having visited a harsh but routine punishment on a child.

Nayce had followed Janey onto the boat. 'What do you know?' he said. Why wasn't she more concerned about Hut? Normally she'd be the first to go up to his room to check he was all right.

With a broad but nasty grin, Janey told him about going to the Palais Royale: how 'Neville' had fucked a dancer and Hut, who'd been trying to shield her from 'seeing bad things happen to bad people', had 'proved what we've always known about him: he can't get a root in a brothel. You've got to love him.'

Nayce had looked at her uncertainly. Though she maintained her smile, there was something sour and merciless in her tone that he struggled to attach to her. For an instant he could almost imagine something going on—something having already gone on—between Janey and Pongrass, as shocking as that was. Nayce had no idea when she'd come back last night. She had lied to him when she'd said she wasn't going out. Could anything have happened between her and that ape? When you boiled them down, even the finest women had a weakness for charisma and good looks. The old story: love and hate. Irresistible bad boys. Nayce tried to shake off this thought, but when he looked at her again she was smiling at him with pointed cruelty. He was here, in this, on his own.

'Just making light of it,' she said, shrugging. 'Gotta laugh, Nayce. Come on! Chill, mate.'

She went to smack him on the shoulder. He caught her arm and queried her with his eyes.

'C'mon, Naycey, you know how it is.' Her eyes crinkled, locking him out. 'Just being one of the boys.'

There—she'd put his finger on it—she was acting *manly*.

The Aquasmith's engines died mid-leap, throwing everyone forward: Jason's equivalent of a handbrake stop.

'Arright,' announced Rip, who had kept his balance with fingertips splayed on the cabin ceiling, like a waiter holding up a tray. 'Sounds like we're ready for a dip. Hope you guys aren't too seasick—though that's the least of your problems.'

They stripped to their swimmers and climbed unsteadily to the deck. They had reached the straits. Patches of spume and surface

211

litter—weed, leaves, a palm branch—floated towards the southern funnel formed by Negociante Island and the Jamaican mainland. It was easy to sense the straits as a narrow drain, sucking water from the Caribbean into the South Atlantic. The open sea's deeper green gave Nayce a shiver; he had to force blinkers over his imagination, to stop his eyes wandering into the infinity. He'd often suffered uncontrollable visions of sharks, whales, eels, sea snakes lunging out of that depthless green.

They jumped in, bobbing to fix goggles and shake water out of their ears. Blackman backstroked a tight curve and shepherded the others into a water-treading cell beside the boat.

'We're only going half a mile,' Rip shouted from the deck. A whistling wind had sprung up. 'I'm gonna stay beside you, just like in the race. But you guys gotta stay together, arright? I can't go off fetching every one of you. Keep someone's feet ahead of you and don't drift off. Okay? You lose contact with the group, the current is gonna be the least of your problems. You're gonna have old Rip to deal with. Arright?' He nodded to Blackman. 'You're the leader, big guy.'

Nayce, bald head stinging in the salt water, fell in behind Janey, who was second in line behind Blackman. Book followed. Pongrass, as the second-strongest swimmer, held the tail. The curled lips of the waves sneered against the current. Given the pulsing swell and the wind chop, Nayce was surprised at the pace Blackman was setting.

Salt water filled his ears and nose, but as a swimmer he preferred salt's buoyancy, organic water, alive with creatures, to the Olympic pool's chlorinated synthesis. He kept an eye on the froth trailed by Janey's feet (and off the great green to his flanks, below), he kept his shoulders rotating, and he felt the familiar flood of feeling towards his oldest friend. His shoulders afire, Nayce knuckled down to concentrate on his swimming; or rather, since the only real painkiller was oblivion, he knuckled down to forget he was swimming.

He was increasingly preoccupied with Hut, a parental frustration: *I can't leave him alone for a minute*. It seemed he had been worried about Hut for thirty-three years, and now, after what Book had let slip last night and Hut's absence today, Nayce's worry spread like ink into a blotter.

He was uneasy about the attachment Hut had formed to Pongrass and Blackman. If Hut wasn't already out of his depth, he was making a grave mistake cosying up to those guys. They boxed in a higher division—they ought only to play among their own kind. By tagging along with them, Hut was inviting derision, if not disaster. These were men who wore a black tie like a second skin. These were men who bet on their own horses at Randwick, then shouted the bar at the Woollahra Hotel. These guys couldn't be bought. Nayce didn't mean this in the moral sense (far from it). But what Hut had—money, only money—they didn't need. What they needed was precisely what Hut didn't have to offer.

Nayce had picked up that morning's sly traded looks, the dry coughs, the spent headshakes, the groans. They'd been to a fuck club. That was what guys like them did. Nayce had done enough of it himself. Janey was in on it with them. But Hut, Hut wouldn't even look at a stripper's tits—he was one of life's innocents; those guys would not be satisfied until they had fucked him up.

Nayce remembered the months after leaving school, sleeping in Hut's car while they did the country B & S circuit. That was where Nayce had first come across Pongrass and Blackman. The B & S circuit was where city kids like Nayce and Hut familiarised themselves with the landed money. In a drunken spree, they'd covered thousands of miles, going to ten balls in five weeks. Nayce developed a taste for kegged beer and rosy-cheeked boarding-school girls. But on their way home Hut had shocked him. He said he'd hated every ball.

'But rooting's the best painkiller,' Nayce had said, 'and at least there was plenty of that.'

'For you,' Hut corrected, clearly remorseful at what he was about to say yet unable to stop himself.

'Come on, everyone was getting some,' said Nayce, who did not yet know that only fear, good form and the protection of establishment stood between animals like Pongrass and rape convictions.

'This is what I'm saying,' Hut went on. 'Sometimes for a guy who's so smart, you're a complete bimbo, Nayce.'

Hut told his story. It was rare for him to show his wounds. That was why Nayce still remembered it; he'd listened with the silent respect that the charmed owe the unlucky.

'By ten o'clock all the good-looking girls get snapped up, okay? Then by midnight all the good-looking guys who're left get their pick of the, you know, the Second XI. So let's say, by this point, about half the guys and three-quarters of the girls are off in their cars playing the two-backed beast. Which leaves the dregs. You know, the guys who are too pissed or too shy or too ugly to get a girl, and the girls who're in the Third and Fourth XI.'

'So there you go,' Nayce said. 'A lid for every saucepan.'

'But the rules change when you get into the wee hours,' Hut said. 'This is what you don't understand. Not everyone ends up getting a root, even a bad root with ugly people. It doesn't just work its way down the line, like a, I don't know, a perfect market, until everyone gets something. When you hit the bottom of the barrel with the girls at those things, what you come up against is *pride*. Ugly girls, plain girls, have *pride*. They're like the rest of us—they start out the night with this hope against hope that they'll get picked early and then gradually it'll dawn on them, like

214

it dawns on them every other party—it's not going to happen. Again. But you see, by the time this becomes clear, they aren't desperate, they're angry. Angry and abusive. Girls are different from us. The plainest girls, you see, are the smartest girls. So you have a bunch of fat, ugly, pissed bovine blokes like me, hoping for anything, and a bunch of smart girls in high fucking dudgeon. And by three o'clock in the morning, it's a *war*. People like you have no idea of this other world. I'm suddenly paying the price for every guy who's got lucky. For every good-looking guy who's overlooked these smart girls, they have payback ready for chumps like me. And these girls are clever—they know how to hurt you. 'Germy Hutchison? Would I pash that?' And stick their fingers in their throats. One chick actually projectile vomited when one of her friends asked her if she'd pash me. That was top-quality insult. That was private-school, dux of the year insult. You've got no fucking idea.'

When Hut had found Pen, everyone celebrated, not least Nayce. A marriage money couldn't buy (and, miraculously, hadn't). That was where you hoped Hut would end up, a rare best-case scenario. All Nayce wanted right now, as he swam, was somehow to stop Hut pissing it all away.

24

ALL MORNING HUT twisted on the balcony. The sun climbed from the bottom of the sea, tinting the bay with colours from the full periodic table, lead to cobalt. He had tried to file into order the previous night's shocks, but his mind refused to run consecutively, or consequentially; it was inventing its own causes and effects in a kind of perverse spasm that, if he could be honest with himself, he had feared all along: a word-association hangover without a sense of humour. He had ceased wondering if he was going mad. He knew he was. He wrenched at the orange fluorescent band around his wrist—the infernal thing made him feel like a hospital patient. God, he whined, is this hangover part of the all-inclusive?

Just as the musical thump of Slashing had fallen silent, the message alert on his PDA blurted. He reached into his chinos heaped beside his cot (leg-holes still upright where he had stepped out of them, like a spacesuit), and fumbled the device from a pocket. The text was from his father, but the first attempt was botched and the message had come through incomplete and corrupt. All Hut could read were the first two words, although those were sufficient to fling him into a new torment.

Bad News, wrote KenH, and of course Bad News could mean only one thing. Hut had been prepared for his father finding out, but his preparations had assumed a baseline quantum of sanity, or capacity, on his own part. He expected to be caught. It couldn't be paid off with some quiet fine (he'd already tried that) or hushed up with the help of his mates (that too). The news of his misdemeanour would ripple outwards—or inwards—until he had to face up to those most hurt: his parents, and finally, if it couldn't be helped (and it couldn't be, it now seemed, despite his best efforts), Pen. The cancer had now spread somehow to Book and Janey. Their knowing, while they were in Jamaica, was not part of the plan. But that blow was superseded on another front: his father. It hadn't quite seemed real when it was just between Hut and the corporate spooks. The whole thing had been less than real for so long. You sat in a manky room with five guys who looked like failed auditors (which they probably were), and they asked you some stupid questions which quite frankly they had no right to ask. You say what you've got to say—it's not as if you have a choice—and that becomes a jailable offence? He was still half-expecting someone to jump out and say he was on Candid Camera, they were only yanking his chain. Perjury! Piss-weak! A Mickey Mouse offence, and there had to be something in the Constitution stopping them sending you away for it. He'd take it all the way to the High Court. He would.

This resolution cheered him for a little, but now his father knew too and what was he going to do about that? Hut had been rehearsing for weeks the speeches he'd make to Ken. His admissions of mistakes, his errors in judgement, and his strategies for recovery would form the first line of defence against his father's initial shock and disappointment. Maybe he could appeal to Ken's better nature. Whenever Hut had been in the shit, his father had taken his side. *My son, right or wrong.* Once Hut had got in trouble for vandalising a public toilet block, smashing a window with a champagne bottle (actually Nayce's fault but no-one had listened), and instead of jumping down his throat Ken Hutchison had snapped into gear like a reservist, a man of action in a state of readiness for just this moment. Ken had gone on the offensive, accusing the local council of various indiscretions that he threatened to make public. His actions gave Hut an effective immunity from prosecution. Privately, Ken told Hut he was a fucking idiot, but in a tone that was more in line with a chief executive upbraiding a senior employee for letting slip a scam in which the whole company was involved. It was as if Ken approved of what Hut had done; or no, not approved—he expressed no judgement on the rights and wrongs—but Ken lived for the challenge of getting out of a scrape, and if a problem could be presented as such, Ken might come on board. He liked to play Superman. Even in his retirement—probably more than ever in his retirement—Ken would be less interested in hiding from the shame, or blasting Hut, than in plotting a miraculous escape. It would prove his powers.

And so, this was how Hut would present his current problems to his father: as a challenge. They were in this together. They had to outsmart the investigators. But when Hut had planned it this way, he saw himself as a man of action by his father's side, not as a sweating, wild-eyed, clammy-pawed, hyperventilating loser locked on a balcony by his friends and unable to sleep for the fourth night running. What he had learnt in the last few days was better not known.

Fifteen minutes after that first text from Ken, a second had come through. Or a second version of the same thing: a complete version. Or not complete. Far from complete, or comprehensible.

Bad news indeed. But not the bad news Hut had expected. His disgrace he was ready to combat. But what his father was telling him was something else, and this, unlike what Hut had been dreading, was a tumult from which he could no sooner escape than conjure the erasure of his own history.

Another hour later (and no more news), Hut writhed around on the balcony like a dog circling some elusive place of comfort that shifted even as he decided on it; he was unable even to keep his mind on his father's message. Hut had been cut adrift into pasts, distant and recent—this was turning into an Alzheimer's hangover—lost in a simmering broth of misplaced images and questions left unasked.

Men like Hut weren't allowed to be unhappy. Money Doesn't Buy You Happiness, but the minute a wealthy person gave voice to his inner emptiness he was shouted down by a peanut gallery denying him the right to anything worse than a common cold. Money can't buy you happiness. But if you're rich and unhappy, you can still go and get fucked.

Hut willed himself to emulate his father. He felt himself dragged towards his mother. Mum's malaise, which nowadays they would call—did call—clinical depression, had looked too much like a lack of gumption. She drifted; she had no excuse to drift; she had no right to complain; it was her own fault. Dad put himself forward as a positive alternative, showing Hut that keeping busy was the secret to success. If you were feeling blue, you could cure it by doing something. Not very complicated. And the bluer you felt, the more you should do. Forward motion was its own reward.

He pined for home. If he ever got out of this nightmare, he just wanted to lie on the couch, all alone, for a few moments before Pen and the boys came home. He saw himself turn the key in the front door and go through the rooms one by one; in close detail he saw the contents, each decorative adornment to Pen's taste. He would be free to wander through, tabulating his home life.

His mind swam to the holiday house at Palm Beach and began visiting all of its rooms. That felt better. The Pizza Hut was even more familiar than his own home; the stigma of renting had been overcome by the constancy of their visits. Dad had been vindicated, at last. 'You never own a holiday house,' he'd always admonished. 'A holiday house owns you.' Of course, it was also a fact that they couldn't quite afford to buy a place on Ocean Road.

You approached the Pizza Hut up tiled steps climbing the grassy slope. The front door, on the ground floor, was clad in beaten copper, a '70s signature. The door went all the way to the ceiling. Its handle, a ring in twisted brass, was too big for one hand, so you had to put your beach things down in order to open it.

The entry foyer, below the main floor and the veranda, was a cool and gloomy space with chequerboard tiles and a great plaster statue embedded with glass mosaic pieces: Michelangelo meets Godspell; you couldn't tell if it was a funky piece of 1970s art or a student project hidden in a dank corner. Flanking the foyer was a big rumpus room with pool and table-tennis tables, the laundry where Fred slept, the garage, and the downstairs showers where everyone had to spend a minute after the beach. Even when he came in from nearly drowning himself two months ago, Hut had followed his reflexes and taken a quick cold one in the recess off the foyer.

A zed of dark-brown tiled steps led up into the heart of the living area. On the walls were unicorn tapestries, yachting prints and bright gluey abstracts. The owners of the Pizza Hut, a property-developing couple, left no personal photos around the place, as if they might be sullied by any kind of intimacy with the holiday renters. (Another of the fine distinctions that Hut had learnt early: paying five million dollars for a second house was class; paying ten thousand for a week in it was crass.)

But the owners were betrayed by their choices in interior design. The kitchen, flanking three walls of the upstairs area into which the steps emerged, was a triumph of chunk and burnish: cupboard handles like the heads of penises, benchtops in some kind of composite gold-dipped metal, a dominating rangehood beaten from copper, utensils hanging from the walls, a chrome-fronted fridge with an icemaker, and every kind of whizzer, blender, mixer, corer, julienner and mulcher. Fuckers even had three pairs of grape scissors. Ken felt right at home.

Hut wandered through the kitchen and fixed himself an orange juice, another reflex action after a morning in the surf. No glasses or cups left, so: Peter Rabbit egg cup.

His towel and rashie over his shoulder, he stepped down into the sunken living room, or 'den'. Shag, pouffes, big telly always a model or two behind the times so you knew this was a redundant one from their first home. They changed tellies a lot. Maybe the old one from the Pizza Hut went to their ski lodge. And the old one from the ski lodge—where would that go?

To the left of the den was the veranda, half-shaded, overlooking the beach. For years they'd had a wooden rail, but as consciousness of young children's safety overtook the world the railing had been replaced by an ugly vertical slatted fence and then by perspex, which would have allowed you to see clear to the water except it was always crusted with salt.

He glanced up the corridor to the guest wing. Most times those rooms were locked up, though for one summer when he was about ten, he and Nayce had taken bedrooms in the bush wing to get as far as possible from the parents. He recalled it was Nayce's suggestion.

The appeal of the guest wing was that the right-hand wall of the corridor, away from the rooms, was all glass and allowed the greenery of the back courtyard into the house. A strip of monstera, elephants' ears, stag ferns and some no-maintenance flowering noxious weeds gave the place a tropical feel. He found Pong, Abo and the Bookalils asleep in the three rooms of the guest wing.

He padded timidly down the corridor to the main bedrooms, all of which had views onto the front lawn and the beach. The first bedroom was his. Or 'his'. It had two single beds against opposite walls, with little-boy spacecraft doonas and posters of Formula One cars. It had pissed him off that that room had always been his. When they'd first come, when he was seven, it was the coolest bedroom, and Nayce was the one, in the double bed and neutral colours of an adult's room, who missed out. But past the age of ten, Hut was stuck in the kids' room with his vroom-vroom cars and flying saucers, and Nayce's room was the one you wanted. There never seemed a way of requesting a change without seeming ridiculous. Hut hinted to his mother that he, the son, should have the bigger room with the double bed, but she waved him off with an airy 'you sort it out among yourselves' gesture. He was afraid to appeal to his father, thinking he would be laughed at.

But he did retain happy memories of that room: setting up a Scalectric and running every car off the same corner; making a home movie with plastic gorillas fighting GI Joes and Nayce doing voice-over; throwing flour bombs from the window onto cars on Ocean Road; shooting birds with his BB gun . . .

. . . Always little-boy memories. The memories seemed to stop when they became teenagers. From then, Hut couldn't remember Nayce ever coming into the little-boy room, and he himself didn't so much go to bed there each night as go into exile.

The weekend they'd had the house party, the other month, Janey had been the one staying in Hut's room, so cute tucked in under the spaceships. Hut and Pen had taken the master suite, and Nayce had claimed the room he had always stayed in.

That morning had an eerie stillness. The beach outside was silent but for the waves and the house more silent yet. Hut had almost died. He was re-entering the house with the tears still caught in his throat, lungs still stretched and wrung from their ordeal, with the mossy-gravestone sense of the end still to be scraped away from his fingertips, blue under the nails.

The house stank of smoke and stale grog. Glasses lay everywhere, as if nobody had deigned to drink twice from the same one. Cigarette smoke clung to the rugs like a ghost's dry chortle. A reeking homemade Orchy bong lay tipped over on the shag pile in the den. He couldn't remember anyone making a bong. Had they? Or was that the bong he and Nayce had made when they were fifteen? Wasn't that when the reeking bong tipped over and soaked the shag? He thought of turning back to the den to verify his memory: was he recalling five minutes ago, two months ago, or twenty-five years ago?

He was re-entering the corridor after nearly drowning. But that had happened before too, hadn't it? Back on that last summer they'd come as a family. A 'family': Mum, Dad, Hut, Nayce. Hut was surf skiing with Dad, and had caught a wave when his father dropped in on him. Hut looked up the face and there was the orange nose of his dad's ski coming at him like a harpoon. There was only enough time to see it and curse Dad; not enough to duck. Hut had been knocked off his ski and must have passed out for a few seconds, because when he got his mouth above the water it was filled with vomit and he knew neither his name nor what day it was. All he knew was that he'd been there before; he had the strangest sense of living inside a dream he'd had the previous night. That was what had happened: Dad had dropped in on him, the orange ski had knocked him out, and he'd woken up vomiting and concussed. Abandoning his ski, he did what had happened next in the dream: he floundered to the shore and collapsed onto the sand, vomiting again, and it was not until his father had come up and started shouting at him—'Where the fuck's your ski, son?'—that the thread of the dream was broken and Hut was once again living his life for the first time.

He had run up to the house, away from his father, leaving him to find the ski. Hut had staggered up the tiled steps and swung open the brass front door with his two hands around the twisted ring handle. He'd had the self-possession to shower—just as he would twenty-five years later—and go up to the kitchen to drink some orange juice. Still heaving, from shock and panic, he had done what any boy who knows he has just escaped death would do: he sought out his mum.

But that was years ago. Now he was in the same corridor, moving towards the same room. Nayce's door had this incongruous nameplate—'Nigel's Room'—a rare personal touch the owners had left.

A shuffling sound within. The door was shut. Its handle was round, chunky, embossed brass with a kind of concentric fly's-wings pattern. Hut pulled the door back into its frame, a trick to stop it creaking, turned the handle, and pushed.

Two pasts, blistered, tears seeping between two skins.

Her back to him. The blackened sole of Nayce's left foot fidgeting on the end of the bed like a security guard. His other foot beneath the cream sheet. The corner of his elbow tucked behind his head.

Why did a kid have to have a room with a double bed? Why did Nayce, who was here on his own, have to have a room with a double bed? Shouldn't the Bookalils have been given that one?

A quick sigh, like a stifled male laugh or female sob.

Two pasts, one possibility. No—one possibility, two pasts.

Hut shut the door as quietly as he had opened it. Now he walked towards the master suite on legs tingling from more than a brush with drowning; now his legs felt like they might fail him.

In the master suite, the bed was rumpled but empty. He went into the ensuite bathroom, dappled from a recent shower, also empty. He couldn't escape himself in the mirror: blue eyes, blue skin, perfect match. His freckles stood out the colour of high, dark grey clouds on a dusky sky, seconds after losing the sun.

He washed his face. This hadn't happened in the dream the night before, or any dream. He rehearsed his speech: 'Hey Pen, you'll never guess who I found in the sack with Nayce.' He would be happy to break the news. It was what they had been wishing for; Pen would be happy too. She would craftily widen her eyes, suggesting she already knew. The news would make him happy too, if only he could find Pen to tell her.

25

Nayce swam into Janey's feet. The five swimmers bunched like a concertina. Jason and Rip hauled them by the wrists onto the deck of the Aquasmith. The five sat around the cockpit, propping themselves on their thighs as they caught their breath. Blackman plugged one nostril with his thumb and eructed through the other. Nayce was grimly pleased to see he was not burning alone.

As they motored back to the marina, Rip spread a big sheet of butcher's paper across the stairwell.

'Okay, listen in,' he said. 'Y'all thought you swam pretty good?'

Cautious nods.

'A little tough?' he said.

'Sure,' said Book.

'Piece of piss,' Janey said, betrayed by the fast-pulsing hollow between her collarbones.

'Arright.' Rip, serious but smug, scratched the hair on his lower lip with his front teeth. 'Lemme show you something.' He drew a cross at the twelve o'clock point on his butcher's paper. 'Here's where you started.' He drew another cross at the six o'clock point. 'Here's where, in the race, you'll be aiming at.' He dashed a vertical line from top to bottom. 'But the current,' he said, 'goes like this.' He drew two big arrows almost perpendicular to the line of the swim, but slightly backwards, rising from eight o'clock to two o'clock. 'And here,' he said, plump with vindication, 'is the way you just swam.'

Slowly, theatrically, his pen started at twelve o'clock, aiming at six o'clock, then bending towards five, curving as it swung around to four, then taking a U-turn before straightening out and following a clear line to two. The course they had swum resembled a fish hook.

'We fell into the current,' Blackman said.

'You fell into the current,' Rip said as if he had won a bet. 'You swim like that tomorrow, we call the whole thing off. I pick you all up and we have pina coladas back at the hotel.'

'Fark,' Pongrass said.

'My words exactly,' Rip said. 'I'm telling you now. This boat is not going to follow you. This boat is going to follow the course. *My* course. And you follow the boat. If that means you dog paddle, if that means you tread water until your half-hour is up, that's fine by me. You stay by the boat, I'll get you out. But if you go off and have a nice free and easy swim with the current and you do what you've just done, either you're pulling out of the race or I ain't picking you up. Capish?'

Book blew out his cheeks and shook his head.

'Fark,' Pongrass said again.

Nayce shrugged: tough. He was looking forward to this. Was he the only one who was excited by their failure? They'd have to sharpen up, but they were strong, they'd make it.

'This what we've trained all these months for, isn't it?' he said. 'Who wanted it to be easy?'

Faithful Book looked at him as if he was a simpleton.

'What's up?' Nayce said, feeling aggressive towards Book. 'You look like you've swallowed a turd.'

Book shook his head: not wanting to talk.

'We went *backwards*,' Janey said.

Nayce smoothed a hand over his bald head, staring out to sea. He said dully: 'You were fine. Don't worry.'

'It's not us,' Book said. 'We'll be okay—I hope. But there's . . .'

Janey was looking past Nayce, towards the jetty. Her face broke into a dewy smile.

'Oh right,' Nayce said, turning to follow her gaze. 'Sure, I'd forgotten about him.'

'How,' she said, 'could you ever forget him?'

On the jetty, waving them in, was a unique figure in a sombrero, mirrored sunglasses, Bermuda shorts, deck walkers and a red and yellow hibiscus-printed Hawaiian shirt so new that the sun shone off its ironed angles. He had pulled up to the end of the jetty in a golf cart loaded with Red Stripe and Gatorade. He semaphored with both arms, their fish-meat undersides glossy and vulnerable in the bright day, like naked truth.

'Eh mon, take the rope!'

Jason came down from the bridge and threw Hut the heavy rope. Hut dodged, ducking under his hands; the rope thumped like a corpse on the jetty. Recovering, Hut wrenched it around a bollard.

Rip turned to the Fast Set and said: 'Okay, okay. And the currents and the sharks and keeping your bearings—they're the least of your problems. Y'know what I'm saying?' He nodded towards the red-gold blur wrestling with the bollard, legs braced, fighting the rope as if it were a giant python. 'The least of your problems.'

Tenderly, on water-wrinkled white feet, the swimmers stepped onto the wharf, Hut helping each to an icy drink, unscrewing the caps himself.

'So, dudes,' Hut said, clapping his hands twice for attention. 'I've organised a minibus for the arvo. We're going on a shopping trip, then a twilight tour of the volcano. Mount John!' He swept his eyes around the group. 'Are you with me, or are you with me?'

26

Penelope Hutchison spent four hours in Kidz Wrrrld at Miami airport. Her attention too blunted to read a magazine, she sipped orange juice and watched Roy and Charlie romp with enervating intensity in a perspex-walled pit filled with slippery multicoloured balls. Every few minutes one of them slid down in this quicksand and Pen readied to spring to the siren of screams. But with a resilient cheer and energy that she found diabolical, they played at drowning in the ball-pit as if it were a running gag.

Men—the lone-wolf frequent flyers—made detours between the newspaper rack and the workstations to take in Pen with transparent rapacity, their inhibitions stripped clean by fatigue and the free-fire zone of an international air terminal. She knew how she appeared and what they were thinking. There never had been any point denying it. To a certain kind of bull, she presented a red rag. She attracted successful men with short attention spans. For the first act of her adulthood this knowledge had scared her, for the second act it had enlivened her, for the third act, marriage, it had become a matter for indifference; but now—the fourth act, yes—she couldn't fend off the prickling in her curiosity. What would she. With that one. Or that. What would they. For the first time in a decade, Penelope Hutchison was speculating.

She was grateful for the flight's delay, happy for postponement. She was racked by questions of process: the When and the How of it. Telling Hut as soon as she arrived would invite a week of suffering, a seven-day window for him to plead and beg, for her the unrelenting pain of saying no. What if he came up with a deal? What if he cornered her, so she had no choice but to give him the definitive *Jeremy, I don't love you anymore?*

Waiting until the end of the week appealed to the coward in her, yet promised a lonely ordeal while she built herself up. Postponing it also seemed unjust, disallowing him a right of reply. Did he have a right of reply? She didn't know about rights. It wasn't a matter of rights.

Could she say it anyway? *I don't love you anymore.* Could she say it? Was it even true? It had to be true—didn't it?—if she was further down the track already, thinking about the practicalities. You wouldn't be calculating logistics unless you'd settled on the truth of the declaration. Would you?

Wavering, she sat and watched the children and tried to draw strength from the days and days at home when she'd thought of him as nothing but an unredeemed shit, an arsehole, a selfish prick. Her very breathing seemed, at times, a single muttered curse. *FuckingHutfuckingHutfuckingarsehole.* But did this mean she'd stopped loving him? Could she tell him? She rejected the each-way bet, the *I still love you but can't be with you,* the self-romanticising soft option she'd heard often enough herself. Before Hut, when she'd wanted out of relationships, Pen had been able to throw a switch and make herself unbearable enough to be dumped. To be dumped was to leave without guilt. Her ego could take it, seeing she had manufactured it. But no matter what she did now, Hut would never leave her—she had to grow up, take the initiative, be the dumper. If she still loved him, she wouldn't want to separate. Would she? She knew (she thought) that she wanted to separate, so therefore she mustn't love him, and she had to have the nerve to tell him so—if she was having doubts, the declaration would be its own test. She had to say it to his face in order to see if it was true.

It was all agony, either way. What if they fought? Hut was not the fighting type, whereas Pen had enough fight in her for two. She loathed confrontation, but once drawn into a fight, Pen had the instincts of a lion. That was one of the secrets of their—success? ha!—their complementarity. Hut knew better than to fight, because a fight with Pen would cost him days and weeks of inconvenience. Their happiness had been built on this curious intermeshing of a gregarious, upfront nature knowing better than to cross a reserved, hard-packed one. And probably, she allowed, he never wanted to fight with her anyway. He never seemed to get angry, the bastard.

Yet an edge of hardness had crept in—to her more than to him. Perhaps it was just symptomatic of parenthood and the forties, but sometimes she felt such a sudden, teeth-baring scorn and contempt enter her voice that she wondered if she might attack him.

Hut had only ever raised his hand at them once, an exception that proved the rule. They'd been on a driving holiday and all the planets had come into alignment: the Hutchisons were late, driving in the dark on their last sniff of petrol, the air in the tyres was down, they were achingly hungry and tired, everyone had a cold, and they'd taken a shortcut that had got them, finally, lost. Then it started pouring and the left front tyre blew. Hut went out into the horizontal freezing rain, jacked up the car and found that the spare was flat too—Pen had forgotten to replace it. Throughout all of this, he retained his Hutness, his irrepressible humour. But as he stood at the side of the road while each of the infrequent passing cars ignored his waving, something snapped. Perhaps it was when a semitrailer seemed to aim at a puddle, splattering him with icy mud. He came back to the car to wipe himself down, reached across Charlie in the back seat for a towel, and the boy sank his needle-sharp milkteeth into Hut's nose just as he heard Pen asking him not to leave mud on the babyseat.

All the planets. Hut's hand recoiled in the motion of a backhanded slap. He caught himself and stared at his hand as if it were someone else's.

'Sorry,' he said. 'I just . . .' He tailed off and got into the car, the dental seam across the bridge of his nose brightening with blood; the scar would take months to fade.

Could he hit her? She wished he had it in him, yes, she wished he could lose his temper and whack her, just as she'd wished and prayed that her father could have whacked her mother. It would make things so much easier.

Another shark glided by. A mako. The corners of his mouth twitched. Pen half-expected to see saliva drip from his incisors. He wasn't her type, but she might have to start rethinking her ideas about types. It seemed cruel to be looking ahead when the present wasn't yet dealt with, but Pen had done her grieving. She had buried and commemorated their marriage. Only now that it felt fully dead did she have the courage to inform Hut.

Cold, cold, she was. But you had to be, or else you simply died. You stayed married to an arsehole, you died. You sympathise with your man, you comfort him, you sacrifice your coldness, and he takes what he can take from you, and then you die. A supporting role is its own punishment.

Now the shark was going by again, and pausing, and now—now—he connected her with Roy and Charlie tossing themselves about in the ball-pit. She read his thought-bubble: *Aha! Encumbered!* He was off.

Pen was familiar with men who toyed with single mothers. Those creeps Hut sucked up to, Justin Pongrass and Andrew Blackman, boasted about their forays into the 'singles' scene (a misnomer—it was not a 'scene', unless it was a taped-off accident scene, and it was much less peopled by 'singles' than it advertised). Pongrass had bragged about the number of 'yummy mummies' he had 'bagged'.

'Yeah,' he'd regaled one of those Friday lunches to which Pen had been dragged along, 'all you need to do on your posting is rave on about how much you love kids and your ideal is a woman with a ready-made family, blahdy blah. They just melt in your arms. All they need to know is that you'd love their kids. I bagged seven hyenas on first dates with three simple words: "I love kids".'

At least Pen was ready for the deception. Men would pretend to love her sons. Then they would fuck her and fuck off. She had this to thank Hut's friends for. Forewarned is forearmed.

How had Hut managed to find himself among such types? He seemed to think he was social climbing, but to Pen it looked more like a sudden and violent fall. They were pure trash. Hut thought they were gods. Sometimes she thought she saw dollar-signs in his eyes.

She couldn't remember, literally, two consecutive ideas from Hut that were not coloured by money. He had changed from a young man who lived amid the invisibility of need into an adult who acted as if he was down to his last coin. So many moments of the day she was desperate to confess to him: *I am not a good mother. You've given me all the help money can buy, and I still can't cope.* She needed him—couldn't he understand that? But he, her third dependant, was swept away on his tidal wave of financial drama. He worried about money, he gloated about money, he foxtrotted with money, he took drubbings from money, he fought (with himself, but not with her) over money, he converted every relationship into dollar terms. He could only understand the world through the language of buying and selling. He cast off friends because they were not money friends. And therein lay (ironically?) his greatest gift to Pen in the last couple of years: his saturation in money drove her to seek people to whom money was nothing; people who inhabited a moneyless world. No matter how primal or tyrannical their yearnings, Roy and Charlie at least knew nothing of money.

On top of it all, as if there could be any room on top of all that, Hut had started coming home coked up on Saturday mornings, expecting her to be as pleased with him as he was with himself that he was mopping the floors or vacuuming the curtains. Pen had tried coke with Hut occasionally before they were married, and couldn't understand the fuss. If grass toasted you into a giggly bore and drink soaked you into an accident waiting to happen, cocaine, instantly and happily, turned you into a dickhead. You snorted coke and fluttered around filling the air with inanity. Coke turned humans into action-figures. Coke stole your inner life. It made you a dickhead while you were on it, and then it made you a dickhead when you were getting over it. It made you a double-dickhead when you were looking for it. Coke was the dickhead drug for dickheads. So naturally it didn't change Justin Pongrass. He was already a dickhead. But with Hut, it soiled what was left of his good nature.

And then, suddenly, he had ceased being a dickhead. He had become an arsehole. That decided it. A dickhead she could put up with.

She could feel his love thinning and clotting, coming in fits and starts. What had he texted her yesterday? *I can't stop thinking about you guys*. His problem was that he couldn't *start* thinking about them. The old steady devotion had clagged into guilt-ridden spasms of overcompensation. Pen was like his farm, his ultralight, his yacht: every now and then, remembering she needed maintenance, he'd spruce her up with a holiday, an expensive piece of jewellery. He'd do nothing around the house for weeks, then hand-polish the cupboard shelves in one manic day. And that was just the coke cleaning, it wasn't him. Did he see what he'd become? When she blew up at him, what did he do? He laughed her off. He hosed her down. He acted his old self, in the hope that his old self would return. But he knew. That was the exasperating part of it: he *knew*. What he didn't know was how to fix himself. He was scared to ask her for help; but he'd forgotten how transparent he was to her. Arsehole.

She could kill him. She could, literally, kill him, take the heaviest Kosta Boda vase and smash it into his skull. That would be easier than telling him she was leaving. Maybe he was good for something: stop her turning her urges onto the kids, or back, as in the old days, onto herself. Maybe she did need him: a punching bag, a pin cushion. But she didn't need what he'd become. What she really needed was the old Hut, the true Hut. She'd been holding on for the purity of that memory. He could find his way back there, correct and renew himself, but he only seemed to be able to do it under the lash of her fury. When her anger subsided so did his contrition; he'd be back to money.

That was the thing: money. Hut was poisoned with it, sick with surfeit, as if, once he had enough, every additional dollar was toxic. When Pen had worked, the exchange of six-minute units of her time for her clients' money had seemed so obscene, so flagrant a transfer from the productive to the parasitic (and its shadow trade, the minutes of her life handed over to death), that her sole and consuming ambition had been to cease billing. She would have preferred that they had nothing. Would she? She would. Hut didn't believe her. He took it as an insult and a lie and a show of contemptible naivete when, at lunch one Sunday with Ines and Ken, Penny said she would prefer happiness, with Hut, over money. She said: 'If we didn't have money, you might work out that there are other ways you can contribute to our family life.'

He replied patronisingly, evilly, sunnily, rosy with his good nature: 'If I was broke, I'd give you five minutes and you'd be out of here. Take away one day of the au pair and you'll be having fits.'

Arsehole. He patted her on the shoulder and winked.

Pen had fled to the bathroom and cried, shedding softness until she was parched hard.

She heard Hut saying to his mother: 'Pen? She's fine, fine. Female issues.'

Ken Hutchison had given an unconcerned shrug and Ines asked for another drink. Something was said, and the three of them laughed. And here was another discovery. The satiety, the completeness that had so drawn her to the Hutchisons was now revealing itself as pure shallowness. They were satisfied and happy because they were doing well. That was all there was to them. They approved of their son because he was making money. Their approval was heartfelt and enthusiastic yet conditional upon that one fact.

He had to have got it from somewhere, and she couldn't blame his friends for everything. The desperate and final truth of it, for Pen, was that Hut was only reverting to what he really was: what his parents were, what they expected of him. His obsession with money wasn't an aberration. It was his destiny, his character. The kindness, consideration and compassion she'd seen in their first few years together: that was the aberration. He was a Hutchison, and he would become more and more a Hutchison with each passing year.

Five minutes and you'd be out of here. There it was. She could not be sure he hadn't spoken the truth. The money. Could she survive without the money? Would she really be happier without it? She could not say. She could not say.

Now a man—a *man*—was sitting down next to her. He dumped himself with a weary sigh, as people never do when they are alone: a sigh for an audience.

'So—where's the father-figure?' He nodded towards Roy and Charlie, who were trying to stand up amid the balls and pelt each other.

'Hey!' Pen wagged a finger. Her sons paused to measure her seriousness; then continued pelting.

'Oh, don't tell me,' said the man, flashing a now-you-see-it-now-you-don't smile. 'He's gone duty-free shopping. In the nick of time!'

'I'm watching you, Roy Hutchison,' Pen raised her warning a notch. Roy's finger shot up his nose like a key into a lock. Charlie continued throwing balls.

'Unless he's . . . he can't have . . . he's left you to it!' The man clapped a hand to his forehead.

Pen smiled a little—an opening.

'So what's your destination?' His accent was American, or North American. You couldn't assume he wasn't Canadian. Money ironed out region. He was well-dressed in a button-down cotton shirt with a fine weave, and smelt expensive. He had silver hair, Cadillac hair, North American teeth so even and white; his smiles—flashed strategically—reminded her of a cartoon character with two sickles of painted whiteness to signify teeth.

'It's not about the destination,' she said. 'It's the journey.'

'Oh my God,' he said. 'You're Aussie.'

He said it with the American hiss—*horsey*, not *mozzie*. Its harshness sounded German, the way Ines Hutchison pronounced it.

238

Oh, how Pen had loved her mother-in-law back in the day, before it had all become too much for her . . .

'You can't be telling me you've flown all the way from Aussie with those two on your hands!'

'You ought to try it one day,' she said. 'It's easier than it sounds.'

Pen found it hard to believe, but she was flirting. She was thinking about making herself witty (rather than just beautiful). Beautiful was nothing. Funny was the full service.

'You know,' he confessed. 'I just *love* kids.'

'You can have them.'

He deployed a lopsided grin. 'I wish you knew me better, because right now I feel like saying, go off, have a shop, take some time for yourself, and I'll look after them. But of course I can't do that. And nor should you let me.'

'Annoying, isn't it?' she said. 'But thank you for the thought.'

'Bing,' he reached out his hand. 'People call me Bing.'

'As in Crosby?' She shook. And God, he was hanging on. It was the handshake of a man who has spent his life thinking about pressure—not too light, not too heavy. And it was time, she had to concede, well spent. His eyes, light grey, toned with his hair better than blue would have, as if they'd been chosen to match. He had a billionaire's even tan, from top to toe as if he had been dipped in a solution the colour of . . . of . . . was Pen alone in noticing that the tan of the five-star set was the exact same golden-brown as baby caca? He looked like he'd been dipped in . . . And oh God, now his hand was loosening into a sheath out of which hers was permitted to slide, each filament of at-attention hair caressed on its way out.

'As in Crosby,' he said. 'You're sweet. Some say as in Bingo. Some say as in Bada-Bing.' As if there were *so many* people.

'Bada-Bing?'

'You're real sweet. It's like, a guy sees a beautiful woman, and it's . . . Bada-Bing!'

'Oh,' she couldn't help giggling and looking down at her lap. She felt his eyes follow hers. She did not have a Brazilian, but she did have a Brazil-shaped stain on her right thigh from where Charlie had vomited his Business Class chicken. She recrossed her legs and laced her hands over the mark.

'Bada-Bing!' he sang, raising his eyebrows, and smiled at his joke.

'This is why I'd never let you look after my children,' Pen said. 'You're not interested in them.'

'What a terrible thing to say,' he smiled. 'Children are our future.'

'Tell me,' Pen said. 'Are children your future?'

He threw his head back in disproportionate merriment. He was rich, he was good-looking, and he probably figured that fifteen minutes in an airport was all he needed to get her phone number—in whatever country, whatever city—and some day in the future, he would be passing by and give her a call, leave the number of his hotel room on her answering service. And she would remember him. Bing.

'So, Mrs Hutchison,' he said, keeping his focus. She didn't panic. He'd heard her call out to the boys. 'You didn't tell me your first name.'

'Ines.' She returned his smile like a cross-court winner. 'Ines Hutchison. How do you do?'

'I could tell!' he said, triumphant. 'When I saw you, I thought, she's dark but has that Teutonic blood. I was thinking Ingrid. Wasn't far off.'

'Wow,' she said. 'Nobody's ever seen through me like that.'

'It's a gift I have.' Bing showed his teeth, like a string of fairy lights.

Boys. They were all boys, just as Roy and Charlie, cartwheeling through the rubber globes, were boys. Every man was a boy at home.

The rest—the money, the rank, the double-chins—was dressing. Pompous judges, dynamic entrepreneurs, eggheads, numbskulls, chatterboxes, silent sentinels, monsters and marvels; they were formed as eight-year-olds in the playground. Hut thought he was the only one, a boy surrounded by grown-ups. He was intimidated by David Nayce, who was cleverer, and Andrew Blackman, who'd been born with more money. He was awed by Justin Pongrass, who inherited talent and looks (so they said; she couldn't see it), and even by John Bookalil, who was born honest. Hut always found something in other boys to elevate, to look up to. He needed to surround himself with the mystique of manhood, totems hewn out of the rough material of his acquaintance. He needed it. And Pen hated that he needed it. Because she knew he was better than any of them.

This Bing, too, was a boy. How would his boyness manifest itself? Not in the bedroom, of course, where he would be the acme of modern man. Not in the restaurant where he would take her for dinner, nor in the private helicopter or motor cruiser. No, he was a sophisticate, a smoothie—although Pen, a mother, knew that the biggest manipulators and oiliest smoothies a woman could ever hope to know were less than six years old. Messing with women's heads was something they all learned early. But a billionaire called Bing? Who, but a through-and-through boy, would take so much *trouble*? Who was furthest from manhood than a millionaire with silver hair called Bing?

Already (she caught herself) she had imagined herself all the way into a king-sized bed with this man. And if she could imagine that, if she was world-weary enough to pre-live it, was there any point in actually doing it?

A wave of loneliness swamped her. She knew how very alone you could be while your days were filled with your flesh and blood and you never stopped talking and they never stopped talking to you; she knew how noisy and populous a lonely day could be. She was a mother of young children. But—this man—or someone like him . . . Pen could submit to the game, perhaps fall in love once more. And it would all start again. It would all start again. She would be a young girl, renewed, eighteen years old, revived by love. She could imagine herself into that as well. And none of it rang true. Or rather—this was it—it rang all too true.

If fifteen minutes was all this Bing figured he needed to get Pen's number, a fraction of a second was all she needed to get his. And there it was. That handsome picture of North American success could never in a million years fuck her like Hut could. She couldn't suppress a private smile. Wasn't that the secret—what nobody else could ever guess—what was theirs alone? She had found the best fuck in the universe in the unlikeliest of places. This cheerful redhead with an inferiority complex who'd cried when he had to say goodbye and worshipped his deadbeat rich mates had turned out to be her holy fucking grail. After the first time with Hut she realised she'd had enough of the beautiful boys and rough types, fair or dark, experienced or virgin, kind or mean, who followed the script, the moves copied from the movies, the lines memorised from magazines, the pride they took in their performance. No matter how *attentive* or *giving* or even *savage* they thought they were, no matter what language they spoke or what persona they adopted, slow or fast they all walked the same path, obeyed the same rhythm. She'd seen enough to know, more than she could count; not that there had been *that* many, but she'd had her time. They were boring—they bored into her with their mass-produced lovemaking. They all worked so very hard at being different, and that was what made them so much the same.

She wasn't ungenerous, at the time. She'd forgiven them all, at the time, found something to remember in every boy. She didn't think she was missing out on anything. At the time. But then came

Jeremy Hutchison, who didn't know what he had, who would never believe it when she told him, who was so wholly *delighted* by every moment he was with her. The world really did feel like it had contracted to the space of their bed, and he had the—not an ability, not even a gift—but the naked enthusiasm to make it feel like an entire world every time. He had no strategy or method. He had the equipment and an endless variety of technique, but it never seemed like *equipment* or *technique*. None of what they did together could be repeated, or learnt. Everything seemed spontaneous and truthful, an answer to the moment's purity.

The first time he'd seen her body, he'd let out a terrible, moving, deep O. Terrible because it came in a voice that was not for others, not even for her: a voice between Hut and himself. She melted, feeling she had invaded him. But he had not heard himself. And through the months and years, gasps like that continued to escape him, never quite the same O but coming from the same place, as if her body had taken him backward in time to the best surviving part of himself and also forward in time to the moment of his death. She could only compare her pleasure to that which killers must feel when life passes from their victims. That power. What that doctor, the one who injected all those old people, must have been addicted to. She'd asked Hut once how he could seem to be discovering love afresh on each occasion, and he'd said, very shyly, *I don't know, it's just I can't believe this is real*. That was five years in, when her expectation that things had to get old was still being surprised. She had come to share his disbelief—for years she had shared it. Was this quite real? Even when things did get a little old, their very routineness delivered a mature kind of comfort, an album of memories and favourites, without ever quite losing the sense that she and he only had one time left together before the end of everything.

So why the fuck had they stopped? Arsehole.

For minutes he had been talking into a vacuum. On cue (he was a proud man and sensitive, twitching to the vibrations rippling off her skin), Bing stood up rather peevishly. A noise that might have been a fart escaped him.

'That airline food,' Pen giggled.

The humour hid itself from Bing.

'Sure, right,' he said, and looked around the lounge as if someone ought to be calling him. 'Okay, Ines! Might get something decent to eat. You?'

Pen shook her head. Her white knight, her silver saviour, vanished behind a row of all-you-can-eat bain-maries. He mustn't have been as hungry as he'd said; she caught a flash of his plateless exit into the rolodex of a revolving door.

There was an accident, and a delay. The accident, fortunately for everyone flying, happened in the perspex box of coloured balls. Roy tried to climb over Charlie's shoulders and kneed him in the mouth. There was shock, and more pain, and panic, and fury, and high anxiety, and pissed pants and incomprehension and the end of the world, but it was only the end of Kidz Wrrrld. Pen Hutchison felt quite sincerely, and not for the first or last time, that she hated her children.

As she got to her feet—'Come on, both of you, come on, time to get out,'—Pen heard the public address announcement that her flight to Kingston had been cancelled and passengers would have to proceed to the service desk where they would be offered a choice of hotel accommodation for the night, and her heart leapt rather than sank, not because the delay had postponed her meeting with her husband for another twelve hours, but because in a crystalline moment between the comfortable lounge chair and the childproof gate of the perspex box, Pen saw just what the problem was and how she was going to fix it; it wasn't sex but a chamber opened by the memory of sex; and now that her solution had come out of the shadows at last, she needed some time alone with it.

27

Two HOURS AFTER Rip had bedded the Aquasmith against its snug fenders, an Australian octoped of Jeremy Hutchison, Janey Quested, John Bookalil and David Nayce was making its wall-eyed way through a neon-lit supermarket in Sandals City. The supermarket was a Wal-K, or a Mart-Mart, some localised a.k.a. of one of the international giants which, Nayce remarked, relied on aliases and shape-shifts to cross borders with the same versatility as organised criminals.

Occasionally one of the four would stop to inspect a Made-in-Haiti toy power-sander or a tea service made out of the best pink polyurethane from Guyana's Export-Free Zone.

'Chop-chop, guys,' chided Hut, making a show of looking at his watch.

Nayce shot him a murderous look. Hut, whose idea it had been to do some gift shopping on their way to the volcano, winked back. This was Hut: in response to adversity, relentless vivacity. Look on the bright side. When the noose tightens, live life, keep borrowing, keep spending, run full-tilt into the sunshine. By promising shopping and the volcano on the one trip, Hut was trying to pack too much in. It was all a frenetic diversion from whatever precious truth was being hidden from Nayce. Hut was in desperate trouble, but he would not allow a pause, a space, for someone to say something. His bubbling chatter closed all doors.

'Get a leg on,' Hut said to Nayce, pushing out a plastic banana made in a banana republic. 'It's not a microphone, mate. Just buy it. Trust me, he'll be happy with the wrapping and won't give a shit about the toy.'

'John's four, Hut. Years, not months.' Nayce's son was named, touchingly if unfashionably, after John Bookalil.

'Whatever!' Hut beamed. 'You want to see the volcano, don't you?'

Book joined them, studying a maze puzzle, beguiled by a skittering silver ball. He showed it to Janey, who read the packaging and said: 'Isn't she only three? It says Eight And Up.' Book examined the puzzle as if choosing between the manufacturer's recommendation and his own instincts regarding Leila, the youngest of his three daughters. He returned it to the shelf.

'You're not getting anything for Roy and Charlie?' Janey asked Hut.

'Nah, I'll be right.' He waved her down, as if any such suggestion were an insult to his hard-won repute as the model father. 'They're getting here tonight. Anyway. Chop-chop!'

Rubbish toys were bought in a rubbish way—panic buying, rush jobs, compromises to get out of the store. Even as he paid, Nayce felt like a process worker, transporting garbage from one dump to another, via, very briefly, his son.

Two hours in a mall almost killed them. Book and Nayce flopped into the minivan, weary from the morning's swim and heavy with jammed-up urgency. Business threw the van up the hairpins and switchbacks of the volcano road while Respect sat beside him rolling joints. Mountainside villages and clapboard churches crawled by in their paint of primary colours. Green fruit trees and wild grasses glowed against the black volcanic soil. Children in startlingly clean clothes improvised games in the skinny margins between housefront and road, while lizardly grandmothers looked on and mothers bustled out of stores. By day, Jamaica's population seemed like one big lifeboat: women and children first.

'This,' Respect said. 'Mount John.'

Hut gave John Bookalil a once-over and shook his head. 'I would if I could, but he mightn't like it. Ha!'

Janey, the only one who seemed able to simulate an agreeable human tourist, chirped about the volcano, showing off what she had read in her guide book.

'Mount John is the highest point in Jamaica,' she said. 'It's active, though, so it could turn itself into the flattest point in Jamaica any day. If that doesn't get your pulse racing, I don't know what will.'

As they rose, Hut gave a running commentary on the scenery.

'Look, guys, there's a big bunch of banana trees . . .'

'Hey, check out the fire in that sugar plantation. It's really burning . . .'

'Wake up, Nayce, your old man would love this church . . .'

He prattled as if chemically catalysed, on and on, in the way a motorcyclist must keep moving or else fall.

'They're like cursive esses,' Janey said, nodding at a line of women moving up the hillside bearing loaves on their heads. 'The upper curve is their bust, the lower curve is their bum. The only thing stopping them falling back on their rump is their bust, and the only thing stopping them falling forward onto their bust is their rump.'

Respect chuckled in a warm baritone. 'The Jah woman be in perfect balance,' he said. Janey rewarded him with a coquettish yelp.

248

Hut, pitched forward between the front seats like an eager child, shook his head like a dog wagging itself dry. 'Cripes, look at that stereo!'

Coming down the hill—heard before it was sighted—was a green Ford Cortina with all four doors spread like wings. Three Rastas occupied the front seat, bobbing in unison. An indeterminate number of Rastas were piled into the back. The doors flapped like Chitty-Chitty Bang Bang; 'It's Spliffy-Spliffy Bhang Bhang,' Janey said. On the Cortina's roof was a black cloth-covered concert speaker eleven-tenths the car's width. It boomed Marley's 'No Woman No Cry'.

Janey whistled. 'That's what I call a car stereo.'

Roused, Nayce and Book sat up to watch it approach, then cross the line down the centre of the road and weave onto the right-hand shoulder before crossing back behind them. Business did the same, so that the passing manoeuvre described a braid, considerate and stylised, like a special local handshake.

'That's called not taking no for an answer when they say your speakers won't fit in your car,' Janey said. 'Those guys are nothing more than a life-support system for that speaker.'

'Respect,' said Respect, nodding appreciatively at the brothers in his rear-vision mirror.

As the van climbed Mount John's shoulder, the villages petered out and the green vegetation turned to black scree. 'That the last of the trees,' Respect said to Janey. 'They be manicheels. You know, they grow fruit but is so poisonous even if the raindrops fall off it they will burn your skin like fire. We call them lava apples.'

'I lava it when you talk dirty to me,' she said.

Nayce shifted in the back seat. He couldn't decipher what had happened. Could he ever? In twenty years, had he ever known what was going on with her?

They passed a ruined church. The switchbacks and hairpins became more improvised—switchpins and hairbacks—and Respect began to offer serious-sounding advice to Business, like a rally-car navigator. Then they got caught behind a hire car which slowed to a walk, then a limp, finally a zimmer-frame shuffle.

'They're doing it on purpose now,' Hut said. 'Get a move on, numbnuts!'

The hire car stopped at the next switchback for a brief view, yet pulled onto the road before Business could overtake. It did the same at the next corner.

'Doesn't he know he's going to miss the sunset too?' Hut said, lip quivering as if he was going to cry.

Nayce felt another swirl of pity mixed with anger. There had been no need to squeeze in the shopping trip this afternoon. As usual, in trying to please everybody, Hut would please nobody.

'Oh Christ,' said Book, who was quietly frowning through his window as if puzzling out a 3D novelty picture whose underlying pattern would soon clarify. 'Take a look at that.'

They had swung onto the volcano's western slope. Business pulled into a gravel parking bay. For a moment no-one thought to get out. The sweep of scree ebbed away beneath them: acres of lava dribbled and folded like capuccino spillage. Far below, resort towns were blinking to life, but in a trick of perspective—or a truth of perspective?—the built-up areas were now revealed as a tenuous fringe, a scumline clinging between the volcano and the ocean, waiting to be boiled away.

This was not what shortened their breath. Slowly they filed out of the van, unaware of each other, gripped by the spectacle. To the southwest, the sun was going down in a blaze. In a slotting of light caused by a shelf of cloud above the horizon, the sun's reddening glow fattened, a vast slash of blood between the greys of sky and sea, and when its reflection started to inflame the water, the sun gained depth and distance, as if, just briefly, they could see the very miles from here to there, the speed of light laid down in a track, just one thing after another.

Nayce, Book, Janey and Hut sat on the verge of the parking area, facing the sunset. They were not close to each other; they sat where nature arrested them. The sun erupted downwards, flattening like a dropped egg, out of the fire into the frying pan.

'Oh wow,' Book pointed north.

'How dull,' Janey said. 'I wish we were still in the shopping mall.'

From Mount John, the aqueous vista swept almost three hundred degrees. Just as the ocean swallowed the sun in the southwest, a clean arc of horizon to the east of it was coughing up a smaller, shapelier, paler body. As the sun fell, like a counterweight the moon rose. Next to the sun—and it seemed, from here, close to the sun—the moon's face was anaemic, tinted rather than flushed. Though for a moon it was red enough.

As the sun lost its shape, the full moon gained, the night committing a theft against the day.

Hut felt a kind of euphoria, or forgiveness: the gods had allowed grace. 'Like *Star Wars*,' he said, wiping a tear of fatigue from his eye. 'You know, where they have two moons?'

The fast-falling sunlight foreshortened the clouds, which stretched to the horizon like patches of lichen, until finally, lasting only the instant of the sun's last bow, a milky green light flashed horizontally across the sky like the wink of an old television being turned off.

Bookalil, overcome, turned to Nayce, his dark face asking if they had seen it or dreamt it. But Nayce was on his feet, his shoulders bunched like a grimace, heading across the scree towards Hut. Nayce had tried to let the scene lift him from the earth, but he would need a month of sunsets. Transcendence was nature's gift to his betters.

* * *

That afternoon, following the swim, Nayce had lain on his bed wondering whom he could call at home to find out what was going on with Hut. He couldn't call his father, who wasn't part of the old-boys' business club.

Nor, due to a colossal fuck-up of his own making, could he call his office. He had no-one there, not even a personal assistant, whom he could trust.

His longtime PA, Joan Randell, was a reminder of how he could get someone completely and utterly wrong, a cautionary tale of books and covers. She had come over with him from the Dutch bank. For fifteen years he had known her as a matter-of-fact, motherly, four-square, dependable administrative foundation. She was one of those people without whom offices fail. A plain, comfortably-built teetotaller, she was what she was: a hardworking mother of four adults.

But then one day, TBG had advertised for an investment manager. Nayce was interviewing candidates, and wasn't even aware Joan had applied until she minced into his office during a ten-minute gap she'd left between a twenty-eight-year-old science/law graduate and a thirty-one-year-old MBA. He said: 'Thanks, Joan, who's next?'

Joan planted herself in the chair facing him, working a smile onto her broad catlike mouth. 'Time for a break, eh?' Nayce said, shuffling his papers into shape and smacking the edge on the desktop. His attention was vacuumed across the table by a silence in the room. Joan was wearing red lipstick. Her eyes were scored in shades that had been researched, tested, and selected in front of a mirror. Her dress was not the usual jumper or casual shirt and faded slacks, but a burgundy pant suit. Her expression was moist.

'Oh, Joan,' he said. 'I didn't realise.'

Joan said nothing as he read her file. Her qualifications were nil. Her belief was that she had seen enough to know she could do the job. And she could. Even though investment manager was a few shelves above her pigeon-hole, Joan could do it on her ear. But Nayce lacked the composure to process all, or any, of this while she was sitting there. By the time he was ready to speak, she had cracked her knees and tottered from his office. She swept up her bag from her desk and was in the lift before he could think of what to say. At lunch, he was going out with his partners when he saw her sobbing in the courtyard, one hand flattening a mobile phone against her ear, the other swabbing her nose. He'd have stopped to say something but didn't want to embarrass her in front of his partners. He had a long lunch, unconsciously—no, consciously—stringing it out to forestall going back to Joan. Go back he did, at five past five, to find her resignation letter on his desk.

That was only the beginning. When Nayce was on a roll, he was unstoppable. As a stand-in for Joan Randell (he was certain she'd come back) he had borrowed one of his partners' assistants, Catriona Finger.

Catriona Finger was built in the shape of a carafe. Her body decanted itself from pin head down through slender neck, pre-shrugged shoulders and sparrow chest, before widening hyperbolically to a three-seater upholstered backside. Nayce couldn't help thinking of Big Bird.

The problem with Catriona was her feelings. Her glandular and genetic misfortunes did not thicken her skin. Catriona's face was red where it wasn't dry and dry where it wasn't red. It was all flush and asperity, like a side of beef you've fucked up in the oven and tried to redeem in the microwave. The only healthy feature on her face was her moustache. Her eyes seemed to swim in their own syrup, the natural moisture of the tea-break smoker double-glazed with her allergies. When she came into his office her eyes addressed him with a horribly embarrassing intimacy that reminded him of his mother. When performing a task as simple as telling him the time, she seemed to be pleading, always pleading: *Don't hurt me! You know how I bruise. Please don't hurt me!* Which possessed Nayce with the urge to punch her.

Sometimes Catriona wore low-cut leotardy tops, originally black but now grey and fretted with over-washing. The sight of her ribbed chest was enough to make the most redblooded heterosexual question his orientation.

So his having tongue-kissed her at the last Christmas party repelled memory and examination. He knew what he'd been thinking: *TBG is about afflicting the comfortable and comforting the afflicted.* The grand arrogance of the do-gooder. He'd wanted to make Catriona feel pretty. But not even twenty-five drinks and a line of coke (it had been a Friday evening) could excuse what he'd done. It certainly stopped him phoning now to ask her to make some calls about Hut. Nayce was scared of his own telephone. This was how simple mistakes turned viral. Joan Randell had led to Catriona Finger had led to this.

Or, looked at another way, *this* led back to Catriona Finger, which led back to Joan Randell, which led to the whole misery of a bad marriage, which led back to the worst mistake of all, which was crouching a few yards away from him on the edge of the volcano, a mistake he kept repeating every time he failed to take the opportunity to speak.

The gods had finalised their exchange. There was one moon and no sun. Perched on the minivan's bumper bar, Respect and Business were sharing a joint the size of a wheel jack. Their pennant of smoke hung in the breezeless air, a signal to the indigo gods. Eventually Book and Janey got to their feet and started wandering up the edge of the crater, where the earth belched rotten eggs. Silently, Nayce walked over and placed a hand on the seated Hut's shoulder. Hut started, then placed his hand over Nayce's and gave it a pat. They watched the moon.

Hut—terrorised by nightmares, wilting with anxiety, sickened by what he had done, dragged down, down, sinking into the earth as if leg-chains were winding him into its core—had been trying to think of good things: open skies, clean slates. The spectacle of sun and moon, far from inspiring him, filled him with vertigo, that old desire to *go*. His wretched three days, his wretched year, his wretched life, swung into alignment.

It was at the worst possible moment for Hut, akin to kicking him as he was already falling, the moment when a playful push could kill a man, that Nayce bent to his ear and said: 'You told me I should be more honest about myself.'

Hut turned his face up and said quietly, the years again moulting away: 'Maybe I should too.'

'Who goes first?'

Hut shrugged. 'Maybe it's the same thing.'

Nayce paused, heart scaling his chest like a caver making for light, and wondered at what he was about to do. He licked the taste of blood from his lips.

'Me first then.'

He sat beside Hut, threw a companionable arm over his mate's shoulder, and started in on the worst news that Hut had heard so far.

5

The Fast Set

28

ON RACE EVE (how rich, how muscular those words) Nayce had slipped notes under doors reminding everyone they were meeting Rip in the hotel lobby at 5.30 am. When he arrived there at 5.25 he was pleasantly surprised to be the last. The air quality had changed. Pongrass and Blackman greeted him with strong handshakes and new faces: abstract, unlined, distant, Nayce observed with a swell of pride. These were professional endurance athletes, and this morning they had woken with their race faces.

Book and Janey were nervously massaging each other's shoulders and making weak jokes. Even Hut looked ready, or as ready as he was ever going to be. He said nothing, which for Hut was quite something. Nayce shoved away the suspicion that Hut was sulking over what had happened up at the volcano. On the return drive Hut had gone awfully quiet, and opted against dinner with the team, instead retiring to his new corner suite alone to wait for Pen and the boys. But some airline snafu had delayed his moment of glory. As if he hadn't had enough to contend with. Surely it was this disappointment, and not what Nayce had said, that silenced Hut now.

Rip swaggered into the lobby with the cultivated matter-of-factness of a man who relished exploiting anxieties. He ordered the group to follow him to the dock. They padded on bare feet with pallbearer faces. From the still-lit hotel, other teams emerged onto the marina, fluorescent orange wristbands glowing in the dawn. Maybe these serious-looking squads had been around all week; Nayce hadn't noticed them. He doubted the other teams could have been jacking off around town as much as the dirty half-dozen. These other teams, their days would have comprised activities ticked off schedules: gym, swim, rest up in room, vitamin supplements, team strategy sessions over salad and electrolyte drinks.

Up to now, Nayce had been unable to escape the feeling that he was participating in some kind of inversion of corporate team-building; instead of a group of strangers coming together in some demanding athletic task with the aim of leaving the island as a cohesive entity, the Fast Set's old bonds were straining and so the race took on the aspect of a last chance. Or else what? Or else they would go home as strangers.

Surveying the dock Nayce realised he was here for a serious race (and was shocked: he had always believed he was coming here for a serious race until the last three days). A pod of women in matching sky-blue towelling gowns formed a peppy huddle in a big motor cruiser. The Atlas shoulders and the muscles-for-tits showed they were real swimmers, authentic competition. The women's vowels—the broads' broad sounds—floated across the water: Os uttered through mouths shaped for an A. Australian. This filed Nayce's competitive drive as sharp as a prison toothbrush. It was one thing to be beaten by women, but another thing again, a far more serious matter, to be beaten by Australians.

Further down the marina other teams settled into their cruisers, engines chortling. Nayce felt intimidated—the competition all looked like Olympians, but unlike the Fast Set's Olympians, the competition looked like Olympians from this century. His flesh prickled, as if being inflated from within, the wrinkles and pores smoothing out. The past few days had been some kind of sick joke, an interim, a phony war, a nightmare of transit and disconnection. Now he was awake, alert, race-ready; those days no longer existed. The race was what they were there for. It was what the internationals were there for. It was on.

The air around the docks tingled. Hulls hugged fenders, ripples kissed fibreglass, propellers cleared their throats. In the Aquasmith's cabin, Rip was quietly counselling an attentive Blackman and Pongrass.

'What a morning,' Nayce said, joining them.

Rip shook his head, as if disagreeing. 'I was just telling these boys that contrary to most ocean races, here no weather is bad weather.'

'How do you mean?'

'Wind and rain and swell are the least of your problems.' Rip stroked his goatee. 'When there's weather, it can counteract the currents. No weather, the currents are able to do their dirty business. Paradoxically,' he glanced around the cabin as if looking for applause at his use of such a big word, 'Negociante is toughest when the surface is calm.'

Nayce monitored Pongrass and Blackman without daring to look at them too directly. They were sombrely intent on Rip.

Cruisers motored out of the marina into the bay. Jason backed the Aquasmith into the fifty-strong flotilla. The team sat around the cockpit jiggling their legs, hands clasped across their knees, heads bowed. Only Rip spoke.

'Hey team, just remember. You'll have a heck of a party tonight. It's only a few hours away. Just remember—time's on your side. Whatever happens, this day will pass like any other.' His prosecutorial eye circled the pale faces like a roulette ball before settling in Hut's slot. 'Well, maybe not like any other. But it will pass.'

The sun rose as they entered the straits, which were, as Rip promised, ominously calm. Foreshortened, the stretch of water looked like a cinch. Nayce swept the fleet from starboard to port with searchlight eyes, always seeking an enemy, until he sighted the launch carrying the team of big-shouldered Australian women.

Rip re-explained the race rules. They were one of forty-five teams entered. Most years more swam, but this year registrations had fallen away. 'Maybe coz a tiger shark followed us all the way across the strait last time,' Rip said with undue relish.

Janey gave a silvery hoot, choosing by force of will to believe that Rip was jesting. Rip gave her a triumphant sneer: *Boot's on the other foot now, eh girlie?* Nayce, who had read about the shark incident on the Net, kept quiet and scanned the water for shapes.

Negociante hunched treeless and grey-green across the channel. With open throttles, the fleet took a dread-filled hour to reach a cove scooped out of the island's near side. The crossing, while smooth, had taken an awfully long time. The start line was on the beach, and the lead-off racer (who they had agreed would be Pongrass) had to run a hundred metres across the sand, then swim the first half-hour. Each leg was measured by time, not distance: you swam half an hour, then you handed over. This was regulated by an honour system, each pilot playing impartial timekeeper. Rip had given no sign that he would do them any favours.

Jason eased the throttle as they approached the shore. On other boats, swimmers had stripped down and their number ones were jumping into the water and stroking slowly to the beach. Some were already wading through the shallows.

On Negociante a yellow banner and marquee indicated the start line.

'Just remember,' Rip emphasised as Jason cut the engine. 'I will not follow the swimmer. The swimmer must—*must*—stick with me. I will navigate the course, and if the swimmer drifts away from the boat, he has to swim back, against the current and all. The boat will not follow the swimmer. The current will be dragging you away from me, but I will not deviate from our course to the finish line. I'll pick the short way. I lead. That, my friends, is non-negotiable. The current and the swim are the least of your problems. Swim away from the boat—then you have a problem. I assure you,' he paused to address each individual with his pebbly eyes, enjoying his part so thoroughly that he risked undermining his gravity, 'you have a problem.'

Pongrass stripped down and exchanged handshakes—no high fives, no gimmicks, just firm grips—with everyone on the boat. He flexed while Janey took his photo. Everyone was going to have their photo taken in the same way. One pose was a full-face shot, and another in profile, clenching biceps like a bodybuilder.

Nayce looked into Pongrass's goggles and saw neither more nor less emotion than usual. He glanced along the seat to where Hut sat, still unnaturally silent. Remembering the words he had spoken up at the volcano, Nayce's feelings of vindication fought with regret, as if he had not been quite careful enough of what he wished for.

Pongrass's tour of the deck reached Hut. He thrust out his hand. Hut took it and, instead of shaking, pulled himself up. Pongrass stood motionless while Hut gave him a hug, slapping his tanned shoulders. Then, as Pongrass pulled away and jumped into the water, Hut faced the team and let out a primal scream.

'Whooo-hooo!'

He punched the sky with his arms, then ripped an air-chainsaw. 'Come on! Let's get it on!'

Nayce cringed, but Hut's eruption found an answer in the Aquasmith and across the cove. Suddenly other swimmers on other boats were hollering. Hut arched his back and howled. A cheer rebounded across the fleet. Competitors were punching the air in a war dance. On the Aquasmith everyone except Nayce leapt up, screaming joyful release, bouncing the boat. Nayce pushed himself up reluctantly, the last man seated during a standing ovation.

Shaking his head, Rip climbed to the helm to talk to Jason.

29

On the beach, forty-five men and women in swimming costumes and numbered caps spread between the yellow flags. Pongrass, hanging back, pressed his palms to his temples to flatten his goggle straps and twisted his neck from side to side. The starter climbed onto a three-step ladder and shouted through a cupped hand. As the competitors went into a choreographic crouch, as if simultaneously ducking a low-flying bird, Pongrass could be seen nudging to the front. The starter's gun coughed smoke, they raced for the water, and the gun's flat report, like a hammer tapping a nail, carried across the cove.

Racers hurtled along the strand—near the back, someone tripped and fell—and fought their way through the shallows, running in slow-motion with ankles waterwheeling above the surface. Soon it became more efficient to swim; the leaders porpoise-dived, six or seven bounds, before the water level rose to their ribs; they fell into frothing strokes. Nayce lost Pongrass in the flurry, but Rip, with Blackman's help, was nodding and pointing and soon the Aquasmith fell in with the other boats flanking the peloton of swimmers.

The pilots sifted into their different courses. Pongrass, under Rip's instruction, swam obliquely towards the eastern headland, face popping up like an otter's to keep an eye on the Aquasmith. Rip took the wheel while Jason gambolled around the deck keeping the boat in order. The Fast Set stood in their team T-shirts cheering Pongrass, except for Hut, who furtively felt his way downstairs to use the toilet.

Pongrass swam sturdily, nailing down the opening leg like a skilled tradesman. Nayce couldn't tell where they were placed in the field, as the boats were fanning out into the strait and it was impossible to know how the different currents would affect them. They'd only know when the boats converged again on the final orange buoy facing the beach seventeen kilometres away.

Reaching the open water, Pongrass fought to stay near the Aquasmith. He'd swim thirty or forty strokes and the current would bear him away. Uncannily, without needing to look up, he was able to prop and churn back towards the boat. Rip had a series of foolscap-sized cards, one for each minute, counting down from 30 to 1, to show the swimmer how far along he was. Jason stood at the rails and raised the 20 card. Twenty minutes to go. He also had a card with a word: SHARK.

Watching Pongrass swim, Nayce felt himself soften. Pongrass had his secrets and his weaknesses too. On his way to the hotel gym Nayce had twice seen Pongrass in the masseur's room getting treatment on his injured back. No monkey-business, no bullshit: Pongrass was moaning as if hot needles were being driven under his foreskin. Once Nayce had heard him weeping like a child. He hid behind a pillar when Pongrass came out of the masseur's room, limping and ashen, looking like a man who had lost everything. And so now, watching him swim, Nayce appreciated and even admired the guy's raw physical courage.

Odd, that a person could reserve so much of his best for one act.

And then there were other reasons to think more humanely, or at least more humbly, towards that bastard. Last night, after the volcano trip, there had been a conversation around the pool: Pongrass, Blackman, Janey, Book and Nayce. Hut had gone to his suite. Nayce, digesting his latest fix of utter chicken, was quietly belching masala fumes. Pongrass was paying out his usual cretinism, talking about the Palais Royale.

'She latched on to me like she'd been waiting all her life,' he said.

'Like an oyster when it sees a good rock,' Blackman nodded.

'Sweet girl,' Pongrass said. 'I don't mind a bit of black, even if their hair's a little coarse, you know? Their skin's a little, I don't know, papery.' He rubbed his dry fingers together and put on a sad face, as if reflecting on four centuries of cross-Atlantic slavery. 'And there's the BO, sheez. Best thing about black fronties is the way they look. They look fucking great.'

'True, Nev.' Blackman nodded like a connoisseur.

The others sat as they usually did, half wanting to stop their ears, half rapt. There was something grotesquely compelling about him. He was, after all, a one of a kind. A first.

'So what was it about her?' Book said. 'What made her a first?'

Pongrass chuckled and swilled his cocktail. 'She was the first who's ever told me, afterwards, that if I don't double my payment she'll have me fucking killed right there and then.' Pongrass blinked around the group, as if surprised at himself.

On the other side of the pool deck, the steel band began packing up early. A burly American couple, second-honeymoon sexy, kept their slow waltz circulating around the jacuzzi.

'You believed her?' Book said.

'You weren't there, matey, you weren't there. I doubled-up

without a squeak. One for the scrapbook. First credible death threat.'

Nayce laughed. For the first time, he was amused by Pongrass. Was he being corrupted? He didn't know, but as he laughed he noticed Janey growing agitated. Then, as if the compression of locking her thoughts away from him cracked her open towards a more general and public candour, she snorted: 'You boys are all the same. Your mothers did everything for you, so you can't respect women.'

Where, Nayce wondered, did that come from? Sails already hoisted by two daiquiris, Janey waved for another. It wasn't as if they didn't deserve some kind of female chastisement. But why had it taken her so long? Why start now?

Book, who always took words literally, responded to what Janey said rather than what she might have meant. 'It's true that my mother did everything for me, but I do respect her. She worked. You've got to respect work.'

'Oh John, maybe *you* do. You're the exception. But,' Janey turned to face Pongrass, 'the rest of you. I'm sure it's why you're all so hopeless with women. Your mothers did too much for you.'

'Mine did sweet FA.' Blackman jutted his blue jaw. 'Didn't lift a finger.'

'And that's why you don't respect us,' Janey said.

'Maybe, but it kind of fucks up your theory, doesn't it?'

'You're another exception that proves the rule.'

'How come everyone who doesn't fit your theory is the exception that proves it?' Blackman said, his turned-down mouth fixed in a Blackman smile.

'It's interesting, Andrew, that you didn't contradict me,' she cocked an eyebrow. 'You agree you don't respect women?'

The discussion had taken place in the lightest tone. Not a twitch of doubt in those privately educated smirks. But Janey couldn't let it go. Slipping out of character—had it all got too

268

much for her?—she needled Blackman. 'So you're agreeing with me. You don't respect women.'

Pongrass had stayed out of it, above it all—or rather, squirming in his chair, kneading his back, enclosed in his pain. 'Fuck it,' he sighed with finality, easing crookedly to his feet. 'You don't understand shit. We hate you because our dads hate our mums. If you'd ever had the guts to get married, you might have a clue. Who are the biggest killers, anyway? Husbands knocking off their wives. Think about it.'

Janey stopped, jaw agape, caught as much by the unusual fact of Pongrass entering the discussion as by what he had said.

'Hate is a strong word, Justin,' she said quietly. 'I only said you can't work out how to deal with us as equals.'

Pongrass tried to stretch his arms above his head in an end-of-night yawn, but was snagged by some new pain between his kidneys.

'Ah, fuck. Call it what you want,' he said with a groan, as if she, Janey—women, female opinion—were another pain to add to his list. He stopped moving and let his arms hang by his sides and stared at her. Janey blushed and lowered her face as if she and Pongrass were alone at the table, spotlit on a stage. 'Call it what you want, Jane. If you want your answers, look at the old men.'

Listing to his favoured side, Pongrass wove through the tables and chairs into the lift lobby. Blackman, as if obeying some secret signal, stayed at the table. Nayce tried not to look at Janey, who had plunged her nose into her fresh cocktail. There had been something unmistakable in Pongrass's tone: some pure intimacy. Nayce's heart began to flutter with the birdlike lightness of confirmed suspicion.

After a short time Janey rammed her straw into her drink like a half-smoked cigarette and bade them good night.

Nayce stayed another hour with Blackman and Book, saying

little. He went up to the twelfth floor around eleven. Briefly he paused at Pongrass's door. He wanted to go in and talk about the race: make one final effort to enlist Pongrass in stopping Hut from swimming. But he felt uncomfortable going into Pong's room informally, as if without an appointment. He was turning to leave when the door opened.

'Oh. You.'

'Hey.'

Nayce and Janey stood facing each other.

She recovered first, smiling. 'On your way to bed?'

Nayce could think of too much to say at once.

'Fuck, Dave,' she said, throwing a glance at the number on Pongrass's door. 'Never quite let go of our firsts, do we?'

Nayce shook his head; or his head shook itself. She'd told him, years ago, about Pongrass. Back in the country days, jolly hockey sticks, racing adolescent hearts. He'd as good as forgotten. She'd been twelve. He looked at the number on the door again: 1212.

'Yes? What is it you'd like to ask me?' Her white smile mocked him. She patted his forearm. He wanted to plant a bruise in her clay-coloured skin. Pongrass was right. Marriage, for some, can be a fatal mistake.

Janey let out a mock-growl. 'Go on, let the animal out, Nayce. Do yourself a favour. We, ah,' she threw another look back at Pongrass's door. 'We all need to be animals now and again, don't you think?'

Nayce watched Pongrass in the water with the humility of the defeated. It was almost a kind of love.

30

Pongrass was twenty-five minutes into his half-hour when Hut emerged from the bathroom. His primal scream at the start of the race seemed to have renewed his licence for frivolity; he cupped his hands and shouted at Pongrass: 'Just—Do It!'

He looked around to see who got it. But Blackman, whose eye he tried to catch first, was sitting, his pipe-cleaner spine bent forward, and frowning at his jiggling knees.

'Just—Do *It*!'

Nor were the others noticing him. They were studying the water abstractedly, lost in their own worlds. Where was the team spirit? Hut grabbed the SHARK sign off Jason and waved it in Pongrass's direction.

'Oi,' Nayce said, stepping up to Hut and grabbing the card away.

Hut's mouth grinned but his eyes were bitter. He spoke to Nayce for the first time since the volcano. 'Ar, lighten up, fuckhead.'

It was as he reached for the duckboards of the Aquasmith, making the contrary motions of lunging forward and arching himself steady against the current, that Justin Pongrass's misshapen first lumbar disc came good on the threats it had been making.

Blackman jumped into the water—'Go-go-go-go!' Rip shouted—and Jason dragged Pongrass out by the armpits. His face and neck, down to his collarbone, were the colour of thunderclouds. Jason propped him on the wooden seat in the stern and produced an oxygen bottle and mask.

'Where did that come from?' Book asked Jason.

'You all need it today,' Jason said without taking his attention from Pongrass, who flung the mask off in a writhing spasm, clutching at his back. His blue-shocked face contorting, he grimaced and whimpered. Jason knelt by him and murmured. Pongrass managed to nod. Jason refixed the oxygen mask to his face and pushed him onto his left side. Pongrass writhed again, maniacally, and flung a fist at Jason. But the boatman pressed him down, leaning on him with his chest as if restraining a criminal or madman, and with his free right hand started to palpate small tender spirals into Pongrass's spine.

The others sat in fright, trying not to watch or listen. Janey took over the minute cards. Every now and then someone glanced at the moaning Pongrass.

Blackman was nearly ten minutes in the water before Pongrass's face regained human colour and he was able to sit upright, Jason still by his side chasing the twitches out of the great slab of his back.

31

BLACKMAN'S HALF-HOUR lifted the Fast Set into the leading third. The swimmers were scattered across the strait—it was startling and not a little unsettling how divergently the pilots predicted the currents—but as Nayce scanned the water he could see that they were keeping up.

Hut was shouting hoarsely and cavorting on the deck, grabbing the others: 'We're gunna win, we're gunna win!'

He did not go near Nayce.

Good, faithful John Bookalil, Iron John, was up next. He perched on the wooden cockpit seat shaking violently, as if seized by malaria.

Sitting beside him, Nayce felt a rising emotion. 'All right, Bookie?' Never in thirty years had he called him Bookie. It was strange, sometimes, the things that came out.

Book hugged himself. Nayce resisted the urge to wrap his arms around his friend's quivering shoulders.

'N-n-no,' Book shivered.

Nayce laid a hand on Book's knee. It felt as clammy as an abalone. 'Shall I tell Rip you don't want to swim?' Yet Nayce, calculating that Book pulling out would hasten his own swim, could hear his voice betrayed by his half-heartedness, his cowardice. They were all scared now, going into the water like condemned prisoners to the gibbet.

Book shook his head with great force. 'I'm o-o-okay.'

'Good stuff,' Nayce patted his knee, but Book edged away from him. 'You'll be fine, mate.'

Book settled himself with a determined volley of deep breaths. Blackman's number had dropped to 7. Once he could stand, Book performed some shoulder and back stretches.

'That's great,' Nayce said encouragingly, but Book shot him a cold look. Nayce watched him stretch until Blackman's number was down to 5. 'What's up?'

Book stopped stretching and stood over him. He had calmed himself, but now that he was still again, the tremor started up in his jaw. His teeth clattered.

'That's what I wanted to ask you, D-Dave. What's up? Between you and Hut?'

'O?' Nayce said, raising his eyebrows innocently. Rarely could one letter of the alphabet feel like such a lie.

'I watched you talking to him. Up at the volcano. What did you say?'

'Nothing! Nothing to worry about.' One more, Nayce thought, and he'd hear a cock crow.

'Okay, keep your secret,' Book said dirtily.

'And you keep yours.'

'That was nothing to do with you, Dave.'

'And what I said to Hut was nothing to do with you.'

No place for a conversation like this. Blackman's card was down to 2.

'Right,' Book gave a withdrawing, hands-up grunt. 'Nothing to do with me. Fine. But you. Know what? There needs to be. Goodwill.

You get me? Goodwill. Here.' His chin was now chattering wildly and he was cutting his sentences into manageable parts. 'Or else. We can't have much. Going for us. As a group. Get me? Fuck I'm cold, my balls are like pistachios.'

Book skidded out of seriousness, as if overloading the moment might tip him over some edge. He had to be this way. Neither of them had forgotten the schoolyard thrashings.

'We'll be right.' Nayce aimed him a warm smile, but Book's white, plasticky back had turned on him.

Although, or because, Blackman swam well, he was hauled aboard the same deoxygenated violet as Pongrass, a ghastly bruise from forehead to shoulders. The oxygen mask was fitted and he fell half-dead against the bulkhead while Book posed for Janey's camera in a grim flex and took to the water.

Hut ran around the deck making jokes about Book's weight. It was true that Book had the aquadynamics of an ice floe, but his swimming technique was sound and, although he kept having to stop and hack his way back to the boat, the Aquasmith was holding position in the spreadeagled fleet.

'Look at it!' Hut cried. 'The great white whale! Ahoy, Captain Ahab!'

The others were paying little attention, either raggedly regaining respiration after their swim, or, like Janey and Nayce, staving off a rampant fear.

'Where's that shark sign?' Hut yelped. 'Hang on, we don't need it—even sharks have to watch their diet!'

After twenty minutes Book began to stop every few strokes to look forlornly at the boat and slug his way back. All his energy went into holding himself to the same place, and soon the boat was stationary. Nayce wondered if he should ask Rip to break his rule and go out towards Book, but Rip preempted him.

'I ain't goin' off course!' he called down from the wheel, singsong rather than snippy. If they had any ideas of bending him, he wanted to show how futile such ideas were. 'He comes back to me or he stays out there all night!'

The current had gathered strength as they entered the central channel. From here the strait was a great gutter sweeping from Cuba to the South American shelf. Nayce realised with a shudder that they had erred by having their strongest swimmers, Pongrass and Blackman, go first. It was all very well to get out to a good start and flatter themselves by keeping up with the faster teams, but now they were paying the price. Or Book was.

The mood in the boat slumped as other teams, other craft, overtook them. Blackman continued to receive oxygen. His colour had improved to an overcast grey. Pongrass wasn't yet able to walk.

Hut danced along the rails like a chimpanzee.

'Come on, sea slug! Christ, did anyone see a dugong float by?' As Jason climbed past him, Hut shouted, so loudly that everyone could hear, 'Hey dude, you're scoring us some coke for tonight, aren't you? You better get it out now and throw a line to the guy in the water—he needs it!'

That old Hut trait. Later he'd be consoling Book—'Mate, you and me, we're the ones who tried hardest'—but now he was nine years old again, glorying in another's failure, overjoyed to have company. A few minutes ago Nayce was regretting having been too harsh with Hut the night before. Now he regretted being too soft. The guy should not have been allowed to come on the boat.

'Carn Rip, you've got a little baggie up there, why don't you throw out a life-preserver for him?'

Rip beckoned Jason to the wheel. Without a word, the pilot climbed down the steps, bracing himself on the guardrails, stepped to Hut and bent down, one hand steadying himself on the deck, the other flopping across his varicose thigh. He said something in a low voice, leagues beneath the surface. Hut nodded once and swallowed visibly. He ruffled his red thatch and screwed his face, a simian mask thrown over the possibility of some other, involuntary, expression. Rip returned to the wheel. Hut didn't say another word while Book swam.

They had drifted into the last third of the field. Book breaststroked the final minutes of his leg. It took two men—Jason and Nayce—to lift him into the boat. Nobody remembered to photograph Janey before she cut like a scalpel into the heart of the current.

32

Janey used to run half-marathons. She'd competed in mini-triathlons. Once she had climbed to the lower camps of Everest. Watching her swim, Nayce remembered their first conversation about the race, more than a year before. In an unusually literal mood, she had tutored him about The End. That was what everything was about: The End.

'What you have to do,' she'd said, 'is switch off all the lights and go to sleep.' Having competed in all those endurance events, she knew what started to happen when your body went into severe oxygen deficit. 'It becomes a little like dying. Your consciousness comes loose from the clock. A minute can feel like a month, a second like a day. You enter the back rooms of your mind, and you've got to stay cool. If you're not careful, if you panic, you mightn't be able to find your way back.'

She knew what was in his mind. This swim was not a fending-off of death. It was the dress rehearsal.

He watched her from the deck with a nameless distress as she stroked through the water. Taking it easy didn't belong in Janey's vocabulary. She had to push herself right to the edge of peril.

She levered her neck upwards, face blackened with dead blood, and the sign was saying: 19. Nayce shivered. Janey's brain would now begin, as she'd put it, to die from the inside.

A victim of her sunny surface-gliding nature, Janey had seemed destined to be too happy for her own good: she'd coast along, ever bright and light, and realise too late that she had needs that were not being met. But now it dawned on him, what she'd been trying to tell him: she had already made her decision, already left him, given up on him, and was only on this trip to say goodbye.

When the card read 1 and Janey paddled towards the Aquasmith they were positioned across the middle of the strait with a freshening swell rising. Nayce was starting to feel seasick, or nerve-sick. Janey hadn't let herself go too far downcurrent of the boat. She couldn't hold their position against the leading groups, but she kept them on course. Nayce was tearfully proud, but the second he saw her come out of the water he was shaken. Janey collapsed, beyond irony, wasted, onto the deck. Jason placed the oxygen mask over her face but she ripped it away and puked on the duckboards.

Pongrass's colour and mobility had returned and he was consoling Janey, tenderly stroking her heaving shoulders.

In that last instant before he dived, Nayce felt both inspired and shut-out; the others formed a club, the club that had done the swim. Very soon he would be a member. If the gods were smiling on him.

But they might not. He plunged into the water and swam against the rising current of his bile and his fury and his jealousy and his regret, his fucking regret, a current that might, if it chose, take his ankle and pull him down into the green.

33

He parachuted out of his blazing body. He switched off the lights and went to sleep.

On summer holidays at the Pizza Hut, ever since the episode on the cliff at Barrenjoey Headland, Nayce wore a disguise. He could not forget how Ines Hutchison had stared at him as he crossed the rock bridge, blotting out her own son. They never went for another walk up the headland, and Nayce was glad for that: when you revisited mythic places the drop would not be dangerous at all, the rock bridge wide enough for a car.

But he had found inside himself a reserve that accrued each summer.

He was showing off for Mrs Hutchison.

As ten became eleven, and twelve, no matter what he was doing or where he was in the house, he was aware of what *she* was doing, where *she* was, to the exclusion of all else. No new mother could have been as aware of her baby as Nayce was of Hut's mother. Her trailing helplessness in domestic matters fascinated him. The meals she served were misfires, bloated with good intentions gone horribly wrong; she brought misshapen dishes to the table without comment or apology, disowning them as she set them out, as if passing on someone else's bad news. But discovering fascination for a parent didn't soften him. He was a teenage boy: strong new emotions flowed like tributaries into the swollen river of contempt.

He saw the way she looked at him, and learnt how to respond. He treated her the way her husband treated her. Ken Hutchison was what Nayce would later know as a *kiss-up, kick-down* kind of guy. In public, in front of their jazzy friends, Ken would sing Ines's praises to the sky, how beautiful she was, how sexy, 'how lucky I am that a Viking goddess would stoop to conquer a Cockney ne'er-do-well'. Their parties were an endless show, Ken crowing about his wife's magnificence, yet as soon as the guests left Ken was all carp and snipe. Ines had forgotten this. Ines had fucked that up. Ines had acted like a goose. Ines had said something so stupid he could only hope that they didn't understand her Kraut accent. She took the abuse with the same countenance as the praise: a million miles away, a wraith of a smile.

Because Nayce was with them after the parties, on the nights and mornings when they weren't living for show—because he saw what Ken really thought of Ines—he was tempted to feel he had become an insider. But he was cunning enough to know he couldn't take too many liberties; the moment he'd join in the teasing would be the moment Ken would go quiet and ask: 'What did you say to my wife?'

Unperceived by Ken, there was something else going on between Nayce and Mrs Hutchison which had started on the clifftop at Barrenjoey. He had got away with something undeserved. She had seen him as heroic in crossing the rock bridge while her son quailed on the safe side. He had bluffed her into believing he was something he was not. Was not yet.

The success of his bluff made him reckless. He wanted to keep getting away with it. She had always seemed to vest higher hopes in Nayce than in her son; now he set out to disappoint her. He was cold to her whenever she sought any softer connection. It was all too strange, an adult wanting to talk to him. He snubbed her. Like a man, he scorned her loneliness. If she feared growing old, if she mourned the boys' growth into men, well fuck her, he'd make sure she saw it happen, he'd rub her nose in it. He walked around the house without a shirt on and chose his routes to make sure she saw him. If he found her bikini hanging in the downstairs shower, he would soak and wring it, as if he could bunch the entire woman in his hands, and leave it thrown on the path outside so she would know it had been interfered with.

A shock: he was now approaching the age Mrs Hutchison had been back then. She had seemed so weakened by life, on the cusp of doddering; he refused to believe that if he met her now, as she was then, he would encounter a slim, blonde, beautiful and *young* woman of forty-four. But maybe everyone was younger these days.

When he'd strutted around the Pizza Hut as a surly, sweaty, silent boy-man, he had only the crudest notion of what he was doing. His only conscious aim was that she see him, notice him, and be hurt by him. He was discovering the thrill of causing an adult pain.

One night, at around eleven o'clock, he marched naked from his bedroom along the corridor to the children's bathroom. Everyone had gone to bed. Nayce made sure to take an unnecessary detour past the open doorway of the master bedroom. He was prepared to be seen by Ines, in his glabrous glory; he was not prepared to be the seer.

He steadied himself to march, cocksure, past the door. But as he stepped out, he heard something—a groan of unmistakable disappointment that sounded so strange to him that he forgot his little parade and threw himself behind the door frame.

Painted silver by streaks of moonlight through the two glass walls, Ken Hutchison, a compact bantamweight braced against the end of the bed, was fucking his wife. Ines lay on her back, legs folded in a limp mid-air crouch like those of a dead spider. Ken's neck was arched at the moon.

Ken rammed her—no other verb for it: Nayce had once seen builders making a rammed-earth wall—he rammed her, thighs slapping like fish in a bucket. Ken released subsiding groans of that odd disappointment. Nayce was twelve. He had never seen a man fucking his wife, or anyone fucking anyone, but he knew what was going on. Ken's groaning wasn't disappointment. This was fucking. This was it.

Ines's face was hidden, sheeted behind her platinum hair, ghost-grey in the moonshine. Her arms mirrored her legs, bent at the joints, suspended by the slack strings of a sleeping puppeteer.

It was the sound more than the sight that stayed with him. In years to come, Nayce would retrofit his memory with new experience. While the groans of coitus could sound deceptively like disappointment, and only a callow twelve-year-old could mistake them for such, just as a younger child might fear that the woman is being monstered and is crying out in terror, for all that, as he relived the scene over and over for years, relacquering the memory, Nayce would return to the clarity of his first auditory impression, his first emotional response; he came to a conclusion that it was indeed disappointment in Ken Hutchison's groans. From Ines he had heard nothing, a silence that echoed as durably as her husband's anticlimax.

There was one more sound as he backed away down the hall, glacially so as not to awaken a floorboard. He heard the smack of

Ken Hutchison kissing his wife: a loud smack, a large action, not unlike the large Ken-like wink Nayce himself had given her that distant afternoon at Barrenjoey.

The smack of a kiss, followed by the chirp: 'Cheers, pet.'

He couldn't imagine, if he hadn't heard those words, that the future would have ravelled the way it did. *Cheers, pet.* Two words taught Nayce the full measure of her suffering. He heard Ken through Ines's ears. He wanted to save her. He wanted to kill her husband.

It was three or four days later that the bottle-smashing incident occurred. The Pizza Hut backed onto a bush reserve, where after a post-Christmas round-up fifteen or twenty overflowing boxes of bottles were piled against the toilet block. Nayce had discovered the bottles, and after dinner beckoned Hut over the back fence.

They picked their way through the lantana and ferns up the gully path to the toilet block.

'Treasure,' Nayce announced when they came upon the bottles.

Hut picked his ears, as if he knew where real treasure was to be found. 'So what? Just bottles.'

Nayce walked over to the first box and withdrew a champagne bottle in each hand. He made as if to juggle them, like a pair of ninepins, but they clinked against each other and fell to the sandy ground.

'Tough glass,' he said, picking them up.

'It's coz people get so drunk they're always dropping them,' Hut said.

'You reckon they don't break?'

'Not easily.'

'How easy's easy? This?'

Nayce hurled one and then the other champagne bottle against the toilet block, careful to avoid the high window of chicken-wired glass. He was only breaking bottles, not vandalising council property. They smashed with a sickening dullness, like human heads.

'Beer bottles are easier,' Nayce said and reached into another box.

'Cool,' Hut said. 'But hey—if we get caught it was all your idea, right?'

Ignoring him, Nayce threw the beer bottles at the same spot; their brown rain splashed into the green puddle of the champagne bottles.

'Shit, don't.'

'Don't what?'

'Someone'll hear.'

'Who? Who's gunna hear?'

At the top end of the reserve, the land sloped sharply. To the south side, separated by a grove of palm trees, was the unoccupied guest wing of the Pizza Hut; to the north was an empty holiday house.

Inflamed by Hut's timidity, Nayce began to load up with bottles—beer, spirits, wine, soft drinks, but the heavy-bottomed champagne ones were the best and this was Palm Beach so the champagne dominated. He javelined them, discused them, shot-putted them, hammer-threw them, into the wall. The sounds they made, the thunderclaps of glass, were exciting; but most exhilarating was the endlessness of the supply. These Palm Beach wankers knew how to drink their holidays away; an entire beach had been blown into glass for them.

'We're just returning sand to sand,' Nayce said. 'C'mon, it's fun!'

Eventually Hut couldn't resist. He stepped forward and plucked a wine bottle gingerly by its throat, as if it were a dead bird. Nayce threw a beer stubby at the wall near Hut's head.

'Oi!'

'Get out of the way and start doing something, ya big redhead girl.'

Hut tossed his wine bottle; it broke lamely into six or seven curved pieces.

'Go pick it up,' Nayce said.

'What do you mean? It's smashed, it's in with all the other glass.'

'Go pick up the biggest pieces, and throw them again.'

'Fuck off.'

Nayce, a jeroboam in hand, strode up to Hut as if he was going to hit him. He hoisted the enormous champagne bottle above his shoulder. Hut cringed.

'You fucking wuss.'

'Shut up!' Hut said from behind barred arms.

'Here.' Nayce lowered the great bottle and held it out for Hut. 'I was just bringing it over for you. It's the A-bomb, it's Fat Boy. Fat Boy for fat boy. Do it properly this time.'

'Shut up,' Hut said again, lowering his arms and fingering the bottle as if worried about leaving prints.

'Make it go boom,' Nayce said.

Hut didn't take his eyes off the bottle. He carried it to the point under an acacia that Nayce had established as his oche.

'Fucking big one all right,' Nayce sneered. 'Bet you can't even dent it. Bet you can't even take a chip out of it.'

'Bet I can,' said Hut, with a tear in his eye. He wrapped both hands around the bottle's neck, as if it might explode in his hands. He started rolling it in slow circles. He stopped.

'It's heavy.'

Nayce stepped forward. 'You want me to show you how?'

'Fuck off!' Hut cried. He swung the bottle twice and in a teary rage launched it in a high arc. Pregnant with Hut's anger, it seemed to hang in the air and keep climbing, above the bricks towards the toilet block window against which it shattered into an epic green firework; glass hailed onto the cairn below the LADIES sign. More glass tinkled, unseen, on a cement floor. Where the window had been, chicken wire hung loose.

'Oh fuck.'

Hut dusted his hands and turned, expecting Nayce to start shouting at him. But Nayce was facing away from the wall with his hands stroppily on his hips. Hut followed his eyes. Standing in the neck of the pathway, in a yellow-check linen sundress, was Hut's mother. Her hair was drawn behind a band, and her face was naked of makeup. The latest Fred, worn out by the walk, fell into a wheezing heap at her heels.

'Oh no, Mum? It was him!'

Ines's face crocheted a mask of anger. 'Get out of my sight,' she said.

'Mum?'

'I'll deal with you later. Go! Get to your room!'

Hut sloped off, leaving Nayce with Ines in the clearing. Once Hut was gone—Fred panting along in his trail, loyal to whoever was going home first—Nayce relaxed and smiled. Just as on Barrenjoey headland, his first instinct was that he was in trouble, but he quickly realised that she was looking at him in a way that demanded words he didn't yet speak. Her hands, which needed something to do, patted each of her cheeks. Her eyes rose to the evening sky.

'The stars,' she said.

Nayce followed her gaze. Pinholes perforated the black sky. He had the feeling, persistent through boyhood, that the universe sat inside something brighter, that we were all bound up like hostages in a hessian bag.

'Can you count them?' she said.

Bloody Ines (he tried out her first name in his head)—dreamy as always. Vague. Spacy. She should have been ripping him apart, if she was any kind of mother. But this was a woman who . . . words came into Nayce's head, without yet being the right ones. There must have been things that she wanted, but to him she was an adult, complete and unchanging in her strangeness. Untouchable. What drove a grown-up? What drove a woman?

'Here, let's try,' she said. She came to Nayce's side and held his wrist. Her hand was dry and cold, his cold and wet.

'One, two, three, four . . .'

He pulled his hand away. 'I'm going back to the house.'

'. . . five, six, seven . . .' Her index finger danced above him. 'Do you know,' she said, and paused until he stopped walking, as she must have known he would. 'Do you know that if you gathered up sand from the beach into your two hands, the number of grains would equal the number of stars we can see on the clearest night?'

Not knowing what to say, Nayce shrugged.

'And did you know,' she went on, 'that the number of stars that exist in the universe equals all the grains of sand on the entire beach?'

He said insolently: 'What beach? Palm? Bondi? Seven Mile Beach? They're all different.'

A smile flickered across her moon-whitened face.

'And who's ever counted that?' he said. 'Who knows how many grains of sand are in a whole beach? And who's counted the number of stars? How do you know for sure? Sounds like bull to me.'

Ines reached her bare arms to the sky. 'That is the whole point,' she said. 'That is the whole point.'

No wonder Ken and Hut were embarrassed by her. Who'd want a space cadet for a wife, let alone a mother? She must be on drugs.

He wanted to be back in the house and in trouble the normal way, with a good talking-to from Ken Hutchison and a thrashing for Hut. They'd been caught smashing bottles. They'd busted the window. They ought to be punished. Nayce ought to be cowering in the house wondering how he could stop this getting back to his parents.

'Oh well,' she said. Her eyes fell to the pile of smashed glass as if just noticing it. 'I suppose if you counted how many pieces of glass you had made in that pile . . .'

'I'm not picking it up.'

A snort, a rare but frustratingly ambiguous reaction, escaped through her nose. 'Do you think that is what I am getting at?'

'I'm not picking it up, that's all.'

'Do you think I could make you?'

'I dunno.'

'No, really.' Her Rs had a glottal hoick, German. She was a Kraut like in war movies. She stepped towards him and took hold of his two wrists. 'Do you think I have any power to make you do something you don't want to do? I am not your mother. I am hardly even Jeremy's mother.'

Later, Nayce would replay these words and wonder if he was being lured into the beginnings of some kind of existential inquiry. But at the moment it was happening, he was still a little boy—or reverting to a little boy again—and he failed to locate the gravitational centre between Ines and himself.

'Okay,' he said, wary of the adult turn the conversation had taken. 'I get it. I'll pick them up if you don't tell my mum and dad. You promise?'

Ines shook her head, disappointed. But at what? With what?

'You won't promise? Come on!' he heard himself wheedling. Disgusted with the speed of his capitulation, he said: 'Okay. I'll pick them up. And if you tell my parents, I'll never come on holidays with you again. Okay?'

Ines smiled forlornly and shook her head, as if asking: *What have I ever done to you? What have I done that you should treat me like this?*

Reading her thoughts, or even discovering that he was trying to read her thoughts, threw Nayce into a panic of evasion. She wanted something from him. What? He lacked the courage to ask. She freaked him out. All the parading, all the merciless, tough poncing half-naked through the house he'd been doing, and he was the one getting freaked out. Did she want him? It was too big a thought, too close, blurring beyond the edges of his vision.

He knelt by the pile of glass and started pushing sand towards the centre. He had an idea of scooping it up with the empty boxes. He used the bottom of a box as a bulldozer, like a kid playing in a sandpit. He was working away frantically, in the yellow toilet-block light, when there was a rustle in the bush close behind him. He jumped and gave a yelp.

It wasn't her. It was a fruit bat taking off from a fig tree. Mrs Hutchison was nowhere to be seen.

When he was sure she was well gone, he cupped his hands and called out, with a snarl: 'Cheers, pet!'

He'd have laughed too, if he could. But a certainty was descending, a correction, as if a beloved schoolteacher was standing over him and asking, generously but with undisguisable disappointment, *David, David, could you have got everything more wrong?*

34

DAVID NAYCE WAS no Olympian but he swam like a dolphin. The Aquasmith overtook two rival boats and came abreast of the blue-clad Australian women's outfit. The sight of Nayce powering against the current, stroking for his life, his bald prow parting the water, revived his team-mates. Pongrass, Blackman and now Janey had regained colour and could contemplate swimming again. Book still sucked oxygen from the tank. Wherever they finished, they must beat those women. Nayce had led them across the worst of the current, and from here the going would get easier.

Pongrass and Blackman, having shed their doubts about surviving the day, began to think about the night. Rip and Jason had promised to deliver seven grams of It. All morning, the boys had stopped themselves thinking about the night, but now that the team was headed for home—you could see the flags on the Sandals beach now—their morale freshened. When Pongrass bent over the prone Book and said, 'Don't worry mate, It will make you better,' even Book raised an injured grin.

Rip kept quiet at the wheel. Jason ran around the deck.

Pongrass and Blackman toasted Rip in Gatorade as their saviour and provider. They were two and a half hours into the race.

No decision had been taken on whether Hut was going to swim. Pongrass and Blackman would have said no, categorically no way. They didn't want to fall behind 'those Aussie fronties'. Janey and Book were concerned for Hut's health, but would have sought a more diplomatic way of exercising a veto. Hut would have seen by now that he was not fit enough to swim—it was obvious—so they would have let him make his own decision, withdraw without losing face.

But a strange thing happened aboard the Aquasmith. The team's morale had re-inflated so quickly during Nayce's swim that Hut felt encouraged. And Hut needed no encouragement. He was on a high: a personal high; a righteous high. He stripped down to his lean new shape and stepped out of his shorts. He flexed his arms. Jason flipped the '2' card over Nayce, and the Fast Set was level-pegging with the women's team. Unnoticed, Hut stepped onto the stern duckboards and winked down at Book.

Book tilted the oxygen mask up from his mouth.

'You're not.'

Hut pulled his goggles over his eyes and gave Book a thumbs-up.

'Ready to roll.'

'Hey,' Book said. His teeth were chattering from loss of oxygen. 'D-Don't.'

Hut gave him a rich smile and said: 'You'll get over it.' Hut could buy and sell Book once a month and still have change. 'You're just having a bad lactic acid trip.'

Book clasped his shoulders to stop himself shaking.

Hut forced out a laugh as sincere as a press release and skipped, shadow-boxing, on the duckboards. 'Look out there,' he pointed to the mainland, still some way distant. 'Trust Papa Hut. I'll bring the mainland, still some way distant. 'Trust Papa Hut. I'll bring this baby home.'

Book glanced over his shoulder towards the others. Nobody seemed aware that Hut was about to jump in.

Hut flexed some last stretches, then crept behind Book, reached out and patted him on the neck. Hut had forgotten the first rule about living with John Bookalil, who, startled by the touch, whirred up and around and flung a balled fist. The oxygen bottle tipped onto the deck. Book's punch swung clear of Hut, who stood still and smiling, palms flattened against the air, a hologram of reassurance.

'Steady mate. It's meant to be fun, isn't it?'

Book, trembling, blue in the face, stared at Hut in confusion. His nerves, like those of airliner passengers who scream at the sound of a raised voice, seemed not to allow any space between composure and blind panic. Hut wore a look of indulgence and perhaps disappointment that Book had missed him. As if he'd provoked the punch on purpose.

'S-Sorry, Hut.'

Hut's eyes clung to him stickily, then his face cracked into a monkey-puzzle of laugh lines. 'Sorry for what, mate? Sorry for what?'

The '1' card went up. Distracted by Nayce's powerful closing sprint, the team members lost count of the minutes and did not notice Hut taking his own photo, holding the camera at arm's length. He didn't have the boobs or the guts of the other boys. He was in the best shape of the lot. As he stood snapping himself, with It as good as in the bag, with Pen on her way, Hut felt as good as he had back at Sydney Airport, in the First-Class lounge. The success of it all.

When Nayce touched the boat it was as if his fingers pressed an ejector button.

35

He'd always been able to swim. His parents had a big pool, and took beach holidays twice a year. He remembered the breathe-bubble-bubble singsong of his swimming teacher. He must've been, what, five or six when he first did lessons? He knew the principles. Breathe, bubble-bubble—breath, bubble-bubble . . . Breathe . . .

The '28' card caught his eye, and he wasn't feeling a thing. Nearly a tenth of the way through! Cruising! He thought, in a delirious moment, that he saw a dark shape. A shark? No, it must be the boat. He swam on, powering, discovering his rhythm.

On the Aquasmith, Rip was ranting.

'Wasn't he fucken listening? I said stick to the boat!'

Hut disappeared into a trough, then rose above a swell. Within the first minute he'd drifted a hundred metres down-current of the boat. If anything, his rate of disappearance was now increasing.

'He going straight to Venezuela,' Jason said. 'Maybe he go there for his drugs.'

Rip rounded on the team. 'Who the fuck told you you could have a sixth swimmer anyway?'

Nobody answered. The ginger-tipped white shape bobbed on the occasional swell, diminishing into the past like a birthday snapshot. Not three minutes in the water, Hut was half a mile away, borne on one of the earth's most reliable undertows.

Rip stepped up to Nayce, who was sitting on the duckboards sucking oxygen.

'Fucker,' Rip said. 'He's yours.'

Through eyes dimmed and ancient, Nayce saw Rip's blurred shape. He tried to shake his head but barely shuddered.

Hut loved swimming; always had. He felt the pleasant strain seep into his arms and legs. He felt his stomach muscles, his new six-pack, tighten up, take shape. No pain, he thought, no gain. It was all about buoyancy: you planed above the water. He'd been to stroke-correction lessons. You tickled your fingers in straight lines above the surface, writing in water, and did your work beneath, pushing the liquid behind you, firm hands pressing it down from the line of your ribs to your hips.

Alone with his body, free, splendid in the wild, he decided to step up his pace and go for broke. He felt that good.

His father had taken him to his first swimming lesson, a memory that opened a door: the recollection (and it did seem like a memory) that he had a father, always up on the latest—like a kid!—and his latest latest was text-messaging.

KenH had texted Hut with the news that. The news that. Better in KenH's own words:

Fred has bowel cancer. Not to worry. They caught it early. Procedure tomorrow. Dont call. Enjoy your holiday. KH.

The horrible thing was. The horrible. Of all the horrible things, it was the self-satisfaction he could imagine on his father's face as he sent the text. Ken was impressing his son with his grasp of the new technology. How many of Hut's contemporaries' fathers could do the same? Not Bill Nayce. Not Joseph Bookalil. Probably not Hilton Blackman or Duncan Pongrass. Ken was in constant competition with the CFs. The Contemporaries' Fathers. His fondness for coining acronyms: more striving to stay young.

The message's brevity was also horrible, though it would be more horrible, in future, when Ken got the hang of abbreviating words as well as sentences. What next? *Fred ok. Op a suxs. CU soon?*

And then it would be Hut who was ready to die.

He could see his father thumb-typing, a gruesome smile playing on his lips. Fucking with Hut's head.

Dont call.

Ken, Dad. He'd done it on purpose.

'Fucken idiots,' Rip said into his goatee. 'Fucken amateurs. Jesus!' He slammed his hand into the GPS and told Jason to bring Blackman and Pongrass up to the wheel. Pongrass was kneading his spine.

'Now listen,' Rip said. 'I'm not meant to leave a swimmer unattended, but this is the way it's gonna work.'

Blackman and Pongrass exchanged a look.

'We're going to leave him behind?' Pongrass said, with the hesitant grin of a schoolboy hearing, but not quite believing, that the teacher has given him a green light to beat the shit out of the class chump.

'Don't tempt me, you crummy bastards. Pretty Boy,' Rip nodded at Pongrass, barely able to meet his eye, 'you're the number one here. You're gonna go in now and do ten minutes. Try your best to stay on line. I'm gonna take the boat over to get the Orang-Utan, and then come back for you. You okay with that?'

'What's the alternative?' asked Blackman, scanning the deep for tiger sharks.

'The alternative,' Rip said, looking over Pongrass's shoulder, 'is that you call the whole thing off now and disqualify yourselves for breaking race rules.'

Pongrass hobbled down to the rails and jumped in, bobbing up every few strokes to keep an eye on the mainland shore. The effort to stop and look wore him down, and he too began to drift, his face twisted by the pain in his back. The boat left him, veering off course towards Negociante, back the way they'd come.

Hut had entered that dreamy state of the long-distance swimmer, counting out each stroke, hearing and seeing nothing but bubbles in his face, when he thought he'd look up to check on the boat.

His first reaction was that the bastards were playing a prank on him. The boat was gone.

His second thought was that the dark shadow he'd been seeing wasn't the boat.

He panicked. He stopped swimming and his lungs began to beat their own quick time, to hyperventilate. His head swung around—no boat, no boat. He'd been left alone in the middle of this channel. The cunts, they'd left him for a laugh. When he was swimming so well! What were they doing? What the fuck was going on? Was there a shark? No—the boat had disappeared, the boys had decided to blow him off. Like the other night, when they'd abandoned him in Kingston. He was a burden, an albatross. He always had been. To his father, to them. And now they were letting him know. They had dumped him here in the middle of the ocean. Could they do that? *They knew*. Maybe in their twisted heads they thought they were doing it for his own good. They'd been talking behind his back. Jail: none of them could face it. They'd decided to save him from his future, cut him loose. That was it. They were faking his disappearance for him.

His breath accelerated, air gulping itself into him, against him, reversing belches. His throat constricted in spasms. He swallowed water. Negociante, Jamaica, Caribbean, the Atlantic: the globe expanded. He was not going to make it home. *Home?* His eyes rolled into the back of his head, and a thought reintroduced itself from the wilds, from the depths: *I have nothing left.*

The boat crested a wave and they came upon him treading water towards South America. His face was not blue with oxygen loss but pale with fright. His jowls sagged; his fat ruby lips were distended. His rusty hair separated across his crown like a '70s centre-part. As Jason lowered the engines and brought the Aquasmith alongside the swimmer, Rip said: 'Aw, the kid's crying.'

Nayce, who'd been ready to give Hut an earful, changed his mind when he saw him so distraught, grief-stricken, tearful. Gently, brotherly, Nayce helped him onto the duckboards.

Jason turned the boat back towards the course, to rescue Pongrass.

'Hey,' Nayce said. 'What doesn't kill us . . .'

He trailed away, sounding hollow to himself. His pat phrases, all the little tics and reflexes of friendship, belonged to a discarded time.

Unlike the other swimmers, Hut didn't collapse onto the deck. Broken, but not by exhaustion, he shook off Nayce's helping hands and tottered into the cockpit. He said nothing, didn't raise his eyes. He sat. As he covered his head with his towel he saw Rip's clock. Hut had been in the water for six minutes.

36

Soon after the Fast Set crossed the finish line, a forty-four-seat twin-engine turbo-prop touched down at Michael Manley International on the far side of Jamaica. Roy and Charlie, docile with exhaustion and the pipettes of Phenergan their mother had droppered into their juice, hung from Pen's hands at the baggage carousel. Pen was not a believer in drugs for children, but nor did she believe in martyrdom. At times during the two-day journey, her dearest wish was to be able to give up those two monsters like a destitute girl surrendering to an adoption agency. Pen loved them, of course, but one of motherhood's many surprises was how love could be poisoned with moments of unspeakable intolerance. How could a mother hate her babies like that? Was it normal? She didn't know, didn't want to know. What she did know was that some day they would repay her in kind.

Feeling she must look like a refugee from some natural disaster, she slopped out of the terminal. The dozen taxi drivers milling around a cold-drinks stand on the concourse looked even more travel-weary than herself. She went with the first who would agree to the five-hour drive to Negociante Bay. Five hours of freedom and then she would have to surrender to the group, those appalling people, her husband's friends.

The boys melted into the back seat and slept. Pen rested her head against a window and rode its vibrations. The minivan broke free of Kingston's outer slums and Pen allowed herself a smile. It was going to be hard, but after everything she was due some kind of recompense.

37

'AND IT WAS John Bookalil who had the honour of the final ten-minute leg and the glory run onto the Sandals sand. Thanks to Justin Pongrass's bold second swim, bravely defying a crippling back injury, and another powerhouse effort from Andrew Blackman, the Fast Set beat off the Australian all-frontbum team, rounding the orange marker buoy in twenty-third place. Bookalil overtook yet another tiring competitor on his blistering final beach sprint. The Fast Set were utterly spent, but had enough breath to cheer their team-mate home. When Bookalil chested the tape, his comrades leaped off the mighty Aquasmith and splashed their way victoriously ashore.'

Nayce's mock-commentary on the race's closing stages, issued over a celebratory round of electrolyte drinks on the grassy dune between the resort and the beach, omitted to mention that the comrades who leaped into the bay left one of their number onboard. While the others mobbed Book at the finish line, Hut was quietly helping Jason and Rip clean up the mess of plastic bottles, tape, numbered cards, leaflets and wet towels dumped around the boat. In shorts and T-shirt, he looked schoolboyishly spruce with his hair combed across his forehead. During the frenzy of the closing legs and the crescendo of cheering, he had hidden in the dark cabin. Only Janey had looked in on him, to see his head buried inside his towel, elbows on his knees, chin cupped in his hands. But she hadn't had time to say anything. There was too much excitement up on deck. Not a word was said, then or now. The five were posing for group photos on the dune, airbrushing him out.

Rip sat by the wheel re-counting the money he'd been given. It was the full five hundred dollars, but he shook his head and said to Jason: 'Fifteen hundred for the coke they want us to get them, bro, but not even twenty bucks to say thanks for today.'

Hut wanted to say he would tip Rip personally as soon as he got back to the hotel, and tap the boys for an even bigger tip later tonight when Rip dropped off the It. But Rip was too stirred up and Hut was afraid to speak. To Rip he was not there.

Back at the hotel, an esprit de fatigue descending on them, the team showered and went to their rooms. All but Hut would be leaving Kingston on a six o'clock flight the next evening, so there was time for a nap, then one celebratory all-nighter before a late-morning drive across the island.

They all napped, except Hut, alone in the family suite, room 1216. He lay on the double bed and stared at the stuccocrete ceiling. Pen would, or might, arrive later, and they could have some time as a family. He ached for her as he'd once ached for his mother. Four days on this island could do it to you. Four days for him to get back to where he started.

He closed his eyes and tried with all his might to put himself to sleep.

The Fast Set woke from their naps in a sullen temper and mooched around the swimming pool. The hotel food plumbed new depths, the bain-maries pooling a sick brown. Nayce had even lost his appetite for utter chicken. As evening fell, hands slapped mosquitoes off faces, necks and legs with a kind of self-flagellating lust. Blowing from the dormitory settlement at the base of Mount John, the breeze smelt meaty and decomposed. Pongrass kept ringing and messaging Rip and Jason, sweatily muttering as he punched his PDA like an auditor who kept getting the wrong sum.

'Greedy bastards, they're thinking we should've fucken tipped them more,' said Pongrass, forgetting that they hadn't tipped them at all.

The Fast Set drank, but the Mai Tais only dulled and flattened them. A presentiment of middle age took hold of Nayce. Trying to stir up teenage blood brought out a weariness. *We are the old men our fathers were when we were teenagers.*

At eight o'clock, Pongrass swore at his PDA, shaking the device as if it were at fault, and said he was giving up. He sighed to Blackman, resuming his subject as naturally as if they, everyone, had been talking about it all along:

'Ever tell you about this thing I had for eastern Mediterraneans: Turks, Greeks, Lebs? I was going through all the races of the world, you know, like colouring in the atlas. Travel the world by front-bum! The inkiness of their hair, you know, that flawless olive-oil skin—Arab, Semitic bints really turned me on. I liked the ones with big noses, bulgy eyes, those huge black upturned bowls of eyebrows. When I saw a Turkish flag, like, I rotated it in my head so that crescent moon became like an eyebrow, the star an eye.'

'Very artistic,' said Janey, her natural huskiness over-salted, wrecked by the sea.

'But you get bored with perfect skin,' Pongrass said, angling his eyes at Janey, a personal rebuke. 'Brown nips: flawless, yeah, but lifeless. So for every action there's an equal and opposite reaction, yeah? I developed this thing for like pink sensitive nips, freckly goose-bumpy flesh. Scottish and Irish girls. I started to go for flyshit-face redheads. When I met a frontie, I hadn't said hello before I was running a book on the colour of her nips—5/4 on pink, even-money brown.'

Janey leaned across the table and said gravely, 'Justin. Don't you ever get bored with all your firsts?'

'Hey, there's always new frontiers,' he said, encouraged. Janey continued to look at him earnestly. He bit down like a trout on a fly. 'Frontie-frontiers! Everything can be a first, if you take the right attitude to life. This is what I don't understand about people who say fucking, good old fucking, one-night stands, are empty and hollow and repetitive.'

'Who would ever think that way?' Janey said, widening her eyes. 'They're just envious. You lead a life that would be any man's dream, Justin!'

'Right! It's a failure of imagination,' he said grandly, a pleased smile skidding across his chubbily retracted handsomeness. 'If you know what to look for, there's always something to take away, some memory, something a little special. You never lose your faith in another first around the next corner. I live in hope. It keeps me going.'

'Hoping for what?' Janey said.

'More of the same!' Pongrass spread his arms, like a king hurling out an order. Janey's attention had turned the tide of his bad mood.

She leaned closer, lowering her voice intimately but making sure the table could hear. 'Justin, don't you ever ask yourself, only yourself, mind you, in your most solitary moments . . . Don't you ever ask yourself if you aren't looking for something, you know, a little *extra*?'

'Sure! I took two fronties, ah, excuse my French, two *ladies*, upstairs from my hotel bar one night on a rowing tour—let me tell you about my first trio!'

Janey narrowed her eyes, a steadiness easily mistaken for flirting. Nayce, trying to hide the ferocity with which he was watching her, ordered more drinks.

'That wasn't what I meant,' she said.

'I know it wasn't,' Pongrass said with a brightness laid over sourness laid over nastiness: a club sandwich of motives. 'So why don't you let me finish?'

He went to pat her cheek. Janey flinched out of his reach.

Nayce felt suicidal. In front of him, in front of all of them: pillow talk. Janey and Pongrass were doing pillow talk. Nayce wanted to pick up a cane chair and smash it over her head. He hated her. He said it to himself, under his breath. *I hate her. I hate her the most.* It swelled in him as a gushing relief. Finally, the truth.

'So we'd been getting down to business for a little,' Pongrass spread a smile around the table like a croupier dealing cards, settling his gaze finally on Janey, 'and they both wanted me to give it to them Super-A. Know what I'm saying? So I did. And it was good. It's always pretty good, A. We had a good time. So then, we were fooling around a little more, and they'd both been a bit coy about their, you know, their parts, didn't want me touching them, but I pressed on and fucking hell, whaddaya know, my mitts stumbled across something I'll take to the grave. *Fuck this!* I did my block. *Get the fuck out, both of you!* They threatened to beat the shit out of me unless I paid up, and being an honourable man, I did. So,' he said, turning fully to Janey, his smile wide, his eyes riverstone-black, 'I go down to the team breakfast next morning and look around the table and then I go: "You'd never guess what, boys—last night I fucked a bloke! A *backie.*"'

He grinned, rubbing his chin. His face was pallid around the gills, still affected by his oxygen loss on the boat. Blackman, inscrutable—was he shaken? had he heard this before?— picked at his fingernails. Nayce wondered if Pongrass had lost enough oxygen to suffer some kind of minor brain damage, popping loose some valve.

Pongrass sighed, lips vibrating. 'I never told them I'd fucked *two* blokes. That might do me some harm. I mean, the boys were very good about it. Everyone knew there were dangers of mistaken identity, and sometimes these chicks with dicks are so gorgeous they really do make you think twice about whether it mightn't be all worthwhile.'

Janey's irises were isolated within white frames. She looked at Nayce, whose heavy-lidded mandarin blandness was a sure sign of strong reaction. Book could hardly wind his jaw off his chest. Blackman shifted in his chair, almost—here was the unbelievable thing—almost embarrassed. Now Pongrass engaged Janey's eye. For a beat, a high-voltage crackle across the table brought hairs to their ends. Janey was the first to drop her gaze, to her brown trembling knees.

'The great thing about all of you,' a drop of mercury ran through Pongrass's voice, 'is that you know two-thirds of fuck-all about anything, so it's too fucken easy to give your chains a little tug now and then. Fuckheads. You're too easy, the lot of you.'

They sat by the pool until the steel band packed up. Pongrass's phone refused to rescue the group from their festering silence. Nayce wanted nothing to do with those fuckwits. Pongrass could stay there and yank his own chain.

Nayce and Book decided to go out for a jerk chicken dinner. Nayce said he had to go to his room for a jumper. Book went to wait for him in the lobby.

'I think I'll just go to bed, take an early one,' Janey said.

Nayce couldn't look at her. She could get fucked too. Except for Book, they could all go fuck themselves. He bit viciously into his cheek and said: 'You're assuming you were invited.'

In the lift he felt light-headed. Was it fatigue or relief? He felt he was watching himself from outside, a bald man saved from his foolishness in the nick of time. Fifteen years late, but still.

He walked down the corridor to his room, weaving from side to side as if drunker than he was. A needle of a headache poked between his eyes, and he stopped, shoulder to the wall, sick. Old regret bounced back at him like Ali at Foreman. His nature had been playing rope-a-dope with him. He wanted to turn back. This was it. In a fit of petulance he was throwing away everything he'd ever wanted.

'What was all that about?'

He turned. Her adorable face smiled at him, its old openness returning. She ran both hands back through her hair. Her dark-blonde tresses fell loosely behind her ears, and she folded her arms. She'd followed him up here. She loved him. *What was all that about? I was just asking myself.*

'What was all what about?' To keep his face hidden, he worked his key card into the lock and pulled it out too quickly. He kept fumbling it until the door opened. Janey kept silent, knowing he could not resist speaking.

'Oh. Right. That? Your "early night".' He made quote marks with his fingers. 'Like "I'll go out for a walk on the beach", right?'

'Try not to be a bastard. For once in your life.'

'I'm a bastard? I don't think I'm bastard enough.'

'What's that supposed to mean?'

'What do you mean, what's that supposed to mean?' Nayce turned his face from her; his confusion, he knew, was advertised in his eyes.

'Do you think he's okay?' she asked.

'Who, your buddy Justin?' he snapped.

'Hut.'

'What the fuck has this got to do with Hut?'

Janey's face fell. 'It's like we're all stuck in a bad marriage.'

'Surely it can't be that bad,' Nayce tried to laugh. 'I speak from experience here.'

'Fuck off, David.'

'Okay. I'd love to fuck off. Thank you. And you can go and take your "walk", and say hi to old Pong for me.'

They faced each other in the door—framed—Nayce neither in his room nor out of it. It came to him that Janey had chosen the corridor for protection. She had to say something—to leave bad blood puddling around the dinner table was too awful, too *unusual*—but to confront him she had chosen a place that was purpose-built to stop confessions, or if they had to happen, at least they could not escalate. They wouldn't want to go back to Sydney and start rumours, would they? They'd have to craft their public relations policy carefully and with a unified front. Because that was the main thing—that was always the main thing. A unified front. Fuck her. Fuck her.

'You've broken my heart,' he said.

He could not see Janey's bowed face. She held her hand like a visor.

'You,' he swallowed. 'You and . . . the other night . . .' He could not bring himself to say Pongrass's name.

'You're such a fucking shithead,' she said.

'Me? Why is it always I'm the shithead?'

She kept her eyes on the carpet and her face screened. 'You think I'd go and . . . do something with him? You do, don't you?'

'You told me you did.' Nayce could hear himself whining, pettish. He wanted to smash his own face in.

'You believe what you want to believe, David. And you want to believe the worst of everyone.'

'So why can't you just be straight with me? Why can't you tell me what's going on?'

'Oh, fuck off. Go away.' She was equal parts irritated and tired. 'That straight enough for you?'

'You're the one who followed me up here.' He heard how childish he sounded. 'Christ, Janey, you're so fucking sarcastic all the time.'

'Oh, you poor thing.'

Now he saw her face, and his own tears responded to hers, like a toddler who cannot let another cry alone. He knew what she was talking about now: what they had been talking about, not talking about, for fifteen years.

He could manage no more than a whisper. 'I want to go back there. Janey. I want us to . . .'

Janey shook her head and laughed through a swollen figure-eight of a mouth. Her red eyes narrowed on him with the first honest expression he'd seen from her in years, and it looked a lot like loathing, the special kind of civil-war hatred reserved for friends and family.

'You do, do you? You want to go back there? Well David, I hate to be the one to tell you, but there's no *there* to go back to. There never was. You want me to be straight? Okay. I was bullshitting you. I was bullshitting about Justin the other night—the fact that you think I'd touch that creep is insulting enough—but that's the way it's always been.'

'You were bullshitting.' Now he wanted to shake her, grab her shoulders and shake her until her head came off.

'You want me to be straight with you? Okay, David. Straight. I'm full of shit. Sure, we're mates. Ha! Mates. I guess we are. We see each other whenever I'm back in Sydney. But that's all. I'm not what you want. If you took a minute to know me, rather than know your little fantasy, you'd know that.'

'*My* fantasy? I'm living in a fantasy world? Yeah, like I'm Cinderella below decks waiting for Prince Charming to come and save me.'

Nayce stood on his dignity, but his dignity wasn't there. He felt he was falling through the door, the floor, into the pitching sea. Nauseated, he steadied himself against the frame.

She tossed her chin. He was boxing out of his division. 'You're unhappy with your marriage, you want a change, you want to turn back the clock? That's just beautiful, mate. Your fucking fantasy, holding a candle for me. It's all yours.'

Nayce slid to his haunches. The fatigue of the race hit him like a shovel to the forehead.

'David, I don't want to be mean, but you asked me to be straight with you. I haven't let Justin Pongrass touch me since I was a girl. Once was enough, I assure you. Why did I say what I said? To wind you up. I like winding you up. I'm sorry. It's a fault of mine. I'm not really very nice. Okay? I'm sorry. But you know, it's gone now, it's dead and buried. You still have this idea in your head that you and I can sort of go back there, but life's not like that.'

She crouched down with him. In response, Nayce let his bottom slide to the floor.

'You're such a fucking *idiot*, you know that?'

'But you love me,' he said with weakening hope.

'No. I don't,' she said, softening. 'Listen. You remember that thing?' As she looked up it seemed that the whites of her eyes trembled with the vibrations of an oncoming storm.

'What thing?'

'That thing. You.'

'No, I don't know what you're . . .' But as he said it, he did know, and he did not complete his sentence. His humiliation. All right.

Taking pity, she changed the subject. 'I'm not Cinderella. I like the way I've got things sorted. I like travelling, I like not being tied to a man. I don't want kids. I told you before, I'm not waiting for you to come back to me and I'm not waiting for anyone else either. I've made my life, and I like it. You, on the other hand—Dave.'

She took his hands. He couldn't look at her. 'You seem to think you can keep all your options open, like your life's still there for the choosing. You think you can just wipe out the last fifteen years, and your marriage, and your son, and live out some sort of movie script with me. You still think you're twenty-five years old and you haven't committed yet. Well let me tell you, Dave, you have. You're forty. You are what you've done. You're a married father of a beautiful little boy. You'd probably love your wife if you gave yourself a chance. Your options aren't open anymore, okay? Forget about me. I'm not here for you. I'm not what you want. Fuck! Why do you have to make me say all this? *Why?*'

Down the corridor, a door creaked open. Hut, red hair still plastered across his forehead, peered out. He was wearing the new red-and-gold Hawaiian shirt he'd had on at the volcano.

'Sure it's interesting and all that for you two, but it's our last night. Wanna hit Slashing?'

Janey was blowing her nose into a tissue. She raised her free hand in apology to Hut, who stepped out and smoothed his hands down his front.

'Coming or staying?' Hut curved his words through an expansive grin.

'Not Slashing,' Janey said with a tepid smile. 'Crashing.'

'What about the big night?' Hut asked, adding, not quite jokingly, to Nayce: 'You fucking pussy.'

'You can come out with Book and me if you want,' Nayce said, an uninviting tartness around his lips. 'We're having a quiet one.'

'You kidding? This is It! Tonight's the night!'

Janey shook her head. 'It's all off. The deal didn't come through, and everyone's buggered.'

Hut began to say something but reconsidered, shooting Nayce a cruel grin. 'Whatever. I'm going down to see how the boys are doing.'

'Hut?' Janey asked. 'You okay?'

'Top of the world,' Hut winked and made a clucking sound. 'Couldn't be better. You kids make sure you have a good time. And Dave? Don't be too hard on yourself. We all have a *thing*.'

Janey mopped her eyes and gave Nayce, who was still sitting on the floor staring at the wall, a gentle kick in the thigh. She bunched the tissue and threw it at him. He watched it bounce off his chest into his lap.

'I guess it makes the trip worthwhile, anyway. Clear the air,' she said, giving a full-stop to the way she extended her arms above her head. 'You'd better not keep Book waiting anymore, he'll be asleep down there.'

Nayce felt again the mass he had been carrying on his own for all these years . . . Janey was right. It was over. The thing, the sex thing: when Nayce had made love with Janey, he had taken a masochistic pride in never coming before she did. It was his way, as a young adult, of defying the badness of men who took, took, took their pleasure from women. Thieves. He prided himself on being *the generous lover*. He strained against himself like Atlas. To make sure Janey got hers. She told him it was wrong, perverse, insane. She didn't want to fuck a martyr. This only propelled him further: eventually he was not only holding himself back until she had come, but he was holding himself back for good. He fell in love with the pain he could inflict on himself. He wanted to be, purely, a giver. Janey could never persuade him that to take could also be a form of giving. He couldn't get it. Locked in his own Presbyterian atonement, messianic inside his stupid stubborn head, believing he could make a sacrifice for all men, he couldn't understand that none of this made him in any way better.

Janey had finally exploded, saying it was excruciating, it was like he was fucking himself. Then Ines Hutchison—of course, of course, the holder of the key—had told Nayce to go and get

312

himself a girlfriend, and Janey stepped aside for Sophie. Nayce fell for the bluff. And with Sophie, Nayce had unfolded himself, allowed himself to take, became a husband—joined the thieves.

Nayce sat in the corridor for a long time after he heard Janey go.

38

WHILE PONGRASS AND Blackman cocktailed their way towards consolation, Hut walked three blocks from the hotel to a service station. The blue Toyota Hilux was already there, waiting by the air pumps.

'Hey, thanks for doing this,' he said, climbing in. 'The boys are gunna love me.'

Jason nodded and, directing his gaze out the driver's side window, slipped the wrap of foil across the front seat. Hut pocketed it and handed over fifteen hundred American dollars. Jason coolly counted the notes.

Hut rolled the cigar-thick wrap in his fingers. 'This is It,' he said. 'This is awesome.'

Jason rolled up the cash and slid it into the breast pocket of his knit shirt. 'You don't want to be having any of that,' he said.

'Eh?'

'You don't want to be having any.'

'Yeah, good one,' Hut grinned.

'Listen, mon.' Jason concentrated his gaze through the windscreen. An empty tourist van drove into the service station and the driver began filling up the tank. 'Only you friends have this. Not you.'

'What the fuck—I'm the one who made the offer, I'm the one who's come and done the deal, buddy, so I'll decide what to do with it. See ya later.'

'You! Australia!' Jason gripped Hut's forearm and pinned it to the centre console. It was odd hearing himself called by his country's name. To Jason, that's what they must have been: Australia. 'I'm telling you, this serious. Rip, he not happy with you and you friends. Rip says you all go to hell. You know what'm saying?'

'He can go to hell too!' Hut said. 'I've paid good cash for this, and not without a premium, so Rip can stick it up his arse.'

'Yah, Rip he can stick it up his arse,' Jason nodded, inspecting Hut's arm which he still held to the console. 'I tell you this so you be warned. Arright? You listen.'

Twenty minutes later, Hut found Pongrass and Blackman supine by the pool. The breeze had swung around to the north, off the bay now, and the air smelt of saltwater, motor oil and chlorine. Blackman's polo shirt was rucked up over his stomach and he panted slightly, like a dog in the sun. Pongrass was staring up at the stars while the ice tinkled in his glass and his free hand caressed his hair. Hut strolled up like the returning conqueror.

'Boys,' he said. 'Voila.'

He slapped the wrap down on the table.

Pongrass sat up.

'Ah! You're alive!' Hut beamed.

Pongrass leaned across and picked up the wrap. 'Is this what I think it is?'

'This is everything you hope it is,' Hut said.

Blackman grabbed it off Pongrass. 'Is this It?'

'This,' said Hut, 'is it.'

'Oh man,' Blackman said. 'I take back everything I ever thought about you, Hutchison.'

Hut nodded, imperiously, and turned to Pongrass for his tribute. But Pongrass had the wrap in his pocket and had sprung to his feet, already halfway to the lift.

'Well?' Pongrass said. 'You blokes coming up? Palais Royale is only open another six hours.'

'You two go ahead,' Hut twinkled. 'I have to go to my room for a minute.'

In his suite, tidy and clean for Pen and the boys, Hut sat at the writing desk and placed in the ashtray the second wrap, into which he had decanted half of the fifteen-hundred-dollar deal. Pongrass and Blackman could do what they wanted tonight, but Hut needed some quality time on his own. He poured two scotch miniatures into a large glass and opened his PDA.

He started typing:

My love, my Pen, my Penelope. It's the end of a big day. You won't understand why I've done this, but I guess I need to unload a few things and I can't do it face to face. You'll understand why. You know I'm a coward.

He paused to compose his words. His mind was clear on what he had to do. He took another sip of scotch and emptied the plastic bag of white powder onto the glass-topped desk. He got up and turned on his television. He rifled through the channels. He sat back down at the desk. It was all in his head; he only had to get it down.

The envelope popped up: mail. Keen for distraction, Hut flipped to his inbox. The sender: RipVan@aol.com.

well congrats you fuckers. you finished the race even tho you cheated. some of you were ok dudes but all in all i can think of better wayz to earn 500 $ than spend my day with a bunch of aussie yuppys specially the lazy redhead cunt who thot he woz goin so fast swimmin happily off to s.america. we didnt leave him for the sharx tho coz thats AGAINST THE ROOLZ!!!!

not that that matters to you prix. but we left the captain swimming alone like bait while we had to get 'the other' guy ie the 'bignoter' as me and jase call him. what in fuck were you dudes doing with that redhead cocksucker??????

he couldnt swim and held up the shark sign like a fucking 5th grader and got in the way and then kept on jases back about scoring him fucking drugs all day. like yeah were really gonna go find some coke for you for 1500$ when you cant even spare a SINGLE MEASLY $ for a tip despite you all being bigtime yuppie millionairs.

how do i know your all millionairs???? who do you think was in my ear telling me how much $$$$ you were all worth????? and how much $$$$ you earn??????

well bigshit bignoters. your not all losers but the ones or one of you who has a big L on his fore head knows exacly who he is.

anyway it was great to meet you—NOT.

hope to see you again next time—NOT!!!!!

yours, Rip.

ps Jase sez he got your phone messages and his reply is gfy which is local for GO FUCK YOURSELFS

Hut read and re-read the email. He put on CNBC and watched the financial news but couldn't concentrate. He went back to the email and read it again. Then he flipped back to his Compose Message screen and tried to continue writing to Pen. But he had nothing to say: a message to Pen seemed pointless now, a pathetically empty gesture. He poked the little teepee of white powder with his index finger and sucked it. Sucked It. Sucked shit. It wasn't going to be pretty. He pushed it around with his room's card key; but first things first.

He re-read the other text from today in his inbox, from his father.

Ken had been texting him frequently, and not just to show off his mastery of the form. For as far back as Hut could remember, Ken had acted out two alternating roles: total stranger and best buddy. For much of his childhood and adolescence, Hut had simply not seen his father, either because Ken was travelling on business or because Hut was busy with school, or because, when they were in the same house for a holiday or a chance encounter, Ken treated him like a junior member of the household staff whose name he would remember in one second. And then, overnight, Ken would become someone different. He would teach Hut how to play cricket, ride a horse, swing a polo mallet. He'd buy him his first computer and encourage him to play games on it rather than study. And then the next day, Ken would again be the distantly congenial yet supercilious employer. Hut had stopped asking himself guiltily what he had done to offend his father to precipitate these withdrawals of affection. It was just the Ken Hutchison way.

When Hut was at uni, during one of their bosom-buddy phases, Ken had hit on his first girlfriend. No subtlety: he marched in on them on the leather couch in front of the living room TV, ordered Hut out to get some cold beers, plonked himself in his son's place and installed his hand on the girl's thigh. Too scared to scream, she had frozen while Ken—who must have been early fifties at the time—tried to give her an exploratory peck on the neck, just to see what happened, forceful enough to show he was serious yet minor enough to be brushed off as a joke if need be. Hut arrived back in the room to find the girl bouncing to her feet, dusting herself off and making excuses to go home. Later, Ken told him what had happened. 'I can't bring myself to lie to you,' he said, itself a lie given that the only reason he had hit on the girl was so that he could tell Hut. 'But don't worry,' he said. 'They're like buses. Always another one coming round the corner.'

If Ken hitting on his son's girlfriend was a declaration of some sort, it was not so much war as the extension of an existing conflict onto a new front. A part of Ken believed the only way to inject Hut with competitive fire was to crush him down. Girls were simply one more game in which the son would do well to learn from his old man, and where the old man would humiliate him before turning around and becoming the sweetest dad on earth.

Fred has bowel cancer.

Hut wasn't fooled by the tone of stoic cheer. There was no put-on jauntiness in his father's text. The jauntiness and the cheer were real.

Back in those uni days, Ken had styled himself as something of a pick-up guru. His sole subject of conversation was girls: chat-up techniques, conquests of yore, the ones that had got away— a running commentary on the passing parade. He talked about women like some kind of monomaniac, a compulsive trapped into a groove. The only woman Ken never talked about (or to, much) was Hut's mother. On weekends he cocooned himself against her by inviting guests—the Hutchison manor was always noisy with friends.

Ines was by no means guiltless in this show. She cared for her husband as little as he cared for her, with equally punctilious observance of the social graces in front of visitors. They had an arrangement. She had always enjoyed, or accepted, her privileges. She went out with her drug-sweetened friends and spent her money and involved herself in her interests. For all Hut knew, she picked up men. If she could be bothered. Mum's one preoccupation in life was to tide herself through to night-time without having to think too much about her faithless husband, her son, her empty self.

Fred has bowel cancer.

Ken's armour of conviviality would survive Fred being diagnosed with or even dying of cancer.

Hut had long outgrown the illusion that his parents loved one another and was fast closing in on the conclusion that they never had. Ken and Ines had constituted nothing more than an alliance for the production of an heir and the maintenance of the pile. They'd finally made it: they were the rich.

Fred has bowel cancer.

Fred, Fred, Fred.

He could see his father thumbing, a gruesome smile playing on his lips. Fucking with Hut's head.

Don't call.

Here was the problem. Fred was the family dog, a basset hound now nearing twelve. The original Fred was meant to be a beagle, but Mum had fucked it up at the vet's and got a mooning basset instead, belly scraping the carpet, jowls painting the floors. Fred, Fred, Fred. How many Freds? The latest one had a dietary problem, an appetite issue: once batteries, once a pack of cigarettes, once a bottle of penicillin. He'd blown up like a sack of onions and the vet had said, 'Either of two things happen to dogs who eat penicillin. They either break out in hives—as Fred has—or they drop dead. You should count yourselves lucky.'

It was only natural that Fred should get bowel cancer. At his age.

But here was the real problem. Nicknaming was one of those little daubings of family cement. Fred. Fred.

There was no way of telling, from his father's tone, whether the text was referring to Fred . . . or *Fred*. He could see Ken at his PDA: speaking of Fred as of some elderly relative.

Fred's time was always limited.

Fred had a long innings.

Fred was comfortable to the end.

The prepared lines were all ready, scored and chopped and ranked across the table.

Which Fred?

And he'd done it intentionally, Hut knew, to fuck him up.

To call his father and ask for clarification was unthinkable. He was meant to know. That was the whole thing about families: if you needed the in-joke explained to you, you weren't really in on it, were you? If Hut called Ken and asked *Which Fred?* those two words would become a family story for the ages. He'd be the butt of every joke from now to kingdom come. '*Which Fred*'? *Did you hear what the kid asked?* '*Which Fred*'?!? *Priceless!*

Her empty self? Not quite. He shouldn't have gone that far, thinking about his own mother. Maybe not empty. Maybe a tumour.

Ken. He'd done it on purpose.

6

All-inclusive

39

SHE HAD NEVER expected it to be quite so beautiful. Some names—
French Riviera, Costa Brava, Jamaica—seemed chipped away by
over-use, left out in the sun too long. The two-lane browntop
crossing the island threaded villages of blue stucco and timber,
shutters carved like lines of a stately dame's handwriting, red
iron roofs, gables crowned by heavenly praise. On the kerbs red-
smocked mothers sprouted from their greens: spinach, limes,
melons, emerald bananas. Shopfronts indicated their wares with
naive paintings, bowls of food traced by black brushes, clothes
hung on stick-figure men. No pavement was uncracked, but the
painted facades of the wooden buildings were splendidly fresh.
As dusk softened the illumination, everywhere, even where there
was neither village nor people, even on the slopes of pineapple
plantations and in the shade of a volcanic plug, came from the
belltowers of churches. Where all else was darkness, churches
glowed. There must, she thought, be a church for every mother in
the country.

Her boys sprawled on the minibus seats, brought down by their
payload of Phenergan. There is a moment when children become

so tired that they are capable only of sleeping or rioting. She had earned their sleep; though when she contemplated the future too closely she had to suppress a wish that the boys would wake and riot and reel her back into the present.

The minibus delivered Pen, Charlie and Roy into the Sandals porte-cochere two hours before midnight. She felt nerved-up and over-bright; it was one in the afternoon back home. Pen paid and tipped the driver, tipped the porters, tipped the man who opened the hotel door and gazed down meltingly at her sleep-puffy redheads.

At the check-in desk, she asked for a key to Mr Hutchison's room. The night concierge said he couldn't hand out keys without the occupant being notified, so Pen asked him to phone up.

'It is very late,' the concierge said.

'Please, we've just come from Australia,' Pen said, nodding to Roy and Charlie slumped against their bags.

The man held the phone to his ear, pressed a number, shook his head.

'Mr Hutchison is not there.'

'He's probably asleep. Listen, can I please just go up?'

'These are resort rules.' He ran his thumb down his computer screen. 'We have no reservation for extra persons in that room. It is only Mr Hutchison in occupation. Would you like me to call my supervisor?' The man's eyelids undraped a little in anticipation of the pleasure of breaching his superior's peace.

'What do you mean? He's my husband—he'd have left instructions for you that we were arriving!'

The man read his computer. He pressed a button, read some more, then pressed another button. Without looking up he said: 'No instructions.'

Pen felt herself coming to the boil, but there was a cry of surprised pleasure from the lobby and she turned to see Janey Quested running towards the children, arms spread.

'Some real men, at long last—thank God!'

Janey bent to cuddle the two little boys. Pen's journey hurt her between the shoulderblades, and she felt her eyes seeping.

'It feels like forever,' she said.

'You're here now, you're here now,' Janey said, holding the boys' hands and guiding them all into the lobby lounge.

'So how's it been?' Pen whispered. She didn't know Janey sufficiently well to lunge into the female confidence she'd have liked, but she was desperate. What Pen wanted, urgently, was a two-minute update of the kind only a woman could give her.

Janey raised her eyebrows. 'It's been . . . interesting.'

Pen put a hand on Janey's arm, but Roy cried out and both of the women bent down. One of his shoes had fallen off. Pen let Janey take it, unlace it and refit it to Roy's foot.

'So how's it been for you?' Pen said, loading her question. How had it been as a woman?

'Oh, the usual,' Janey said, breezily across the action of tying Roy's shoelace. 'They manage to be rude to everyone, and I smooth it over. The Jamaicans think that if I'm with these guys, they can't be all bad.'

'And are they? All bad?'

'Nah, they're cool,' Janey said, her lie so plain it started to break like a wave across her face. Things weren't all that bad. They were worse.

Walking across the marble floor into a darker, carpeted lounge, Pen was frightened by Janey's demeanour. This hard little brown nut who'd always intimidated her, who seemed more one of the boys than the boys themselves, was putting everything she had into not weeping. 'Me being here—I'm their licence to behave like shits. Here. Look at these two.'

On facing naugahide couches in the lounge, David Nayce and John Bookalil were sitting in their blue Fast Set T-shirts. Book gave a purr of delight to see the children, took them on each of his knees and made faces. No words could better have expressed how he was missing his daughters. Shy with sleep, Charlie and Roy hid their grins behind their hands. Nayce, Pen noticed, hung back.

'They won't let me have a key to our room,' Pen said. 'They phoned up to Hut, but I was telling them he's probably just asleep.'

She saw Janey and Book swap a look.

'What? What is it?'

'Oh, nothing,' Janey said. 'Hut's gone out with the others, Justin and Andrew. They'll be back soon.'

'With *them*? It's pretty late—when did they go out?'

'I went and took a walk,' Janey said. 'Then I came in and found these guys just now.'

'Ah, we went out for a light dinner. At about eight?' Book questioned Nayce for a nod of confirmation.

'Why's he out with *them*?' Pen's eyes sought help from Nayce, who was studying the sparked glow of what appeared to be a fire out the window, beyond the pool.

'New best friends,' Janey said. 'You know what he's like.' Before Pen had a chance to absorb or query this, Janey went on: 'We're all pretty tired after the race.'

'Oh, of course!' Pen said. 'So how did you go? Well enough to be wearing those ridiculous T-shirts!'

Pen gave a brittle laugh, but noticed that again Janey and Book seemed to be watching each other, agreeing on a version. Nayce was still detached, hovering on the fringe.

'We went great,' Janey said, but her eye-sockets were bruised and there was something guarded in her tone. John Bookalil, trying his best to amuse the boys, had the hollowed-out look of a grandfather.

'Did my husband stay afloat?'

As synchronised as a choral duet, Janey and Book burst into a song of too-loud hilarity.

'He went great, he went great,' Janey said.

Pen again sought David Nayce's eye, but he was changing the subject.

'Book, why don't you two take the boys up to our room. They can sleep there tonight, there's heaps of beds,' he said, turning to Pen. 'And you and I can wait down here for Hut.'

'You're sure they won't let me into our own room?' Pen said. 'This is ridiculous!'

'Believe it or not, they're quite strict on their house rules,' Nayce said. 'I've been trying to get ladies of the night up for a party all week, but it's no go.' He made a paltry run at a smile.

'Bloody Hut,' Pen said. 'When will he grow up and be reliable for once?'

'That's a lot to ask,' Nayce said.

'I think it's a great idea,' Janey said, though the stiff way she stood showed that she was suffering. They were all middle-aged tonight. 'Book and I can put the boys down in our room, and give you a break.'

Pen bent to Charlie and Roy, who were hiding gleefully from Book's faces. 'No, thanks, I want them to get a good sleep. It's okay.'

'What, and deprive me of my regular dose of other people's children?' Janey said. 'I'm suffering withdrawals here!'

'Oh, twist my arm,' Pen said, her face settling between a frown and a smile. 'I guess I'm owed a pina colada.'

40

CHARLIE AND ROY went without a backward glance, and Nayce led Pen to the late-closing outdoor bar. He ordered a cocktail and a Red Stripe, and she followed him outside across the pool patio to a wooden gate, which he opened with a four-digit code.

'Leave your shoes here,' he said.

Pen kicked off her espadrilles. Her feet felt like zeppelins. She followed Nayce up a short sandy path between palm trees, over a slight dune and onto a crescent of beach, pewter in the moonlight. To the right was a jetty and a marina, to the left a craggy headland.

'Nice haircut,' she said.

'You like it? I've been thinking it was a mistake,' he said, compulsively rubbing his now-stubbled head.

'You're right,' Pen said. 'You've turned yourself from a reasonably good-looking guy into something, I don't know, criminal.'

'Ha. I don't think Janey liked it either,' he said heavily.

Nayce gave a cough, and finished his bottle of beer on the third swig. At the base of the eastern headland, a bar emanated a hooting human treble over a 4:4 thud.

They walked to the edge of the water, a buffering smell of rotten palm trees, seaweed and diesel oil. Pen read her watch. It was deep into tomorrow back in Sydney. She covered a yawn and swirled her cocktail. 'This is going to finish me off.'

'Nah, nah, nah,' Nayce grabbed her wrist in a rough, brotherly way. 'You don't have a bed to go to. Come on, let me show you the marina.'

'I don't know.'

'Just thank me that I'm not dragging you to Slashing.' He nodded towards the thumping beach bar. 'It's owned by Lawrence Welk, you know.'

'Who?'

'Jamaican Test cricketer.'

'Somehow I think you've got that a little bit wrong.'

'Oh well, some day I'll care.'

They walked to the wharf's chickeny neck. Nayce held Pen's half-empty cocktail glass while she climbed over the steel guardrail, then she helped him follow. They stepped down the wooden jetty. Boats rocked in their sleep.

'Good flight?' Nayce said, woodenly.

'Forty-eight hours with two toddlers?' Pen shrugged. 'Life doesn't get any better.'

'Right,' Nayce nodded seriously. 'It doesn't, does it?'

Pen pushed him in the arm, to make him listen. His distraction scared her.

'David, where are you?'

'Me? Right here!' He gave her a pleasant smile, coming-to. But he couldn't hold it. His face darkened again. 'You know,' he said, 'you saved him. When you married him, you saved him.'

'Oh? From what?'

Nayce wanted to say: *From me.* From what had happened.

But this was not for Pen. Nayce hugged his sides and stepped to the jetty's rim. Certain things he had to take home with him, and certain things he had to leave in Jamaica.

'This is where we left,' he said. 'Before six o'clock this morning. Seems like a week ago.'

At the steps declining from the end of the decking Pen sat down and dangled her toes in the water. 'That's better.'

Nayce sat, his thigh touching hers. He had sunk beyond weariness. With everything else, there had been the self-imposed effort of respecting Book's reticence and going through dinner without probing him about Hut. In response, Book had elected to say nothing. Nayce was still shut on the outside.

'So,' she said. 'How did the race really go?'

'Great. We came twenty-third. More to the point, we all came back. It was tough.'

'You know what I mean.'

'Ah.'

'How was he?'

Nayce massaged his scalp and ran a tired sigh between the tip of his tongue and his teeth. 'It hasn't been Hut's best week.'

'I got that feeling.'

'You'd better ask him.'

'What am I going to get out of him? "It's been great, had a ball!" You know what he's like. I'm the last person he'll tell.'

Nayce sighed again, blowing through rubbery lips.

'Let me give you the short version. He got into a bit of trouble one night in Kingston. Then he got into a bit of trouble in the warm-up swim. Then he got into a bit of trouble the first night here. Then we went up the volcano, and he got into a bit of trouble there. And then we had the race, and well, that's when his troubles really got started . . .'

'Stop it.'

'You asked.'

332

'I asked for the truth, not some comedy routine. You're as bad as he is—everything has to be a joke.'

'You don't want to know the truth, Penelope.'

Pen hawked up the last of her cocktail through her straw. Slashing was growing rowdy. Someone had brought speakers and a car and set them up on the beach; a reggae beat bounced off the igneous headland.

'You're not a very good friend to him, are you?' she said.

'How's that?'

'What's he doing out with those cokeheads tonight, those arseholes? Why isn't he with his friends?'

'I guess you'd better ask him that.'

'How was he—really—during the swim?'

'You sure you want to know?'

'David.'

Nayce told her, without gilding the lily, how Hut behaved in the race. How he horsed around with the cards, how he raised the false shark alarm, how he made fun of everyone else but particularly Book, and how he nearly derailed the whole venture and put Pongrass's life at risk by swimming away with the current. Nayce did not tell her how quiet Hut had gone afterwards, head in his towel, and how he had withdrawn alone to his room earlier in the evening.

'So. He made a fool of himself,' she said.

'Oh no. He'd already finished making a fool of himself. This was just the cherry on the icing.'

'You really aren't a good friend to him.'

'It's my fault for trying to talk him out of the swim? It's my fault for trying to get him to train for the last six months? It's my fault he wouldn't listen when I told him this was exactly—exactly—what was going to happen?'

'Calm down, David. He's so easily led, you know that. I

shudder to think what he's up to with those fuckwits.'

'I'm not his babysitter, Pen. This is the guy who sets out to insult our friendship at every opportunity.'

'You know he doesn't see it that way. Don't twist it.'

'Oh, sure, he's not malicious. Hut's never malicious. He's got a good heart. It's like—you know what he said to me the other night? He had this just-fucked radiance about him because he'd been allowed to hang out with bloody Justin Pongrass for an hour before those pricks dumped him in Kingston. They dumped him. But you know what he said? He said: "You know, people from our background are just . . . nicer".'

'Present company excluded.'

'Well yeah, that's what I'm saying. We forgive Hut anything because he's so optimistic and generous and he's got a *good heart*. He forgave those guys, so we all forgive him. Everyone gets away with everything. But has he really got a good heart? Has he? Or is he just desperately scared that anyone's going to think ill of him? How long can he keep getting away with everything because he's *likable*? When does he start facing up to his own responsibilities? How long is it before someone says, Hut, we don't give a shit whether you've got a good heart or not, because beneath the good heart is . . . a . . . I don't know, a . . .'

'A perjurer.'

'Yeah right, and that's just the start . . . What did you say?'

She wouldn't repeat it. She sat and watched the water, considering the word as if she had thrown it in: *perjurer*. It sounded technical, non-venomous.

'Apparently he's about to be charged with making false statements about some of the companies' financial positions,' she said mechanically, exhaling.

'False statements? Hut? No, I'd never believe it!' Nayce laughed, then winced. 'You're serious, aren't you?' There were everyday white lies, garden-variety business bullshit, but there were also people you didn't lie to under any circumstances. 'Who did he make the statements to? Someone bad?'

Pen nodded in glum assent.

'Who?' Nayce repeated.

Pen's Adam's apple bobbed over an audibly dry swallow. 'You didn't know?' she said.

'Ah, the others, Book and Janey, were talking about something . . . But no, nobody would tell me. Pen—who did he lie to?'

'ASIC.' The securities regulator. 'They interviewed him over some irregular share trading. I don't know what he was trying to hide, but whatever it was, apparently he saw fit to tell them a tarry-diddle.'

Nayce felt stung by the condescending way she was telling him, as if explaining to a child. 'Under oath?'

She nodded.

'Fuck, that's criminal. You're sure?'

'So I believe.'

'It actually means,' he let loose a shrill laugh. 'It means he can go to jail?'

He could see, from a loosening in her neck, that she might not have wanted to tell him but her body was nevertheless relieved that she had.

'*Fuck*ing perjury!' he spat. 'Fucking bullshit!'

'I'm sure that's what Hut thinks too. Knowing Hut, he probably can't quite believe that lying to ASIC is any more serious than, I don't know, lying to his wife.'

Nayce found the flat, even pulse of her tone unsettling. Pen seemed cold, as if watching from the outside. Keeping him away from the core of it.

'You haven't spoken to him yet?'

She gave off a humourless laugh. 'He ran away with his mates rather than tell his wife. He probably thinks he can fix it all without my knowing.'

'How *do* you know?'

'His father told me.'

'Does he know his father knows?'

She raised an eyebrow. 'Hut wouldn't know if his arse was on fire. And it is. It's blazing.'

'Jesus, Pen. This is bad.'

'Well,' she said, frosty towards him—adult, more adult than Nayce, in the way Book was. This was knowledge that killed off innocence. 'It answers your question. How long can Hut keep getting away with it? Until some actual physical force—say, the law—catches up with him.'

They sat on the jetty, fishing without lines. Nayce twiddled his fluorescent wristband. A mother-of-pearl mist was settling on the bay, drawing in the horizon to give the scene a stagey closeness. From the hotel behind the dunes came a clatter of crockery, as penetrative as a sudden truth that had been under their noses all along. Nayce thought about Janey, how stiff their encounters had been. Book, too. It was all over. Things would look very different when they got home. Pen's arrival, an outside pair of eyes, was already making things look different here: a lot less flippant.

'He really fucked up on this trip,' Nayce said.

'Have you always been this angry with him? He's been your best friend for, what, nearly thirty-five years? Is this always the way you've been?'

Nayce feigned a coughing fit, buying time, then shrugged. 'I've spent my whole life being angry with him, then having all that anger fall away when I see him. It's like he robs me of it. And his doing that only makes me madder.'

'He worshipped the ground you walk on, David.'

'Ach. That's just his way of disarming me.'

'And when you die, this will be the way you look back on your best friend.'

He scratched his head and rubbed his fingers together. 'I'm dying every day,' he said.

Pen got to her feet, uninterested in hearing Nayce talk about himself. Aboard one of the boats in the marina, a light switched on, then off.

'He's got to be back now,' she said irritably, as if whatever was going wrong was all Nayce's fault.

41

THEY PICKED THEIR way around the jetty's loose boards and up the
sand path. Nayce punched the four-digit code into the keypad
and led Pen back across the pool patio. When they entered
the ground floor of the hotel, something seemed reordered. An
unnecessary number of lights were on, and instead of the one
somnolent concierge at the desk, six or seven uniformed staff
crisscrossed the foyer. Nayce and Pen rounded a corner into
the desk lobby and saw an ambulance, lights mutely rotating, in
the porte-cochere.

The lift bell rang and the metal doors opened. Out of the lift
came two paramedics pushing a person covered to the neck on a
gurney. Following them, ruined in a towelling dressing gown and
shorts, picking his nose unselfconsciously like a small boy, trailed
the ursine wreck of Andrew Blackman.

'What's happening?' Nayce grabbed Blackman's arm.

'Jeremy!' Pen ran to the gurney. But as she lunged at it—the
paramedics accelerating it past her—she saw the face. It wasn't
Hut. It was Justin Pongrass.

'What the fuck happened?' Nayce asked Blackman.

'Oh dude,' Blackman shook his head. He smelt of spirits and chemical piss. 'It wasn't It, it was shit.'

'What?' Nayce pinned him by the elbows against the concierge's desk. Pen came briskly, her face wrestling with itself. 'Where's Hut? What have you done with him?'

Now there were staff rushing across the floor, holding urgent conversations. The paramedics loaded Pongrass into the ambulance. The driver revved the engine.

'Man, it was shit.' Blackman complained, holding his ribs. 'I need another ralph.'

They found a couch. Nayce and Pen sat on either side of Blackman, who slumped against the cushions deep-breathing with his eyes closed.

'Just tell us what happened,' Nayce said.

'Oh, you fucking arseholes . . . !'

Nayce caught Pen's rising claw before it could slash Blackman's face. He held her while Blackman let out his story in dull tone-waves.

'We went up to the room. We were getting ready to go out, we did a couple of lines. Pong went first and he just sat down sharp. I did two, bang bang . . .'

He stopped, made a square mouth and wriggled his jaw from side to side, palpating it with his hand. 'I need a glass of water.'

'Fuck that,' Pen said. 'You piece of . . .'

Nayce squeezed her wrist. 'Just tell us what happened, Abo.'

'Dunno,' Blackman hacked up phlegm; swallowed. 'Next thing I know it's . . . what time is it now?'

'It's just past eleven.'

'Right.' Blackman nodded as if he already knew it. 'That's the night then. I passed out. It was only nine or something. Then I wake up and Pong's in the bathroom on the floor with blood and shit running out his nose. So I called downstairs . . .'

'Where's Hut?' Pen said. 'What have you done with him?'

'It was shit, not It.' Blackman, fogged, shook his head like a quiz show contestant who had stumbled at the last question.

'Andy,' Nayce said. 'Abo. Just listen. You're okay. Pong'll be okay, right? Just tell us what happened to Hut.'

'The fuck would I know?' Blackman scratched his armpit. 'He was the one who gave it to us. I never saw him again.'

Pen stood up and said to Nayce, 'I can't listen to this man.' She marched to the reception desk and clapped the bell, striking it as if hoping to break something, the bell or, preferably, her hand.

'So Hut didn't go out with you?' Nayce asked Blackman.

'Fuck no. We never went out.'

'Think hard now. Was Hut with you in the room when you did the lines?'

'Fuck off,' Blackman said painfully, his eyes wrinkled shut. 'He was the one who scored for us, the prick.'

'So where is he?'

'The fuck would I know? We went to our room. He was going to his room then coming out with us. Oh dude, my head.' He was speaking in slow, hazed motion, the words limping out.

'Piss off back to bed.'

'Is Pong okay? Man, I need some water.'

'You just look after yourself, buddy,' Nayce said, grimacing at the redundancy of his suggestion.

Nayce left Blackman and walked to the reception desk, where Pen was trying to compose herself while demanding the key to the Hutchison suite. Eventually the concierge relented, but said he would have to escort her.

Nayce, Pen and the concierge rode up to the sixth floor. The concierge couldn't have been more than eighteen. He had a pad of beard, like a protection against wear and tear, on the tip of his chin. When the lift doors parted, Pen ran ahead down the corridor.

She tried to run the card through the slot but kept fumbling it. 'Shit! Shit! It doesn't work!' The concierge took it from her and slid it slowly.

Suite 1216 was dark, and the concierge lit it while Pen and Nayce ran from room to room calling Hut. The bathroom light showed around the frame of the closed door; Pen pushed it, heart in mouth, fully expecting to find her husband face-down in the tub. It was empty. Nayce looked under the beds and in the wardrobes.

The concierge waited by the room door, arms folded. 'I could tell you he's not here,' he said.

'What's this?' Pen was at the glass-topped desk. Beside a row of empty sample bottles of spirits was a smear of saliva and white powder. Nayce put his fingertip to the smear and tasted it.

He nodded to Pen.

'Oh no,' she said.

'I've only ever tried it once, but . . .'

'Shut up! Shut up!' She clutched at her hair, ripping out her scrunchie as if it had been the problem all along. 'What's this message?'

Pen was bent at the desk chair. Upon the cushion Hut's PDA lay open.

Nayce came behind Pen and read over her shoulder.

'What is this?' she said, a crack through her voice like a pull in fabric. 'Who's this Rip? Why's he saying . . .' She read on, lips moving with the words as if stress and panic had sucked her back into childhood. 'Why's he saying this about Hut? Who's Rip? Oh my God!'

She fanned her mouth as she read.

'Oh, how can . . . ? God!'

'Come on,' Nayce coaxed her to her feet. 'Hut's not here.' He hauled Pen away from the device, to the door. 'We'll find him.'

The concierge held the door open. 'I tell you he not in here. I see him earlier tonight. He go for a swim.'

'What?' Nayce grabbed the man by the lapels. 'You saw him go swimming? You fucking deadshit!'

'What time?' Pen screamed in the concierge's face. 'What time did he go out?'

The man's eyes memorised Nayce; he said nothing until Nayce let go of him and Pen backed off. Rich, spoilt, stupid Westerners: Nayce wondered why the man would tell them anything. This was the black man's consolation, wasn't it? For everything? How could he ever resist the opportunity to exploit their fear, to return the favour? With grave dignity the concierge led them out of the room, closed the door and measured his pace along the corridor to the lift. He pressed the button and spoke without facing them.

'More than one hour ago. Late to go swimming, I said.'

42

At the ground floor, Nayce said, gnawing his lips: 'I'm sorry, sir. Sorry I grabbed you. But can you please tell us—this is our friend—this is her husband . . .' He indicated Pen, who had run to the lobby phones and was pressing numbers. 'This is serious, sir. I'm sorry if I touched you . . .'

'Okay, *sir*,' the concierge said, flinging the word back like a counterfeit coin. 'But I have to go back to work now.'

He sauntered to his desk, every muscle a sand grain through an hourglass. Nayce crossed the marble floor to Pen.

'You're sure?' Pen said into the phone. 'We don't know . . . David and I are going to go looking . . . Are they? Good. Oh, Janey, I don't know . . .'

She plugged the receiver down like a stopper, as if to prevent herself from coming apart. She took a moment to adjust herself, pushing bangles up each wrist and tucking her dark hair behind her ears. Eyes closed, she took a breath, then fixed Nayce with a crooked, old smile. 'At least the boys are happy. Janey's put them into bed. They haven't moved.'

'Right.'

'So where do we start looking? Where would he have gone swimming?'

'This way.'

They went out through the front of the hotel. The ambulance had pulled away, empty, and now the night staff were huddled around a coughing Jamaican laugh, end-of-the-world humour, under the portico.

'What happened?' Nayce said, looking after the ambulance.

'You friend, he mess up,' one of the staff said, singsong. 'But he okay. He sleep it off in the hotel sick bay.'

'They didn't take him to the hospital?'

'He be fine by the sun-up.'

'Have you seen our other friend?' Nayce asked the ring of faces. 'The one who was with them? Red hair?' He mimicked a clown's frizzed wig.

Grizzled heads shook; bony shoulders rose and fell. 'He go feed the sharks,' said a uniformed porter.

'Come on,' Nayce took Pen's arm. They ran across the road and into the park where Business and Respect were lying in the minivan. Marley sang them their 'Exodus'. A mighty spliff ebbed. When they opened the window and the smoke escaped, Pen recoiled, her face a clenched fist.

'Hey Business,' Nayce said. The driver held out his knuckles. Nayce brushed them with his.

'Respect,' Respect said.

'Oh. Sorry. It's dark in there.'

'And cloudy!' Business said from the passenger seat. He and Respect echoed past laughter.

'Have you seen Hut?' Nayce said. 'You know, the one with the . . .'

'Fuck-up,' Respect said. 'We call him Fuck-up.'

'Whatever,' Nayce said, glancing at Penny guiltily, as if she might care what they called her husband. 'Have you seen him tonight?'

344

'Yah mon. He come out late, in he swimming trunks and he towel over he shoulder. He tell us we can have the night off, we not needed.'

'What happened?'

'Me no driving tonight. Me too stoned, man.'

Business chortled, or coughed, in the sweet darkness.

'So what did he do?' Nayce said.

'He ask where is a good place for a night swim. Me say if he want to drown heself, he go in the bay. So he go back through the hotel and out into the bay here.'

'How long ago? What time?'

'Mon, what is time? That me cannot know.'

Pen bustled to the window. 'How was he?'

'Fuck-up? He was fucked-up.' The driver collapsed into wheezy laughter.

'What state was he in? Please! Please!'

'He kinda loose, but he no more fucked-up than he always be.'

'And he went back to swim in the bay?' Nayce said.

'Yah mon.'

'But we've just been there. He wasn't there.'

'This time use you eyes.'

Nayce and Pen ran back across the road into the hotel. No longer pretending that to walk, to act normally, to keep their voices steady would be enough to retrieve Hut from the night, they sprinted through the pool area, through the wooden gate and back out across the sand dune to the beach. The surface of the water was horribly smooth, like a canvas stretched freshly onto its frame.

Pen cupped her hands around her mouth. 'Hut! Hut! Jeremy!' The misted bay swallowed her cries.

Nayce leapt over the guardrail and ran to the end of the jetty. He also started shouting his friend's name, but his calls felt soundless, like shouting in a dream. He peered over the water—for anything, any bump on the glass—for what he dreaded, a floating shape. Already his mind was constructing a picture of how Hut would look, his colour, his bloat, his popped eyes. This was it, wasn't it? Could it be? Financial problems, perjury, the humiliations from Pongrass and Blackman, the final shame of the race—it had to be too much for him. Even Hut must have his limit. And then there was what he, Nayce, had said. He couldn't go near that.

Nayce screamed Hut's name, grating it against the back of his throat.

'Oh God, Oh God!' Pen was hyperventilating beside him.

'Jeremy! Jeremy?' Nayce shouted. Reverting to his friend's first name seemed theatrical, but called for.

'Oh God,' she wailed.

'Come on, let's go along the beach. We might see . . . something,' he said, diverting her from thought into action. Diverting himself.

They climbed back over the jetty gate and fast-walked, half-stumbling, along the beach towards the headland.

'You wait here,' Nayce said to Pen and started running. The Slashing party raged on—senselessly, vilely. How could people be enjoying themselves? What kind of monsters could do that, now? The enormity of the situation enclosed all else, enclosed the whole island. Hut was gone. How could anyone be drinking and laughing and shouting and dancing?

Forty or fifty shadows ground around a stage, under a thatched roof. Most of the dancers were Jamaicans, salted with a handful of whites. Tears curdled in Nayce's eyes; he felt like charging in and tackling them into the flame lanterns, teach them a lesson. Music and ganja floated above their heads. How could they? But he didn't see the point in running into a party and causing a fight. What was he going to do? Ask them all to come diving into the

346

bay? Make them apologise for enjoying themselves? He couldn't. It wasn't their fault. He returned, breaking into a run, along the beach to Pen.

Waves lapped against the rockpools; the tide hadn't quite given up on Jamaica. The full moon's shadow-casting light gave a clear view of the shoreline. How could the waves still come in? How could the moon dare to shine?

'Nothing,' Nayce said. 'Let's go back to the hotel. I'm sure he's turned up.'

'How? How can you be so sure?'

'I . . . I just know he has.'

43

Nayce poured out six vodka miniatures, three into each glass, and sat on the bed. Pen took her drink and moved away from him, as if from a contagion. She stood with Hut's PDA and re-read the last message.

'Who's this Rip?' she asked. 'Why does he say such horrible things about Hut? Could Hut—maybe he went to see Rip? Can we call him?'

'Rip was our pilot,' Nayce said.

'Where is he? Where can we find him? He's responsible for . . .'

'He's not responsible for anything,' Nayce said. 'We'll find Hut and he'll be okay. We're panicking over nothing.'

'These terrible things!' Pen's pitch rose. 'How can he say that? What if he's done something to him?'

She flipped the screen to get rid of it, and the last composed message popped up: the unsent text Hut had half-written to her. His misspelt apologies. His ungrammatical contrition. Pen's face fell into her hands. Nayce, drawn to her, patted her shoulders, torturing himself. He sat again on the bed. Pen wiped her nose, got up and fixed herself another drink: three miniatures pell-mell, gin this time, neat.

'I don't know why I'm going to pieces,' she said. 'He's going to turn up, isn't he?'

'Of course he is,' Nayce said. 'In half an hour we'll all be laughing about it.' The other night, when Hut was lost in Kingston, Nayce had scoffed at Book's wishful thinking. Now he'd adopted it himself, as a last hope. Hut *had* to be all right. The alternative, now that it seemed a real possibility, was too horrible to let in. Now that it was thinkable, it was unthinkable.

Pen looked at him. 'Do you think . . . do you think he might have staged a . . . made himself disappear?'

Nayce thought for a moment and said: 'I guess he had his problems, but is that really what Hut, as we know him, would do?'

'I know far more than he gives me credit for,' Pen said, more to herself than to him. She was standing at the window and Nayce was seated on the bed, feeling redundant. 'The scariest thing for him, when he was first investigated, was that I might find out. It's like I'm his parents, and he's going through childhood all over again.'

As if he'd ever left it. 'You think he might have run away?'

'Oh, I don't know.' She sighed with the same impatience as before, ready to blame Nayce. He was there.

'In a way,' he said, 'I hope that's what he has done.'

He stood and joined her at the window. Down on the beach he could see the party at Slashing—cunts.

He put an arm around her shoulders. She felt as responsive as a side of meat hanging in a freezer.

'Ha!' Nayce said mirthlessly. 'We give each other a cuddle, that's when Hut walks in. Lurking, spying, getting the wrong idea.'

In the window he saw warped facets of himself, caricatures and impressions. As he withdrew his arm, Pen's icy hand held his wrist to her collarbone. 'Wouldn't it be worth it? Just to see if we can conjure him up?'

'Okay,' he said, his voice misting the glass. 'I'm really, really worried now.'

Where he'd made the mistake was in not saying what he'd meant to say. He could see that now. The irony—and this was irony—was that he'd changed tack out of deference to Hut's feelings.

They'd been sitting on the lip of Mount John, watching the sun go down and the moon come up. The heavenly bodies seemed to be calling on him. Nayce knew that now was the time to do the right thing. Nayce wanted nothing more than to help Hut, and for the first time he could be his benefactor, he could play giver. What had he to give Hut if not the truth?

It seemed so easy. Why had he waited so long? Under the intoxicating serum of sunset and moonrise and the green flash, Nayce sat next to Hut on the soft bent grass, ready to iron out the past.

'You told me I should be more honest about myself.'

'Maybe I should too.'

'Who goes first?'

'Maybe it's the same thing.'

'Me first then.'

The air smelt of sulphur. Nayce felt so warmly towards Hut that he reached to hug him. It was as Nayce tilted against him that Hut woke from his trance and half-jumped away.

'What you doing?'

Nayce's eyes filled, his stomach cartwheeling. 'I . . . I just wanted to ask you about your, you know, your problems back home.'

'What?' Hut blinked at him. 'Get fucked.'

It was here that Nayce saw how wrong he had been. Best friends, yes, but there are things best friends cannot offload to each other. There are things they can give to anyone but each other. Hut would have been able to mayday an absolute stranger without a qualm. But—it was now blindingly obvious—he would rather die than confess his problems to Nayce.

'Don't you think we should talk about it?'

'Talk about what?'

Hut glared at him with such hostility that Nayce wondered if Hut even liked him. Maybe thirty-three years had finally worn thin. Maybe Janey was right, and their friendships were a matter of geographical coincidence that had exhausted their natural life. Perhaps it was all for the best; and yet the suspicion that he was being abandoned gave birth to a spike of such silvery violence that he said to Hut the worst thing he could think of. It roared out fresh from oblivion.

'How well do you remember those holidays?' Nayce began.

Hut wouldn't look at him. 'Jesus,' he muttered. 'Aren't you always having a go at me for living in the past? Anyway, I saw you and Janey.'

'What?'

'You and Janey. All on again. It's never really stopped, has it?'

'What?'

'Oh, don't play coy with me. I saw you.'

'Saw us? I swear, I haven't touched her since 1992. In fact,' Nayce scratched his stubbled head, 'you couldn't be further from the truth.'

Hut glared at him with a toxic mixture of hostility and need. He had blunted Nayce's charge, sat him back on his arse. You couldn't underestimate Hut. Beneath all the masks, he was an angry man, combat-ready.

'Liar. I saw you.' Hut gathered up a pile of shale and threw the pieces, one by one, onto the grassed slope.

'What do you mean?' Nayce said, letting out a shrill laugh that sounded more derisory than he would have wished. 'When?'

'At the Pizza Hut.'

'What Pizza Hut?'

'The holiday house. What you were about to tell me.'

'Eh?' Nayce was genuinely perplexed. 'When?'

'When we had that party there a couple of months ago.'

'Me and Janey? You've got to be kidding. Is that what you meant about me being honest? When?'

'Ah, come on, don't lie to me, buddy. I went out for a swim, and none of you knew it but I nearly drowned. I was out in the surf on my own, and lost it. It was only because this fisherman guy saved me that I lived to tell the tale.'

'You are such a bullshitter.'

'But I didn't really get to tell the tale, did I? Because when I got back to the Pizza Hut, everyone was asleep. Or so I thought.' Hut's face met the sunset and stole its colour. 'I had a shower, got some juice, and came to find Pen to tell her how I'd nearly come a cropper. She wasn't in our room. I came to your room— *your* room, Dave, all yours—and when I opened the door, I looked inside, and . . .'

Hut twisted his mouth to one side, then the other, as if easing a cramp.

'And? And?'

Hut seemed to be struggling with an uncertainty of vision; as with an instant childhood memory or a dream, it overcast itself in doubt. His face moved both ways at once.

'Oh, shit,' Nayce said.

Hut came over dark, like a child being punished, grasping the idea of punishment, for the first time. The unhappiness was profound, but so was the revelation. He knew something was wrong, and he knew in what way it was wrong, but the jumbled

352

parts of that wrongness were recombining in his memory only moment by moment.

'Nah,' Nayce said. 'Oh. Oh, Hut . . .' In spite of himself he began to giggle. He could see what it was that Hut was thinking, or trying to think, or trying not to think; the bastard had come up with the wrong memory.

Hut had finished throwing away all his rocks. He pushed himself to his feet, dusting his hands down the front of his Hawaiian shirt.

'Hut, Hut,' Nayce got up. 'You're mixing up a whole lot of different things.'

Hut kept his face averted, as if the very sight of Nayce might make him sick. He walked towards the minivan, where the others were collecting for the trip back down to the resort. Not even when Nayce ran around in front of him to cut him off would Hut look at him. Hut paused and tried to sidestep him. Nayce blocked his way.

'Hold it,' Nayce said, putting his hands on Hut's shoulders. 'You've got it all wrong. You walked in, and now you're thinking . . . Oh you fucking fuckhead, when will you learn? You go around peeping into people's rooms, you're always going to get the wrong idea.'

Hut breathed so rapidly Nayce wondered if he would faint. Darkness was falling swift and silent as a curtain. The moon climbed, and the chain of lights around the shore began to glow. Sulphur thickened in the still twilight. 'So,' Hut said, short of breath, not taking his eyes off Nayce's feet, 'did I imagine that or did it really happen?'

'Hutchison.' Nayce put his finger under Hut's chin and tilted it up, like a lover. 'You know damn well what happened. And when.'

There: the worst he could say. Nayce felt thrilled and disgusted with himself. He had got Hut back, for everything. And his pleasure in seeing Hut's face crumple, lose its constituent parts, told Nayce that he had no right to call himself this man's friend. Wasn't that what he wanted? Was that the point of it, of the torture, the cruelty? You never knew how strong friendship was until you found its breaking strain.

Hut's eyes dropped back to Nayce's deck-walkers.

'You need a new pair of those,' he said with a fatherly kind of quiet. 'I'll get you some when we go back home.'

Nayce watched Hut climb past him into the minivan. The trip down Mount John passed in silence and darkness. They each stared out of their own windows. Even when Business stopped to get out and smoke a fresh spliff with Respect, Hut didn't stir in his seat. When they arrived at Sandals and Nayce touched his shoulder, Hut twitched, his face puckered in pain.

David Nayce did the right thing, and suffered for it. That was another of his personal myths.

44

Pen gaped at him as though she wanted him dead.

'He thought I was *with* you?' she said, shaking her head hard, as if to physically throw off the misconception.

'He walked in on us that morning. He thought it was Janey and me, and he had this idea that she and I were back on and sneaking around together. But then, I could see the wheels working in his head, he gave it a re-think. See, he'd come in to talk to you, and he couldn't find you anywhere. So he jumped to a conclusion.'

'He nearly drowned? He never told me!'

'He said he was going to, but he must have . . .' Nayce tamped his head with an open palm. 'He must have had some kind of suspicion all along. He couldn't find you, he'd seen me with someone in my bed, but he never saw her face. Because he didn't want to let himself contemplate that it might be you, he settled on this idea that it was Janey.'

'Oh, David! I wasn't *in* bed with you!'

Nayce, his back to the window, banged his head against the glass twice. He finished his drink and took his tumbler to the bathroom where he refilled it with water. Back in the room, he made as if to sit beside Pen on the bed, but thought better of it and perched on the writing desk.

'You were. I was there. I do remember.'

'Well, yes, but I wasn't *with* you. We were just having a post-mortem on the party, weren't we? You were lying in bed and I was on the end.'

'Hut only looked in for a flash. He got it all mixed up in his stupid head.'

'But why didn't you just *tell* him that?' She flung herself backwards onto the bed, clenching her fists and pummelling the mattress in frustration. Sitting up, she composed herself with a deep breath and cleared loose hair from her eyes. 'You are a— what are you, David, how can you leave him with that idea? Why couldn't you have set him straight and told him the truth for once in your life?'

Nayce swivelled on the desk, where Hut's PDA lay open. Rip's message and a message to Pen. All these mistakes curled up in bottles.

'I figured that if he can think that of you,' Nayce said, turning back to her, but unable to meet her eyes, 'if he can think for one second that you were going to do something like that with me—and if he can think that of me—then he deserves to be left with it.'

Pen's mouth opened to say something but words shrivelled away.

'What kind of a friend are you, David?'

Nayce scratched his chin. 'Bad friend. Bad apple all round.'

'And . . . and he's . . . How could you? How *could* you?'

'Because it wasn't about that day at all,' Nayce said coldly. He fiddled with Hut's PDA, snapping it open and shut. He planted a fingertip on the smear of powder on the desk, and licked it again. Surprising, he thought, how much heroin tastes like garlic. 'Something happened there, at the Pizza Hut. But not then. Years ago. Hut was mixing it all up.'

'I don't want any more of your—your bullshit,' Pen said. 'I'm going out to find my husband.' She rose from the bed and made for the door.

'Pen.' Jumping from the desk, he took hold of one of her arms.

'Fuck off, David. Fuck off!' She fought free and left the room, running past the lifts to take the fire escape down.

Nayce, feeling wretched, yet, after his confession—or part-confession—monstrously relieved, stayed in Hut's room. He was getting used to being told to fuck off by women. He felt light-headed in all this cleared air. When he got home, things weren't going to be the way they used to be. Not such a terrible thing, really. He picked up Hut's PDA and scrolled down. Below the messages was another, sent today, from KenH. Ken Hutchison.

This one, now, this one was puzzling.

45

THE MIST ON the bay smelt of rot and smoke, like an old carpet that needed a shake. Nayce paused and took in the scene. Jamaica: a beautiful woman who hates herself. From the moment he'd landed, he'd had a presentiment of death in the island's foul beauty, sweet as fruit on the turn; but he'd only seen his own, always his own.

Feeling like a murderer, he followed Pen's footprints. By the time he made it down to the shoreline she was a hundred metres ahead and walking with the brisk limping pace of someone too tired to keep running but unable to let herself stop. He jogged to catch up.

'I've already been to the beach party, Pen. He's not there.'

She pressed on, tears painting her face, teeth tight down on her lip.

'Pen. There was something on his PDA about Fred.'

'Fred?' Pen stopped and let him come up to her. She stared at him, half bent as if her spine was melting. 'What do you mean, something about Fred?'

'There was a message. From his dad. About Fred.'

'What did it say?' Torn down by the need to know, the promise of a clue, her hostility fell away.

'It said Fred has bowel cancer.'

A noise of finality escaped Pen's mouth. Her knees buckled and her hand reached for Nayce's shoulder. 'What else did it say?'

'Everyone was rallying around, don't call, enjoy your holiday, just some bullshit.'

'And it said Fred had cancer? Oh . . .'

'Pen. I don't think Hut's going to go out and do something silly because of Fred . . . It was just weird, the tone, somehow. Ken messaging him about the dog.'

She was shaking her head angrily. 'That bastard,' she muttered. 'That arsehole.'

'Who? Hut?'

'You don't understand anything.'

'So you keep telling me, but I . . .'

'Fred is the dog's name. But Fred is also what Ken and Hut call his mother.'

'Whose mother?'

Pen was clutching her hair. 'Oh my God! Oh God, what have you all done to him?'

'Ines?' Nayce grabbed her wrists. 'Fred is Ines?'

She tore away. 'You—what have you all done to him?'

'Pen . . .' he called, but she took off along the shoreline, not in search of Hut, it now seemed, but escaping from Nayce.

'You fucking idiot! You're all fucking idiots!'

'Penelope!'

She ran ahead. Nayce's skin prickled. He stopped at the shoreline and cast a hopeless eye like a baitless hook over the water. There was nothing, less than nothing, the ironed sea massively indifferent. Nayce tried to arrange events in his mind, a worst-case scenario. Hut was in financial trouble. Then he'd

359

been interviewed by the regulators, and had lied under oath. He might be going to jail. He had come to the island and fucked up, embarrassed himself in front of everyone night after night and then made a fool of himself on the swim. He had some self-inflicted but not baseless idea that something might have been going on between Nayce and Pen. Which Nayce had stoked. Then there had been this news, like a taunting bad joke, from his father, that either his dog or his mother had been diagnosed with cancer. His dog or his mother? What the fuck? Hut had gone out and scored heroin, given some to Pongrass and Blackman, kept some for himself, had last been seen heading for a swim, and—there was no point trying to imagine—or there was plenty of time, a lifetime, left to imagine . . . No, it was impossible to stand at the edge of Hut's skin and slide in, impossible because of what he, Nayce, might see of himself in there.

46

By the age of fifteen, Nayce had figured out the beautiful simplicity of how things worked in the adult world. To see Ines Hutchison as the prize, the trophy, the touch of dazzle, was to view through the eyes of an outsider. Once inside, he could see Ines the way Ken saw her: the skeleton in the closet, the deadweight, the bit left over. *Cheers, pet.* Her otherworldly vagueness had nothing ethereal about it. She was bent under her load the way Caribbean women bent under their baskets of fruit, and no number of tranquillisers and charge cards, no excess of drunken afternoons and saunas and overseas trips, could straighten her. She lurked on the fringes of family life. What must it have been to be Ines Hutchison? By the age of fifteen, Nayce had neither the sympathy nor the curiosity, nor indeed the personality, to ask.

She lurked. This was what he understood now: her gauzy drift through the world wasn't aimless; it had its own concentrated intent. The day Nayce and Hut had gone for the bushwalk at Barrenjoey, and Nayce had defied Hut's craven appeals to 'fall'— Ines had followed them, to spy. She hadn't caught them doing something wrong; *they* had caught *her*. The night she had come upon them smashing bottles against the toilet block—again, the boys weren't the ones who had been caught.

He didn't think of it as the day she caught him, because he knew there had been other days. He would come up from the beach alone, shower, and go to his bedroom. He would draw the curtains and lie on his back. Sometimes he let his mind wander, knowing it would come in its own time to where it had to arrive. As he grew confident, he would tease himself cold by trying to think of his parents, or his school, or church. He knew that it wouldn't be long.

There had been days when a floorboard creaked or a blind rustled. Afterwards, he would come out of his room in a pair of shorts and Ines would make him a glass of lime juice with ice-blocks. She would sit across the kitchen table and pretend not to watch his Adam's apple bobbing down the frosty drink. By now, Nayce had found the word. *Avid*.

The tension could hold as long as they did not catch each other. Whatever it was they were doing could be maintained as long as the performance—for that was what it was—was a peepshow. Neither the watcher nor the performer was allowed to acknowledge the other's presence. But on the last day of that last summer Ines changed the pattern. It was the day Ken Hutchison had announced that they weren't going to come to the Pizza Hut the following year because the Hutchisons had been invited by some business contacts for a fishing holiday in South Africa.

Nayce had come up from the beach as usual a half-hour before Ken and Hut. He was lying on his back when she revealed herself at the door wearing a plain turquoise bikini under a parted white cotton robe. There was nothing accidental or inadvertent about her appearance. She stepped timidly but defiantly into the doorway and held her position, her hands loose against her thighs, wrists turned out.

Nayce's hand flew off his cock as if scalded. He pushed himself upright against the bedhead and reached for a pillow or sheet to cover him, but they were caught under his legs. He quickly realised the futility of disguise. His penis, filling and lengthening as he had lain on his back with her image in his mind, now stood like an unfinished sentence.

She was not quite looking at him. Her eyes were fixed a few degrees to his side: at a bedside lamp, or at his suitcase gutted on the floor. He understood—she was looking at nothing. He blanked his face and resumed, seeking the same nothing. He did it as he always did it, here at the house: his hand moved vaguely, distractedly, with a lightness that he tried to make random, unpredictable, autonomous, the flighty feeler of another.

He stopped himself from looking up when he heard her footsteps pierce the silence in the bedroom. He paused for a moment but, as if understanding an instruction, resumed his airy strumming. She stopped beside his bed, next to his suitcase. Her hands went to her hips, pushing the flaps of the white cotton robe aside, and her thumbs hooked over the side strings of her bikini bottom. His throat dry, Nayce closed his eyes and wished, and when he opened them again she was answering him. Her hands had slithered up her midriff and now her white-painted fingernails were untying the bow of her bikini top. Sensing an imminent seizure or spasm, his focus bore into her fingers. Her chest—he knew by heart the placement, size and pigmentation of every freckle, dark, light, mulatto, every signature of time and age. He loved her sun damage. She took the two strings, now free, between her thumbs and index fingers and drew them apart like curtains. Her bare breasts wore precise white triangles, a ghost bikini. Her nipples were pink with a just-showered pucker. Now she cupped her breasts in her hands. She didn't move them, didn't crush them together or jiggle them or play with them. She simply cupped them and looked at them curiously; she stood with her breasts in her hands and listened to that music, faraway in the past or the future, that only she could hear.

He closed his eyes and wished again, and again she heard. Ines's right hand came down (he heard her knees crack as she bent) and with her palm she pressed his penis against his belly as it ebbed its way out. She held it there, gently firm, until the end. Then, knees re-cracking, she got up and crossed the room to the dresser where a mostly spent box of tissues sat. She withdrew the last two and handed them to him, without showing him her face. He never dared to meet her eyes, or to say anything. After she touched him, he never again shot any kind of look, insolent or grateful, in the direction of her body.

She had spent three or maybe four minutes in his room. Or maybe longer, because when Ines left and Nayce cleaned himself up and got dressed, and went out to flush the tissues down the toilet, he came back to find Hut in the room. Usually, when Hut came up off the beach, he was with Ken and they would make a great ruckus, dragging in their surf skis like kangaroos' thumping tails. But this time there was no Ken, only Hut, and he was perching on the end of Nayce's bed looking at his hands, thunderstruck by his own simple existence, just like his mother.

'What's up?' Nayce said, drilling a fingernail into his ear.

'Nothing. Just thinking about all the good times we've had here.'

It was such a strangely sentimental and adult answer, and it blended so finely with Nayce's attentive guilt, that he knew what had happened.

The easy habit was to rub Ines out of the genetic picture and see Hut as Ken's son, only his father's son. That was Hut's aim. It was Ken's aim. It was, even, Nayce's aim. But as he stood over Hut on the end of his bed and understood, with a panicky climbing heart, what had just happened, he knew that his friend was equally his mother's son.

He loved Hut for it. That was the truth. Nayce sat on the bed and put his arm around Hut's shoulder.

'Hey.' His voice was a barren croak. 'What doesn't kill us makes us stronger.'

Hut sprang to attention halfway between the bed and the door. He mastered his features with a bright smile—the front teeth prominent, the eyes gregariously atwinkle like his father's. In that moment Nayce saw everything it cost Hut to summon up that expression, the price a complicated boy will pay for the thing to which he believes he owes his success: his easy smile, his satisfaction with himself. And Nayce saw how upside down and back to front Nietzsche had it. It's the things that make us stronger, in the end, that kill us.

He waited for Hut to respond, but nothing came out, not a word.

47

On the dune in front of Slashing, a green Ford Cortina was parked. Someone had built a bonfire, a flagrant totem pole, its flames brushing the beach and kissing the stars. As Pen approached she could see that the party was smaller than it had seemed—only ten or twelve dark shapes still danced around the fire.

She started up the incline to the base of the dune. There was laughter and singing, some aggressive male shouting. Then more laughter. She heard a heart-rending cry.

She started running again, stumbling in the sandy slope. At the rim of the firelight, a gust bent the smoke and blinded her. Voices hooted and whooped, party ejaculations. Someone wolf-whistled.

Crabwise, a hand cupped over her leading eye, Pen blinked her way into the circle. A music system the size of a telephone booth sat on top of the Cortina playing some kind of nightmare reggae, a voice from hell. Two girls, white and black, danced in shorts and bras. The air reeked of salt and smoke and weed, and seaweed and fire smoke. She began whimpering—'Oh God! Oh God!'—in a released way. Clownish faces mocked her. A white man walked on his hands with his feet tucked into the crooks of his elbows.

A black man naked beneath his waistcoat walked around with an armful of Red Stripe beer. The music was African, new, electric, a beat that Pen had never heard and would never forget.

'Oh God!' She was wailing, abandoned, in the sand, beggar-like. 'Oh, God . . .'

Standing above her, a Sandals bath towel around his waist, grinning with a kind of diabolical mock-triumph, a family-sized smile, was her husband.

'Hey, babe,' he said.

Pen gasped, slowed, controlled her breathing so that he could not mistake what she had to say. She hauled herself to her feet and, beginning a retreat into the dignity of small acts, began to brush the sand off her shins. She glanced up at him—he wore his wide eyes, his blameless *What?*—and, unable to countenance him, so scared was she of tearing his face from its bones, she kept brushing the bridges of her feet even after the sand was all gone, and when she spoke it was with her eyes on his silly towel. Sandals.

'You have made my life hell and you have fucked up everything for your family. How dare you call me *babe?*'

Then her legs gave way.

48

'Bloody hell,' Nayce said, arriving. 'I thought I'd looked here.'

Although he was crouched on the sand beside Pen, Hut seemed to loom above Nayce, not merely happy but glossily triumphant.

'Hey, buddy. What's wrong with the wife? I can't get a word out of her. She's gibbering.'

'Come on,' Nayce bent to the ground and started to lift Pen. 'Come on.'

'Whatup, everyone?' Hut called to the crowd, playing ringmaster. Voices echoed happily. 'Whatup, mon!'

Nayce helped Pen to her feet. She pushed him away and hurled herself like a deck quoit around her husband's neck. One of her feet gave a blind kick at Nayce. Then she started scratching at Hut. He yelled at her, jokingly at first, but she continued clawing and was now screaming abuse.

'You arsehole . . . you fucking . . . you inconsiderate selfish fucking *arse*hole . . . !'

'Hey, Pen. Penny. I know it's been a long trip. You're here now.' Hut wrestled her down, patting her shoulderblades until she gave up, gagging for breath. She wrung her hands beside her ears and began sobbing, shrinking. Hut sank to his haunches and patted her lightly until she had used up the last of her attack. She let him hold her to his chest. 'Hey, everybody!' he called. 'This is the hottie I've been raving on about! She's here!'

Around them, the party's welcoming cheer was that of old, old friends.

49

Hours later the rising sun laid out a pink blanket for the setting moon. Hut and Pen were perched on the end of the jetty, not touching. Nayce sat one length of planking to their right. The Slashing party had ended, and the revellers had retired to their homes and hotels. Hut had carried a half-case of Red Stripes along the beach, and he, Pen and Nayce had come to the end of the jetty to drink their way through the bottles like laboratory workers, replacing each empty neatly in the box until they were through.

As Hut prattled on with cheerful evasiveness about his night at the party, Pen sat numb and dry, her insides scooped out. She drank the beer to fill herself up, but it pooled in her arms and legs. She wished Nayce would go away, leave her alone with her husband. Noticing Nayce's silence, she suspected he would like to leave them alone as well. But Hut was being Hut: trying to please everyone, pleasing no-one, slyly serving himself. Hut claimed to feel bad for Nayce—'Come on, this is our last night, come and have a few cleansers . . .' Yet Hut also wanted to shelter behind Nayce. So terrified was he of being alone with her that he used

Nayce as a shield, like a skittish debutante needing a chaperone. She was so tired of it.

'So I threw it away,' Hut said. He was talking about the heroin. 'Jason met me in a service station and warned me. He said Rip had scored it to fuck us all up. Tell us it was coke, give us a nasty surprise. But Jason—he must have taken pity on me or something—he warned me not to take it. I split it in half. I didn't want Pong and Abo to, you know, OD. But I didn't see any harm in giving them some, let Rip have his practical joke, you know? Probably not the smartest move I've ever made.'

'They'll be right,' Nayce said. 'Pongrass is sleeping it off in the sick bay. Blackman's in bed.'

'Whew. I'm glad curiosity didn't kill the cat.'

Hut couldn't conceal his glee, Pen noticed. He had turned on those bastards, given them their long-overdue kick up the arse. Maturity? They must have hurt him. Something like hope rose in her. She wanted him to scar, to know at last how she was scarred. And there was something beyond that, she realised as she finished her sixth Red Stripe. She felt his body's heat, across the close yet still unbreachable width of one jetty board. She tried to will Nayce, telepathically, to *piss off*. Piss *off!* She wanted her husband.

'I did think about having a taste myself,' Hut went on. 'I was in my room looking at it, feeling like shit about the race. I mean, I was up for a party I spose, but in the end I thought, fuck this, I don't want to do this.'

'This Rip,' Pen said, opening another Red Stripe. 'What had you done to him to make him hate you so much?' She took a swig from the bottle, her question hanging over the water. What on earth had she meant? Rip was a boatie, some ordinary hardworking man. It would have been stranger if he hadn't hated them. Yuppie scum. Sometimes she wanted to give herself a shake, scrape off

371

this tan of wealth that had grown on her, and see her life the way an ordinary person would see it. Renew her old eyes. She'd served too many years under the blinding sunlamp of all that Hutchison money.

'Old Rip, he's fine,' Hut said pleasantly. 'He just didn't appreciate not being tipped a dollar when we could chip in fifteen-hundred for drugs.'

'But that awful email,' Pen said, tailing off, not wanting to think about it. How bitterly Rip had singled out her Hut, her man. But then, the other one, Jason, he'd cared, hadn't he? Cared enough to warn Hut against taking the smack?

Hut laughed. 'Rip and his poison pen! Yeah, what did I ever do to him, Dave?'

Nayce said nothing, the jetty boards creaking like something caught in his throat.

Hut continued: 'But Rip didn't write that email, did he?'

'He did, I saw it,' Pen said miserably. 'It was horrible.'

Hut shook his head and nodded towards Nayce. 'The author,' he said.

'What—him?' Pen blinked at Nayce, whose eyebrows made startled arches.

'What, ah, what makes you say it was me?'

'Come on, Nayce. Underneath it all, Rip loved me. You'd need to know me a lot longer than three days to hate me that much.' He clapped Pen heartily on the thigh. She gave a shiver and rubbed the outsides of her arms.

'Is that true?' she asked Nayce. 'You were the one who wrote it?'

'I . . . I don't know how you can be so certain . . .'

'Shut up, Nayce,' Hut said. 'When you wrote that stupid email, you had no idea that Jason was about to save my life. It was Pong and Abo they really hated. Not me. So when I read that bit about

372

Jason telling us to go fuck ourselves, I knew it wasn't fair-dinkum. It stank of phony. Believe me, Nayce, never bullshit a bullshitter. I can smell it a mile off. And the only person who's a big enough cunt to go to the trouble of creating a new email address for Rip and writing that email . . . well, I'm looking at him, aren't I?' He leaned back and folded his arms.

Nayce gave a smile that turned into a cough. 'I only meant it for a laugh.'

'Well, you are a cunt,' Hut said amiably, as a courteous assassin might say as he points his gun at his victim's temple. 'I've always said it.'

'I guess I am.'

'If only you meant that,' Pen said. 'Because Hut's right. You are. And,' she felt herself thawing, marvelling at that indestructible thing in her husband, 'people *like* him. They can't help it.' She turned to Hut. 'It's a miracle, because he's such an arsehole.'

Hut was looking squarely at Nayce. 'I'm not surprised you'd be able to channel him. I mean, it takes a cunt to get inside the head of a cunt like that cunt Rip. Cheers, mate. And Dave?'

'Yeah?' Nayce looked at Hut like a puppy at its master. Pen felt ashamed for him.

'Why don't you leave me and my wife alone?'

They watched him limp away down the jetty and struggle over the fence. It might have been the race that left him crooked, a tight-hamstringed old man, yet it seemed more than that.

Pen and Hut fell silent until they were down to the last of the beers. Without his audience, Hut had gone shy. The sun hauled its full circumference above the horizon, burning off the bay mist as if shrugging itself out of a bad dream. Fishing boats motored towards Negociante Island. The first of the tourist skin-diving operations, a shoal of bristling snorkels, appeared off the eastern headland.

Pen was pleased to see that Hut, even if thirty-odd years too late, was beginning to understand the depth of Nayce's hostility. But she wasn't prepared to concede or forgive any more than that. Her relief at finding him unharmed had been succeeded by anger at his blitheness, as if he'd been in some minor scrape, no bruises, no broken skin, no problemo! Didn't he know how worried they'd been? Fucking arsehole. And she couldn't ignore the elephant, the herd of elephants, in the corner. She needed to talk to him about their marriage and the terrifying prospect facing them. She wanted to shake him and scream in his face: *You are going to jail! You can't laugh it off!* But her weariness now weighed on her like a chemical fact, as if she'd taken a handful of sleeping pills. She had nothing left.

'I'm a cunt too, scuse my French,' he said at last. 'But at least I know I am.'

Pen shook her head. 'It's not important.' She edged closer so their thighs touched, and she leaned towards, if not quite against, his arm. 'We have too much to sort out.'

'You bought a lemon,' he said. 'It's my mission in life to stop you ever knowing that and hope like hell you don't wake up to yourself.'

'Oh, Hut. You had me worried.'

'Nah. I don't have the guts to top myself.'

'I could have killed you,' she said. 'If you'd done that, I'd have killed you again.'

'Hey. There's two little friends of mine, and the minute I get down, I only need to put those two faces into my slide-show, and I'm fine.'

'So why don't you . . .' He could talk like such a wonderful father; why couldn't he start *being* one? She was about to launch herself at him, but was overcome again by waves of tiredness and, bizarrely, perversely, irresistibly, desire. How good they'd been. How he had loved her. What was the point in starting the conversation about them, their future, their past, the ordeal that was to come, the *business* of planning? There would be time for that. Now she felt the desire that comes at the end of the world, an hour until annihilation.

'Hut, can you carry me up to our room?'

His eye caught hers and crinkled evilly. Why, she wondered again, had she and he ever stopped doing it?

'Don't you dare think you're forgiven, Hutchison. We have a lot of talking to do, and you have to hear me out.'

'But tomorrow.'

'You've got an hour until your two little friends wake up.' She let her hand enclose his, squeeze down. 'And did I mention it's your morning? My turn to sleep in.'

'Better hurry then,' he said.

50

Nayce, Janey, Book, Pongrass and Blackman were booked on a flight leaving Kingston for Miami at six-oh-five Friday evening. They would have to leave Sandals before midday.

Nayce was in his room alone, packing his suitcase. He unsnapped his fluorescent wristband and dropped it in the bin. Books, magazines, DVDs and the rest of his good intentions lay unopened beneath his folded clothes. He had not turned a page in earnest since the outward flight. Sometimes, he thought, leafing through one of the books he had planned to read, fear of death can mask a fear of life. Self-improvement is a way of eluding experience. He had been distracted from all of those things that he wanted to do, and instead had frittered away the time with— with what? What had he done here? Nothing, it seemed. So why did these five days feel like months?

That morning, on the jetty with Hut and Pen, he'd had the feeling they were rounding on him, cornering him. It was what had been rising for a few days, ever since Janey had begun closing doors in his face. He was being cut loose. Yet he couldn't help feeling a sense of gain, the enrichment of defeat. When he'd left Hut and Pen—*Why don't you leave me and my wife alone?*—he had made an effort to anticipate his return to his wife and son, Sophie and John. He forced their images onto his mind but they wouldn't stay. While in Jamaica, he'd made the phone calls at the pre-agreed times, asked the right questions as if working down a checklist, listened to his wife's and son's monologues with regularly spaced vocal prompts—'Uh-huh', 'Really?'—and made certain to buy gifts. Only when he stopped trying so hard might he have a chance, and maybe not even then. But he had no choice. Every other road out of here had been cut.

He lugged his case down to the lobby and put it with the others in Respect's car. Janey and Book were eating breakfast in the hotel restaurant with Pongrass and Blackman, who looked healthy enough for men of fifty-five, shattered ruins for men of forty-two. They couldn't eat, but they could breathe and (Nayce's nose twitched) they could smell.

Nayce sat at the edge of the group while they finished eating. He caught a glimpse of the way those two men would look in twenty years: faces chafed by nor-easters and raddled by booze, lips basal-cell pale, the whites of their eyes the tan colour of cigarette filters, paunches cantilevered over their shorts, legs still dainty and slim and shoulders pulled back in obedience to the mirror-mirror's lies. Their future was already written: these were the brick-red white men of the Cruising Yacht Club, the Australian Jockey Club, stepping off their boats, perusing their stables. He had seen them before. They were their fathers.

'Rough night?' Janey grinned at Nayce malignantly. There was the sharpness of finality in her eyes: no regrets.

The Hutchisons were at a separate table. As Book went to sign the bill, Nayce followed Janey, almost hiding behind her, to Hut and Pen's table. Janey crouched, grimacing with the pain in her thighs, and talked softly with Charlie and Roy.

'So,' Nayce said to Hut and Pen. 'The end of the trip.'

After spearing, smearing and inserting in his mouth a brief marriage of egg yolk and toast, Hut hitched his eyes up from the plate and gave Nayce a nod.

'Later then.'

'Ah.' Nayce reached out his hand for a shake, but Hut went on with his breakfast.

'Hut,' Pen said.

Hut wiped his hands on a napkin. 'Oh. Sorry, mate.' Politely, he shook Nayce's hand and went back to his eggs.

'Listen,' Nayce said, eyes darting, edging closer like a racecourse tout. 'When we get back home, ah, if there's anything you need, I mean anything at all . . . There are lots of good biotech stocks we have, and, um, I know you've kind of dissed it before, but these are pure gold-plated investments, I'm not selling them to you for the ethical side, though if that interests you, then I'm quite certain we can . . .'

'Listen to him,' Hut said to Pen. 'The salesman now. Over breakfast. In front of my kids. Cheap.'

'Hut, be nice,' Pen cajoled.

Nayce looked from one to the other, his eyes being bounced like loose ball bearings. Hut chewed serenely on a slice of bacon. He cut a little triangle of toast and pushed it around his plate to mop up the last of his eggs.

'Hey, I'm serious. I know things are . . .' Nayce gestured emptily. 'All I want to say is, I'm your friend and I want to help you out. I can, you know, help you financially . . .'

Hut gave a pious sigh. 'In front of my kids.' He dabbed at the corners of his mouth.

A flight of nerves in his stomach, his calm swirling out of him like water down a plughole, Nayce pulled up a cane chair and slid beside Hut, knocking his knees against the table. 'Come on,' he pressed. 'I just wanted to do you a favour.'

'Well, let me do you a favour,' Hut said. He shifted in his chair to face his friend. 'Have a really good flight. Get some sleep.'

Nayce could feel his sweat changing, into a sour, toxic effluvium.

'Now.' Hut shrugged as if to say that anyone else in his position would call for security, but he would restrain himself out of the goodness of his heart and respect for an old friendship. 'Trying to flog me your business in front of my kids. It's cheap, Dave. Cheap.'

'I'm glad your mother's okay,' Nayce blurted, almost shouting, with a monumental awkwardness, his shoulders slumping under the weight of the platitude.

Hut wiped his mouth again and folded his napkin before laying it on his plate. Then he called for coffee. He said nothing until the waiter had filled his cup and he had stirred in two sachets of sugar. Nayce perched at his side, waiting, fighting back his confusion, the galloping sense that he was giving away everything, that he was shrinking into the size of a fly on the arm of Hut's chair.

Across the table, Pen felt Hut enjoying the silence, his sadistic pleasure in leaving Nayce hanging. She felt another tingle of desire, a transport to some memory. Since he'd come to Jamaica, something had altered in Hut—setting up Pongrass and Blackman, turning the tables on Nayce. And his bitter reaction to Ken's practical joke. Last night, Hut had called Ken, who'd clucked away: *You didn't think I meant* Fred, *did you? You bloody idiot. It's* Fred, *not Fred. Vet says he'll be fine.*

Hut hadn't yielded meekly the usual way. He was livid. *Thanks, Dad, thanks a lot. And by the way, there's something I've never asked. Why exactly was it that we started calling Mum Fred? How did that happen?*

In the phone a staticky snort: *You don't want to know, son.*

Hut had wanted to know. *Tell me.*

379

I can't even remember. Doesn't she remind you of the dog, in a way?

No. No, she doesn't.

Hut, she saw, had become starched up. Some essence in him had gone from wet to dry. He wasn't nicer, but he was firmer.

'Yes, David,' Hut said with pert mockery, as if they were actors. 'My mother is all right. My father, on the other hand, is one sick puppy.'

'I'm glad,' Nayce said, robotic. 'I mean, about your mother. Hut. I'm sorry for what I said.'

'Which bit, mate?'

'On the volcano.'

'Oh, that?' Hut angled his mouth at Pen as if he were the deadpan artist, she his audience, Nayce his dupe. 'He didn't say anything. That was the worst thing he said. Nothing.'

'Sure, sure.' Nayce got up to leave.

'And don't pretend to be concerned about my mother, will you? Have a great trip home.'

While Janey and Book finished their goodbyes to Hut and the boys, Pen followed Nayce to the forecourt. Business was loading Pongrass's and Blackman's bags into his white minivan.

'Don't be offended,' Pen said. She had a dry, corporate manner with him now, the precise cost of what he had given away.

'Offended? I'm confused.'

'Well, don't be offended either.'

'What's to offend me?' Nayce laughed weakly. He was slipping, slipping.

'David?'

'Yep?' He panted a little, seeing himself in Hut's words: cheap, snaky.

'Don't take this the wrong way,' Pen said. 'But Hut doesn't want to see you for a while.'

'He doesn't want to see me?'

'He thinks it's best if you had a break from each other.'

'God, you make it sound like I'm being dumped.'

'Well, you're too much a part of each other's lives for that. But you've been hurting each other for a long time now.'

'Fuck! He is dumping me!'

'We'll call you. We're going to take a break from the city, get ready for all the bad stuff coming up. Hut wants to spend some time with me and the boys. And with his mother.' Pen blushed, tellingly.

She knew then. She knew. Hut had told her. This was what it was, why Pen and Hut seemed arrayed against him. Hut's cowardice was no longer big enough to protect Nayce's secrets.

'Give us a few months, and we'll give you a few months, I'm sure he'll call. And David.' She cast him a lingering look, not unmerciful. 'Give yourself a chance, won't you?'

Janey and now Pen: he'd never given himself a chance. He'd accepted too easily that he wouldn't be happy, bending to his selfless consolation prize, accumulating a legacy for others. His middle-class martyrdom. He'd built his little mollusc-shell of perfection—photogenic wife and son, the trappings, the job that *did genuine good*, a clean moral slate—and derived from it not a whit of happiness. He'd laboured to impress whom? Himself? His friends? No-one was impressed by him. His mother and father? He'd been a good son, phoning his parents every few days and bearing their questions, their questions, their desperation to keep him on the phone as if he were a fugitive and they were fixing a trace on him . . . He had worked as hard at loving his parents as he worked at everything else. Yet he hadn't given himself a chance to be happy, and what was the value in any good works if they weren't coloured by happiness?

'I don't believe it,' he croaked. 'My oldest friend, dumping me.'

'Well, you said it yourself.' Pen gave him a world-weary smile. Her face twitched as if she might ordinarily have laughed. 'You're a cunt.'

51

THE FAST SET left the all-inclusive resort in two vehicles. They forgot to gather for a team farewell, or a photograph. Hut was busy walking his boys to the beach, and Pongrass and Blackman had gone to their room to pop Valiums for the five-hour drive. Pongrass was still grizzling about the shit, convinced that Hut and Rip had set him up. Hut knew this was what they were thinking. As he played on the beach with Charlie and Roy, he saw Business's minivan chug smokily up the headland. God knows, Hut thought, how anybody ever thought this was a good idea.

The island nation hadn't had much chance to impress its charms upon Justin Pongrass and Andrew Blackman. They would not have a lot to report to their friends and family back home. *How's Jamaica?* Justin, or Andrew, would reply: *Shithole.*

As he swung the minivan onto the inland road, Business looked into his rear-vision mirror and said: 'You boys not yet go up the volcano?'

Pongrass, in mirrored sunglasses, glared out of his window.

'Nope,' Blackman said. 'Means we'll have to come back again some other day.' Under his breath, to Pongrass, he mouthed: 'Not!'

'You miss the sight of you life,' Business said.

'You can take us next time,' Blackman said.

Pongrass snickered effortfully, as if hoping that a tail of laughter might wag the dog of an unfelt humour.

'Eh mon, me take you this time!'

'No time,' Blackman said. 'We've got five hours to get across to the airport, in, ah, the airport city.' He had forgotten the name of Jamaica's capital.

Business waited at an intersection for a truckload of goats. Now on the main road, they were stuck behind the lorry.

'We could walk faster than this,' Blackman said as Business crunched down to first gear.

A whistling sigh, a breeze cutting through a scene of havoc, came from Pongrass's nose. He ran his tongue along his still-numb lower lip.

'Me tell you this,' Business said. 'There is one shorter way. We go round the volcano. Mount John. It get us past these goats.'

'Yeah whatever,' Pongrass said. 'Do your worst, Bidnid.'

The van took the next turn-off, to the east, and the road began to circle Mount John's wide base.

'You sure we'll make it to the airport in time?' Blackman said.

Business raised his thumb. 'No worries, mate,' he chuckled.

Half an hour later, the road was still climbing.

'Me tell you what,' Business said. 'We so close to the volcano now, it be no time at all out of you way. You boys got to see this.'

Blackman made coathanger eyebrows at Pongrass, who shrugged, surly.

'That a promise?' Blackman said.

'That a promise,' Business nodded. 'If me no get you to the airport by four o'clock, you no have to pay me.'

'Good way of doing bidnid,' Blackman said. 'Glad to see he's getting with the real world.'

'He a real bidnidman.' Pongrass's private cackle was that of a senile comedian remembering a long-gone highlight.

Business took another turn-off, onto the unpaved one-lane road snaking up the volcano's cone. He explained the sights as they climbed.

'This volcano born four hundred thousand years ago. See those peaks over there?' He pointed to warty knolls on the slopes. 'They called breccias. They parts of lava that break up when it flow down the mountainside. You see those spikes?' He nodded to the car's left. 'They be called pitons. Everything in a volcano has a name and none of it in English. Volcanoes they don't speak English, yah mon?'

The road emerged from the plantations onto the grassy upper slope. 'This a classic volcano,' Business said. 'This a stratovolcano, and it get steeper as it rise. See all that rock on the slope? That is pumice. You take that home to you lady and she rub it on she heels. You children love pumice too—it be the rock that float on the water.'

'You sure we've got enough time for this?' Blackman said. 'I mean, the geology lesson's great, Bidnid, but we've got a plane to catch.'

'Like me say,' Business said. 'We no get there by four, me no get paid.'

'Okay,' Blackman exhaled with showy patience, 'but you'd better make sure.'

They drove past a stone ruin. 'That the oldest French church in the new world,' Business said, 'but it get blown to pieces by a *nuee ardente* in 1840. That mean,' he checked his mirror to see if his passengers were curious; they weren't. 'That mean, "glowing cloud". That a beautiful thing to say, but a bad thing to happen to you.'

Soon they were at the pull-over where two days earlier the others had got out to watch the sunset, the moonrise.

'Smell that,' Business opened his nostrils to the sulphur. 'That be the devil's fart. Hee-hee! Come on boys, get out, sniff it!'

Blackman and Pongrass gave each other questioning looks and consulted their watches. Disordered by the previous night, they were finding it hard to make calculations. They had a sense that they were losing valuable time, but had no fix on precise quantities.

'How's your back?' Blackman said.

Pongrass put his hands to his spine to verify what he was feeling. 'Strange thing is, what happened last night seems to have clicked something into place. It's never felt better.'

'Good. Let's do what he says. Sooner we get out, sooner we get off this stinking pimple,' Blackman said.

'One thing,' Business said, tilting his mirror as they unclipped their seatbelts. 'Why you boys call me "Bidnid" all the time?'

'Duh, because it's your name?' Pongrass said, nudging Blackman's ribs to hurry him out.

'Me wonder why you boys call me Bidnid,' Business continued, 'when my name is Clarence. "Business" the name of my car. And my friend Brian. His car's name be "Respect". It be the name of the car, not the mon.'

'You know what?' Pongrass, outside the van, leaned in the window. 'We really don't give a fuck.'

'Oh,' Clarence said mildly. 'That okay. Me no give a fuck either.'

Pongrass winked, and started across the scree after Blackman, who was climbing to the lookout over the volcano's crater. Pongrass massaged his loose back as he walked, uplifted by the thin air and the view to Negociante, a vista that felt like a trophy. He and his old mate Abo would take a photo. A good long look into Mount John's core, oodles of time to read the informative plaques, maps and diagrams on the walkers' route around the rim. They would have all afternoon to enjoy the spectacle of the sun setting over the Straits of Negociante while the moon rose over Cuba. Abo would have time to reveal to Pong that he was going to get involved in politics when he returned home, perhaps make a run at the rural seat once held by his grandfather. Things he'd seen in Jamaica had politicised him. He'd never have expected to get interested in politics, but there were certain issues he wanted to deal with before it was too late: for instance, protecting his homeland from becoming a place like this, populated with such sorry excuses for men as Bidnid and Respect.

The island nation would at last have its chance to impress itself upon Pongrass and Blackman, and they would be able to remember something of its beauty, for they were destined to spend many hours at Mount John that day.

As they stood at the lookout, below them Clarence's minivan revved in the carpark, reversed, turned a careful half-circle to avoid a rubbish bin, and made its way towards the first hairpin on the descent. After negotiating that turn and checking on the silhouettes of his guests up at the lookout, their backs to him, pointing down into the volcano, Clarence pulled the handbrake, opened his door and walked around to the back of his van. He lifted the two suitcases onto the side of the road. He went into the main cab and picked up the two leather bumbags on the centre seat. From one, he took the wallet and taxed five hundred American dollars. Tenderly, he replaced the wallet in the bumbag and laid it by the suitcases. As he climbed into his seat, Clarence checked his rear-vision mirror again, to see that the Australians had still not left the lookout. He gave a silent chuckle as he started rehearsing the story he would tell Brian when they met up, as arranged, in Kingston later that night: *Brian, let me tell you about the first passengers I ever dumped on Mount John . . .*

52

At six-oh-five that evening, Nayce, Book and Janey were asleep in their seats as the connection from Kingston to Miami left the ground. Pongrass and Blackman were walking down Mount John. Eventually they would come across a pineapple farm and offer the owner a thousand American dollars to drive them to Kingston. He asked for five. They paid him three. He ran their credit cards through his own machine.

Jeremy and Penelope Hutchison were sitting on the beach in front of Sandals, their toes driven into the sand, a daiquiri each, their little boys chasing each other in and out of the water. The sun was three fingers above the horizon and the sky was beginning to deepen. Hut had an uncoordinated, uneasy feeling, as if he and Pen were on a first date and might run out of conversation. Their real first dates all those years ago had run as smooth as silk, impelled by destiny, a downhill ride greased all the way to the safety of marriage. But life can't be evaded; its patience is eternal. The night before, or that morning, their attempt at lovemaking had burnt itself out, a bubble popping in the dead air of self-consciousness. Sex was their touchstone, but this time it had failed them. As if the awkward first time, the unconcluded collisions, had arrived late.

Hut hoped to seal over the unfortunate start by playing good father and attentive husband. Efficiently he'd got the boys dressed and out to breakfast, and brushed off Nayce and the others. Then he'd let Pen go back to the room for a sleep while he brought the kids down for some sand play. He'd taken them up to the hotel for lunch and a nap, and Pen had joined them down on the beach for the afternoon.

Hut paused to watch his sons, who were bartering with two American toddlers at the water's edge to get hold of their buckets. Roy and Charlie succeeded in offloading some colourful but dime-a-dozen hunks of chipped coral in exchange for the buckets and ran back with their booty, as pleased as colonists who have just scored a province for a handful of beads. The American children's father followed the transaction. Hut gave him a wave to show it was all in fun and he'd make sure the buckets boomeranged.

Hut, Charlie and Roy began building an ornate Gaudi-like sandcastle, dripping sand onto their little towers to make a globulous citadel. Roy was holding out the bucket and saying, 'Here, Charlie, it's your turn to go and put more sand in.' Charlie, being a second child, accepted the responsibility with great seriousness. Roy played voices around the citadel, having all the fun while his helper did all the work.

Hut lowered his eyes. His red fringe fell over his shame. *It'll be fine, look at these boys, nobody could send away their dad.* But the plain hardness of the truth cut him down. He was fucked. He'd tied himself up in a bag he couldn't talk or buy his way out of. He got to his feet and walked away from the boys, to the edge of the water.

He saw Pen's shadow come beside his on the sand.

'You never thought I'd do anything that stupid, did you?' he said.

'I don't know, Hut. You haven't been a model of rationality lately. And between us, things haven't been too good, have they? I didn't know. I was worried. Yes.' She flinched. 'Don't touch me. Sorry, I'm not in the touching mood.' And then, softening, 'Don't cry, darling. There are a lot of things we need to talk about . . .'

Before them, the evening was spreading itself out under slants of sunlight: the smell of pineapple and coconut wafted from a fruit-hawker's stand; two buxom middle-aged women in sun visors pedalled a yellow plastic aquatic bike; up the beach a pick-up soccer game was under way between Jamaicans and tourists; the horizon was cut by a green, gold and black paraglider; somewhere a metal shutter clattered down, a wheezy snicker.

'Dad messaged me again. He said everyone was "rallying around" Fred. Great in a crisis, he is, the old man. It's like you've always said: the only time he's ever been great was in a crisis. Sometimes it's like he needs to bring one on to remind everyone how great he is. Shithead.'

Pen studied the boys. Roy had Charlie picking up shells and stones to decorate the citadel. Roy had also recruited the American boy and girl to dig a moat. He strutted around, a diminutive monarch. He was Ken Hutchison's grandson. And Ines's grandson, too. Great in a crisis? Great only in a crisis? She and Hut had a crisis to face; time to see how great he could be. It would be a matter of endurance, not discovery. She had to wait and see if being Jeremy Hutchison was enough to satisfy him. A couple of years in jail, if it came to that, could even be turned to some good. He could learn to sit on his own and be silent and listen to his heart. But. *Jail*: the moment she pictured it, Hut in over-laundered greens, she and the boys visiting him in some supervised cafeteria, the publicity, how it would affect them all—she flared again with anger. They must fight this, battle their way out of it, exercise every possible challenge, do whatever it took, before she could let herself think that it could be *turned to some good*.

'That time at the beach,' he said, 'when I nearly drowned. Do you know what I wanted to tell you, why I was so desperate to find you when I came back to the house? It was because when I thought, you know, it's all over—I didn't really care for myself. I've been lucky. It's only fair if I cop a bit of bad luck, and that's the end of me. On my own account, I was ready to give it all up. But what kept me going, and what made me so angry and upset, was you guys. I don't want these two to grow up without me. I don't want to imagine your face. And my mum's.'

'You had your great spiritual conversion.'

'Don't make a joke of it.'

'Sorry, sweetheart.' She patted his arm, then, seeing the gesture as merely friendly, guilty for having stopped him touching her a few minutes ago, she stroked his neck with the backs of her fingers.

'You know, the one who I really thought might be in danger of, well, of topping himself, was him.'

'Nayce?'

'Miserable bastard. Always carping, you know, criticising, getting in the way, it just wears you down in the end. Why go through life being a critic?'

'That's just him.'

'Yeah. It's always been him. You know, once we went for this walk, at Barrenjoey. I can't remember how old we were. About nine? We climbed through the bush and we came to this kind of bridge of rocks to get out to the very point of the headland, where there was this cliff with a two-hundred-foot drop. Sheer. Anyway, it was hairy, really dangerous, and I didn't want to do it. But Nayce—he just gets this self-destruction thing going, you wonder if he cares whether he kills himself or not. And this is when we were nine. He was a miserable bastard then too. Always on about death, and what was the point of anything, and we're all just specks of useless dust—the usual Nayce bullshit. That's what you get when you grow up inside a church, I guess. Anyway. He decided to cross this narrow ledge, to get to a cliff, I mean, it was insane, and I remember thinking—actually this guy does want to die. If he's so obsessed with the pointlessness of everything, and criticising everyone, and hating the world, then maybe he should just get it over with. So I said to him, like, "If you're going to go on the way you are, why don't you just jump?"'

'What did he do?'

'I can't remember him saying anything. But he crossed it, and came back, and we walked back to Mum, and I could tell he was really really angry with me.'

'Why with you?'

'I couldn't work it out. But I think now—and I can remember this so well—I just think he misunderstood me. When I was saying, "Come on, if you don't want to live, give up, but if you want to live, do it properly, you know, be happy . . ." When I was saying that, he thought I actually wanted him to fall. And I never did. I never did.'

'You were nine years old. You weren't ready for that kind of conversation.'

'Yeah, well, we never had it later either.'

Pen watched her boys, her two strawberry blonds, the physical image of their paternal grandmother. There was something assertive about some genes, the way they bullied their way through. Nobody would have expected it to be Ines, of all the grandparents, who ran into the third generation. And yet here she was.

Hut pushed his sunglasses onto the crown of his head. 'Careful!' he called out to Charlie, who had waded into the water up to his thighs. The little boy threw a testing look over his shoulder and continued in up to his waist. Hut took a step forward but Pen stopped him, sliding a hand to his hip.

'Wait,' she said in barely more than a whisper so the children wouldn't hear.

Charlie flopped into the water. Hut started, but Charlie's head bobbed up and his feet kicked behind him. He grinned, half-swallowing the water, swirling his arms in a wild dogpaddle. A few seconds later his face rose again and he was stepping up, coughing water triumphantly onto the sand.

Hut turned to Pen. 'He can swim?'

'They can both swim. You arsehole.'

Hut pinched his forehead.

'It's okay,' Pen said. 'It's okay.'

Hut reckoned with her, his eyes the glaze of fish skin. He shook his head again: in pride, in shame. He was about to speak but his lip quivered like the white of a soft-boiled egg and he hooked his chin over her shoulder and kissed the back of her neck, hiding his face from her. Above the horizon the sun was beginning to fatten. The sky was mossed with green-tinged cloud.

'Look at this,' he said, releasing his embrace and throwing an arm around his mate's waist, turning her so she was facing the sea. His unsteady finger cross-hatched the outline of Negociante Island. 'No, serious. Look at this.'

He was still afraid to check if she was looking.